I0760743

Tikiri

Copyright

• • • •

THE GIRL WHO BROKE Free

The Red Heeled Rebels Series

Book Four

www.RedHeeledRebels.com[1]

• • • •

Edition: 2020

Library & Archives Canada Cataloging in Publication

ISBN: 978 1 989232 53 8

• • • •

AUTHOR: TIKIRI HERATH

Publisher: Nefertiti Press

1. http://www.RedHeeledRebels.com

Copy Editor: Stephanie Parent
Cover Design: Angela Oltmann
Back Cover Headshot: Aura McKay

The Girl Who Broke Free

Book Four
Red Heeled Rebels Series

A Gift

Don't forget to download your personal copy of the epilogue short story. Access is at the back of this book.

Other Titles by Author

• • • •

The Red Heeled Rebels Thriller Novels[2]

The Girl Who Crossed the Line
The Girl Who Ran Away
The Girl Who Made Them Pay
The Girl Who Fought to Kill
The Girl Who Broke Free
The Girl Who Knew Their Names
The Girl Who Never Forgot

• • • •

Asha Kade Murder Mystery Series[3]

Merciless Legacy
Merciless Games
Merciless Murder
More to come

• • • •

The Accidental Traveler

An anthology of personal short stories based on the author's sojourns around the world.

• • • •

The Rebel Diva Nonfiction Series[4]

Your Rebel Dreams: 60 Days to discover your purpose and passions and power up your life.

---

2. http://www.redheeledrebels.com/
3. https://tikiriherath.com/mysteries/
4. http://www.RebelDivas.com

Your Rebel Plans: 30 Days to create a masterplan for your career and life change.
Your Rebel Life: 100 habit hacks to transform the ten most important pillars of your life.
Bust Your Fears: 3 easy tools to conquer your fears and upgrade your career and life.

• • • •

Collaborations

The Boss Chick's Bodacious Destiny Nonfiction Bundle
Dark Shadows 2: Voodoo and Black Magic of New Orleans

Part ONE

Chapter One

It was the shrill scream of a terrified woman.

The sound reverberated through the house, sending a shiver down my back.

I whipped around, my heart racing.

My best friend, Katy, had been strolling around the room, admiring the murals on the walls—the ones with dark men in white robes riding Arabian horses across golden dunes. She was standing next to a display of scimitars now, those ancient curved weapons of the desert, and was staring at me with a horrified expression on her face.

"Did you hear that?" she whispered.

"I think so," I said, unsure myself.

We remained motionless, heads tilted, waiting to see if we'd hear the cry again, wondering if we'd imagined it.

We were alone in the dining hall that morning, one of the many rooms in this luxurious apartment in downtown Manhattan.

This room was unlike any dining hall I'd been in. That was what the ambassador's head of staff had called it when she'd ushered us in an hour ago. I thought it was more like a mini-museum dedicated to the Orient, not a room where they served you meals.

Until that strange cry, I'd been sitting deep in thought, reviewing the official papers the head of staff had left on the antique dining table.

I still couldn't believe I was holding this contract in my hands.

I'd been waiting for this moment my entire life. A jolt of pride went through me when I spotted our new logo on top of the document. I'd pointed it out to Katy.

"Check this baby out," I'd said with a grin.

"We've made it!" she said, giving me a high five.

It was our brand new Red Heeled Rebels logo. It had been Katy's idea. To make us official, she'd said. And now, next to the Saudi Arabian Embassy's formal insignia, it made us look distinctly professional.

Katy was right. We'd made it. Finally.

This was my foot in the door to my dream career and good money. Respectable money. Made legally, for a change.

But I couldn't ignore the eerie feeling I got every time I stepped into the ambassador's sprawling residence in the sky. Even Katy said this place gave her the heebie-jeebies.

Something didn't feel right.

Neither of us could pinpoint what it was. But I felt a warning tingle on my back whenever I walked out of the fancy elevators and in through the front doors of this apartment. Every time, it felt like I was entering a time machine and taken back to a medieval world where I'd get trapped. Never to escape.

But that was ridiculous. We were in a modern apartment, in a modern city.

This luxury penthouse was eighty-five floors high in an exclusive residential skyscraper in midtown New York.

In this house, multi-million-dollar sculptures that looked like they'd been loaned from MoMA sat awkwardly next to antiquated Bedouin furniture right out of Lawrence of Arabia. They bunched together everything wherever they found space. Whoever decorated this place had been more concerned with showing off their possessions than creating a pleasant interior.

Then, there was the sickly smell of expensive men's cologne that pervaded every inch of this home. Maybe that was what made the house claustrophobic. All this opulence sucked the oxygen right out.

I looked at the contract in front of me again. The offer on the table was good. It was so good I was forcing myself to ignore my instincts.

"Lemme go!"

I jumped.

This time, I didn't imagine it.

It was a girl's cry. With a distinct Arabic accent.

"I heard that!" said Katy, looking around nervously. "That was real."

I swiveled around to check the door.

It was still closed. The head of staff had shut it behind her. I'd thought it was to give us privacy while we looked over the contract, but now, I wasn't so sure.

Katy and I stared at each other, wondering what we'd got into this time.

I pushed my chair back and stood up. Reading my mind, Katy followed me to the door. I was halfway there when the door banged open.

We jumped back in alarm.

"Bibi!" Katy and I cried out at the same time.

Without acknowledging us, Bibi whirled around, closed the door firmly behind her and turned the bolt, locking us in.

"What's going on?" I asked.

She looked like she'd seen a ghost.

"You okay?" asked Katy, concern on her face.

"They're coming," Bibi hissed.

"Who?" I asked.

"Those bad men," she replied, wiping her nose with her sleeve.

"Which men?"

"When they come, act normal."

"Normal?" I asked. "But you just...locked us in here."

She averted her eyes. I noticed the sweat running down her face, ruining the cheap goth makeup she insisted on wearing. Yes, even to our diplomatic client visits.

"Bibi, hun," I said, putting a hand on her shoulder. "It wasn't you that screamed just now, was it?"

"No," she said and gave a furtive glance behind her. "But we need to get out of here."

"Why?" Katy asked. "And who are these men?"

Bibi's face scrunched like she was about to cry. "Bad people. Can we go now?"

Bibi was multilingual, English being her fourth language, which she'd only learned recently. But something besides language had her tongue-tied.

Her past gave her ample reasons to not trust anyone. Even us. She'd gone through more in her seventeen years than most adults did in a lifetime. Even now, I'd forget she was just a teen, unpredictable at times, struggling to adjust to a normal life.

"Hey, you can tell us what happened," I said. "Do you know who screamed? Is someone in trouble?"

Bibi's eyes darted from side to side.

"It's like I'm back home. This is a bad place." She sniffed and looked away. "Can we go now?"

Katy and I glanced at each other.

I was supposed to get back to the head of staff with a signed contract in half an hour. We were invited guests at the Saudi Arabian ambassador's house. We couldn't just walk away. Or lock ourselves in our hosts' dining room. That just wasn't done.

"Why don't you two stay here," I said. "I'll go talk to the head of staff and ask her what's going on, okay?"

"No!" Bibi said, clutching at my arm. "They'll come and get us too."

"Sweetie," said Katy, "we're in New York. No one can hurt you here anymore."

A scraping sound on the door made us turn around. Someone was trying to open it.

Bibi slipped behind Katy and hunkered down. "It's them!" she whispered.

I felt the hair on the back of my neck stand up.

The door handle depressed slowly. It didn't sound like a bunch of scary men trying to swarm in. It was more like someone was trying to slip in. Stealthily.

My mind raced. It was my turn to overreact.

Katy and I had stopped carrying our weapons to business meetings after we moved to New York. Not because it was illegal, but because we never had a reason to. But Bibi's reactions had unnerved me.

David kept a small Japanese tanto-style knife in our vehicle's glove compartment and a handgun in the overhead bin. "Just in case," he'd said when he'd tucked them there months ago. But our car was now eighty-six floors down in the underground parking garage.

I crossed the room and pulled a small dagger from the open scimitar display. I touched the blade with my finger and pulled away quickly. The knife was ancient, but it had been sharpened recently.

"Better than nothing," I whispered to Katy. "Just in case."

I stepped up to the door.

Chapter Two

I reached for the door handle, holding the dagger behind my back.

Part of me felt silly. We're here to sign a catering contract, for heaven's sake. But I wasn't a little girl anymore. I'd seen enough in my twenty-one years of running around the world, escaping people who only meant harm. Being paranoid, for me, meant staying alive.

I turned the bolt.

The person on the other side depressed the handle.

The wooden door creaked open.

I stepped back, gripping the knife tighter. I could feel Katy and Bibi behind me, holding their breaths.

The door opened wider and a solitary, petite figure appeared on the threshold.

I let out a sigh of relief. It was the young Indonesian maid. Part of the kitchen staff. She was carrying a silver tray laden with a Moroccan teapot and gold-rimmed teacups.

"Good afternoon, mademoiselle." She gave me a confused look. "Everything okay?"

"Ye...yes," I stammered, feeling my face go warm. "Sorry, must have, er, locked the door by mistake."

"Your tea, mademoiselle."

I opened the door fully for her.

"Thank you," she said in a soft voice.

"No, thank you," I muttered. My hand holding the knife was all sweaty now. I clutched it tighter, so it wouldn't slip.

The girl stepped out of the shadows and into the room.

I'd seen her before, scuttling around the house, cleaning, and serving, bowing low whenever she encountered a family member or a guest. She had good reason to fear the family. The only person in this household who was nice to her was the ambassador himself.

I remembered how on our first day here, Sarah, one of the many daughters in this multi-family Arab household, had barked at her.

"Stop being lazy and get me my soda, you useless thing," Sarah had screeched. "Do your job. I want it now!"

The servant girl had stumbled into the kitchen and brought her mistress her precious soda bottle, all the while keeping her head bent low, showing her deference. Sarah had snatched the bottle without a word of thanks. She hadn't even noticed Katy and me cringing at the scene from our corner of the room. I'd wanted to say something, but I'd held my tongue.

The girl was treading softly toward the dining table now.

After a quick glance at my friends who were still hovering by the doorway, I followed the girl and slipped back into my chair at the table. Katy came over and sat next to me. With a wary glance behind her, Bibi joined us reluctantly.

Without making eye contact, the girl placed the cups in front of us and poured the tea. The smell of fresh mint wafted to my nose.

I couldn't help wondering if she knew anything about that hair-raising scream we heard just a few minutes ago. Or if she knew the men Bibi had mentioned.

If we ask her, will she answer? Or will she get scared like Bibi?

The only reason I'd asked Bibi to come on this client visit with us was because she spoke Arabic. She was one of two in our team who did, but David was teaching a Krav Maga class at the martial arts dojo that day. So, Bibi it was.

Over the years and through her travels, Bibi had picked up Urdu, Hindi, Arabic, English, French and a smattering of Spanish. She had a natural talent for languages. In a different life, she'd have ended up as a translator at the United Nations or some other international organization.

But now, her multilingual skills came in handy whenever I dealt with the diplomatic households of New York, courtesy of my partnership with Chef Pierre, the world-renowned celebrity baker. Katy and I frequently asked Bibi to translate client emails and documents from various embassy staff. Sometimes, though rarely, she even sat with us at client meetings.

I was still puzzled why she'd run out of her "secret spot" in the kitchen where she usually liked to lurk alone, engrossed in her phone, unless we needed her. But Bibi was too freaked out for us to ask her anything now.

With a sigh, I reached to pick up my cup. I needed a tea badly.

That was when I noticed there were three cups on the table. They hadn't known Bibi was with us. Or had they?

"Is Madame joining us for tea?" I asked the girl, wondering if the ambassador's wife had changed her mind.

"She very busy," she answered, still not looking up.

I noticed a tremble in the girl's hand. There was a strange tension in the room like both Bibi and she knew something important. Something urgent. Something unpleasant.

Bibi was ignoring us now, playing nervously with the tablecloth with one hand, holding her phone in the other. And the girl from the kitchen had been trained too well. Making eye contact with her master's family or guests was forbidden. Speaking anything more than necessary was also not permitted.

She looks scared, I thought. One sideways word and she'd scurry off in a heartbeat.

After pouring the tea, she slipped her hand inside her apron pocket and rummaged for something. She pulled out a white index card and set it next to my cup.

"For you, mademoiselle," she said.

I picked it up.

A handwritten note.

I read it silently.

Girls, you wait in room. I will join to discuss contract soon. Madame is very busy. Not disturb us right now. - head of staff, Saudi Arabia Embassy Household.

I flipped the card around. There was no further explanation or even a please or a thank you. But I was used to that now.

The head of staff wasn't the most gracious person I'd met. She was cold, curt and had little time for people lesser than her. As a senior staff member in the ambassador's household, I suspected she considered herself above us mere caterers. At least, that was the impression I got.

But Chef Pierre had been clear.

I had to ignore all cultural idiosyncrasies. If I satisfied this household's special event needs, it would lead to bigger and more lucrative catering contracts with the other embassies in town. Foreign diplomats talked to each other and paid well. Supremely well, he'd told me. Like him, I didn't want to lose this once-in-a-lifetime chance to make a splash on this side of the Atlantic.

This was why Katy and I were in our smart black dresses with matching jackets, our signature red heels, and briefcases embossed with our logo. The Red Heeled Rebels were an official partner to the most famous baker in Europe and we had to look the part. Especially in front of our wealthiest clients.

Katy and I always found it fun to put away our baker's aprons and dress up for client meetings. But Bibi refused to wear any formal attire. She'd spent her entire life suffocating under the head-to-toe veil her family had coerced on her. The scars on her face were still visible under that heavy goth makeup, a testament to how they'd treated her. The last thing any of us wanted was to enforce another dress code on her. Or any code, for that matter.

In the beginning, I worried how our upscale customers would react to a plaid-kilted girl with spiky hair, nose ring, and bright red Doc Martens. But Bibi had flown under the radar. She'd stayed quietly in the back kitchens, playing on her phone in a corner, unless we called on her to translate a word or two.

I looked up at the servant girl who was waiting for me to reply.

"Thank you so much," I said. "It's super nice of you to bring our tea. You can tell the head of staff we'll be right here waiting for her."

I also wanted to ask her what the heck was going on in this house. I wanted to ask if she was okay. But she kept her eyes averted and her lips tight. She picked up her tray and gave us a low bow.

"Aw, come on!"

Katy had had enough.

She reached over and touched the girl's arm. The girl flinched as if Katy had tried to hit her.

"Sorry, honey, didn't mean to startle you," Katy said with a friendly smile. "You're in America now. You don't have to bow down to us or anyone like this."

The girl didn't smile back. She gave that sideways head nod I'd seen so often in India, the one my Aunty Shilpa used to give. I wasn't sure if that meant a yes or a no. But the girl didn't linger. She slipped out of the room as silently as she'd come in.

The door closed behind her with a click.

I passed the note to Katy.

"Look at this."

She read it out loud. "Not disturb us right now?" She frowned. "Why? Are they trying to hide something?"

"That girl who screamed," whispered Bibi.

Chapter Three

Bibi reached over to take the card from Katy when my phone buzzed.

I pulled it out of my purse and frowned at the screen.

How did Sarah get my number?

Then I remembered.

I'd left a handful of business cards on the kitchen counter on our first day so anyone could call me with questions. I was eager to please the entire family and get this contract in the bag. With such a large household I didn't know who had sway, whose words meant more than the others, and I didn't want to take a chance.

I accepted the call and punched the speakerphone button so the others could hear the conversation.

"Hello, Sarah."

"Can you come up?"

"Pardon me?" I said.

"Come to my room."

"May I ask what this is about?"

"So we can talk about my birthday cake. I wanna see what it looks like."

My first task, once we'd agreed to and signed the contract, was to cater to Sarah's sixteenth birthday party. It was coming up in a week. But nothing had been arranged. I hadn't even thought of the menu yet.

"I'd love to, Sarah, but I'm meeting your head of staff in a few—"

"I want to see you in my room now!"

An infuriated snort came from Katy's direction.

I bit my tongue.

This girl was as nasty as her older, obnoxious brother. For a second, I wondered what would happen after I signed the contract, how quickly we'd go from coveted caterers to mere household help. Maybe the transition had already begun.

On our first day, the head of staff had taken Katy and me upstairs to meet one of the ambassador's wives in the women's quarters. When we'd passed by Sarah's open door, she'd called out and demanded to know why she hadn't got her lunch yet. Sarah lived in her bedroom, spending her days binge-watching Netflix, gorging on chips, cakes, and soda and commanding her servants on a whim.

I let out an inaudible sigh. *Isn't there an easier way to make money in this city?*

"I'm so sorry, Sarah, but your head of staff asked us to stay—"

"She works for me!" snapped Sarah. "I give you orders, not her."

"Orders?" This time, I didn't mask the distaste in my voice. "Really?"

"Manners." I heard Katy hiss under her breath. Sarah probably couldn't even spell that word.

The girl's voice dipped a notch. "It's super important. Can you come to my room, please? Please?"

Now she sounded like a sniveling child. She was trying, at least.

Sarah could be as haughty and bossy as the rest of her family. The only reason they didn't treat us as badly as they did their servants was because we had Chef Pierre's name behind us. I wondered how long that would last.

"Alone," Sarah was saying, "I want you to come alone."

Before I could reply, she hung up.

I stared at the phone.

"Wow," Katy said. "What a hysterical brat."

Bibi glanced around quickly, as if to check if anyone had come into the room while we weren't looking.

"This is not a good place," she said. "I told you so."

We turned to her.

"What happened in the kitchen, sweetie?" asked Katy. "What made you run up?"

"These two men came and asked the head staff woman if the girl was ready," replied Bibi, lowering her voice.

"The girl?" I asked.

"They didn't see me 'coz I was in the back, near the pantry, but I heard them. They were talking in the corner. One man was carrying a rope."

"A rope?" Katy asked, her eyebrows shooting up.

Bibi nodded. "And they had these huge black sports bags."

"Duffle bags?" I said. "Sounds like the ambassador's security detail."

Bibi shook her head. "No, they were new men. They didn't look like the other men." She paused. "They looked like really bad people who do bad things."

Katy shot me a warning look across the table.

I knew what was going through her mind.

Maybe it was wishful thinking, but I'd hoped we'd put these kinds of things behind us. We couldn't live a normal life if we kept jumping to crazy conclusions every time something out of the ordinary occurred. Our pasts were behind us. This was a fresh new life we were building, a life of running a prestigious business in one of the best cities in the world.

"But, we don't know that for sure, do we?" I said, gently.

Bibi scrunched her face as if she was ready to cry. "They looked like those men who used to work with Zero. They looked....." She paused. "I know what bad men look like."

I looked away, feeling slightly nauseous.

Bibi's brothel-running brother, Zero, had made her life a living hell. I could only imagine the men she was talking about.

Thank goodness that man was dead. My only regret was I hadn't been there to watch him get his just deserts. Tetyana told us he'd screamed to the high heavens. Or to the low hells, in his case. She did a good job. She always did.

Katy leaned over and squeezed Bibi's arm. "Hey, maybe they were going to drive one of the wives to the doctor or something."

But fear had clouded Bibi's face. She shook her head. "I think they're coming for us."

Katy and I exchanged another glance.

"Why would they do that?" I said. "We're here on official business, under Chef Pierre's name. There's no reason for them to do anything bad to us."

"The head staff woman saw me in the back listening and she got real mad," said Bibi, looking down. "I thought she was going to hit me."

"What?" I said.

"She shouted at me. She told me I'm not supposed to be in the house. Then she told me to get out. She told me to wait in the garage until you were done."

My heart fell. "Oh, no. I'm so sorry, Bibi. That shouldn't have happened."

"What a nasty piece of a woman," said Katy, frowning. "What a crazy house."

"I told you," said Bibi. "When she went back to talk to the men, I came upstairs to find you." She gave me a pleading look. "Can we go home now?"

I nodded.

"There's a real weird vibe in this house," said Katy. "Even without Sarah's creepy brother around."

Though I'd been pretending otherwise, I'd felt it too. This was the last straw. Paranoia or not, it was time to leave.

From all the contracts I'd worked on under Chef Pierre's umbrella, this had to be the most bizarre.

In this house, the women's quarters were separated from the men's. The women wore traditional black garb that covered them from head to toe while the men wandered freely in comfortable modern attire.

Here, the wives mostly stayed cloistered at home while the men traipsed to the glitzy diplomatic events of New York, openly flirting with other women.

Here, the women didn't dare make eye contact with the men, and the servants didn't dare make eye contact with anyone lest they got yelled at, grabbed at, hit or worse. This was a place where everybody played a strict role in a draconian hierarchy.

Besides, the idea of multiple wives per man was revolting and unjustly one-sided. Cultural idiosyncrasies or not, there were serious issues in this household. Boys, even as young as ten, had more freedom than their own mothers.

I remembered how Sarah's disgusting brother had groped Katy the first day we came for the interview. His ogling and leering had made me want to go home and take a shower.

Every time I'd walked in, I'd felt like I'd been transported back to the Middle Ages. But we were in modern-day New York. Inside a six-thousand-square foot, three-story apartment in Manhattan.

The catering contract in front of me was mouth-watering, and the money was more than I'd made before. If only I could stomach this unpleasant place.

The strange thing was, out of all the people in the house, it was the ambassador who was the most normal and the nicest. *Why can't the others take his lead?* I wondered.

My phone rang again.

I turned it on.

Sarah's voice came loud and clear.

"Are you coming?" she shrieked. "I asked you ages ago! I need your help!"

"Sarah," I said. "Please be patient—"

"Come now! Please! Help—!"

Something or someone cut her off.

We stared at the phone.

Bibi's face had gone paler.

"That was freaky," I said. "Something's wrong."

"Sounded like she's having a panic attack," said Katy. "I'd normally say a bitch attack, but this was just...weird."

I slipped the phone in my pocket, gave one last glance at the contract on the table and pushed it away.

"Let me check up on her quickly and we can get the heck out of here."

Bibi turned and clutched my arm. "But..."

"You two wait for me here," I said. "Someone needs to go check on that girl."

"Want me to come with you?" asked Katy.

I shook my head. "I've pushed you both enough."

"Take this," Katy said, passing me the dagger I'd placed on the table earlier.

"No," I said, pushing my chair back and getting up. "This shouldn't take ten minutes. Wait here in case the head of staff comes. Let's be nice and then I'll go ask Chef Pierre for another contract."

"That's too bad," said Katy, glancing wistfully at the contract. "That's good cash."

"Yes, but we can't let them treat us like this."

I looked at my friends sitting at the table with apprehension on their faces.

"If I'm not back in fifteen, call Tetyana, will you?"

Chapter Four

W*hat are they doing to her?*

I peeked from behind the pillar in the corridor.

It was the sound of male voices in Sarah's room that had stopped me in my tracks. Hushed, low voices. Strange. It was rare to see men in the women's quarters in this house.

I'd stopped just in time and slipped behind the nearest pillar.

From where I was, I could see a part of Sarah's bedroom. The curtains were drawn, but I made out two silhouettes. There were two men in there, working urgently and silently. They were searching for something, bending down and pulling up bedcovers, opening and shutting cabinet drawers, pushing papers off the nightstand.

What's going on in there?

It had taken me a while to get through the winding corridors of this mansion in the sky. I hadn't met a single soul on my way up, unusual for this busy household.

The sickly sweet smell of frankincense oil cloyed the air and the sound of soft Arabic flute music echoed from the home sound system. I'd muddled around, peering into every open doorway, half expecting to see troupes of belly dancers inside, but it had been deadly quiet. Then I remembered. It was a Friday afternoon, so everyone, including the servants, was at their prayers.

Except for these two men in Sarah's bedroom.

One of them turned on a table light and started rooting through a drawer.

Where's Sarah? Didn't she just call me from her room? Like five minutes ago?

I checked my phone to see if I'd missed a call or text from her. Maybe she'd wanted to meet elsewhere. Maybe I'd misheard her. But there were no recent calls or texts. I turned the ringer off quickly.

Something told me the two men would not be happy to find me here.

From behind the pillar, I peered into the room again.

It was a nauseatingly gaudy room made for a teenage princess obsessed with glitzy pink. Exactly the room you'd expect Sarah to have.

Enormous posters of Middle Eastern pop stars adorned the walls, oversized stuffed teddy bears sat on the bed, and pink cushions were strewn across the floor in between half-eaten plates and overturned cups. It was a mess, even without the men throwing things around.

The second man turned on a flashlight and pointed it across the room. The light crossed the bed. I nearly gasped and pulled back.

There was a shapeless body on the bed.

I leaned in to get a better look.

Sarah?

I was sure of it. She was a big girl for her age. I was positive it was her lying motionless on the coverlet.

My mind swirled with questions.

What did they do to her? Was it Sarah who screamed earlier? But didn't she call me after we heard that cry?

Something had happened between that last call and now.

The two men continued to work hurriedly, like they didn't have much time.

Every bone in my body screamed at me to get out.

Whatever was going on here wasn't my business. Sarah's family wasn't the most charming to deal with, and I was already practicing my future conversation with Chef Pierre where I'd tell him I was pulling out of this contract.

Sometimes, it felt like the only goal of New York's high society was to outdo each other's parties. Foreign delegations were no different. In fact, they were worse. Everyone clamored to be on Chef Pierre's list, even if it meant they'd have to make do with his partner, me, to cater his signature cakes. All to take pictures, put them on social media and brag about it.

The Saudi ambassador's head of staff had called me a week ago for an introductory meeting. The impending birth of a son and a series of lesser birthdays were coming up, on top of a national day and religious festivals, all for which they wanted the best "Western cakes"—Chef Pierre's cakes.

That was the day I'd met the full family.

Katy and I had arrived alone and had been ushered into the dining room to meet everyone. It was there we'd first been introduced to the ambassador's four wives. All four, or so we were told, wanted to outdo each other and were ready to fight tooth and nail for the most impressive cakes at their personal events.

Chef Pierre's instructions had been simple: Do your best each time and stay diplomatic. Easy for him to say. I was the one on the front line.

The first family member to walk into the dining room that day was Ahmed, the ambassador's pudgy twenty-something son, who looked like he had an even bigger sweet tooth than Sarah. He'd come into the room by mistake, looking for his father. But then he spotted Katy.

He came over with a big grin on his face. Katy had politely offered him her hand to shake. Instead of shaking her hand, he rudely pulled her toward him and slid his hand down her back to grope her bum.

Katy pulled away in shock, but his lecherous grin told us he'd got what he'd wanted. He'd laughed a crude laugh. The head of staff had been too engrossed in her phone to notice. Even if she had, I doubted she'd have cared.

I'd stood frozen, mouth open, feeling sick to my stomach. I knew I had to say something. *This is wrong.* It was a relief when one of the staff members popped in to say his father needed him in the upstairs office immediately.

That was when I should have walked away from this place and never looked back.

But I hadn't.

I'd chickened out.

Instead of confronting the ambassador's son right there, instead of calling Chef Pierre to say this job wasn't for us, instead of doing the right thing, I'd stayed quiet. Like a coward. I'd let the size of the contract color my thinking.

Katy had told me it was nothing. It's fine, she'd said. But it wasn't fine.

It was soon after that we'd met Sarah. She'd walked into the room, loudly slurping a can of soda.

With an icy look my way, she'd turned to her mother and declared she didn't want Indian people at her party. It was the mother who'd reminded her that having Chef Pierre's coat of arms on her cake would make all her friends jealous. Not to mention their extended family, who'd be looking up their party pictures on social media from the Middle East.

Katy had turned to me in shock. I'd given her a look that said, *let it pass. We need this contract.*

I shuddered at the memory. I cringed at how I'd sacrificed my team for the sake of money.

The Red Heeled Rebels were a mixed bunch.

Katy was the redheaded Irish Canadian and Tetyana was the Ukrainian brunette. Peace and Chanda were from Tanzania, Bibi was from Pakistan, and Win was from Laos. David was a refugee from Yemen, Luc was French, and I was half-Sri Lankan, half-Indian.

We were a ragtag group of misfits, survivors, discarded by our own. But we were a family now. We may not always agree with each other, but we treated each other with love and kindness. At least, we did our best.

And here I was, trying to do the impossible: cater to the birthday party of an over-privileged daughter of a sour, dour family who cared not an iota how they treated each other, let alone those who worked for them.

I'd made a mistake. I just hadn't realized how big of a mistake I'd made.

I leaned in to get a better look inside Sarah's bedroom.

The girl on the bed hadn't budged.

The men were still bustling around, moving things, then wiping things down. Seeing the silhouettes of these two thugs in that pink-washed bedroom gave me the chills. If I'd have been more paranoid, I'd have suspected they were covering up a crime scene. *A murder? A rape?*

Suddenly one of them pulled the curtains closed, darkening the room even more. The second man walked over to the bed and crouched next to the girl on the bed.

Is that a needle in his hands?

He touched Sarah's wrist like he was checking her pulse. Then he checked the syringe.

I watched, frozen.

Something's wrong here. Very wrong. Sarah's either drugged. Or dead.

"What you doing here?"

I spun around.

It was Ahmed, the ambassador's son.

Chapter Five

I blinked.

Ahmed glared.

I hadn't heard him sneak up.

He stood ten feet from me, arms crossed over his flabby stomach, an ugly scowl on his face.

"What you doing here?" he growled. "You not allowed here."

I swallowed. I remembered how he groped Katy on our first day here, but here I was, feeling like I was the one who'd been caught doing something wrong.

"Your sister asked to see me," I said in the calmest voice I could muster. "She wanted to talk about her birthday cake."

"This place off-limits!" barked Ahmed. "Servants not allowed here!"

I pulled myself to my full five feet and looked him in the eye. I couldn't stand him. He was the type of man who thought petite Asian women made easy targets. I wasn't going to humor him.

I squared my shoulders, lifted my chin and kept my voice steady. "Look, I was only responding to your sister's call—"

"Hey, Asha!"

We turned to look.

Katy?

She was stepping out of the elevator.

"You forgot this in the dining room."

In her outstretched hand was my tablet, which contained photographs of the desserts we made at the bakery. But something told me she didn't pop up to just bring me cake designs.

Behind me, in Sarah's bedroom, someone bumped against the door. I heard shuffling inside. The men were moving something heavy. Then a cry. A low, feeble cry.

A chill went up my spine.

I turned to the ambassador's son. It was my turn to ask questions.

"What's going on in there?"

He gave me a startled look.

"What are they doing to Sarah?" I couldn't help myself. "Is she okay?"

"Get out!" he yelled. "Or I will teach you good lesson. You belong in kitchen, kafir!"

I flinched, but I didn't look away.

"Your sister called me just now. She called for help. Shouldn't someone be checking up on her?"

A curious mixture of emotions went through his face—anxiety, shame, rage.

He took a menacing step toward me.

I stood my ground, frozen more from terror than anything else.

"If you ever tell what you saw," he said, in a low, guttural voice, "remember, I come from very, very important family."

His dark eyes bored into mine.

My legs felt like jelly, ready to give way any moment, but I didn't budge. I didn't break eye contact. My mind swirled with questions. Why would a girl's own brother not care she was lying limp on her bed with two thugs inside her room?

"Oh, is that so?" I asked between clenched teeth. "What does that have to do with what's happening to your sister right now?"

"You stupid girl!" he bellowed. "Do I need to beat it into you?"

Beat it into me?

I knew what bothered him. I wasn't cowering or breaking into a blathering mess in front of him, which was what he probably expected all women to do.

I clenched my fists involuntarily.

A long time ago, I learned the Indian half of me had given me a gift. The gift of Kali. Maybe it was all in my imagination. Maybe it was a story I'd conjured up as a kid. But I knew that goddess of doom and destruction lived inside of me and could come out at the most unexpected of times. This man would have to work harder than that to rattle me.

"Are you threatening me?" My eyes flashed angrily. "How dare you?"

That didn't faze him. "I'll beat you and your friend to pulp!" he shouted, frothing at the mouth, furious I hadn't succumbed to his anger.

I glanced over at Katy.

Her red hair was a fiery mane now. Katy always reminded me of a lioness when we were in danger. She was standing strong, only a few feet behind him. I'd seen what happened to anyone who pushed this Irish-blooded redhead to the extreme. The ambassador's son didn't know who he was messing with.

He may have got away with pushing us around the first time, but....

I stopped, feeling a cold shiver go through me, realizing something I should have figured out a while back. With diplomatic immunity, Ahmed could get away with anything.

Anything.

I took a deep breath to settle myself.

This wasn't our fight. Plus, we had a bigger war to wage. It was time to go.

I looked the man in the eye. "We're leaving," I said. "There's absolutely no need to shout at us, grope us or threaten us. For the record, that's illegal in this country."

His face turned purple, like he was about to implode.

"You dumb woman! Bow down in front of me now! I teach you to talk to me properly!"

"That's enough," I said, and turned away. "I said, we're leaving."

"Asha!" Katy called out in warning.

That was when I saw his fist come toward my head.

My instincts kicked in. I ducked. Just in time. He missed me by an inch, and his hand hit the cement of the pillar.

"Aaargh!"

His roar almost deafened me. But he wasn't done. He turned and hurtled toward me like a rabid dog.

I felt the adrenaline rush through my veins. I stepped to the side, thrust my forearm up to deflect his punch and slammed my other hand, palm up, to the soft part of his nostrils. Before he could figure out what had happened, I smashed my red heel on his foot, grinding his toes.

I'd practiced this maneuver so many times on Bob, the Rubber Man, back at David's dojo that it came naturally to me.

Ahmed screamed and staggered back, clutching his face. Red liquid spluttered from his nose.

I wasn't sure if he was howling in rage, pain, or shame. But I didn't wait to find out.

I ran toward Katy, suppressing the urge to look behind me.

Katy was already jabbing at the elevator button.

Behind us, Ahmed was screeching in Arabic. A door banged open. Someone bellowed.

"Get in!" Katy shouted as the elevator doors slid open.

We jumped inside.

I jabbed the down button and the doors began to close.

Thank goodness.

But my relief was short-lived.

A split second before the doors touched, a hand slammed through.

We screamed.

Chapter Six

A brutish face sneered at us, showing off yellow smoker's teeth. It was one of the men I'd seen in Sarah's room.

Katy and I took a few steps back. I felt the cold steel of the elevator wall on my shoulder blades.

We were stuck.

"You think you run away so fast?" The man spoke in heavily accented English.

The elevator doors closed on his hand and opened again with a loud clatter. He didn't even flinch. He smiled an ugly smile and leaned my way. I smelled his stale cigarette smoke.

"I saw you looking, you nosy girl. You know what I do with nosy girls?"

I kept my eyes steady on him, but my mind was racing, trying to hatch an escape plan. We were in a confined space with our backs against a wall. One swipe of this brute's fist, and Katy and I would be finished.

His eyes narrowed dangerously.

"This is family business. If you talk to anybody about this, I will cut your throat open and make you bleed like cow."

Behind him, Ahmed was screeching like a madman. I remembered the second man in Sarah's room. I wondered how Katy and I could take them all on.

I desperately tried to recall more techniques David and Tetyana had taught us in our self-defense classes, but my brain was feeling mushy. All I could think of was I could poke my fingers in his eyes, then slam my knee between his legs.

That's what I'll do if he gets one inch closer.

"I make you disappear fast. Very fast." The man snapped his fingers as if to show how quickly he could make us vanish.

A shiver went through me. I needed to summon Kali *now*.

“Get away from us,” I snarled. “You touch one hair on us, and we will fight you to death!”

The man’s face went red.

“You hear me? One step closer and you’re toast!”

“You dare talk to me like that, woman?” The man spat out his words. “I will smash you and thrash you and cut...aargh!”

He pulled his hand and staggered back with a cry, giving Katy a wild look.

“You!” he roared. “I will kill you, you fu—”

I jabbed furiously at the elevator’s close button. Once. Twice. Three times.

The last thing I saw was the thug hopping in pain, clutching his left hand, screaming obscenities at us.

Mercifully, the doors closed shut.

I turned to Katy in shock and saw the curved scimitar in her hands. She’d drawn blood.

Katy wiped the knife on her skirt.

“Bibi was right,” she said, slipping it inside her pocket. “This is a bad place.”

“This is all my fault,” I said holding onto the steel bar, feeling like my legs were about to give way any moment. “I’m so sorry I brought you here.”

Katy shook her head. “Forget the contract. Let’s just find Bibi and get out.”

The doors pinged and opened.

We were on the second floor.

We ran out toward the dining hall, with me cursing silently. *What a madhouse. Didn’t I see the red flags from the beginning? Why didn’t I take them seriously?*

When we got to the dining room, I noticed someone had flung the door wide open.

Sitting at the table, in the chair I'd vacated only minutes ago, was the ambassador, himself.

He looked up as we ran in.

We stopped in our tracks.

He beamed.

In his expensively tailored suit, the ambassador looked the part of the dignified foreign delegate. He always carried himself with a regal bearing. He was also the only person in this entire household who'd treated us with respect on our first day.

But what's he doing here?

"Ah, ladies," he said with a friendly smile, waving us in. "Come. Come in. I wanted to say hello to you both. I've heard so much about your work, and I hear you will cater to my family's special functions soon."

I glanced around the room. *Where's Bibi?*

"I, er..." I said, my heart beating fast. "Mr. Ambassador, we promised your wife some samples from our car. We were just on our way out."

"I am so happy to hear that. That's *excellent*, as you say in America. I'm very pleased you have agreed to do this for my family." He tapped the contract in front of him. "Everyone's asking for Chef Pierre's special cakes. Even my relatives back home. All over the world."

I scanned the room as discreetly as I could, checking every potential hiding spot.

No. Bibi's not here.

"Your wife asked us to rush," I said.

"Which one?"

"The second one," stammered Katy, taking my cue.

I nodded.

"Oh, that one? She's always in a rush. She can wait a few minutes," the ambassador said, his smile broadening, "I have a plane to catch soon myself, but I'm not rushing like a madman, am I? Haha!"

He gestured wildly with his hands. We stared. It wasn't the most diplomatic like thing to do, I thought.

He caught himself and smiled. "Don't be shy now. Come, come in and join me. I see you haven't signed the contract yet."

Before I could reply, his phone rang.

He fumbled in his jacket pockets, momentarily forgetting we were there. "Now, where did I put this thing?" he muttered to himself.

I tapped Katy's arm and took a step back toward the open doorway.

"Hello?" the ambassador said, taking the call.

Katy and I quietly stepped out to the corridor and walked back to the elevator, picking up our pace as soon as we were out of the ambassador's line of sight.

Is that call from his son alerting him to us? Does he know what's going on upstairs? And where's Bibi?

"Must be in the kitchen," whispered Katy, reading my mind.

We jumped back into the elevator and headed down to the first floor, where the kitchen and the servants' quarters were located. I tapped my foot, praying for the elevator to work faster, my mind whirling with worst-case scenarios.

What if more goons are waiting for us downstairs? What if they've already got Bibi?

Within seconds, the elevator doors slid open.

We were in the kitchen.

No one was around, but the smell of saffron, cumin, and coriander filled our noses.

We stumbled out in a daze.

If that was Ahmed or his goons calling the ambassador, they could say anything to him. Who would he believe? His own family and people, or two catering girls?

Katy and I walked shoulder to shoulder through the maze of countertops and shelving toward the back door, scanning our surroundings. We walked as casually as we could, so as not to arouse attention. But my heart was thumping so loudly, I was sure the entire house could hear it.

Where is that girl?

When Bibi came on client visits with us, she always found a spot at the very back of the kitchen where she could play on her phone without getting in the way. If I knew her, she'd have gone to her usual safe place to wait for us.

Katy and I passed a sous chef rolling pita bread dough near the stone oven. Two teens were washing dishes in an oversized sink. An enormous steel pot sat on the stove in the middle of the room. It bubbled as we walked by, smelling of stew.

Any other day, I might have lingered, taken in the smells and asked a million and one questions. But not today.

The chef, an obese man with a knife scar on his cheek, glared at us before turning back to the stove with a dismissive grunt.

"There!" Katy whispered, nudging me. "I see her!"

Chapter Seven

Bibi was in the shadows at the back of the kitchen. She was hovering near her "secret spot," which usually meant somewhere near the delivery entrance.

She was holding our briefcases in her arms and was glancing around nervously.

Her face lit up when she saw us.

We dashed toward her.

"You okay?" I asked.

She nodded. "The ambassador man came to the room. He told me to stay, but I ran out." She shot me a strange look. "What about the girl?"

I glanced behind us. It wouldn't take long for the goons to find us.

"We have to get out of here," I said, taking her by the arm and propelling her outside, into the back corridor.

"But—"

Katy turned to her. "They're coming after us."

Bibi gave her a wide-eyed look.

"No time for questions," I whispered urgently, shaking her arm. "Now! Run!"

That did it. Bibi turned and fled.

Katy and I followed, running helter-skelter, past the entrance to the main lobby, with Bibi leading the way.

"Wait!" I called out, trying to keep up with her in my heels. "We just passed—"

"Look!" Katy said.

She was pointing at the lone industrial-sized elevator hidden in the back corridor, next to the recycling and garbage containers.

The service elevator.

"Genius!" I said, as we caught up to her and jumped inside.

I felt relief wash over me as the doors shut firmly and we started moving.

The only sound now was the whir of the elevator as it whisked us eighty-five floors down at high speed. I was thankful no one else had called it, or we'd have been in trouble.

My heart was still pounding hard. It took a minute for me to breathe normally again.

"My goodness," I said, looking at Katy, who was trying not to hyperventilate. "What the crazy heck just happened?"

Bibi turned to us with bug eyes. "What did they do to Sarah?"

"No idea." Katy shook her head. "Looked to me like they were removing evidence of a dead body."

"Did they kill her already?" Bibi asked in shock.

"What do you mean *already*?" I asked, my eyes narrowing. "How—"

The elevator dinged, announcing our arrival at parking level one, where we'd left our SUV more than an hour ago.

The doors slid open to the well-lit open garage, and Katy moved to step out.

"Wait," I said. "What if someone's waiting for us?"

She pulled the dagger out of her pocket and held it out. "I'm ready."

Bibi's eyes widened when she caught the sight of the blood on the weapon.

I peeked out first and scanned the area.

No one was around.

Katy and I stepped out and crept toward our car, swiveling our heads in both directions and Bibi following closely at our heels.

I was thankful the Red Beast was exactly where we'd left it.

This was my primary vehicle. David had procured it from a used auction site soon after we arrived in New York and I used it almost every day.

Other than the Japanese knife and handgun, he'd also stashed a box of ammunition and two wooden nunchucks in the overhead compartment, should we need them. This SUV came with eight seats and oversized cargo space at the back. It was the perfect team car for the Red Heeled Rebels.

Right now, I was just happy to see its tires hadn't been slashed.

I relaxed and unlocked the vehicle remotely.

Bibi pushed past me to get to the car when I remembered.

"Hold on," I said and bent low to peek under the carriage.

Tetyana had trained us to look for booby traps or tracking devices under the car when leaving hostile environments. This was the first time I'd had to check. Something told me Ahmed and his goons wouldn't hesitate to play dirty.

"Clear," I called out.

Bibi ran over, opened the back door and jumped in.

Katy scrambled into the passenger seat.

That was when I realized we'd left my best serving trays behind, including the samples we'd painstakingly made to impress this diplomatic family. The lucrative contract on the dining-room table flashed into my mind. I pushed that image away. I had more urgent things to focus on right now.

I'd have to tell Chef Pierre it didn't work out. He didn't need to know the details. He was the only reason we were allowed in New York. In the USA at all. I couldn't jeopardize my relationship or my credibility with him.

I slammed the driver's door shut and started the engine, relieved to be getting out of this place.

"Oi!"

Startled, I glanced at the rearview mirror.

"Stop!"

A man in a black suit was running toward us.

What the...? Is that a gun?

It was the goon with the yellow smoker's teeth who'd accosted us earlier. He'd found us.

"Go!" Katy screamed.

I put the car in drive and punched the accelerator with my foot. The car leaped over the small barrier in front of us. I swerved to not hit the other cars and maneuvered us onto the middle lane of the parking lot.

A glance in the side mirror showed two men jumping into a black sedan. The men from Sarah's room, I was sure.

Space was tight. I had to focus.

"Exit!" yelled Katy, pointing to a sign.

I revved the engine and gunned in that direction.

"They're catching up!" Katy hollered. "Bibi, head down!"

I put my weight on the accelerator.

"Down!" screamed Katy.

Crash!

One quick look at the rearview mirror and I saw our back windshield had cracked.

"Jeez!" I cried. "Is everyone okay?"

"Okay!" shouted Bibi, her voice muffled like she was huddled inside the footwell right behind me.

"It didn't break through," Katy shouted and jabbed her finger toward the exit sign. "Go! Go!"

From behind us, I heard the squeal of tires skidding on the concrete floor.

I gripped the wheel and scanned up front, trying to get to the exit without hitting anything or getting jammed into a corner.

"Hold on, girls!" I shouted as the SUV gathered speed.

I turned a sharp corner.

"Nooo!" Katy screamed.

We were hurtling toward the exit gate. A thick plastic pole barricaded our way.

When we arrived at the building, we'd collected a token to get inside the parking lot. That token would get us out.

Forget the stupid token!

We were seconds from the barrier. I felt a powerful shot of adrenaline course through me.

"Hang on, girls!"

I leaned into the wheel and pushed the accelerator to the floor.

This is it.

Katy screamed. Bibi shrieked.

Our car slammed through the barrier. The pole shattered into pieces.

"Oh, no!" cried Katy, clutching her head.

I followed her eyes and looked up just in time to see a metal barrier slowly come down on us. It was there to stop crooked drivers from running out without paying.

"Oh, my god!" cried Bibi from behind me.

I ducked involuntarily as the metal scraped against the roof of our SUV with a deafening screech. Sparks flew around us. I kicked down on the accelerator and roared the car up the ramp. For a split second, we were airborne.

We landed with a crash a few inches from the main road, whiplashing us.

"Watch out!" shouted Katy.

I veered to the curb to avoid hitting a yellow Mini Cooper speeding by.

It dashed by us, horn blaring angrily.

Ignoring the smell of burning rubber, I gunned our car toward the traffic and followed the Mini.

Chapter Eight

The driver of the Mini rolled down her window as I passed. A woman's angry face popped out, shouting something nasty.

When I didn't respond, she gave me the finger.

I revved up, overtook her and disappeared from view. I had much bigger stresses than local traffic to worry about.

I was thankful we were in New York and not on a remote strip in Dar es Salaam or Goa. The streets here were busy, and it would be harder for the men to chase us, guns blazing.

Though I knew the scenario was unlikely, I kept checking my mirrors. No sign of a black sedan. Yet.

Katy and Bibi had gone silent, probably trying to digest what had just happened.

My eyes swept the inside of the car.

No blood. No wounds. No panicking.

My friends looked eerily calm.

Katy was sitting quietly in the passenger seat, eyes focused forward, her face taut. Bibi was lying in the back looking exhausted, her feet on the seat. Any other time, I'd have asked her to put her feet down, but right then, I was just glad she was breathing.

"You two okay?" I asked. "No one hurt?"

"I'm fine," said Bibi. "I was hiding behind you."

"Not a scratch here," said Katy.

I took a deep breath in.

"What the heck just happened?" I said. "Whatever's going on in that house has to be pretty serious."

They didn't answer.

"I mean, they shot at us!" I banged my palm on the steering wheel. "Can you believe that? And we survived. What are the chances? Do we go buy a lottery ticket or what?"

"Good thing we're proofed," said Katy in a quiet voice.

"Proofed?" I said. "What do you mean proofed?"

"The Red Beast," she said. "It's bulletproofed."

"When did that happen?"

"Last summer. I took ten thousand bucks for it."

"Wasn't that for the dojo, for gym equipment?"

"It was to upgrade the car."

I raised an eyebrow. In every family, there's one person who is the last to hear the news, and in this one, it was me.

"Are you serious?"

"*I* knew," quipped Bibi from the back. "I knew the car was bulletproofed."

"Why didn't anyone tell me?" I asked. "How can you do things like that without even telling me about it?"

"Because you never approve security stuff," said Katy. "So Tetyana, David, and me made an executive decision."

"An executive decision?"

"Besides, every time I talk about David, your brain shuts off."

"Not true."

I felt my face go warm.

"I'm busy with Chef Pierre, getting clients, trying to set up a business so we can actually stay here."

I was learning fast that starting a new business was hard. Doing it in a new country was harder. Even more challenging was setting up a new business in a new country as an undercover operation.

I glanced at Katy. "Without a business, we don't have money, and without money, we don't have any security. I thought I told you, Katy, setting up the business was our priority."

"It saved our lives today, didn't it?" she replied.

I sighed. She was right.

"Wait." I sat up. Something didn't add up. "Ten thousand to bulletproof this SUV? What did they do? Half of the back window?"

"David swapped a year's worth of Krav Maga training for the armored company's team," said Katy. "Every Wednesday morning from six to eight he teaches their factory workers and staff. It's part of the company's team-building plan now. Tetyana and I convinced their HR department."

"You talked to their *HR department*?"

"It's a two-year contract. That's fifty grand right there to bulletproof the panels and windows."

"Wow." I didn't realize how resourceful my team was. "So that's where David goes on Wednesday mornings."

Bibi's face popped in between the front seats.

"Hey," she said, her face scrunched up in concern. "What about the girl—"

"Bibi, please sit back and put your seat belt on," scolded Katy. "They could come after us any minute, and we'll have to speed up."

With a groan, Bibi pulled back, and I heard her belt being buckled.

"Don't think we have to worry about that," I said, shaking my head. "First, they know where we live so they don't have to chase us down the streets. If they chase us with their diplomatic licensed cars, it'll be an international scandal. The cops will have lots of questions for them. That's for sure."

"For us too," said Katy quietly.

I felt a cold sting of fear go through me.

"Us too," I repeated softly to myself.

We drove in silence for a while.

We were heading back home now, toward the bakery and the dojo. I felt a headache coming on. The adrenaline had run its course and my brain was coming to terms with what we'd just seen. I'd experienced some strange things in my life, and this wasn't the first time we'd been shot at. Or threatened. We'd been through much worse than this, but this was just plain bizarre.

"We have our powwow tonight," Katy said, interrupting my thoughts. She checked her phone. "Tetyana said we're starting a half hour early because Peace has a meeting at the university."

My head throbbed more. I'd forgotten our weekly get-together. It had been a long day, even without the men in black suits and the gunfire.

I'd started work at four in the morning to prepare a delivery for a high-society luncheon at the Thai embassy. It was a client who demanded perfection and was always particular about everything. And now, I'd got my team almost killed by some diplomatic henchmen. What a day.

What do I tell Chef Pierre?

I wasn't going to put any of us in danger by returning to that house. Ambassador or not, they'd have to find a new caterer.

I massaged my temple with one hand, trying to think this through.

If I told Chef what really happened, there'd be lots of questions, maybe even the authorities visiting us. Surely an investigation. They'd wonder about the bulletproofed car. They'd want to know why.

"Is Chanda calling in?" I asked, trying to think of something else for the moment, if, for any other reason, to reduce the pounding in my head.

"She's in Nairobi this week," said Katy. "It'll be early for her but she's going to make it. Peace will call in from Boston as usual. Everyone will be there."

I glanced at the clock on the dashboard. Our digs in Harlem weren't that far away, but there was traffic to contend with. "We won't make it on time," I said.

"How late?"

"Ten minutes, give or take."

"I'll text Luc to let everyone know."

Thank goodness for Luc. I didn't know what we'd do without him.

Luc kept shop at the bakery while we were out in meetings with clients. For a nineteen-year-old who'd spent most of his life as a small-time drug dealer, he'd surprised me by becoming the best cake decorator I'd encountered.

It had taken a year and a half of training—training he'd asked for, begged for. His detailed and creative modern designs were so spectacular even Chef Pierre bragged about it to our clients.

Ever since I made fairy cupcakes with my mother as a little girl, I'd dreamed of baking delicious goods for a living. And here I was, finally, working with my mentor, Chef Pierre, the most renowned culinary artist in the world, catering to the über-wealthy of New York.

I wished my mother was here to see me now. She'd be proud of me.

Chef Pierre and I had a symbiotic relationship. I shared with him my mother's fusion recipes that delighted and surprised his most discerning clients, and in return, he gave me credibility with his brand and prestige, and opened doors for me—doors I'd never imagined would open for someone like me.

More doors meant more work. More work meant more money. More money meant we could finally do what we wanted. That meant redemption for everyone in the Red Heeled Rebels team. This business was more than a childhood wish. This was a call to duty for all of us.

A white card waved in front of my face.

"Bibi, honey, I'm driving," I said, pushing her hand away.

"Read it," she said in a firm voice, pushing it under my nose again.

A quick glance told me it was the card the servant girl had left on the dining table. "I already did," I said, keeping my eyes on the road.

"Okay, let me read for you."

With an exasperated sigh, Bibi plopped back in her seat.

"SOS. Help me. SOS."

I squinted at her through the rearview mirror.

"Is this a joke?"

Her eyes were two inches from the card, scanning it, with a serious expression on her face. "There's a long string of letters and numbers after that."

"What are you talking about?" I said.

"Can you read it out loud for us, hun?" asked Katy.

"Okay," said Bibi and began to spell. "B3A1D3D4A5B4C3 E2A5A1D1B3D5A5." She paused. "There's a number after that. I think it's a telephone number. 653-208-6753."

"Wait," I said, turning around to get a better look at what she had in her hands. "I thought it said, *Girls, here's your tea. Stay till I come.* Or something like that."

"You missed the pencil marks scribbled on the back," Katy said.

"What pencil marks?"

"They're hard to see, but Bibi spotted them right after you left. I came up to find you because I knew something wasn't right then."

"Why didn't you tell me this before?"

"We were in the middle of getting chased and shot at."

I blew out from my mouth.

"Hey, Bibi, did you say six-five-three?" Katy asked, turning around. "That's not Sarah's number, is it?"

"Nope," said Bibi. "I called when you were upstairs. It rang and rang, but no one picked up."

"Strange," I said.

"Maybe Sarah didn't write this," said Katy.

"Who then?" I asked. "Someone else in the house? Maybe that servant girl?"

"Maybe that's not a telephone number," said Katy in a thoughtful voice. "Maybe it's code for something like that long word and number sentence."

"I'm sure it's Sarah," said Bibi, "I know it's her. She wants our help. We have to do something."

Her face popped in between the seats again.

"Bibi," said Katy, "you really need to sit back."

"Where's your phone?" Bibi said, poking my elbow, ignoring Katy.

"My phone?" I asked.

"Yes. Give it to me."

"Don't you have your own?"

"I need yours."

Bibi could be stubborn, and I already had a headache to contend with. I pulled my phone out of my pocket and held it out.

Within seconds, I heard the sounds of dialing. Then ringing.

Who's she calling?

"Allo!" a man's gravelly voice barked. "Allo?"

I recognized it instantly. *Ahmed.*

Bibi hung up and threw the phone on the seat beside her.

"What did you do just now?" I asked, swiveling my head. "Who did you call?"

"Sarah."

"Oh, my god," Katy said.

"I wanted to see if she'd pick up," said Bibi. "She'd know it's you, so why didn't she pick up? Why does Ahmed have her phone? Sarah's in trouble. I tell you we need to help her."

I sighed. "We have our own stuff to manage. Much more urgent and important things."

Katy glanced at me. "You realize that wasn't a normal family spat?"

"Yes, but we can't get involved in it, whatever it is. We can't go running around helping everyone. We're not superwomen."

"It's freaky crazy for sure," said Katy. "This is not like some dude stealing an old lady's purse on the street. They shot at us for good reason."

"We did the right thing," I said. "Got out fast to live another day."

"We have to help her," Bibi said from the back, her voice a pitch higher than normal. "Even if she's a nasty donkey's tail. We can't just run away."

I shook my head. "Not our business, honey. We don't have the bandwidth to handle this. David and Tetyana will agree. So will Chanda."

The image of the girl's lifeless body lying in that gaudy pink room loomed before my eyes. I pushed it away.

Bibi was right. Sarah was a "nasty donkey's tail," but we shouldn't leave her like that. I just didn't want to think about it right now.

"Maybe," Katy said, hesitating, "we call the police on an anonymous tip line? Tell them we saw something suspicious?"

"No," I said, "you know we can't do that. They'll track us down and come asking questions. Then we'll be in real trouble."

I sat back with a sigh.

Why can't we just get a normal catering job for once? Why do we always have to find drama?

I glanced at the rearview mirror. In the backseat, Bibi was staring out the window, her face pointed, her dark lipsticked mouth looking more melancholy than ever. Next to me, Katy was gazing outside, one finger twirling an errant red curl, her face grim.

I knew what they were thinking. I felt it too.

If a young girl was in trouble, we should help. That's what we did. But calling anyone, let alone the authorities, meant unwanted attention on us.

That would risk our entire operation in New York. And that was something none of us wanted.

Part TWO

Chapter Nine

I parked the Red Beast in its usual spot in the alleyway.

I'd taken the fastest route home, and we were only two minutes behind now.

There was one other car here, the two-door green Subaru hatchback David had found in a used car lot when we first moved to the city. This was Bibi's baby, the vehicle she used for our routine deliveries. It was old, but it did its job.

Parked under the faded awning in the back was also our fleet of two-wheelers. Katy's red Vespa, Luc's scooter, David's Yamaha motorcycle, and Tetyana's black Ninja were all lined up, chained and padlocked.

The bakery was now closed, but the martial arts dojo had its lights on. Classes were done for the day. David and Tetyana must have locked everything up and the entire team must be inside, waiting for us.

I jumped out and surveyed the Red Beast.

This was my ride, the one in which I shuttled back and forth between clients and Chef Pierre's downtown offices. I'd become fond of this car. I sighed in dismay. There was no hiding that offensive bullet crack in the back window and the glaring dents and scrapes on the front panels where I'd rammed the parking lot barrier. I didn't even want to think what the top of the car looked like from that metal barrier scraping it.

"We'll get it fixed," said Katy, putting an arm around my shoulder. "We have a contingency fund for emergencies."

"Thank you, Katy," I said giving my friend an appreciative look, "for being super prepared. Don't know what I'd do without you."

"It's my job. Isn't that why you hired me?" she said with a smile.

I shook my head at the thought. She'd been my BFF since high school in Toronto. She was the friend who'd stuck with me when I was at my lowest. She'd come with me across four continents and, together, we'd hatched plans to escape our captors and bring them down. Without her, I'd be enslaved or dead. Katy was no hire. She was family.

"The armored company did an excellent job," Katy said. "It saved us today."

The back door opened and Bibi slid off her seat, her nose stuck to her phone, pouting, looking like the teenager she was for once.

Anyone would need some TLC after what we'd just gone through. I walked up to her and pulled her in for a hug. She tried to half-heartedly wiggle out, face away.

"Hey," I said, holding on to her, "we had to get out of there fast. Now we're home, we can try to figure out if and how we can help Sarah."

"Promise?" she asked, suddenly paying attention, hope in her eyeliner smudged eyes.

I stared at her for a moment, trying not to think of the lifeless girl I saw lying on the bed. I wondered why Bibi was so bothered about a stranger she barely knew, an insufferable one at that.

"We'll talk to the team and decide together, okay? That's the best promise I can give you right now."

With a shrug, Bibi turned around and walked inside, her body language saying *you just don't care.*

Katy and I exchanged glances.

"Traumatized by the whole thing," she said.

"It's not the shooting that's got to her," I said, shaking my head. "Something else is bugging her. Something from her past."

After locking up the Red Beast, we entered the building through the back door. The heavenly smell of butter cakes and chocolate icing hung in the air. A part of me wished I could just bake all day, but someone had to meet clients and rustle up contracts so we could make money.

On paper, I was the president of the Red Heeled Rebels catering company and the head baker. Katy managed the books while Luc was our cake decorator and Bibi, our official delivery person. In reality, everyone pitched in and helped each other out. Tetyana and David were also on my payroll as assistants, though they rarely came into the bakery, unless we were tight.

The bakery and the dojo gave us legitimate reasons to stay in the USA. We had business licenses for both, so no one had questioned our arrangements. Yet.

Over the past few months, we'd slipped into a daily routine. During the day, we baked and delivered our cakes to upscale clients while Tetyana and David taught martial arts classes next door. In the evenings, we shut down the ovens, put away our supplies and skipped across the hallway to start our night classes.

Katy and I made our way to the dojo now, walking through the connecting doorway inside the building.

It was here we apprenticed under Tetyana and David every evening. We trained in self-defense, knife handling, sword fighting, hand-to-hand combat, grappling, and every martial arts technique they'd learned over a lifetime in the real battlefields. On weekends, when business was slow, they took us to the gun range half an hour from town to give us weapons training. We even tried David's sniper rifle for target practice, the weapon I enjoyed the most.

We'd been lucky to find two connected spaces for rent side by side, one for the bakery and one for the martial arts school. It had taken us ages before Tetyana had finally got wind of a rundown two-story brick building opening up for lease in Harlem.

There had been graffiti on the outside and a mess inside. The hall, which was now our dojo, had been an illegal makeshift indoor skate park for the local kids. They'd used discarded wooden sheets and beams ripped from the walls for their covert playground. On the bakery side, there had been a foul smell like someone had been squatting inside for months.

But we'd grabbed it, even if it had meant months of cleaning and renovations to bring the building to livable conditions and to code.

This wasn't a part of town Chef Pierre or any of our upper-end clients would walk into. We heard police sirens all day and all night long, and most businesses had iron bars on their windows. The best thing was the landlord didn't ask too many questions and collected rent via a third-party agency that conducted their business online.

This served us perfectly.

There was only one entrance to the room inside the dojo we were heading toward, and that was through David's corner office.

At first glance, the entrance looked like a door to a typical janitor's closet. If you looked closely enough, you'd notice a keypad and two deadbolts on the door, painted white so they wouldn't show.

The numbers on the keypad had been whitened out too, so we had to use our memory to punch in the password. The last thing we wanted was the backlight to attract someone's attention.

This was our War Room.

The door to the War Room was now wide open, and it seemed like everyone was gathered inside.

"He came by again today." I heard David say.

"The construction worker?" Luc asked.

"One of the skate kids said a city pipe had busted."

"Doubt that," said Tetyana. "Something smells rotten and I'm not talking about a city pipe."

Katy and I stepped inside the War Room and shut the door behind us.

Once this door closed, the room became fully soundproofed. It was a windowless oblong space tucked at the edge of the gym with only one entrance. David had walled up the entire back section of the dojo so no one could guess there was a room hidden in the back. A room within a room. Just the way we wanted it.

Inside, everyone was settled in their usual spots around the oval boardroom table.

Tetyana sat across from the door. At twenty-three, she was the oldest among us and had more street smarts than any of us. With her athletic build, dark brown hair cut military style and steely green eyes, she looked like Charlize Theron from Mad Max. And that could be imposing.

There were only a handful of people in the world who knew her true story. Starting as a shy, young English school teacher in a Ukrainian border town, she'd been forced to join rebel fighters against the ruthless Russian militia and then work in London's Red Light district to pay for her brother's ransom. Her past life was one she rarely talked about. No one would believe her journey seeing her now.

I looked to Tetyana for security advice. Though we didn't always agree on everything, I trusted her astuteness and her experience.

David was sitting at the end of the table where he had access to the control panel for the equipment in the room, including the drop-down screen. It was on this mega screen that Win, Chanda, and Peace would show up soon. Behind him was a bank of computer screens lining the back wall, which Win had hooked up before she'd taken off to college.

I always felt a funny frisson go through me when I saw David. His workout regime and martial arts classes kept him toned and fit. His muscular arms and abs made more than a few girls in his classes go all gooey around him. I knew exactly how they felt, though I did my best to hide my crush.

Bibi was sitting in the chair next to David, her legs curled underneath her, her nose in her phone, looking decidedly unhappy.

"Hey guys," said Tetyana, waving at Katy and me. "Everything all right? Bibi doesn't want to talk to us anymore."

"Was it something we said?" asked David, giving Bibi a friendly poke. "Do we smell?"

Bibi studiously ignored him.

Katy shook her head. "It's not you. It's us."

Katy and I took our seats and plopped down.

"Wow," said Luc. "What the heck happened to you? Did you run through a hurricane or something?"

"Pretty much," said Katy.

"You've no idea," I said.

A loud "ping!" distracted everyone.

All heads turned to the huge screen that hung against the far wall.

A familiar pixilated image appeared on screen.

Chapter Ten

The image on the screen crystallized, and Peace's friendly face appeared.

Every time we see him, he looks more and more like a younger Idris Elba, I thought.

"Hey, sweetie!" Katy called out, blowing him a kiss.

"Katy!" Peace replied, his smile widening. "Sorry, I'm late, guys. Was stuck at my prof's office. I'm assisting his freshman class now. How is everyone doing?"

When we met Peace in Dar es Salaam, he was preparing for law school in Nairobi just as Mr. Mudenda, his father, had wished. Then, he won a scholarship to the Boston University School of Law, making his father even more ecstatic.

Katy had been thrilled. This meant Peace was only a four-hour drive away. He came up to Harlem every few weekends to join us, but mostly to see Katy. Seeing them together made me happy. For once, my BFF had chosen a good man.

Peace was smart, studious, and learning a topic very relevant to us. He took his role in the team seriously and signed off all emails with, "Red Heeled Rebels—legal adviser on retainer."

He still had law school to finish and a bar exam to pass before he became a full-fledged attorney, but as usual, I took help from wherever I could. Besides, Peace was happy to accept free meals and a stay at our digs in lieu of exorbitant legal fees.

Another *ping* came from the speakers.

The face of my childhood friend, Chanda, showed up on screen, next to Peace.

"Chanda!" we all cried out.

"Hey, everyone, good to see you all." She smiled elegantly. It was an ungodly time in her part of the world, but she looked better dressed and more energetic than any of us.

The last time I saw her in real life was six months ago, when I'd hugged her goodbye at the Dar es Salaam international airport.

Chanda now lived with her mother, Mrs. Ngozi, in the guest wing of Mr. Mudenda's home in Dar es Salaam.

Peace's father had lived a reclusive life for many years after his wife's death. But when we all turned up at his doorstep after barely surviving a brutal mission, he'd opened up his executive mansion to us all. That was almost two years ago. I knew he held a lot of guilt about my parents' deaths, so embracing me and my orphaned friends into his family was his way of trying to heal old wounds and find redemption.

"How's everyone doing back there?" Tetyana asked.

"All well here," replied Chanda. "Mom's volunteering at the hospital. Peace, your dad's keeping busy at the office. And Mama Gladness is bossing everyone around as usual."

Chanda leaned into the camera. "Hey Asha? Preeti has some news for you. She'll call you on Sunday."

I sat up, a pang of worry going through me.

My cousin, the only real family I had left in the world, had stayed behind at Mr. Mudenda's home. She'd gone through hell and back and needed a stable place to recover. Also, having grown up in a tiny seaside village in India, she didn't want to have anything to do with New York. Even Dar es Salaam was too big for her.

I knew she was safe in the hands of Mr. Mudenda and his stern but kind housekeeper, Mama Gladness. Still, there were days I wished she were closer.

"Is she okay?" I asked, feeling my back tensing up.

"It's all good. She got into the Kilimanjaro Medical College."

"What?" I said, sitting up. "Are you serious?"

"Mr. Mudenda's over the moon like she's his own daughter. Telling anyone who'd listen, even the delivery guy this morning.

Preeti was so embarrassed. But don't tell her I said anything, okay? She wants to give you the news herself this weekend."

I sat back, trying to soak this in.

Going to medical school had been Preeti's lifelong dream. That was before our traditional grandmother had forced her to become a child bride. *A daughter for cash.* I'd seen it happen in so many places, but it hurt the most when it happened to my own. But now, Preeti had got her life back.

Thank goodness, I whispered to myself, blinking away tears. *Thank goodness.* Maybe an angel was watching over her after all.

Another *ping*.

"Hey, Win!" Luc cried out, a broad smile breaking out on his face, his blue eyes twinkling with happiness.

Luc and Win had got close during their last few months in Dar es Salaam, so Win's move to California had been a sore point with him.

A college education was good for Win, and it was only for four years, anyway. But Luc couldn't wait for her to finish and join us in New York. He was already researching tech companies in the city, worried she'd get recruited into Silicon Valley and decide to stay.

"Hey, Luc!" Win squealed. "Guess what? I'm number one in my coding class again!"

"That's ma girl," said Luc, a proud smile on his face.

"Congrats!" I said.

"Proud of you, sweetie," said Katy.

"Hey, that's awesome," Bibi said, looking up, forgetting she was supposed to be sulking in the corner.

We were getting used to Win's news now. She was raking in award after award in her program. At seventeen, she was the youngest of us, younger than even Bibi, or so we suspected. But her life hadn't always been about good grades and school awards.

Win had spent most of her childhood in a brothel. The men who ran the trafficking ring had roped her into setting up and managing their global online network. For her, this work had been an escape from her environment and a way to get out of other duties forced on the girls. She'd taught herself well in the most adverse circumstances, and it was paying off in spades now.

It had taken a year and a half of therapy with psychiatrists, child psychologists, and anyone Mr. Mudenda could think of, to get Win to return to a semblance of a normal life. We never knew if she had fully recovered, but the girl had a sharp mind. She'd buried herself in her studies and aced exam after exam, getting a full scholarship at Stanford, of all places.

I turned my attention to the conversation around the table.

"...been hanging around outside for three weeks now," David was saying, "pretending to fix a water pipe. Either we're sitting next to the crappiest pipe in the city, or he's doing something else."

"Won't other city employees notice and report him though, if he doesn't work for them?" asked Katy.

"It's a big city with a huge maintenance department," said Luc. "No one's gonna stop to ask."

"Maybe he's a cop?" Peace asked from the screen. "NYPD? FBI?"

"Don't think so," replied Tetyana, shaking her head. "I can smell a cop from a hundred yards. He's not one."

"It's also not the Mossad, then?" I asked, giving David a sideways glance. The Mossad had many good reasons to track down their former employee.

He shook his head. "If they're here, we won't even know it. I know their tactics. It's not them."

Tetyana looked worried. When she was worried, I got worried too.

"Someone hired that man to watch us," she said, drumming her fingers on the table thoughtfully, "and they want us to know we're being watched."

Chapter Eleven

"I put my money on Black Sphere," said David.

"What the heck's *Black Sphere*?" asked Luc.

"Mercenaries," said Tetyana. "Retired operatives. Ex-military. Ex-paramilitary. But mostly badly trained bullies from the streets."

David nodded. "They'd sell their grandmother for a good package."

"Who'd hire someone to watch us?" Chanda asked.

"More importantly," said Peace, his forehead creased with worry, "who'd hire anyone to watch us so openly?"

"Sophie?" Katy whispered, as if too scared to speak her name out loud.

A silence fell in the room.

Tetyana turned to Chanda on the screen. "Seen anything unusual on your end?"

Chanda shook her head. "Geoffrey has a good team. They're always on the watch, and I can rely on them. I get security reports daily." She looked at the camera in the direction of Tetyana. "Which I send to you every night too."

"Yes," Tetyana nodded, "your team's doing a great job. And thanks for the reports. I haven't seen anything noteworthy in them either."

"Do you think Sophie's here in New York?" said Luc, making my heart skip a beat.

Oh, god, I hope not.

"She has a good reason to come after us," Katy said.

I tried to control my nausea. But I couldn't stop those memories from crashing into my head like a tsunami wave.

I'd never forgotten the look on Sophie's father's face as he wavered in front of my gun. He'd been on his knees, hands in the air, pleading with me to spare his life, a life I didn't think deserved to continue. A life that had destroyed too many innocents to count, including my own parents. It hadn't been my first kill. But it was the one that haunted me the most.

Something bitter came to my mouth.

Everyone was avoiding eye contact with me now. The feeling of regret and dread can be contagious, and no one wanted to catch it.

"I don't think it's Sophie," David said, finally. "She's more interested in money than people. She's also not one to do her dirty work herself. I'm sure she's still in Johannesburg, but I wouldn't put it past her to hire people here."

"What puzzles me," said Tetyana, looking thoughtful, "is I'd expect her goons to come rushing in here and hit us hard, not watch us patiently for days."

"Maybe it's a threat?" said Luc. "A warning?"

"Or, maybe," said Win, "they're after the money?"

We all looked at the screen.

Win was leaning in, a frown on her pretty face.

She pushed her spectacles up her nose. "Maybe they want to know where I put it?"

My stomach flipped.

What have I got her into?

I wanted to reach through the screen, give Win a long hug and apologize for everything.

"You know, Win," Luc said, his face darkening. "I really don't like it when you're alone in California. What if they come for you there?"

Luc was protective of his girlfriend. Perhaps a tad too much, some of us thought.

"It's safe here on campus," Win said. "Everybody's super nice and I've got tons of friends. All my profs love me."

"Yes, but they're not with you twenty-four-seven," said Luc. "It would be nice if you could stay with us. It's so much safer."

Katy and I exchanged glances. We couldn't sabotage Win's education. Not now.

"Or," Luc said and paused. I noticed he was deliberately looking away from me. I knew what was coming and knew that would not be possible. Not legally, anyway. I held my breath.

"I can quit the bakery and come over there. I can find another job. We don't have to tell Chef Pierre or immigration."

He glanced at me from under his eyelids, half-afraid I'd stop him.

"Hey," said Win before I could answer. "You sound like an old grandma. Did you totally forget I'm coming home for spring break this weekend?"

Luc's face lightened up. "Oh, yeah! That's awesome. I mixed up the dates." He rubbed his eyes. "Sorry, I'm super tired. Been working since four this morning while these guys were getting the royal treatment from ambassadors."

"Oh, yeah," said Bibi, her lips curled in scorn. "They gave us the royal treatment all right. We're lucky to be alive. No shi...sugar!"

All heads turned her way.

"What do you mean 'lucky to be alive?" Tetyana asked, her eyes narrowing.

I massaged my temples. My headache was turning into a migraine. It was time to tell them what had happened.

"Bad news," I said, "I lost a big contract today."

Tetyana squinted her eyes even more. "Why do I feel there's more to this than just losing a business deal?"

"We walked into a private mess. A family affair."

"It wasn't *just* a mess!" cried Bibi from her corner.

"Not sure what it was," said Katy, trying to explain. "But we saw something we shouldn't have at the ambassador's house."

"Like what?" asked David.

Katy cleared her throat. "Could have been a kidnapping."

Gasps went around the table.

"Or an attempted murder," she added.

"It's Sarah," wailed Bibi. "She's the ambassador's daughter, and she's in a huge lot of trouble. Maybe she's already dead!"

Between Katy and me, and with angry interjections from Bibi, we shared our full story.

"What the frigging heck?" Tetyana said, slapping the table when we were done. "Why didn't you call us for backup?"

"We were too busy trying to get away," I said.

"But they shot at you!" said David. "Who shoots at their caterers?"

I let out a sigh. "We should have never taken that job. Should have left the day that creep groped Katy."

"Wasn't your fault," Katy said. "I pretended it was nothing too."

"But if we didn't go back today, we'd never have seen what happened to Sarah," said Bibi, her voice rising.

"Here I thought Nairobi was dangerous," said Chanda from the screen. "New York sounds scarier. I don't know guys, maybe you all need to come back home."

"The thing is you got away safely," said Peace, who was, as always, the one who calmed things down. "That's the most important thing."

"Oh, I forgot." Katy pulled the dagger out of her pocket and held it high. "Got a little souvenir from our incident."

Tetyana reached over and took the knife with a low whistle. She held it to the light while everyone watched, fascinated.

"Nice little knife."

"A scimitar from the Middle East," said Peace, looking closely into the camera. "Could even be an antique. Where did you find that?"

"In a display case in their dining room," Katy said. "Good thing too. Without that, we'd be at the bottom of the Hudson with cement blocks on our feet."

"Oh, man," Luc said, leaning back in his seat, looking frazzled. "I take everything I said back. I'm happy I get to ice cakes. Asha, don't ever ask me to do these crazy-ass client meets."

David turned to me, his face grim. "Next time, I'm coming with you."

"No one else around when this happened?" asked Tetyana.

Katy and I shook our heads.

"It was one gunshot in an empty garage below ground. I doubt anyone heard it," Katy said. "Sounded like a car misfiring."

"But someone will ask about a car that broke through the parking lot barrier without paying," I said.

"I'm sure they'll come up with a good story," Tetyana said, her brow furrowed. "You guys didn't call it in, did you?"

"Nope," replied Bibi, shooting me an accusing look. "Asha said we weren't allowed to."

"Good," said Tetyana.

I sighed, trying to ignore the feelings of guilt washing over me. "It was us against an ambassador's son and their security team...."

"All of whom have diplomatic immunity," Peace said, finishing my sentence.

I nodded.

Chanda spoke up. "I know a group who takes care of kids in trouble, especially immigrant kids. This girl, if she's still alive, might be eligible. They're called Safe Horizon and I have a contact in their New York HQ. Maybe someone can call anonymously?"

"Great idea," I said. "Better than calling the cops directly."

Katy nodded. "Not much we can do when the family's shooting at us."

"You did the right thing," Tetyana said, "Otherwise, we'd have the NYPD, FBI, and Homeland Security here asking questions."

"With a SWAT team in tow," added Luc with a grimace.

"But what about Sarah?" cried Bibi. "If it was me, are you guys just gonna dump me too?"

"Bibi!" I said, shocked she'd even think that.

"Of course not. You know that," said Katy, giving her a stern look.

"Don't ever say silly things like that, my girl," said Chanda, wagging a finger from the screen. "We're family, for goodness' sake. We never leave anyone behind."

But Bibi looked like she was going to burst into tears.

Then I remembered. "Do you still have that card?"

It took a second for my question to register. Bibi hastily pulled the note out of her pocket and placed it on the table.

Tetyana was the first to grab it and scrutinize it. "What the heck is this?"

"Hey, Win," I called out. "We think there's a secret message on the back of this card. Can you check it out?"

"Totally. Can you send a photo?"

Bibi grabbed the card back from Tetyana's hands and took a picture with her phone. "Sent!" she called out.

Win scrutinized the image, her eyes whizzing across the photo, her brain working a million miles per second. It didn't take more than ten seconds for her face to clear.

"Who wrote this?" she demanded.

"Probably Sarah or someone in the house," said Katy.

"We think it's a call for help," I said.

"How old is this Sarah?" said Win, scrunching her nose. "This is kid's stuff. Even you guys can break this." She typed something on her screen. "Just use the grid and you have H-A-S-T-E-I-N space W-E-A-R-H-U-S-E."

"Can you show it to us on screen, Win?" asked Chanda.

Win put her screen on display. "Here you go."

"Hastein Wearhuse?" said David. "Is that a name?"

"Hastein's Swedish, I think," said Katy. "I had a teacher with that family name in Toronto."

"Never heard of a Wearhuse," said Tetyana, frowning at the screen.

"Wear huse, maybe?" I tried. "Wear, I get, but what kind of a "huse" can you wear?"

Everyone had their phones out now and was Googling.

"Hey, did you know Hastein's a card trick?"

"No, it's a Viking king. You were right about it being Swedish, Katy."

"It's a town in Alberta. Settled by Swedish immigrants."

"I think I found it!"

We all turned to Peace.

"It's the head of the Department of State, USA."

Chapter Twelve

"Jacob Hastein," said Peace, "that's his name."

Chanda frowned. "What does the State Department have to do with the Saudi ambassador's household?"

"A lot," said Peace, scrolling through his phone. "The State Department is the primary federal contact for foreign embassies on US soil."

"What does that mean?" asked Luc.

"It means the department is very familiar with the ambassador, his household and his staff. They should have settled them in New York, if I'm not mistaken."

"We saw a girl getting drugged or kidnapped," said Katy. "Gory stuff, but there's nothing political about it."

"It's farfetched to think this has anything to do with the State Department," I said. "Or any government."

"I think you're right." Peace nodded, still not looking up from his phone. "I wonder if the connection has to do with this Hastein guy himself, the head of the department. He's very wealthy and owns several businesses. Shipping. Trucking. Logistics. He's got quite the reputation too."

"What kind of rep?" asked Tetyana.

"Partying. Hanging out with celebrities and diplomats. Got caught inviting a bunch of underage girls to a party at one point, but got away over a technicality."

"Sarah's family would kill her if she went to a party," said Bibi. "They'd never let her."

"Sarah isn't the playing kind anyway," Katy said. "She's a stay-at-home, sixteen-year-old stuck in an ultra-strict family. She has the usual teen issues on top of a real nasty attitude if you ask me."

"I can understand not wanting your child to party," said Chanda, "but who watches quietly while their daughter's in a room with thugs?"

"I keep telling you. How come no one listens to me?" Bibi's voice rose in exasperation. "Happens all the time. Sarah did something really bad, so they're punishing her."

"I'm sure that scream we heard was Sarah," said Katy. "That's probably when they dragged her to her room. Then somehow, she got a hold of her phone and called you, Asha."

"And you got to her room just when the men came back to do whatever," said David.

"This is a tad unbelievable," said Chanda, shaking her head. "Perhaps there's a perfectly suitable explanation for what you saw. Maybe you didn't see the full picture. Maybe you—"

"We didn't imagine them shooting us," Bibi said sharply.

"She's right," said David. "We can't ignore the damage to the car. It's there in black and white."

Tetyana nodded. "You guys saw something you shouldn't have. That's why they came after you."

"But why would your own family drug you or harm you?" asked Chanda.

"I can tell you why," said Bibi, sitting up, her eyes flashing in fury. "Maybe she wanted to go out of the house without her head veil. Maybe she wanted to go to a high school party. Maybe she went to a party and got caught. Maybe she had a secret boyfriend. Maybe that boyfriend was white. Maybe she'd gone on a—"

"Whoa, slow down there, cheetah," Tetyana said, putting her hands up. "We can sit here all night and come up with many assumptions and twist our knickers into knots. But they'll be wild guesses, and we have serious work to do. We still haven't got to today's agenda yet."

"That's true." David nodded. "We have bigger priorities than diplomatic goons harassing their kids."

"They're evil!" howled Bibi.

I let out a resigned sigh. "You're right. They're a strange bunch for sure. And we lost a good contract. But it's time to move on. I'm sorry, Bibi."

"So you're just gonna forget about Sarah?"

"I don't think I'll ever forget what I saw, honey. But we can't run around trying to help everyone, especially now."

She gave me an angry look that said I'd let her down. My heart sank. Bibi glanced around the table with tears in her eyes, trying to rustle up support.

"Sorry, hun," said Tetyana, shaking her head. "Believe you me, we all feel terrible for this girl, and it pisses me off to no end to hear they came after you with a weapon. But right now, we've got lots of other work to do."

"What if they're torturing her?" Bibi's voice rose. "Like they did to me!"

The room fell silent.

It was remarkable how quickly most of us had got accustomed to our new freedoms. Our lives had turned one hundred and eighty degrees over the past two years, but not everyone was taking this journey to "normal" at the same speed. Bibi was having the most difficult time.

We each had our coping mechanisms. For me, it was setting up the business with my childhood idol, Chef Pierre. The scars of my past simmered beneath the surface, but I'd buried them well. Kali only woke up when someone cornered me now.

David and Tetyana poured their energy into their martial arts school and into training us. Win forgot by getting lost in anything digital and hackable. Luc had recovered by immersing himself in a new culinary skill that was legal for a change. Chanda coped by taking on the complex job of managing our orphanages in East Africa.

Katy kept the bakery's finances, but there was one activity that made her forget everything. The gun range we trained at on weekends had an archery program. The day she discovered it was the day we lost her to it completely.

Bibi was a sharp girl with a knack for languages and really should have been in school. But she'd appointed herself as our odd-job-delivery-girl and hadn't budged when we'd suggested a local trades program or catch-up high school classes. Unlike Win, school wasn't important to her.

"Hey, Bibi," I said, "We'll try to contact Safe Horizon, okay?"

She didn't even look at me.

"And I'll check on this Hastein guy to see if there are any connections to the Saudi ambassador's family," said Peace. "How does that sound?"

"Thank you," Bibi squeaked.

"I'll ask my contacts if they have any intel on the goons who work for the Saudi embassy," said Tetyana. "Or that son of his."

"And I'm gonna recheck this code you gave me, okay?" said Win.

Bibi nodded mutely, wiping a tear-stained cheek.

"Honey," said Chanda, "I want you to know we all love you. We can disagree and debate, but that doesn't mean we'll ever leave anyone behind. I truly hope you understand that."

Bibi nodded.

"Sending you a virtual hug, sweetie. I love you."

"I love you too," Bibi mumbled, miming Chanda's hug back.

I caught Katy's eyes.

Yes, we still had to get to today's business.

"All right, everyone," I said, sitting up. "What's this week's tally?"

David went first. "Six thousand from my end."

"Seven thousand here," said Katy. "Expenses down five percent so we can send a good chunk your way, Chanda."

"Except we now have a car to fix," I said. "An expensive repair. Sorry."

"I'm not worried about a few thousand dollars," Chanda said, leaning in, her face suddenly serious. "There's something bigger happening here you all need to know about."

Chapter Thirteen

I felt everyone in the room brace themselves.

"We did a rescue from the Congo and I'm running out of space. We're using makeshift buildings to house everyone, but it's not sustainable. And we got news of another camp last night. We need more funds."

"How much are we talking about?" Katy asked.

"Still doing the math, but it'll be around two hundred grand for accommodations, security, staff, and I need to hire another nurse next month."

Luc let out a low whistle. "That's a lot of moola in a short time."

"I'll send you the budget next week. We'll need half of it in three months. If we can't get it, I'll have to stop the rescues."

"Want me to take it out of the Jamaican account?" asked Win. "Or the Barbados one?"

I shook my head. "We have to be careful. We already dipped into those for the reno work. Constant large withdrawals will send red flags to the banks."

"I'm worried they're already on to us." I heard Katy mutter next to me.

David nodded. "I wouldn't touch those accounts for eight months at least. We have to find another way. We can top it up at the end."

The room fell silent.

Everyone sat deep in thought, trying to figure out how to rustle up that kind of money quickly.

Tetyana spoke first. "We can start small. I'll schedule more classes. David, maybe it's time to up your rates. You're getting a good rep in the neighborhood."

"Sounds good," he said. "I'll hustle more at the basketball courts and the gyms too."

"I'll try more embassies and big clients," I said. "See if I can get more referrals from Chef Pierre."

"What about the Saudi embassy? Won't they give us a bad reference or something?" asked Katy. "I mean, they were really unhappy with us today."

"I've got a funny feeling we won't have to worry about them," I said. "They'll want to bury this. They're official diplomats and all."

A wicked smile crossed Tetyana's face.

"Actually...," she said, picking up the dagger and turning it in her hand slowly, her smile broadening. The knife glinted under the boardroom lights. "We've got the upper hand here, folks." She looked at the screen. "You need more cash for the kids, Chanda?"

"Er..." Chanda hesitated, leaning back with a worried look. She knew Tetyana well by now. "Yes, but we can't—"

"I think I know where we can find some hard cold cash fast."

"You thinking what I'm thinking?" Luc asked, a wonky grin appearing on his face. "I was going to suggest it. You beat me to it."

"Jeepers," said David, raising an eyebrow. "That's gutsy, folks."

Bibi swiveled her head around, trying to follow. "What are you all talking about?" she asked. "What?"

"Blackmail," I said, shaking my head.

"I'll admit it's crossed my mind," said Tetyana.

"Guys," Peace said, his forehead lined with worry. "Remember, we promised to keep our affairs legitimate from now on? This is why I'm here. As your legal adviser, I don't recommend this."

Katy nodded. "No more shady stuff. We've got to stay clean. Besides, this sounds dangerous."

I looked around the table. Everyone was staring at Tetyana, half the team thinking of how to make her idea work, and the other half wondering how to stop it.

We'd already racked up enough points to land each one of us in jail in several countries. We couldn't afford to play in these gray areas any longer. I rubbed my temples. This meeting had taken far longer than we'd planned. It was time to pull out my leadership card.

"All right, everyone," I said. "Why don't we chew on this tonight? It's been a long day, for everyone. Unless someone has more news, this meeting's adjourned."

Chanda nodded. "I'll get the financial statements so we have a clearer picture of what we need. Love you all. See you next week, same time, same place."

She waved and her picture went blank.

"I have an exam tomorrow and need my beauty rest tonight," said Peace. "Talk to you soon, Katy. I'll be driving up next weekend. Sleep tight, everyone." With that, his picture went blank as well.

"Hey, don't forget to pick me up at the airport tomorrow!" Win called out.

"I'll be three hours early waiting for ya," said Luc with a grin.

She blew him a kiss. And her face disappeared from the screen.

Everyone pushed their chairs back and stood up, yawning, stretching, then slowly shuffled out of the room, one by one.

Our sleeping quarters were on the second floor over the bakery, so we didn't have far to go. Soon, a troupe of tired footsteps trudged up the stairs on their way to hot showers and warm beds.

I stayed behind to help David shut down the audio-visual equipment.

This was usually Win's job when she was here. She called the War Room her "office" because of the computer equipment. David considered it to be his because of the weaponry stored in here. It was a friendly sibling rivalry that amused us all.

But the items inside the weapons cabinet were no smiling matter.

The storage was made of hardened steel and had digital, physical and biometric locks that only David or Tetyana could open. Besides our emergency stash of cash, inside were a series of handguns, semi-automatic rifles, David's sniper rifle with the scope, the crossbow

Katy practiced on and Tetyana's grenade launcher, which only she was allowed to touch.

Why we needed a grenade launcher, I didn't know. I just hoped we'd never, ever, have to use it.

While it was David's task to secure the weapons, it had been Tetyana's job to procure them. But she wouldn't tell us where she'd got the stash from.

I knew she had connections to the underworld, so Peace and I made her swear that nothing had been stolen. The last thing we needed was more gangsters on our tails. In response, she'd shown us the firearms licenses for each piece in the cabinet.

"You even got a license for that bazooka rocket thing?" Peace had asked, his eyes wide in shock.

"Grenade launcher," Tetyana had corrected him with a disdainful sniff. "This is America, guys. The second amendment rules all. Best danged country on earth if you ask me."

Peace had been skeptical, but we had to trust her. Besides, we had to be prepared for anything. Without Tetyana and David and their skills, we'd be naked and vulnerable.

David was going around the room now, doing his routine checks, locking up for the night. I'd just finished bringing up the screen when he turned around and gave me a strange look.

"Hey, Asha?"

"Yup?" I said, latching the screen in place so it wouldn't fall.

"Just wondering if, er..."

"What?"

I hadn't seen him this way before, eyes averted, face slightly red. David was a doer more than a talker. But when he talked, he was more confident.

"What is it?" My headache was still throbbing, and my brain was fuzzy. "Are you worried about today? Don't think it's connected to us. It was a random event."

"No, I mean, do you want to get a bite to eat?"

"Right now?"

I glanced at the clock on the wall. It was nearly ten, and I hadn't eaten, but I had to get up at four the next day to open the bakery.

"No, er, I mean maybe on Saturday?"

I stared at him. *Is he asking me on a date?*

I felt my face go warm again. I hoped it wasn't showing.

"You mean d...d...dinner?" I heard myself stammer and cursed silently. I hoped I didn't look like the girls in his class who gave him gooey eyes every time he walked past.

"Yeah, if that's what you—"

My phone rang.

I recognized the tone.

"I have to get this," I said.

Chef Pierre rarely called me directly these days. It was Anne, his administrative assistant, who did, and it was always early in the morning and always regarding the orders of the day or to confirm a meeting with the Chef.

Why's he calling this late?

I turned on the phone and put him on speaker.

"Bonjour, Chef," I said in the brightest voice I could muster.

"What in the name of goodness gracious is going on, mademoiselle?"

"Is everything okay?" I asked.

"I just got an absolutely torrid call from the Embassy of Saudi Arabia."

My heart sank.

"Oh?" That was all I could come up with.

"It was extremely unusual. And a most serious offense. It wasn't a handler or even the secretary. It was the ambassador himself."

I felt sick to my stomach.

"What...what did he say?"

"He said you assaulted his daughter."

Chapter Fourteen

"It's a dreadful allegation."

The Chef's voice was strained.

"I cannot understand this. How can such a thing even happen?"

Chef Pierre was typically a jolly man with a cheery smile on his plump face, but this time I heard a tremor in his voice I hadn't encountered before.

"This will hurt our reputation. No one will want to do business with you or me. What do you have to say for yourself, mademoiselle?"

I took a deep breath before answering.

Do I tell him what we saw? The gunshot? What really happened?

"I didn't touch her, Chef. I'd never hit a girl. This is ridiculous." I paused. "What exactly did the ambassador say he saw?"

"Well," the Chef hesitated, "he said it was his son who's accusing you of this scandalous crime."

"Oh, is that right?"

"He phoned from the airport, saying his son just called about an incident at their home. Apparently, you and Katy had gone up to the daughter's room, had an argument over the cake design, got into a fight and slapped her around so badly, she'd fainted. That's what he'd told the ambassador."

I was speechless.

"So, what do you have to say to that, mademoiselle?"

"Chef, Kat...Katy and I would never hit a kid even if you held a gun to our heads," I sputtered. "I don't know what that son's up to, but that's a preposterous lie."

"I can't imagine this in a thousand years, myself. I am appalled. What happened in that house?"

"Chef, I don't think we can trust that man."

"If you'd pardon me for being so direct, you are a petite woman. I mean, anyone could crush you in seconds, even that girl."

I stared at the phone. *What's he getting at now?*

"And Katy's such a sweet girl. I cannot imagine either of you being violent. This is madness."

I let out a small sigh of relief. He was partially right. I was on the small side, and Katy could be very charming. But Chef Pierre had never seen Katy angry or seen me when Kali was fully awake. I was glad he didn't know that side of us.

"This is a grave misunderstanding," I said.

"I can't afford to let misunderstandings ruin my business, mademoiselle. Neither can you."

I hated it when he became all "mademoiselle" formal with me.

"Madame Bouchard will have a fit if she gets wind of this, and she is well connected to this community, as you know."

He's bringing her into this?

Madame Bouchard had given me my first break in Toronto almost three years ago. But she'd let me down. She'd let all of us down when we'd needed her support the most. I no longer respected The Diplomatic Dragon Lady, my private name for her. Just the thought of that woman strutting around in her fancy Chanel pantsuits and pearls, acting like she owned everyone, made me queasy.

But it was Madame Bouchard who oiled Chef Pierre's connections with the glitterati and referred all diplomatic businesses to him. This business trickled down to me. I couldn't afford to mess with either of them.

I steeled myself. "Chef Pierre, there's something you need to know."

"Oh?"

"On our first day, the ambassador's son came on strong to Katy. When she went to say hello, he pulled her in and, er, groped her. She tried to brush it off, but it was horrible. We said nothing then, but I think it's time to tell you."

The Chef was silent for a few seconds. Then I heard him blurt out, "my goodness!"

I glanced up at David who was following the conversation, hands on hips, a frown on his face.

"The head of staff was in the room, but she ignored it," I continued. "It was uncalled for and not right."

An idea was forming in the back of my head. Maybe I could keep this lucrative contract intact and redeem myself in Bibi's eyes too. If Sarah was in major trouble, we may even get to help her. I could feed three birds with one hand if I played my cards well.

"The family also made it clear they didn't appreciate...." *How to explain this?* "Their idea of a perfect caterer is a blonde version of Julia Child. One of them took exception to me being half-Indian and was pretty vocal about it."

"Did they actually *say* that?"

"Yes."

"That's terrible. Why didn't you tell me this before?"

"It was embarrassing, Chef. And I didn't want to lose the contract, so I tried to ignore it all. But now..." I trailed off.

"Did anything else serious happen?" His tone had changed.

So far, I'd told the truth. This was where things would get tricky. I swallowed hard. I felt like I was standing at the edge of a cliff. One wrong move and I could fall and take my friends down with me.

"Today," I said, turning away to avoid eye contact with David, "we spoke up. I told them we wouldn't sign the contract if this carried on. I also told them I would talk to you. That got them upset, especially the son. He was angry and said something about their honor. He said we were going to regret it."

David gave me a funny look. I ignored him.

Better to beg for forgiveness than ask for permission.

"It's only an assumption, Chef, but I think that's why he's accusing us of this outrageous claim. He didn't like us speaking up. Why else would he make up something outrageous like this?"

The Chef was silent on his end for a long time.

I remained still, holding my breath. My palm was so sweaty, I worried the phone would slip out.

"Is there anything else I need to know?" Chef Pierre asked finally.

The image of Sarah on the bed flashed across my mind. I ignored it.

"No."

The bullet hole in the back window of our car came to mind. I pushed it away.

"Nothing else."

"It was a terrible misunderstanding all around," I said. "I'd be happy to return and finish this job, but under one condition. They must promise to treat each of my team with respect. And no more crazy accusations."

A longer silence on the other end.

Is this it? Is he going to break our partnership? Will we get kicked out of New York?

"Well," said Chef in a normal tone of voice, "that explains why the ambassador didn't want to answer my question."

"What question?"

"I asked if he would talk to the police and he quickly changed topic. Evasive, if you ask me. Then again, he wouldn't want any scandals. Funny thing is he still wants me to cater his events. Strange reaction, I thought, given the enormity of their accusation."

I waited. Let him come to his own conclusions.

The Chef let out a loud sigh. "It's always some drama or the other with these diplomatic families. My life was so simple when I catered to local birthday parties."

I raised my eyebrows. He didn't know half the drama we'd seen that day.

"They're a bit of an entitled, elitist bunch. Especially that son. I met him once at a diplomatic party, and I must admit his manner left such an unpleasant taste in my mouth. Those rumors about him must be true."

I was dying to ask about the rumors, but this wasn't the time.

The Chef sighed again. "I'd believe you any day over that nasty young man."

"Thank you, Chef. I appreciate you saying that."

"We have such a good contract, it would be a shame to lose it. These people could make up more stories and hurt our reputation in the city. It's best to make amends, I think."

Thank you, I whispered silently.

"But next time, please take one of the boys with you. I hate to say this, but that son won't pull tricks like this in front of the men. It's cultural. Make sure you have a witness at all times. And stay professional."

Stay professional? I bit my tongue. At any other time, I'd have been mad, but I had to play this right.

"I understand, Chef," I said, gritting my teeth.

David spread his arms wide as if to ask, *What are you doing?*

Chef Pierre was prattling in my ear. "You never know what kind of people you'll meet these days, and these diplomatic missions are the worst."

"I'm really sorry for the trouble, Chef. I'll be more careful next time."

"Listen, Asha, I know what you and Katy went through. I've had my fair share of creeps. Some hate gays. Some hate the French. That's two strikes against me. It's just the way the world works. We shouldn't apologize for them. Next time, call me when it happens. Don't wait until a crisis."

"I will do so."

He let out another heavy sigh. "For a moment there, I was sure I was going to lose all my hair. Well, whatever's left of it, anyway. Maybe Madame Bouchard can sort this out for us, get the contract back on the road and make sure they treat you right while on the job."

"That would be lovely, Chef."

"Okay, got to join hubby now. He wants to watch the latest *Game of Thrones* and insists on watching it with me."

After wishing me a good evening, he hung up.

I put the phone away, feeling jittery. I hated lying, even though it was a lie-via-omission.

David was staring at me in shock.

"You want to go back to that madhouse?"

"I know what I'm doing."

"You're inviting trouble."

"The son lied to the ambassador. He doesn't know what really happened to Sarah."

"These families are tight. They have no secrets. The whole house smells."

"The ambassador's the most normal person in that house. He shook our hands, didn't make nasty comments and didn't try to grope us."

David raised an eyebrow. "That's your baseline for normal now?"

I sighed.

"Firstborn sons are precious in Arab families," said David. "They have more power than their mothers. I come from that part of the world, remember."

"Yes, but you're from Yemen."

"It's worse in Saudi Arabia. There's no difference when it comes to family matters. Besides, that man's crafty. He's a diplomat."

"What do you mean?"

"He's an ambassador. It's in his job description. He's supposed to make himself, his family and his country look good. They'll never accept a scandal."

I shook my head to clear it. I'd already said yes to going back. I couldn't pull out now.

"That call was a warning," David was saying, his forehead creased with worry. "You're playing with fire. Be careful."

"Hey, David?" I said, putting up a finger to shush him. "Can I take you up on that dinner offer?"

"Now?" he spluttered.

"Please? I need some air. And I'm starved."

That did it. We closed up the boardroom and walked out into the fresh night air.

No, it wasn't a date. Or maybe it was.

Either way, I was happy to have his company, even though he was miffed at my idea. I hadn't eaten much all day, and Chef Pierre's call had rattled me. There was no way I could sleep after that.

It was a Wednesday night, but the city was still alive and humming. We headed down an alleyway near our bakery. Too busy debating, we took a detour without realizing it and ended in a side street I'd not seen before. Neither had David.

We were in an even grittier neighborhood a few blocks from our home. It was a place that had yet to catch up with the gentrification elsewhere.

We stopped to take in the unfamiliar facades and graffiti-covered storefronts. Black garbage bags and empty cardboard boxes were strewn against a wall and an unwashed, unshaven man was squatting nearby, eating out of a Chinese takeaway container, his eyes in a drug-infused daze.

I wondered if we should head back when David nudged me.

"Hey," he said, "been there before?"

I followed his eyes to a large dingy bar that took up almost a third of the block.

The Troika.

A Russian bar.

"Why does that ring a bell?" asked David.

The establishment's name was set in severe black letters on top of the building. A neon sign on a windowpane flashed "Welcome," but the restaurant looked anything but. It was the type of place where you'd expect to see a grand fistfight break out over the tables.

"Never been there, but I've heard that name too."

I frowned, feeling like I was seeing something important. I tried to recall something someone had said about this place.

But who?

Chapter Fifteen

Three hefty Harley-Davidson bikes were parked in front of the main doors.

Leaning against them, having a late-night smoke, were three men in leather vests and red scarfs tied around their heads. Their hair was gray, and their faces were weathered from age. Whoever wanted to walk in had to get past these old sentries first.

"Doesn't Tetyana hang out at a bar every Friday night?" I said as we scoped the place from afar.

We all needed time away from work and each other, so we each had a designated "off-day." Friday evenings were Tetyana's time to get away from it all.

"This is where she comes on her off-day?" David asked in surprise.

I shrugged. "Have you seen any other Russian bar around here?"

He shook his head.

"Maybe she told us about it. That's why the name's so familiar."

The restaurant had been grand once. The immense wooden door, the stained-glass windows, and the high ceiling were impressive. It had probably been a place where people arrived in top hats and tailcoats, driven in old-fashioned horse buggies.

But the building hadn't been taken care of for decades. The brick wall was peeling, and the door needed a paint job. Two sets of red rope barriers lined the entrance, but they looked like faded throwaways from a hip-hop bar.

"Guess she gets homesick sometimes," said David.

"At least she's got a place to go to."

David nudged me. "You're not the only one, you know that?"

"What do you mean?"

"You think I have a place to call home?"

"I'm sure there's a Yemeni-East African-Jewish restaurant somewhere. You just have to look. But I'll never find a Sri Lankan-Indian-Tanzanian-Canadian spot. That's for sure."

"You never know. This is New York."

We stared at the facade for a while, feeling nostalgic for things that didn't even exist.

"Didn't she say she gets her perogy and cabbage roll fix on Fridays?" I said, suddenly remembering how hungry I was. I pulled David by the hand. "Let's check it out."

One of the motorcycle men gave us a quick nod as we walked past.

"Zdravstvuj!" he said.

I'd heard Tetyana use a similar greeting on the phone. I remembered thinking I'd never learn how to pronounce that word myself.

"Hey, hello," David and I replied at the same time.

I could feel the watchful eyes of the men on our backs as we climbed the short flight of stairs toward the main door. It was late, and the street was getting quieter. I wondered if this had been a good idea after all.

David opened the door for me. The smell of alcohol and guffaws of male laughter hit us as we stepped in.

Inside, the dark red wallpaper and low lighting from ancient chandeliers gave the place a sinister, gangster-like feel.

At a round table in the middle of the room sat six men with an open bottle of vodka. They held thick cigars in their hands and were talking boisterously in Russian. It was illegal to smoke inside restaurants in New York, but I was sure no one would call these men out. They didn't even notice us coming in.

A handful of derelict men were watching a game of pool on the side of the room, hanging on to their whiskeys and vodkas, lost in their worlds. Regulars, I guessed.

We took a window seat furthest away from the main table, closest to the door. Just in case we had to leave fast. *Just in case* was our mantra these days.

When the waiter came, I didn't even refer to the menu. I didn't have to. I ordered cabbage rolls and perogies, eager to try Tetyana's favorite foods.

David shrugged and said he'd have the same. The waiter gave us a quizzical look but took our order without a word. When I asked for the vodka brand Tetyana enjoyed, he lifted an eyebrow, but again said nothing.

David and I devoured the food when it came. Now I knew why Tetyana was always going on about her grandma's cabbage rolls. I made a mental note to ask the waiter for the recipe if he'd be willing to share.

The waiter didn't return to our table until we'd finished eating. But he had a question for us before I could ask mine.

"Excuse me, but I have to inquire," he said as he picked up our empty plates, "Are you with Tetyana?"

I froze.

David stiffened.

I looked the waiter over carefully. He seemed a normal, friendly person, but you never knew with Tetyana.

"Who is that?" I asked, putting on my most innocent expression.

"She's the only one in this city who orders Ukrainian cabbage rolls with Morosha Vodka."

I glanced at David, who had his poker face on now.

"Morosha is banned in Russia, but we serve it here. Only place in town."

Oh, no.

"But we're in America now, eh?" he continued. "Ukraine? Russia? Who cares? We're all immigrants with funny long names here. Haha!"

I gave him a frozen smile. "We're new to town. Heard you serve good Ukrainian food here, so we had to try it out."

"We have the best Ukrainian cook in town," he replied, pointing at the kitchen. "Only time he gets to make what he wants is when Tetyana comes in. They're best friends. They sit in the back kitchen talking for hours. Sometimes I think they're planning an insurgency in Russia! Haha!"

I fought the urge to glance at David.

The waiter paused and gave us a strange look. "Hey, but you two aren't Ukrainian. Or Russian. Or European, even."

"We're not," David answered curtly.

"So this woman comes here often for cabbage rolls and perogies?" I asked, trying to defuse his attention from us.

The waiter nodded. "And to chat with Olek. Every Friday night."

"Olek?"

"The Ukrainian cook."

A woman's annoyed voice called out loudly from the kitchen. The waiter jerked his head up and yelled something back.

He picked up our glasses and turned to leave. "Welcome to New York," he said, flashing a friendly smile before leaving.

"Do you know this Olek?" I whispered to David.

"Never heard of him."

"A new friend?" I wondered. "Or an old one?"

"Weird," said David, glancing around to make sure no one was within hearing range. "She's not a huge fan of the Russians. They shot her mother and tortured her brother. She fought them back home, so why would she come here?"

"Like he said, this is America. Everyone mixes and forget old fights, don't they?"

David shrugged. But he was right, there was something peculiar about Tetyana hanging out in a Russian bar.

We left the money on the table and stepped outside.

The motorcycle gang had gone.

It was getting chilly, and the vodka was making me sleepy. All I wanted was to fall into my warm bed and close my eyes.

Within fifteen minutes we were back at the bakery. The lights were off. Everyone had gone to sleep.

We tiptoed inside, barricaded the door and turned on the alarm system as usual. I always felt a sense of relief when I heard that alarm beep three times to indicate the building was secure.

David and I trudged upstairs to our sleeping quarters.

We'd used most of our funds to renovate the bakery and the dojo. We still had to put stronger bars on our windows, another expense for our books, something Tetyana had been pushing for. But I'd told Katy to make that a lower priority until we got the business up and running. That meant equipment for the dojo and bakery came first.

This also meant less money for our living quarters. We were a little too old for bunking with each other, but it saved us money, money we could send back to Chanda or put back into our business.

When we got to the landing, David gave me that funny look again.

My heart skipped a beat.

He leaned in as if to say something. My heart leaped, then did a cartwheel. I hoped I didn't look as ditsy as I felt.

He got closer as if to whisper something in my ear, but at the last second decided against it and stepped back.

"See you tomorrow," he whispered with a smile.

I nodded mutely.

He turned around and walked into the room he shared with Luc.

They had two bunk beds in the boys' room, where Luc and David slept and where Peace stayed when he visited. The girls' room had three sets of bunk beds, so Win could join us during college breaks.

I stumbled toward the girls' room where Tetyana, Katy, and Bibi were now asleep. I turned the doorknob and pushed open the door.

A dark shadow was sitting up on the bunk below mine. Someone was crying.

Chapter Sixteen

"Bibi?"

I closed the door gently behind me and walked over to her.

I peeked at the beds. Tetyana was dead to the world, snoring softly on the top bunk next to us. Below her, Katy cuddled with her pillow, sound asleep.

"What's going on?" I whispered, kneeling next to Bibi.

She sat crouched at the edge of her bunk in her purple pajamas, phone in her hand, tears streaming down her cheeks. She wiped her face with the back of her hand.

"Hey," I sighed, "I know you're mad at me, but can you tell me what's going on?"

"It's Sarah," she whimpered.

"What about her?"

"She just texted me."

"What? How—?"

"I texted her."

"I thought they took her phone away."

"I tried the number on the card and she wrote back to me." Bibi thrust her phone in my face. "See?"

I leaned back and squinted at the screen. The text app was open, but the words were squiggly. It was in Arabic.

"What's it say?"

"She's saying everyone's mad at her. Really mad." Bibi gave me an accusing look that said, *I told you.*

"Why?"

She shrugged. "That's all she said."

"How did she get a hold of that phone?"

"It's Reza's phone. When she came to give her food tonight, she gave her this phone in secret."

"Who's Reza?"

"The servant girl."

At least she has an ally, I thought. *And at least she's still alive.*

"So, was it Reza who wrote on that card, then?"

But why would that servant girl help Sarah, putting her employment or even security at risk? I wasn't sure who to feel worse for: Reza for trying to help her mistress who mistreated her, or the ambassador's daughter now in uncertain danger.

Then again, it was hard to know if Sarah was telling the truth. She wasn't the most reliable person I'd met. No one in that family was.

Bibi shook her head. "She said she can't be on the phone long, so she stopped texting."

"Did you tell her to call the police? They can help her. Text her back and tell her she needs to call them ASAP."

Bibi gave a strong head shake. "That's the worst thing to tell her."

"Why?"

"Her brother will really kill her then. Then, he'll run away to Saudi Arabia and they'll never catch him 'coz he's got that special passport."

That damned diplomatic immunity again.

Tetyana groaned and turned in her bed. We stayed silent for a minute, waiting for her to settle back down. I glanced over at Katy, but she was still lost to the world.

My phone buzzed in my pocket, making me jump. I almost hit my head on the top of the bunk bed. I pulled my mobile out with shaking hands, wondering if Sarah was trying to reach me now. I unlocked my phone and checked my messages.

"Win!"

Bibi peered over my shoulder as I clicked on the text.

"Heya," said the message, "broke rest of code. Hastein is correct. Last word spelled wrong. It's Warehouse."

"Warehouse?" I said, puzzled. "Hastein Warehouse?"

The phone buzzed as another message came in.

"Don't forget me! Flying tomorrow. Want to try new cakes please."

I typed a response. "Can't wait to see you too, honey. Lots of new recipes."

Win's reply came in seconds. "Searched for Hastein warehouse. Found 2. 1 in NY. Going to bed now."

Bibi nudged me and whispered, "Say hi for me."

I typed: "Bibi sends love. Pick you @airport at 4:30 PM EST tomorrow. Sleep tight. Love ya. Hugs & kisses from all."

I got a row of heart emojis back.

I put my phone away, glad she was coming home soon.

"So what do we do about Sarah?" Bibi asked, giving me that fiery look again. "You're not going to ignore her again, are you?"

I now knew why she was so concerned. Bibi saw herself in Sarah's shoes. Her own family had punished her for "dishonoring" them and now, this strange girl from a different social strata, but bound by the same cultural values, was in similar trouble.

I couldn't tell Bibi of my plans yet. I didn't want to get her hopes high for nothing.

"I need to have a chat with Chef Pierre. Can you give me another day, please?"

I reached out to give her a side hug. She pulled away.

"Hey, I know you're scared. This is probably triggering a whole load of bad stuff for you. But will you promise me something?"

She shot me a suspicious look.

I pulled her in and held her. This time, she didn't wiggle out.

"What?" she said.

"Get some sleep and stop worrying. That's what I need you to promise me now. We need to stay healthy, so we can think more clearly and get ready to do the right thing, okay?"

With a small nod, she turned around and slipped under her sheets, and placed her phone next to her pillow.

"Good night, Bibi," I whispered.

"Don't forget her, okay?" she whispered back.

I sat next to her, a hand over her arm until she fell asleep.

Bibi was an enigma. No one knew how old she truly was. Sometimes she was confident and mature, then within minutes, she'd act out like a petulant child. Bibi had lost her childhood a long time ago and had experienced violence none of us could even imagine. But now and then, I'd glimpse the cheeky girl still inside her.

Her transformation from a frightened, burqa-clad young woman to the plucky girl she was now had been remarkable. Even more phenomenal was how she'd tracked us down in New York after we'd lost her in Europe. By the time she found us, she'd ditched her robe, spiked her hair, got a tattoo, a nose ring, and her favorite pair of bright red Doc Martens. She was finally free to be herself.

I pulled the blanket to her chin and tucked her in.

I changed into my pajama shorts and climbed up to my bunk, thinking of the growing list of things I had to do. We needed to make more money fast. Lives were at risk if we didn't.

Win's final heart emoji message popped to mind. Luc was right. I'd also feel much better once everyone was under this roof together.

A buzz from my phone made me pick it up. It was another text from Win, just one short line this time.

"Check Main Email. NOW."

I clicked on my email icon, but there was nothing new. I hit refresh. Nothing.

Maybe the email's still on its way. But why didn't she just text me?

I frowned at the text. Why did she say "Main Email"? Why not just say "check email"?

I had only one email account. Strange. I opened my email again. Nothing.

The words *Main Email* kept swirling in my brain. I suddenly realized Win wasn't referring to my email. That phrase meant something else, something key, but for the life of me, I couldn't put my finger on it.

It was getting late, my head was still throbbing, and I needed sleep. I slipped under my sheets and closed my eyes but, as usual, sleep didn't come.

I tossed and turned, willing myself to sleep. That, of course, never worked. My brain was refusing to relax because that was when my past sneaked into my head, bringing nightmares to life.

I'd learned a valuable lesson over the years. Revenge absolved nothing. It only haunted your dreams, forever.

But this night, other worries were crowding my head on top of old memories. My gut was telling me we were heading into a storm.

How big of a storm, I wasn't sure yet.

Chapter Seventeen

"She's not here!"

Luc swiveled around, eyes darting in all directions.

"Did you check the carousels?" I asked.

"What do you think I've been doing?" he snapped.

We'd been waiting at the airport for two hours.

I was getting fidgety. *Where's this girl?*

Win's flight from San Francisco had arrived on time and all the passengers had disembarked. But neither Win nor her luggage had shown up. She wasn't returning calls either.

I'd been hanging near the baggage pickup area, the one designated for her flight, my eyes trained on the arrival gate like a hawk. All I wanted to do was pluck Win from the crowd as soon as she came out and whisk her home as quickly as possible.

After the first wave of passengers had trundled through the gate, Luc had talked to the airline. No luck. They wouldn't share any information as he had no proof of being a family member. He'd returned crestfallen, his eyes ringed with worry.

After two more planeloads had walked through the gates, I'd asked Luc to stay and keep watch while I had a chat with the airline. Maybe they'd be more receptive to a woman inquiring.

It took me a while to get the attention of the harried, impatient clerk. They'd had several last-minute cancelations, but they wouldn't give me names. Showing my driver's license and pleading didn't help one bit. I tried the other airlines with flights coming from San Francisco that day, but getting them to talk was even harder. They dismissed me before I could even ask a question.

All flights had been overbooked that day, so none of the clerks felt any desire to dig in and check. Passengers were mere numbers to fill seats, and I was wasting my time. At least, that was the impression they gave me.

Why didn't Win call or text to say she canceled or changed her plans? Why isn't she picking up her phone?

"We got the right date, didn't we?" I asked when I returned to a nerve-wracked Luc near baggage claim.

I always worried about being unreasonably suspicious. After what we'd gone through, we had the right to be, but I'd also seen how paranoia could worsen a situation.

I glanced at my phone for the hundredth time. Win hadn't answered any of our text messages or phone calls since the night before. Early that morning, I'd asked her to send an anonymous distress signal to Safe Horizon on behalf of Sarah, but I hadn't heard back. Not even an acknowledgment. That was unlike her.

I read and reread the last texts she'd sent the night before. She'd confirmed she'd got her tickets, and she'd confirmed she'd be here at four thirty in the afternoon, Eastern time. So what happened?

Luc was pacing in front of the arrivals gate, jerking his head nervously every time the doors slid open and someone walked out.

While I'd been away pleading with the airlines, Luc had called Win's dorm room at Stanford. A university receptionist had picked up the phone. Win had already left and had returned her dorm room key. When Luc had asked her to open the room and double-check, she'd said that was against university policy.

"Was she heading to the airport?" I asked.

"She had her suitcase and got into a rideshare, she said."

"So we know Win left the dorms," I said, trying to think. "But did she get to the airport?"

"Anything could have happened!" Luc said, looking at me bug-eyed. "Maybe she got into an accident and is lying in a ditch somewhere. Maybe someone kidnapped her or—"

"Hold on now, we don't know any of that. Win's a smart girl. Wherever she is, she's not going to just let anything happen to her."

Luc started hyperventilating. I put a hand on his shoulder to calm him. I was apprehensive too, but we had to think clearly right now.

"What I don't understand is how come she didn't contact any of us," I said. Win loved to broadcast blow by blow accounts of her travels to the point it annoyed Tetyana. "She didn't even text us to say she was waiting for her rideshare."

Luc pulled at his hair. "I think they got her!"

"Who?"

"Whoever's watching us. Have you forgotten that?"

I stared at him helplessly. He had a point. We weren't operating under normal conditions.

"What if Fred or the men we fought in Tanzania or Brussels have tracked us down?" said Luc. "What if they're coming for the money we took from them?"

I swallowed hard. I took full responsibility for that heist. It had been my idea, but it was Win who had done the work, which meant all electronic fingerprints would point to her.

Luc looked like he was about to have a heart attack. "What if they're torturing her right now to find out where we put the money?"

In my lifetime, there had been a few times I'd wanted to call the police despite all the risks that would entail. This was one.

I knew better than to trust the authorities in the many countries I'd traveled to. They'd given us more grief than help. But here, in New York, I knew if I'd called the cops about a missing seventeen-year-old college kid from Stanford, an entire army would rally behind us and help to track her down.

But that would expose us all. Win's alias could get blown. She could get kicked out of college, or worse, the country. And the rest of us could end up in jail.

Still, any of that was far more palatable than the thought of Win getting tortured by goons.

Luc stopped pacing and gave me a wild look. "I'm going," he said and turned to march off. I caught him by the arm just in time.

"What are you doing?"

"If she's not here, she's back there. Somewhere. And she needs me. I'm gonna find her. Next flight to San Fran is a red-eye at nine."

I nodded. "I'm coming with you."

His face cleared. He looked relieved.

"I'll get the tickets."

Before I could say another word, he pulled away and jogged toward the airline counters.

"Time for backup," I mumbled to myself, punching Tetyana's number.

It was Friday afternoon, which meant she was at the Russian bar. I just hoped she had her phone turned on while she was hanging out with this Olek guy, whoever he was.

Please, please pick up.

My call went straight to voice mail.

I punched in David's number. He picked up right away.

"Hey," he said.

Behind him, I could hear the loud thumps and cries of *Kia,* as his students worked their exercise routines on the mats.

"It's me, Asha."

"Is this urgent?" He never liked to be bothered when he was teaching. "I'm offsite at a client's place."

"Win didn't show. It's been two hours."

"Serious?"

"She didn't text or call. And she's not picking up her phone."

"Oh, no."

"Called Tetyana, but got voice mail. I left a message."

Silence on David's end. I could almost see him frowning, thinking of the next steps.

"David?" I said. "Luc and I are flying to San Fran tonight. He's getting us tickets."

"Hold on. I'll be right there."

"There's a red-eye at nine."

"Be there in forty minutes tops."

"What about your class?"

"I'll take care of it," he said, "just keep your eyes open and wait for me."

"Do we get a tick—"

But he'd already hung up.

I stared at the phone for a few seconds before checking my messages for a sign from Win or Tetyana. Nothing.

I turned around and scanned the ticket booths.

The desks were short-staffed, and Luc was in the middle of a long line of travelers snaking around the terminal. He stood impatiently, tapping his right foot, a deep frown on his face. Seeing him like this was hard. I knew how close he and Win were. I prayed she was okay and tried to not let grisly worst-case scenarios take over my mind.

It took thirty-five minutes for David to race to the airport. He arrived just as Luc returned with our tickets. An anxious Katy trailed behind David, carrying a black motorcycle helmet.

We moved to a quiet corner to talk.

"Any news?" asked Katy, reaching out to Luc to give him a hug.

I shook my head.

"I'm sure she's fine," David said. "Maybe she took the wrong flight. People make mistakes all the time."

"Not Win," said Luc. "She'd never do that. And we double-checked."

I nodded. *We quintuple-checked.*

"The airline won't give us any info," I said, "Privacy laws and all that."

David frowned. "I think I know someone who can help. Worth trying anyway. He works for one of the airlines."

"Who?" asked Katy and I at the same time.

He shook his head. "Gonna make a quick call." He walked off to the side with his phone in his hands.

I sighed.

That was the problem with us. We all had pasts. We shared a lot with each other, but there was also a lot we didn't share, like our personal contacts.

Katy, Luc and I stood in a circle, waiting for David to finish his call. Luc shifted from foot to foot, looking devastated. I racked my brain to think of what would have made Win not show up. I wondered where we'd search for her once we landed in San Francisco.

The image of her sweet face popped into my head, and my chest tightened. *I swear to god if anyone hurts her, I'll make them pay—*

My phone rang.

Unknown number.

I fumbled to turn it on.

"Who's with you?" came Tetyana's voice through the speakerphone.

I glanced around quickly. We were in an isolated corner, away from the crowds. No one could overhear us.

"Katy, Luc, David are all here," I said. "Bibi's at the bakery."

Katy called out to David and gestured for him to join us.

"Just you guys?" asked Tetyana.

I raised my eyebrows. "Just us."

"Can you guys join me outside?"

We swiveled around. Outside the terminal, we could see taxis, shuttles, and people disembarking. It was busy, but we'd spot that tall, athletic brunette anywhere.

"Where are you?" asked Katy.

"Tetyana, there's no time for games," Luc said, his voice strained.

"Luc and I got tickets to San F—" I started.

"Guys, it's time to talk to the authorities," she replied, cutting me off.

"What?" I said.

"Are you outta your mind?" Luc said.

"That's insane—" Katy didn't get to finish.

"Calm down, people." It sounded like she was gritting her teeth. Something was up.

I caught David's eye. He felt it too. She wasn't telling us the complete truth.

David put a finger to his lips and leaned into the phone.

"David here. What do you want us to do?"

"Join me outside. The NYPD has a few questions for us."

Chapter Eighteen

Outside the airport's departure terminal, a long line of cars had formed to pick up passengers. People were dashing in and out, rolling luggage carts, bumping into one another, calling out to friends and family in a hundred different languages.

No one seemed to notice us, but this was New York. Everybody was busy. No one had time for anyone else's problems.

I scanned the area.

"Where is she?"

There was no sign of police officers. There was no sign of Tetyana either.

"We don't have time for this," said Luc in exasperation. "We gotta find Win."

"You know," said Katy. "Tetyana didn't sound like herself just now."

David nodded. "Someone's with her."

A chill went through me.

I hit reply on the last number that called me. It rang, but no one picked up. Strange, I thought, that she hadn't called us from her own phone.

Looking like he was following a hunch, David walked down the ramp toward the car park, away from the pandemonium. We trailed behind him, anxiously panning our surroundings, hoping to glimpse her.

Small groups of airport security guards huddled here and there, casually watching the crowds. None of them seemed overly concerned. There wasn't one NYPD officer in sight. In uniform, anyway.

I caught up to David, who was hurrying toward the bus terminal now.

"This way," he said with a wave. "I think I know where she is."

We picked up our pace.

"There!" he said, pointing to the parkade behind the bus terminal.

In front of the drab multistory structure was an open parking lot assigned to motorcycles. Right up front, perched on her black Ninja, with her helmet in her hand, was Tetyana.

She waved as she saw us.

We ran up to her.

"What's going on?" demanded Katy.

I grabbed her by the arm. "You okay?"

"I'm good," she said without a smile.

I glanced around. There were no cop

s, not even a police car in sight.

Tetyana's face was taut, as if she was on high alert. She looked over our shoulders and waved at Luc to hurry. He'd been trailing behind us, stopping and going, looking for Win in every corner. He walked up, ready to jump at Tetyana's throat.

"Win's missing and you're playing these—"

"Shh..." Tetyana put a finger to her lips.

She pulled her phone out of her pocket and pointed to it wordlessly.

What's she up to now?

With her other hand, she made a gesture that said, *Hand over yours.*

Katy opened her mouth to say something, but Tetyana shushed her.

David didn't hesitate. He pulled his phone out, turned it off and passed it to her.

She gave a nod and turned to the rest of us.

I wavered for two seconds. I had no idea what she was doing, but I had to trust her. This was the woman who'd fought for us, put her life on the line for us. I pulled out my phone and set it on the motorcycle seat behind her.

Katy did the same.

Luc reluctantly passed his over, but not before checking to make sure Win hadn't replied.

As we watched, Tetyana removed the SIM cards from each phone. Then, phone by phone, she began dismantling them, shushing us immediately if we tried to speak. When she was done, she collected the pieces and walked over to the nearest garbage bin.

We looked on, mouths agape.

As she opened the bin's cover to dump everything in, a middle-aged man rushed by her, sweat streaming down his face, pulling along a suitcase. She froze. He barely glanced at her and kept running. She threw everything in, slammed the bin closed, turned around and marched back to us huddled around her bike.

"No one followed you?" she demanded.

David shook his head. "No, I've been keeping watch."

"Good. We can talk now."

"What the heck's going on?" I asked.

"What about those cops?" asked Katy. "Where are they?"

Tetyana shook her head. "That was a ruse in case someone was listening in. Guys, I just found out the bakery and dojo were bugged."

We stared at her, openmouthed.

"Bugs?" Katy asked. "I guess you don't mean bedbugs."

"Wiretaps," said David in a quiet voice.

"Someone was listening to us?" I asked, finding my voice.

"For at least twenty-four hours from what I can see."

A family of six strolled by, talking loudly, fighting over who had dibs to the window seats. We waited for them to pass.

"When you called me earlier," Tetyana said, looking at me, "I was running a sweep through the bedrooms. I couldn't take your call before I checked everything. I also didn't want to talk to you in the open on my phone."

"But who would do that to us?" I asked.

"They were generic devices. Nothing high-grade or pro. And it was all in the perimeter."

"Not inside?" David asked, looking partially relieved. "Nothing in the War Room?"

Tetyana shook her head. "Found one behind the bakery's back door and another outside the dojo. Nothing inside. I checked both change rooms, the office and the boardroom."

"So, it could have been anyone at any time, day or night." David said.

Tetyana turned to me. "What about the bakery help? Do you trust them?"

I'd hired a part-time team of five students from the local culinary school for whenever I needed extra help. I'd promised to mentor them to make up for the low student pay. I'd interviewed every one of them with Luc, and Luc had done all the reference checks.

I couldn't imagine anyone going to the trouble of applying to an exclusive culinary school with the remote chance of getting selected by my bakery so they could bug our premises.

"There's always a risk," I said, "but it's a tiny probability."

"Plus," said Katy, pointing at Luc, who'd stepped away from the huddle and was scanning the area. "He watches them like a hawk. I don't think we have to worry about our kitchen help."

Tetyana nodded. "I'll go through the security camera footage when we get back. But that'll take a few days because I have no idea how long those were around. I might have missed them before."

"At least they didn't pick up our weekly meetings," I said.

"This is recon work," Tetyana said.

"What does that mean?" Katy asked.

"Reconnaissance," explained David. "Their goal is to check the perimeter and work their way in, slowly. Undetected."

Chapter Nineteen

"We have to stay vigilant," said Tetyana, picking up her helmet. "And we don't want to hang around here too long."

Katy and I exchanged a concerned look.

Tetyana called out to Luc. "Oi, get back here!"

He turned to her, his eyes lined with frustration. "Are we done here? Asha and me have a flight to catch."

"You don't have to do that," she replied, putting on her helmet. She looked like she was in a rush now.

"What do you mean?" I asked.

"I have news for you all."

"Unless it's about—" started Luc.

"Win's in town."

"What?" I said.

"Oh, my god," said Katy.

Luc jumped on her and grabbed her by her jacket. "Are you kidding me?"

"No, I'm not joking, Luc. Yes, she's here," she said, gently pushing him away. "But I don't want to leave her for too long."

"Where—"

She grasped Luc by the shoulders and looked him in the eye.

"I'm sorry I couldn't tell you this before, but I had to make sure no one was listening or following. Win's here. She's fine. Got here an hour ago."

"How did she come?" Katy asked.

"That girl's a heck of a lot smarter than any of us. I'll let her tell you herself." She turned to Luc and gave him a wink. "You ready? She's been asking for you."

Poor Luc. His face had turned a deep shade of pink, like he was about to have a heart attack.

"Where is she?" he squeaked.

"In a secret place. Follow me."

She straddled her bike and turned the key. The engine roared. She glanced at us. "You wanna hang around here, gawking, or come with me?"

"Let's go!" cried Luc, pulling me by the arm roughly. "Get the car!"

"My bike's right here," David said, pointing at his motorcycle just a few spots away.

"Get your vehicles and meet me here," said Tetyana, "Make it fast."

David marched over to his bike, putting his helmet on. Katy, Luc, and I dashed into the parkade to get the Red Beast. By the time we pulled out, Tetyana and David had their bikes side by side at the entrance, revving and ready to go.

They took off in a roar as soon as they saw us coming out.

I followed, keeping my eyes trained on their backs. They weaved in and out of highway traffic at high speeds, turning corners with their knees nearly touching the asphalt. There was only so much I could do in my eight-seater SUV, but I kept up. In twenty minutes we hit traffic and things slowed down. We crawled along, keeping as close together as possible.

Katy was in the passenger seat next to me, helmet on her lap. Luc was in the seat behind me. He was quiet, but I noticed he was biting his nails. He was struggling to keep composure like he couldn't decide whether to cry or rejoice.

My thoughts turned to Bibi. I hoped she was okay, alone at the bakery. I wished I'd had my phone to call her. I hated being the last one to know these things. *Why does Tetyana have to be so cryptic?*

There was one other thing that was worrying me.

Three of us had no valid identification.

David because he was on the run. Win and Bibi because they'd both been ripped away from their families at such a young age.

They'd had nothing on them when we found them, not even something to indicate their birthdays.

When we were making plans to come to New York, Tetyana had promised to take care of their official documents. She hadn't told me where or how she'd got them, but their passports had mysteriously appeared the day of our departure. David, Win, and Bibi had sailed through Homeland Security inspections.

I knew what we'd done was wrong, but it kept us together and gave the girls opportunities they'd never have anywhere else. But this meant I lived in constant fear of them being found out. If that ever happened, it would be the end of everything.

It didn't take much for this fear to get fanned to life, like a cinder catching fire.

It took a full nerve-wracking hour to get back home with the afternoon traffic. Nobody had been in the mood to talk, everyone lost in thought, trying, like me, not to let their imaginations run too wild, I guessed.

I was half-surprised to see Tetyana head toward our home. I'd expected her to lead us somewhere out of town, into a secret warehouse or some obscure hiding spot. But she drove right past the bakery. I glanced at our home quickly. All lights were turned off, and the blinds were closed. The place had been shut down.

Where's Bibi? I didn't want to lose one girl after finding another.

"I'm sure she's okay," Katy said, seeing me looking. "Tetyana's always got us covered."

"Where's she going?" Luc asked, leaning forward.

I turned my attention back on the road to not lose sight of the motorbikes.

Tetyana signaled and turned into a small alleyway. David followed.

I slowed down and put my turn lights on too.

A memory stirred in me. I'd been here before. At night.

"Are we going to fit in there?" Katy asked.

I slowed to a crawl and nudged the Beast through the narrow alleyway. We still hadn't fixed the car, so I didn't have to worry about scratching it, but I didn't want us to get stuck.

We inched forward, following the two motorcycles to the end of the alleyway. Tetyana and David turned right and pulled into a parking spot where three massive Harley-Davidsons sat parked side by side.

That's why I remember this place.

"The Troika?" asked Katy, squinting at the sign.

"This is Tetyana's Friday night hangout."

"Here?" asked Luc, bending in his seat to get a better look. "But it's Russian."

I shrugged. It was a mystery to me too.

I put the Beast in park mode and pushed the handbrake button on. Maybe it was a good thing the car was busted on the outside. It fit right in in this neighborhood.

We got out and followed Tetyana and David inside.

The waiter who'd served David and me the night before walked up to us with a friendly smile.

Tetyana turned to him. "Girls okay?"

He nodded. "Keeping Olek busy," he said, motioning us to follow him.

Luc pushed Tetyana aside and marched on the heels of the waiter toward the back of the restaurant.

We trooped behind them, stumbling over each other to get to the kitchen.

It was a larger than usual kitchen for a grungy New York restaurant. And it was a noisy, busy place.

A team of sous chefs was preparing for supper. A woman looked up, irritated at these strangers trooping through her workplace. The waiter walked past her, toward a walk-in refrigerator in the back, and opened what I thought was a closet door.

He ushered us in.

It was a prep kitchen with a smaller stove and oven. The place was steaming and smelled heavenly.

Luc spotted Win first.

Chapter Twenty

Win and Bibi sat perched on high stools at the kitchen counter in front of a plate of perogies.

Home-cooked smells filled the warm air.

Across from the girls stood a mountain of a man wearing a faded chef's apron. His tattooed biceps bulged as he rolled pastry dough on the counter with more force than necessary. From where I was standing, he looked like an unrefined cousin of Chef Pierre.

He glanced up as we walked in and gave a salute to Tetyana.

With an ear-splitting squeal, Win jumped off her stool and landed in Luc's arms.

The rest of us ran up and pounced on them both.

"Oh, my god! I'm so happy to see you guys," shrieked Win as she hugged each of us. "I missed you!"

She still had her school backpack on, the one with the Pokémon key chain dangling from the back. On the floor, next to the counter, was her small suitcase with a fresh airline tag.

"*Mon Dieu!*" Luc said, lifting her up, backpack and all.

"How did you get here?" I asked. "We waited for you at the airport for hours."

Luc pulled out the tickets from his pockets and waved them in the air. "I was even going to San Fran to look for you. You scared me."

"She's here now, isn't she?" said Tetyana. "And I'm starved with all this running around. What a day." She placed her helmet on the kitchen counter and leaned on it with a tired sigh.

"Get that thing off," said the man gruffly. "This is my kitchen, not a bike garage."

He spoke with a thick Eastern European accent, sounding a lot like Vlad from our former life.

Is this Olek?

"Okay, okay," Tetyana said, picking up her helmet and finding a spot for it on a wooden bench near the door.

The man turned back to his work, feigning hurt. "Just 'coz they stick me in the back doesn't mean you treat this place like a dump. In my kitchen, food is god. You have no respect for Ukrainian any more?"

"Hey," Tetyana said, giving a friendly punch on his arm. "Don't be such a dork. You cook as well as my mother. Don't you know I come here for your food?"

He brightened visibly. "And the documents."

"Of course," Tetyana said, nodding amiably. "And the documents."

What documents?

"And the hardware," said the man.

"And the hardware," echoed Tetyana.

I frowned. I didn't like the sound of this.

"Everyone," Tetyana said, looking around the room, "I want you to meet my good friend, Chef Olek."

Olek stopped his work to give us an exaggerated bow. "It is a great pleasure to finally meet Tetyana's good friends. I've heard a lot about each and every one of you."

I glanced over at Tetyana.

Can we trust him?

She smiled at my hesitation. "He cooks way better than your fancy French chef, Asha."

"Oh, you don't get nothing fancy from me," said Olek, shaking his head. "Just good old Baba's food from the old country. That's what you'll find here."

"Olek's my key contact in New York," said Tetyana, noticing our confused frowns. "We go a long way back. I can vouch for him." She jerked a thumb at him. "He's the one who helped me get those toys in our cabinet."

Olek's a weapons trader?

"Bibi, honey," I said, turning to the girl who'd been silently watching the reunion from the corner of the room. "When did you find out about this place?"

"Just now. Tetyana told me to close the bakery and come here two hours ago."

"I needed some space while I swept the building," explained Tetyana. "I sent her to the only safe place I knew."

"These are really yum," said Bibi, pointing to the pastries on the table. "I don't mind hanging out here." She grinned at Olek. For a moment, I thought he was going to reach over and ruffle her spiky hair.

I looked over at David who was standing across from me, regarding the man warily.

"You're a businessman," David said. "You're here because it gives you connections."

"I won't disagree with you there," said Olek with a slight nod.

"So, who are your contacts in Russia?"

Olek paused and surveyed his dough.

"You know that thing they say?" he said, still looking down. "If I tell you, I'll have to kill you?"

Nobody spoke.

"Well, if I tell you, they will kill *me*." Olek looked up, his face grave. "So if you will be very kind, I'd prefer to keep certain private things private. Please?"

He gave a polite smile at David. David didn't smile back.

"I thought we were doing everything aboveboard," I said, shooting Tetyana an accusing look.

"Don't worry. I bought everything we have in the cabinet," she replied. "One hundred percent paid for."

"Yes, but who did you buy them from?" I asked. I was tiring of these mysteries. *Why can't everyone just be upfront with me?*

"Look, I get what we need wherever I can find them at the price we can afford. It's not like you give me a big budget."

I felt my back go up and my hands clench.

"Tetyana, don't play games with me."

"I don't play with our lives," she said, returning my dark look. "You want security? I'll give it to you the best way I know how. But if you want someone else for this work, go right ahead."

"Fine!" I snapped, instantly regretting my words.

"Asha!" cried Win.

"Merde!" I heard Luc swear.

"Don't fight, you two!" said Bibi.

I felt Katy's hand on my arm. A slight squeeze to calm me down.

I closed my eyes and took a deep breath.

"Look," said Tetyana in a calmer voice. "I know security is not a priority for us right now. Setting up the business is. But we have to watch our backs and I'm doing my best with what you give me."

I bit my lip. I knew she was trying. I nodded. "I know and I appreciate that."

No one spoke for a few seconds.

"Here, why don't you all sit down?" Olek said, breaking the silence. He gestured at the stools across the counter. "Sit. All this running around and yelling is not good for your health. This is how you die young. Sit and eat. Take it easy and relax. Celebrate your reunion!"

No one moved.

"Are you people going to let me feed you old Baba's food or not?" he asked, looking genuinely hurt.

David made the first move.

With a decisive nod, he deposited his helmet next to Tetyana's and took a seat at the kitchen counter.

"Okay, Olek, feed me," he said, spreading his arms wide. "Let's see if your perogies are as good as they say. Though I think I've tried them already."

"I heard," Olek said and put his hand out to shake. David took it. Olek pushed a second platter of perogies in front of David with a friendly nod.

With that exchange, the tension left the room.

I felt my shoulders relax.

Using Win's fork, David reached over for a perogy, dropped one on Bibi's plate, then helped himself to one.

I walked over and took the seat next to him.

I need a drink, I thought.

As if reading my mind, Olek took out four glass tumblers and pushed them across the table toward Tetyana, David, Katy and me. He plucked a bottle of vodka from the top of the cabinet and poured us a few fingers each.

With a tired sigh, Katy plopped next to me, picked up her glass and downed it in one gulp.

This is how we become alcoholics, I thought as I watched her worriedly.

I gave a side glance at Olek, who was now pouring orange juice for the underage members of our crew. At least he respected some laws. I wondered about his relationship with Tetyana. They had a friendly vibe between them, but he didn't look the boyfriend type. He was old enough to be an uncle of sorts.

Olek started packing perogies in neat rows on a stainless-steel baking tray, promising to not send us off hungry.

"Okay, Tetyana," I said. "How did Win get here? Who bugged our place? Tell us everything, please."

She leaned over, her elbows on the counter, a somber look on her face. "Someone's been watching us for a while now."

"Other than that lone construction worker?" asked Luc.

"He's a decoy, I'm guessing, to keep us occupied, our attention away from what they were really doing."

"What do they want?" asked Katy.

"And who?" I asked. "Who are they?"

"Ah," said Olek, without looking up, "that's the one-million-dollar question. I don't know exactly what you kids are up to, but you're playing with big fire, that's for sure."

"Could be anyone who chased us in London, Brussels, or Nairobi. Maybe even India," Tetyana replied. "Until I have evidence, I don't want to make the wrong assumptions and run in the wrong direction. Also, I don't want us to get unnecessarily nervous."

"Tetyana," I said, leaning toward her, "when someone's tracking us, I need to know. Pronto. Like right now. Not tomorrow."

"I swear I didn't know till this afternoon. When I figured it out, everyone except for Bibi was out. You were at the airport, David was offsite and Katy was at the grocery store. I couldn't call you because we were all being tracked."

"How did you find all this out?" Katy asked.

"Not me," said Tetyana and pointed her chin toward Win, who was nuzzling against Luc at the end of the table now.

"She's the one who alerted me last night."

Chapter Twenty-One

"Win?" I called out.

Seeing everyone look at her, she leaned away from Luc and sat up.

"How did you know we were bugged?"

She pushed her glasses up her nose. "Someone hacked my college account yesterday. Our IT department totally sucks so anyone can get in. But I was super busy with my exams, I didn't even see it till this morning."

"Who hacked you?" Katy asked.

"Dunno. They covered their tracks. Didn't have time to check it out 'coz I just wanted to come here fast and warn everyone that someone's watching us."

"This all happened online, right?" David asked. "No one following you around campus or anything like that?"

"Nope." Win shook her head. "All online and on our phones. I knew for sure someone hacked us when I got that funny text from you last night." She pointed a finger at me.

I frowned. "Which one?"

"You asked me for our Barbados account number."

I looked at her aghast.

"I know. It's weird you'd ask me something you already know. Somebody spoofed your number to mask theirs."

"Someone spoofed me?"

"They were pretending to be you. It's easy. That's how they do spam calls. But I didn't know if they hacked all our numbers. I couldn't call you, 'coz maybe they bugged everything."

"My goodness," I said with a sinking feeling, "So whoever it is knows about the money..." I trailed off, realizing Olek was still in our midst. Tetyana may trust him, but I'd just met him and we'd already shared more than I was comfortable with.

Tetyana spoke up. "And this morning I woke up to a three-word text from Win."

"What'd it say?" Katy asked.

"Check Main Email," she replied. "I kept checking my normal email. Took me all morning to figure it out. That's when I realized I had to check for physical bugs in our building too."

"I got the same message," I said, turning to Win. "But I never got an email from you."

"Check main email?" Luc asked, puzzled. "Which email?"

"I was really hoping one of you would remember from last time," said Win.

"What last time?" Katy asked, scrunching her forehead.

"Remember Nairobi?" said Tetyana.

Katy's and Luc's faces cleared. Then I remembered.

Two years ago, we went to East Africa to locate and rescue Chanda and Preeti from traffickers. During that mission, Win had created a group email account for us. There, we put down our plans and sent warnings to each other. But we never hit send. The emails stayed in the draft box. All we had to do was log in and read each draft email to know what was going on or who needed help.

Because the messages never got out on the Internet, no one could intercept them. Our email account was hosted by the second-largest tech company in the world with a reputation to uphold. What that meant was, as Win had explained to us, we were as secure as we could be.

We'd called it our *Main Email,* so no one would guess. It had been the perfect channel to talk to each other secretly. But so many things had happened between then and now, I'd forgotten about it. In my defense, we also hadn't been watched. Or hacked. Until now.

"Is that still active?" Katy asked.

Win nodded. "Dormant. Nobody touched it after our last job."

"Good thing I remembered," said Tetyana. "I checked it and found her notes."

"That's why you got rid of our phones," said Luc.

"But Win," I said, "how did you fly in? Luc and I parked ourselves in front of the arrival gates at JFK all afternoon. Did you wear a disguise or something?"

She shook her pretty head. "Nope. I bought a standby ticket on the first flight to Newark. Then, I wrote another email for you guys saying I was landing over there. Sorry, you waited."

"I guess we should have checked the other airports." I looked at Luc, who replied with a shrug. He'd calmed down considerably after seeing Win and was back to his normal relaxed self.

"I didn't cancel my ticket to JFK in case anyone found out," said Win.

"Smart move," Katy said.

That was one mystery solved. I turned to Olek, who'd been listening keenly in between checking up on his pastries in the oven. He and Tetyana were standing shoulder to shoulder behind the counter like old friends.

"I'd like to know how you two know each other," I said.

"We go way back," Tetyana replied.

"How far?"

"Olek's from my hometown. We're fourth cousins or something like that. He was there when..." She stopped and lowered her head. She was unusually quiet for a few seconds. Olek stood by her, clutching his oven mitts, eyes averted, a serious expression on his face now.

Tetyana took a deep breath. "He was there when the militia gunned down my mother."

The room froze.

"He tried to help her, but it was too late."

"I could have saved her," said Olek in an almost inaudible voice, looking down at his mitts. "But I was a coward. I didn't—"

"You did what you could," said Tetyana quickly. "That's what matters." She turned to us. "He escaped to America on a boat three years ago, but we kept in touch."

No one spoke for a long time.

"When we were looking for a home here," said Tetyana, breaking the silence, "I asked him to keep an eye out for us. That's how we found our building. Thanks to Olek." She gave him a weak smile.

Olek gave her a subdued nod.

I softened my voice. "What were those documents you two talked about earlier?"

To my surprise, Olek blushed.

"Everyone says I'm a good cook," he said. "But in my spare time, I make permits, passports and visas for clients. They're outstanding quality, if I may say so myself. Even better than my perogies."

"But isn't that, like, illegal?" Bibi asked in a hushed whisper.

David knew his passport was a forgery, but we'd kept this information from the girls. I had hoped they'd never have to find out.

"I do it to help good people," Olek replied, looking at Bibi. "There are so many good people who want better life in America. Hard-working doctors, nurses, teachers, journalists, and good boys and girls too." He gave her a genial smile. "They just want a new life. To get away from nasty governments, rotten police, and the mafia. I charge less than snakeheads. I make it easy for them."

I looked at Tetyana. She gave me a discreet nod back.

Olek saw the exchange and pointed at his chest. "I always do excellent job. You will have no problem." I noted a slight infliction of pride in his voice.

I rubbed my face, trying to soak this news in. At least I knew who made their passports now. And the permits for our weapons.

That was when the door opened with a bang.

Everyone jumped.

It was the waiter who'd showed us in earlier. His face was pale, like something had terrified him.

"You have order for me?" asked Olek, looking up.

"No, er..." He gave a furtive glance behind him. "Someone wants to talk to you."

"To me?" said Olek, pointing at his chest.

"No..."

"Us?" asked Tetyana, standing up, her hand going under her jacket where she usually carried her sidearm.

Next to me, David pushed his stool back and stood up too, one hand hovering over his belt.

The waiter opened the door wide with shaking hands.

A small man stepped inside.

We stared.

He was wearing dark brown pants, a tweed jacket, and an old-fashioned waistcoat. The man was a cross between a staid university professor and a boring corporate middle manager.

He scanned the room, looking at each of us, expressionless.

"The Red Heeled Rebels, I presume?" he said with a polite bow of his head.

His Midwestern accent and his professional attire didn't belong in a rough restaurant bar on this side of Harlem. I felt a nervous tick coming on my neck.

"Who's asking?" I said, giving him the steely eye.

"The CIA."

Part THREE

Chapter Twenty-Two

No one moved. No one even twitched a muscle.

The only sound in the room was the hum of Olek's oven, baking his last batch of pastries.

The man in the tweed jacket held up his hands, palms out, as if in a gesture of peace.

"I didn't come here to make trouble. I came here to negotiate."

Negotiate?

The waiter was still standing silently by the door, as if in a trance. When the man turned to give him a nod to say *that will be all,* he scampered back and shut the door with a thud. He'd ushered a lion into the room and he didn't want to hang around to see the consequences.

From the corner of my eyes, I saw Olek hunch over the counter, his face pale like he was about to pass out.

Everyone else looked comparatively calm, wary but calm, I thought, despite this unwelcome intrusion.

"May I take a seat?" the man asked.

No one replied.

Ignoring our chilly stares, he stepped up to the kitchen counter, pulled out a chair and settled himself comfortably, adjusting his glasses. He threw an appreciative glance at the perogy plate on the counter. Then, he turned to give Tetyana and David a nod each, to acknowledge their presence.

They glared back.

Does he know who they are? Does he know they're armed?

I spoke up.

"Who are you?"

The man reached into his waistcoat pocket.

Next to me, I saw David stiffen. Tetyana put her hand inside her jacket.

I took a sharp breath in.

To my relief, the man pulled out his wallet and flashed an ID card. He turned it around slowly so we could all get a good look at it.

It looked official enough from where I sat, but he could have flashed anything at us. If Olek excelled at creating identification that fooled airport security and the feds, this man could surely recreate a CIA ID card.

Sensing our mistrust, he handed it to Katy who was the nearest him.

Katy passed it to me and we scrutinized it together.

It was an employee ID card or an excellent imitation of one.

The CIA logo was embossed on it and it came with a name. William LB James. The title underneath said *Special Field Agent.* The security clearance beneath that said "*Level five,*" whatever that meant. Employee Id No. was followed by a fifteen-digit number and a bar code.

"Check the back," the man said. "There's a QR code. Scan it with your phone and you'll get my boss at the CIA. Deputy Director of International Ops." He paused. "She's high in the echelons, part of the agency's politburo, so you'll find her name on our website. Feel free to call her office and check up on me right now if you'd like."

I turned the card over. Sure enough, there was a QR code.

"I can wait," said the man, settling back in his seat. He eyed the perogy plate again, but Olek was too panic-stricken to offer our undesired guest anything.

None of us had phones anymore, but I wasn't going to admit that to him. With a grave nod, I passed the card to David. I noticed him take a pen and scribble the number down and pass the card to Tetyana next.

William James was a small man, maybe only a few inches taller than me.

Olek could have crushed him with one hand if he'd stop hyperventilating in his corner. Then, there was the gun power and combat prowess Tetyana and David brought, not to speak of the training the rest of us got each night. Even without the weapons and fighting skills, we outnumbered him. But he didn't seem too bothered. He was as relaxed as if he'd been at a tea party.

And that worried me.

"Mr. James," I said, "why are you here?"

"I'm here to discuss a proposal with you."

"What does the CIA want with a bakery in Harlem?"

"That's not all you do."

"You're correct. We give martial arts classes to school kids and office workers." I paused. "Does the CIA have issues with that?"

He brought his fingertips together and contemplated me silently.

I kept my gaze steady.

"You need help," he said.

"We don't need help from the CIA," I replied bluntly. "Now if you happen to be a local business financier, I'd love to talk to you. I was thinking of expanding soon. Maybe even franchising."

He merely raised an eyebrow. "What if I tell you you're being watched?"

We already knew that.

"What if I also told you, your premises have been wiretapped?" He paused. "But you were already aware of that, weren't you?"

I hoped to god everyone was keeping a straight face.

Katy spoke up. "Mr. James, why would anyone want to bother with a bakery and a school?" She tilted her head. "What you're saying sounds out of this world. Are you trying to scare us?"

"Not at all. That wasn't my intention."

"But we're not doing anything wrong," she replied.

"No one said you were doing anything wrong." The man paused. I caught a glint in his eyes. "Not now, anyway."

I bit my tongue. The less we said, the better. Despite his claims, we had no proof he was from the CIA. If he was, it could a good thing or a bad thing, or both. If he wasn't, I was glad David and Tetyana had come prepared.

James glanced around the room casually.

David and Tetyana were standing on either side of the counter, frowns on their faces, arms crossed but ever ready.

Bibi was looking down, shoulders stiff, fiddling nervously with the edges of her skirt. Luc and Win were holding each other's hands under the table, watching the man bug-eyed. I wasn't sure if they were more curious than nervous, but on the surface, they could have passed for innocent college kids.

Next to me, Katy was sitting up, maintaining eye contact, looking for all the world like a concerned citizen. She was a good actor.

Among all of us, Olek appeared the most suspicious.

He was staring unblinkingly at his pastry tray, refusing to look up. His face was beetroot red. Sweat dripped from his forehead to the counter and his breaths came loud and fast.

I wished he'd excuse himself. I knew Tetyana trusted him, but with this stranger in the room, Olek's presence only made things worse.

"It wasn't *you* who tapped us, was it?" I asked the man.

He shook his head quickly. "We certainly did not. I can promise you that. We don't even have jurisdiction in this country. Our work happens overseas." He stopped, and a faint smile crossed his face. "In many of the places you all come from."

My stomach flipped.

"Then again," he continued, "we have no need to put a tap on you. We know everything about everyone here. You see, we have a dossier for each of you at HQ."

My heart sank. I heard an almost inaudible gasp from the other end of the table where Bibi, Win, and Luc sat. I struggled to maintain eye contact.

"A CIA dossier?" asked Katy, looking shocked. "On *us*?"

James cleared his throat. "Look, there is no need to act surprised. Besides, I'm here to offer my support." He spread his hands magnanimously.

"Why?" I asked. "Why does the CIA want anything to do with us?"

He leaned in. "Ms. Kade."

I froze, hearing my family name.

"Let's stop playing games. We know what happened in Nairobi."

He locked eyes with me, challenging me to look away first. My stomach did another sickening flip. Something came up to my mouth, and I swallowed it. I took a quiet, deep breath to steady myself.

"I'm on your side," the man was saying. "We're already trying to track down the people watching you."

"You can start with the man in the construction overalls up front," I snapped.

"Oh, him? He's one of us. We wanted you to see him. He's simply there to make sure nothing bad happens to any of you. Think of him like a day security guard."

"So you *are* watching us!" Katy said. "Isn't that illegal or something?"

"I like to call it risk management. You're too valuable for us to lose sight of." He let out a sigh. "Listen, ladies and gentlemen, I came here to have an amicable but serious conversation about working together."

We stared at him.

"I have a good deal to offer you."

"You sound like a used car salesman," I said.

"You might be right, young lady. But would you at least hear this old car salesman out?"

"Sure," I said, with what I hoped was a nonchalant shrug. "I'm taking in offers for sous chefs this week. Would the CIA like to bake some cakes for me?"

His face fell like I had disappointed him.

"I don't have time for juvenile jokes," he replied. "My message is this: you're in more trouble than you think. You're dealing with powerful people. And you've made quite the ruckus on four continents." He paused. "You think no one noticed what you did?"

He glanced at each one of us, his eyes resting a little longer on Tetyana, David, and then on me. I noticed his jaws were clenched and his gaze was piercing. For a moment, I felt like he could see right through us.

He leaned in.

I felt the entire room brace.

"There are many who believe you all should be behind bars."

Chapter Twenty-Three

Silence.

We stared at this strange man in front of us.

Who is he?

I struggled to speak. "You can't come in here and make threats like that," I said, trying not to stammer.

I thought I saw a faint smile cross William James's face. I felt a shiver go down my back.

"What do you want from us?" said David, stepping closer to me.

James's eyes fell on him and stayed there for a while. David didn't waver. He returned the man's look, his face stony.

"Ah, Mr. Basha," said the man, shaking his head sadly. "Employee number three-five-nine-one-one."

David didn't flinch, but I did. I had no idea if that was number correct, but even if it wasn't, this man was scary.

"An idealist when you joined and an idealist when you left. You never grew up, did you?"

David remained silent.

"You do realize you have an internal arrest warrant from the Mossad? They stripped you of your rank and you can never go back."

David's expression didn't change, but I felt a chill go through me. *How does he know so much?*

"Part of the equipment you took without asking in Nairobi belonged to us. The CIA. Even though you returned it all, I admit, in good condition, you were clearly in insubordination. Then, you have the temerity to take off without formal leave. What makes you think you can go back?" The man leaned in. "In *any* official capacity?"

"I have no idea what you're talking about," David replied in a low voice.

"Don't be so coy," the man said with a dismissive wave, "One call, just one call and I can have a team of military police here in minutes to haul you away." His eyes bored into David's. "And you'll never see your friends again."

Stay strong, David, I said silently.

"What I'm proposing is an offer." The man glanced around the room. "An offer that will eliminate all of your problems. And your pal, David here, will be exonerated. We will make sure his records will be wiped clean."

Everyone instinctively turned to David. *Isn't this what he wants?*

But he still had his best poker face on.

The man gave him a stern look. "Mr. Basha, you left us with a lot of administrative headaches, for both your organization and ours." His voice had changed. There was something hard underneath that calm demeanor. He sounded less like a college professor and more like a boot camp instructor holding his anger in check.

He pointed a finger at David. "The Mossad should have arrested you a long time ago. You got off easy. If you'd been part of my team, I'd have court-martialed you."

David looked stoic on the outside, but I could feel him breaking down.

"One call and your little friends here will all be locked up for good."

"Leave them out of this," David said between clenched teeth.

Oh no.

"Take me on if you want, but they had nothing to do with anything."

I closed my eyes.

"You were all in this together!" the man shouted, thumping the counter, making us all jump.

"They're civilians!" David shouted back, making us jump again. "Leave them alone. You want to haul me away, haul me away."

James's face turned red. "You broke the rules!"

"I saved lives!" David hollered right back.

The man snorted.

"I did what I did because you couldn't finish the mission," said David, his eyes flashing with fury. "I got the job done while you were shuffling paperwork. I worked while you played politics and went to cocktail parties with criminals. I did in one week what you failed to do in years."

James and David stared in each other's eyes, furiously, silently, challenging each other.

The rest of us waited. For what, I didn't know.

I glanced at Tetyana, but her eyes were focused on James, her hand on her belt, alert and ready for anything. That made me wonder. *Is there a team of cops waiting behind that door to arrest us? If they burst in, will she shoot at them?*

My mind raced, trying to figure out how to extricate ourselves, but something heavy had settled on my shoulders. Whatever it was, it had shunted my brain. I was having a hard time breathing.

It took forever for someone to speak. It was James who went first.

"Newton's laws apply to everything," he said with a sigh. "Whenever there's an action, there's always an equal and opposite reaction. You can't possibly believe you could have done what you did and get away. Even if you were after madmen, the scum of the earth. There are always consequences."

"I'll pay for breaking the rules," said David, stepping forward. "I'll do whatever you want but on one condition. You don't touch a hair on the others."

No! Don't do this.

The man shook his head. "I'm not here to arrest you, Mr. Basha. As I mentioned, this is not my jurisdiction, anyway. What you don't realize is when, not if, *when* the authorities take you away, you will all get separated."

I heard gasps from Win and Bibi.

My throat went dry.

"You will get detained in different cities, different countries even, depending on extradition treaties. You may never see each other again." He paused, his eyes watching us keenly for a reaction.

We were standing in front of him exposed, naked, while he sat back and taunted us. Gloated even. I wanted to punch him.

David had already given his position away. There was no use pretending anymore.

"What do you want from us?" I snapped.

"Ah, I thought you'd never ask." The man adjusted his glasses and gave me a fatherly smile.

I didn't smile back.

"Here's my offer. Why don't the Red Heeled Rebels join us and do some important work instead?" His smile broadened. "You're such a talented group of young men and women. Wasted talent, really. Come work for us and you will get a good salary. We will even give you a nice pension. You'll be set for life."

Is he blackmailing us?

"We don't need a government pension." Katy spat the words out.

Ignoring her, the man continued. "You don't have to steal equipment or vehicles anymore. We will give you everything you need to get the job done. It will be good work. Work you love doing."

He settled back casually, waiting for our reply like he had all the time in the world.

I sat up. My brain kicked into gear and started to whir again.

"What kind of work?" I asked.

"Special projects involving high-profile traffickers. You'd be the perfect team to infiltrate them. It's work you already know. Work you did back in East Africa, in India, and on continental Europe. It's work that will save lives. Children's lives."

His eyes flitted over to where Win and Bibi were sitting.

He knows about them too.

He noticed my face.

"Ms. Kade, one of your formidable former compatriots, Julia Child, was a valuable intelligence officer turned chef. Being a chef gave her access to levels and people she'd never have had otherwise. Do you believe she stopped her important work when she started baking cakes?"

Where's he going with this?

"Between you all, you speak several languages. You have skills in weaponry, martial arts, and computer hacking. You have an exceptional cover and you make a great ready-made team. Plus, you will fit in anywhere we take you. So, what do you say?"

"What's in it for us?" I asked.

"Ah, that's a good question." That sickly fatherly smile again.

For one crazy moment, I wondered if I could bargain with him to help Chanda's orphanages. I pushed the thought to the back of my mind. That would mean confessing to way more than we were comfortable. The less we said about that, the better.

"A great compensation package for life for the adults here. College paid for the girls. Your troubles taken care of. No more worrying about your future. And an identification overhaul."

"What does that mean?" Katy asked.

"It means, young lady, there will be a tragic vehicle accident on Route 110." He shook his head, seemingly upset at the very thought. "A very sad day indeed. The loss of so many young lives. All in one go. Tsk. Tsk. The newspapers will talk about it. Television crews will come out. But no one will be allowed near the incident. For safety reasons, of course."

He paused and looked at us.

"And you will find yourself in Washington with brand-new identities, awaiting instructions." He looked at me. "I can make anything happen."

"What if we say no?" I asked.

His eyes gleamed. "Ah, but I haven't told you the best part of the deal. You won't have to worry about Homeland Security knocking on your door. You will get to stay in America for life. What do you think of that now, eh?"

He let the words sink in and sat back, bringing his fingertips together, appearing more professorial than ever.

I took a few seconds to choose the right words.

"I have a formal business partnership with Chef Pierre," I said. "You know very well we're here legally. We don't need you or anyone else to legitimize us."

"Is that right?" He regarded me keenly. "And what would happen, pray tell, if I called immigration to scrutinize your youngest members' papers?"

"Are you talking about us?" I heard Bibi say in surprise.

Someone shushed her. Sounded like Luc.

I stared at the man, struggling to keep my face straight.

How does he know all this?

Olek started to hyperventilate louder.

"Ah, I thought so," he said, after what seemed like an eternity. "You see. If you come with me, you will all receive a Green Card. Do it for the young 'uns."

"If we say yes," I said, finding my voice, "what will happen next? Hypothetically speaking?"

"Not hypothetically, there's a small team in Washington who will get you geared up," he said with a smile that didn't reach his eyes. "You will train with us for eight months before we send you on overseas missions. We say when and what and how. This is an exclusive deal. No side projects. No negotiations. We decide. You execute. In return, you will be paid a handsome salary from day one. Enough that you'll each be able to purchase a brand-new BMW of your choice in a few months."

No one spoke.

"Trafficking is a hundred-and-fifty-billion-dollar dirty industry. We have much work to get done, and our superiors are depending on my department to show results. You can help bring these sick men down. Men who make millions of people suffer around the world. This is an opportunity to save those who desperately need help, people from the very places you all came from."

He paused and regarded us gravely.

"There are plenty of local caterers who can bake cakes in this town. That's just menial labor."

Menial labor?

"You're capable of much more important work. Work that will change the world."

I glared at him, wanting more than ever to punch him on the nose.

"I'd like to remind you that you don't have many options."

"Is that a threat?" David asked.

"Perhaps you didn't hear me," James replied, sounding ticked off now. "Your past will catch up to you sooner than you can imagine. I suggest you consider my offer seriously."

He pushed his chair back and got up. He reached over to pick up his ID card, which Katy had left in the middle of the table. He tucked it back in his wallet.

"I will give you five days to reflect," he said, looking at each of us, letting his eyes linger uncomfortably just a little before moving on to the next person.

A small knot of fear had formed in my stomach and my throat had gone dry. I wanted to tell him to leave and never come back, but the words died in my mouth.

"One more thing," he said, wagging a finger. "Take some advice from an old man, will you? Stay away from that ambassador's son."

I heard a sharp gasp from Katy.

"With his diplomatic status, he gets away with a lot. He fools everyone, but he's a mean one. Trust me, I've seen what his thugs are capable of. Even we can't help you if you get yourself entangled with that bunch."

Chapter Twenty-Four

William James turned to Olek.

"Mr. Babyak?"

Olek flinched at the sound of his name and looked up. He leaned away with his back hunched like he was expecting to get hit.

"Yes, sir?" he squeaked.

"You don't recall a word that was spoken in this room in the past hour. Am I correct?"

Olek stared at James mutely.

"Do we have an understanding?"

"Yes, sir. Absolutely, sir."

"I appreciate your discretion. Thank you, Mr. Babyak. That's very wise of you."

James reached into his waistcoat pocket, took out a business card and placed it on the counter. He held up a hand, fingers spread out. "Five days," he said. "You know how to find me."

With that, he walked out of the kitchen.

As soon as the door closed behind him, Tetyana drew her pistol. After a quick check outside, she shut the door, bolted it and leaned against it.

We stared at each other silently.

I let out a long slow breath, feeling like I'd been holding it in for the past hour.

Olek grabbed a dishcloth and wiped his sweaty forehead.

"God almighty good mother of sweet baby geez!" he blurted. "They're going to arrest me. I swear I'm gonna end up in a detention camp and get electrocuted." He wheezed into his cloth. "They'll put me in Guantanamo Bay and waterboard me or something. I just know it. I swear to God I know it. I'm done!"

"If they wanted to do that," Tetyana said, speaking slowly, "you'd already have found yourself there."

"Just in case," I said. "I'd tone down the documentation work for a while and stick to the kitchens."

While Olek tried to calm his nervous heart, the rest of us gathered silently around the kitchen counter, trying to make sense of what we'd just heard.

"Wow!" said Luc suddenly, slapping the table and making us all jump. "Wow. Wow. Wow."

We stared at him.

"Think about it, guys," he said looking around the table, his eyes shining. "The CIA wants to recruit us. How cool is that?"

David and Tetyana gave him an icy look. Katy shook her head. And Olek's face turned a deeper red. I bit my tongue for the third time that day.

Luc didn't notice our reactions. He turned and elbowed Win, then Bibi. "Guys, just think. We'll be like James Bond, but a super-duper team of Bonds. Like, imagine that."

"You mean like the famous Five?" said Win.

"Yeah!"

"Famous Nine," said Bibi. "We're nine, not counting Preeti."

I picked up the business card and flipped it over. There was no logo or any sign that man was a government employee. It was a bland white card with the name he'd given us and a telephone number.

"For starters," I said, "we don't have proof he's with the CIA."

"He sure knew everything about us," said Katy. "He's been listening in. How else did he get all that information?"

"He said he had a dossier," said Bibi. "What's that?"

"It's an official file," David explained. "What it means is they have our history, our backgrounds, our past, all documented somewhere, to use whenever they need it."

Win gave us a wide-eyed look. "So they know everything we've done in our whole entire lives?"

"He made a pretty good show of it tonight, didn't he?" said Katy.

"I don't trust him," Tetyana said, shaking her head. "He's not here to help us. That's bull crap if I ever heard it."

I held the business card to the light. "Don't see any chips or anything. Looks legit to me."

Without a warning, Tetyana reached over and plucked it from my hands. Then she turned the oven off and pulled the door open. The cooling fan began to hum.

"What are you doing?" asked Olek. "They're not done yet."

"It will burn!" cried Bibi.

"Fahrenheit four-five-one," replied Tetyana, sticking the card on a half-baked perogy and slamming the door shut. "That's the temperature paper burns. The card will be fine."

We stared at her.

"It will muffle the sound. Just in case," she said. "I'll scan it at the dojo to double-check."

"This is all my fault."

We turned to David.

He was sitting at the edge of his stool, elbows on the counter, head in his hands.

"If that's really the CIA," he said, "I'm the one who brought them to you. Between the CIA and the Mossad, we're talking about the most powerful intelligence agencies in the world. I was stupid to think I could outsmart them."

"Don't take all this on your shoulders," Katy said, reaching out to squeeze his arm.

He shook his head. "That's why they haven't hauled me off to military prison yet. They've been waiting for the right time to find out how they can use us."

He looked pale, like all the blood had drained from his face. Tetyana put a hand on his shoulder and shook him. "They'd be after us even if you hadn't defected, my man. None of us are clean. They picked the lowest hanging fruit and pushed all your buttons."

"He was right about one thing," I said. "We made a ruckus everywhere we went, even before we met you, David. And people noticed."

"So, what do we do now?" asked Luc, looking around the room. I noticed the excitement in his voice hadn't faded.

Nobody replied. I was still trying to sort things out in my head. I suspected most of us were.

"Come on," Luc said. "We're not gonna let that old fart push us around. We're smarter than him, right?"

"Of course," said Win and Bibi at the same time.

"So? What are we gonna do?"

Win sat up. "I can hack into the CIA and check out that dossier thing. Then we'll know if he's lying or not."

Olek shot her a frightened look. "You will do no such thing, young lady. We're in enough trouble as it is."

"That's so dope," said Luc, ignoring Olek. "But getting in is gonna be really tough."

"I can do tough problems," said Win. "I won a gold medal at the hackathon last month."

"Geez," Tetyana swore. She plucked the vodka bottle from the counter and poured herself a glass.

"Hey, guys," said Katy, "I don't think that's such a good idea. We have to be careful here."

"But this kid in his mom's basement got in last year," said Win, "from London."

"The reason we know about him is because he got caught," I said. "Katy's right. Not a good idea."

"But I'm not a dumb little kid in a basement. I go to Stanford."

Katy and I exchanged glances. Win had developed a superiority complex ever since she started at her college. The only other school she gave leeway to was the Boston University School of Law where

Peace studied, but that was only because she had kin there. Anywhere else and anyone else was open game.

"Exactly," said Luc, nodding. "If anyone can get into the CIA, it ma girl."

"You guys have no idea who you're dealing with," said David, shaking his head. "Absolutely no idea."

"Hey," Bibi poked Win in the arm. "Can you teach me too? I don't want anyone to have a dossier on me. I wanna get rid of it."

"That would be super cool," said Win. "You can be my hacker buddy."

"If you two get into the CIA," Luc said, "I'll buy you slush puppies every day for the rest of your life."

"Deal," said Win. "But you gotta help us too."

With a frustrated yell, Olek threw his towel in the sink and leaned across the counter toward the three of them.

"Are you kids out of your flaming mind?" he shouted as he pointed at the door. "Do you realize that was the CIA that just walked into my kitchen right now? And you're planning a major crime? You'll go to jail for life!"

Chapter Twenty-Five

Luc, Win, and Bibi leaned back, trying to avoid Olek's spittle more than anything else.

"Didn't you hear what that old dude said?" said Luc, talking right back.

"What did he say that didn't frighten you?" roared Olek.

"The CIA *needs* us," said Luc sitting up, "Can you imagine? When does that ever happen to anyone? We got the upper hand here, man."

I was glad Peace wasn't here, or he'd have fainted by now.

Tetyana slammed her glass down on the counter. "I never thought I'd have to say these words in my entire life." She looked at Luc, then Bibi and finally at Win, a somber expression on her face. "Please don't hack into the CIA, okay?" She gave a weary shake of her head. "Just don't."

"You two are the most vulnerable," I said, pointing at Bibi and Win. "Without proper ID, they can send you back to who-knows-where and we won't be able to do anything. Do you really want to go back to Pakistan? Back to Laos?"

"That's why we need to get in and change that dossier," said Win. "If we change it, they'll never know. Maybe I can even delete it for good." She pointed at Bibi and Luc next to her. "If they help me with the easy bits, like monitor the front end, I can work fast on the back end."

"And what happens if, I mean, *when* you get caught?" Katy asked. "Have you thought of that?"

"Win won't get caught," said Luc. "She's too smart for that."

"You guys told me I could hack into Vlad and Zero's Swiss bank account, didn't you?" said Win. "It was super hard, but I did it, didn't I?"

All the adults, even David, who hadn't even been there when we'd asked her to commit that heist, looked away.

Win was right.

We'd been desperate.

But we'd targeted criminals, despicable men who'd made money off the backs of innocent girls like her. Katy had called it *blood money*. Those trafficking kingpins deserved everything they got. But this was different. This was the government of the US of A.

I stared at her, wondering what we'd done. We'd created a monster. With two eager helpers.

Except for Olek, none of us were that much older than Luc, Win or Bibi. I wondered if we had any authority over them. Or even any credibility, anymore.

"Win, honey," I said, leaning in toward her. "We're proud of you. And yes, that was a huge job you did, and you had no problems with it. But we're not talking about gangsters now. This is not a hackathon or a coding competition. This is not a video game. This is serious stuff with serious consequences."

Flanked by her sidekicks, Win gave me her most stubborn pout.

"God almighty," Olek said, throwing his hands up in the air. "I swear you're all going to get yourself killed." He turned to Tetyana. "Don't get me involved in this." He tore his apron off and threw it on a chair. "I'm going home to take an Advil and watch TV with my cat."

We watched silently as Olek marched out in a huff.

"It's time for us to go, too," I said, pushing my stool back and standing up. "We've got lots of orders for tomorrow."

One by one, everyone got up and started to clear the kitchen. It was the least we could do for Olek. I'd just opened a cupboard to get containers for the perogies when a loud ping echoed through the kitchen.

I looked around, trying to locate the sound.

"Did Olek leave his phone behind?" David asked.

Another ping, sounding like a text message had just come in.

"Bibi!" cried Tetyana.

I turned around.

Bibi was curled up in a corner, head down, scrolling through her phone.

"Didn't I tell you to get rid of that?" asked Tetyana.

Bibi looked at her, a guilty expression on her face. "Yes, but Sarah—."

Tetyana gave her a furious look. "This is how they're learning everything we're up to!"

Bibi's face went red. "I just wanted to—."

"Gimme that," said Tetyana, snatching the phone from her hands.

Bibi jumped across the room and grabbed it back with such ferociousness that Tetyana let go of it in surprise.

"Whoa!" she said, "What's got into you?"

"I was hoping we'd washed our hands of that family," said Katy, making a face.

"She asked for our help," said Bibi in a defiant voice.

"How do you know she's not playing games with us?" asked Tetyana.

"I know. This was my life. They're going to hurt her. You have to believe me."

We stared at her.

Her lips quivered. A tear ran down her cheek and she wiped it away quickly.

"You don't understand anything!"

Sarah has really got to her, I thought.

"Why doesn't she just dial nine-one-one?" asked Katy. "She has a phone now, doesn't she?"

"You don't get it. They won't come. She's just a girl." Bibi swallowed a sob. "It was the policeman in my village who told me to go back to my family. He beat me with a stick. He said he was going to lock me up if I didn't go. And then, and then, when I went home..."

And Bibi burst into tears.

Win put an arm around her shoulder. "Heya," she said. "It's gonna be okay."

But Bibi was crying uncontrollably now.

With every tear she wiped, she removed her heavy makeup, and in a few seconds, her scars came to light. Those ugly scars that reminded us how a family can punish their own daughter.

"I'm scared for her," she mumbled through her sobs.

"Oh, honey," Katy said with a sigh. She poured a glass of water, set it in front of Bibi and rubbed her back.

With an exasperated sigh, Tetyana pried the phone gently from Bibi's hands. "All right, let's see what this diplomatic brat wants," she muttered to herself as she scrolled through the messages.

"Frigging heck!"

David stepped up and peered over her shoulder. His eyebrows shot up.

"What's it say?" I asked.

"It's in Arabic," said Tetyana, "But the subject line's in English. 'He's gonna kill me.'"

David leaned in and translated the rest. "He wants to make me pay for everything. It's planned already."

"What's planned?" asked Luc.

"Who's this *he*?" Katy asked. "Her brother?"

I remembered my promise to Chef Pierre. I was supposed to meet him the next morning to discuss renewing the contract.

"I think it's time to tell the ambassador what's really going on in his own house," I said.

Another *ping* came from the phone.

Tetyana clicked on the message and David read it out loud.

"He told me he will kill me on my birthday. I'm so scared. Help me!"

Chapter Twenty-Six

The Diplomatic Dragon Lady looked as stunning and as terrifying as she always did.

If there was a real-life Cruella de Vil, she was it. Almost six feet tall, and impeccably clad in her signature pearls and a white Chanel pantsuit with real fur trimmings, she looked like a supermodel for the older, wealthy woman.

Every time I saw her, I felt like a kindergarten kid in front of a mean school principal.

A clerk from the Department of Diplomacy, Development and Foreign Affairs had told me Madame Bouchard was rumored to have hit her seventieth birthday but wasn't anywhere near slowing down.

She was sitting primly in an empress chair in Chef Pierre's ritzy downtown Manhattan office now, looking down her perfectly sculptured nose at Katy and me.

Katy and I had worn our best business suits and had even bought brand-new red heels for this day. We knew a meeting with her and Chef Pierre meant we had to double our efforts to impress. What we hadn't been prepared for was the bombshell she was about to drop.

"The Saudi ambassador's household is requesting an official letter of apology," Madame Bouchard said with a disapproving sniff.

"An apology for *what*?" I asked.

"You've got to be joking," said Katy.

"The family was deeply disturbed by your actions," said the Dragon Lady.

"Disturbed?" I spluttered.

"It's the most discreet way to settle this sensitive matter," Chef Pierre said, looking unhappy. "It'll put this whole thing to bed quickly."

Chef Pierre hated debates of any kind. Sometimes, I thought, he liked to escape to make-believe worlds of prancing unicorns and sweet-smelling roses made of sugar. It was one way to survive this industry.

He'd come far from his coal-mining roots in the outskirts of Brussels to the cutthroat mercenary world of catering to celebrity brides. The critics hadn't approved of this upstart baker getting all the attention. They hit back harder when they found he was engaged to one of the most flamboyant male models in Milan. The old guard found him a double threat. That made him a hero in my eyes.

But I also knew Chef Pierre picked his battles carefully. I suddenly realized this wasn't going to be one of them.

Whenever we visited the Chef's office, we relaxed on the comfortable couches in the corner from where we could see New York's magnificent skyline. The Empire State Building rose in front of us, reminding us where we were. And here we'd sit, sipping wine, sharing stories, gossiping about clients, and coming up with fun and tasty party menus.

Not this day.

The tension in the room was thicker than the fondant on a cheap wedding cake. For this meeting, Chef Pierre was staying safely behind his over-sized mahogany desk. He looked like he was hiding, wishing this conversation wasn't happening, yearning to be elsewhere.

Anne, his personal assistant, sat behind him in a straight-backed chair, pretending to be working on her tablet, but I was sure she was listening to every word. Katy and I sat in equally uncomfortable chairs across from the Chef's desk. Just like how some offices use stand-up meetings to cut discussions short, this was Chef Pierre's way of making sure we wouldn't stay for long.

"This risks becoming an international incident," the Dragon Lady was saying. "Best to nip it in the bud and not make a mountain out of a molehill."

"A molehill?" Katy tossed her hair, something she did when she was getting angry. "But we saw—"

I nudged her foot. "Didn't you say yourself, Chef, that we shouldn't be apologizing for creeps?"

He sighed and spread his arms.

"I don't like this any more than you do. The ambassador said he felt bad about this entire thing too, but his son had been adamant and now they have to save face. At the end of the day, my reputation is on the line. Yours, too. And business is business."

I looked at him in surprise.

This was my childhood role model, the man I'd admired, respected, even revered. He was the one I'd looked up to in my darkest days, the man I'd dreamed of meeting one day and working with. He'd given me so much hope for my future. A cold stab of disappointment shot through me.

I wasn't looking forward to returning to the Saudi house. But that last message from Sarah had unnerved us. We all knew what it was like to be helpless and alone. We also knew what a death threat felt like.

Bibi was right.

A girl was in trouble and was asking for our help. We couldn't abandon her now. Not if we wanted to look ourselves in the mirror every morning.

"Did he talk to the girl directly?" I asked. "Didn't he ask his daughter what really happened?"

The Chef shrugged. "The ambassador called me from Zurich on his way to Vienna. He's a busy man. Look, I really don't know, and I certainly wasn't going to probe him any further than I had to."

"The ambassador's being very gracious," said the Dragon Lady. "They want you to return. This means they're willing to forget whatever happened and move forward. They would love it if you would cater to their daughter's birthday party."

She gave me an icy smile.

I knew it wasn't me they wanted. They wanted Chef Pierre's emblem on the cakes.

Madame Bouchard was here because the party was in four days. It was too late for them to find someone else, especially after they'd announced to the world Chef Pierre was catering the party. The Lady was wrong. They didn't want us back. They *needed* us back.

"Did they promise to treat us properly?" I asked.

"They have always been professional with me," said Madame Bouchard, with another disdainful sniff. "I think it's a given—"

"It's not a given!" I said, only half realizing I'd just interrupted The Diplomatic Dragon Lady herself. "They treat you well because of who you are. It's different for us. Have you seen how they talk to their help?"

She looked at me like I'd ripped off someone's head.

"We're not going back if they can't promise to not grope us or shout at us. I'm not having anyone in my team face that kind of harassment again." I glared at this grand dame in front of me. "They have to promise to be decent human beings. Otherwise, this deal is off. We're not going." I turned to the Chef. "And you can keep the advance."

"I second that," said Katy next to me. "We're not going to be mistreated like that again. We're not sadomasochists."

With a shocked look, Anne brought her tablet to her face. I saw a frightened blue eye peek from behind it. Chef Pierre looked down at his phone on the desk, as if trying to block the conversation out, but I could see his chest was heaving.

The Dragon Lady stared at me for a long time.

I wished I could melt into the floor. I wondered if I'd ever walk in here again, whether I'd ever work for Chef Pierre again.

Then, suddenly, I decided I didn't want to be in this stifling room anymore.

Did I really believe I'd make it big in New York? Maybe it's time to pack my bags and go back to Dar es Salaam—

"Well," said Madame Bouchard finally. "Well, well, well."

She paused and stared at me.

Say the words, I thought, just say it and get it over with. *You're fired.*

Chapter Twenty-Seven

A slight smile appeared on Madame Bouchard's face, a genuine one, this time.

"You have spunk, my girl."

It was my turn to stare at her in shock.

"So what do you think, Chef?" she turned to Chef Pierre who still had his head down, inches from his phone.

He looked up and cleared his throat. "I think it's, er, important, Madame Bouchard, that our, er, clients treat us, er..." He stammered, his face slightly pink with embarrassment, but at least he was trying. "Can we ask discreetly at least?"

We waited.

Madame Bouchard sat up with a determined look on her face. "I will make that imperative."

To my surprise, she gave me a nod. "I agree with you. We can't have these people come here and push us around. I was going to ask my assistant to settle this, but I will call them myself."

I felt relief wash over me and resisted the urge to exchange a triumphant smile with Katy.

The Lady leaned in, pointing her beautifully manicured finger at us.

"There is, however, something critical you both need to know, mademoiselles."

I watched that pointy finger hovering a few inches from my face and wondered if it could be used as a weapon.

"I'm going to share some confidential information with you both," Madame Bouchard said. "Information that must never be repeated outside this room."

My mind raced. *Does it have something to do with Sarah? Is it about her family? Or about us?*

"This birthday party is an unofficial, preliminary affair. I hate to use this word, but it's an excuse."

"An excuse?" I asked. "For what?"

"For the right people to get together." Her eyes gleamed. "You see, ladies, the US, Saudi Arabia, Jordan, and Turkey are negotiating an armament trade, but it stalled a few months ago. The Middle Eastern countries want more for less, but the Americans are holding out."

Katy and I exchanged quick glances. *What does this have anything to do with us?*

"These Orientals, as you know, never like to do business cold," the Lady said with a glance in my direction. I ignored the comment, more interested in what she had to say next.

"They have to meet your entire family, family's family, and your dog's family before they even start talking to you," continued the Dragon Lady with a sniff. "They believe inviting their American counterparts to a friendly event will assist them. They'll get to know each other better, show their friendship, build trust at a personal level, and set the stage for the deal to get back on track. On their terms, of course."

"So," I said, trying to wrap my mind around this explosive news. "This party has nothing to do with Sarah's birthday?"

"Who's Sarah?" asked the Lady, brow furrowed.

"The birthday girl. The ambassador's daughter."

"As I mentioned, that's inconsequential in the scheme of things."

I felt goose bumps spring up on my arms. It was like a whiff of evil had just crossed the room.

"Wow," said Katy, staring at the Dragon Lady in disbelief. She turned to me, lost for words. I had nothing to say. This conversation had gone to a whole other level.

"Wow is right," Chef Pierre said, as he scrolled through his phone.

"I didn't know till this morning who would be there on Saturday. Other than Madame Bouchard and the mayor, of course, there will be two Saudi princes, the ambassador of Kuwait, the ambassador of Egypt, the Turkish commissioner, a well-known imam, and the US Secretary of State. This is a serious business gathering."

"Secretary of State?" I said. *Where did I hear that name before?*

"You mean Hastein?" asked Katy, jogging my memory. "I mean, Secretary Hastein?"

Madame Bouchard gave a dismissive wave. "I can't recall all these petty bureaucrats' names. Just remember there will be many things happening that evening. Everything will be choreographed tightly. Your products are just one part of this picture. It's a status thing that will allow the family to say they had celebrity Chef Pierre's desserts that night."

She turned to the Chef. "Well, enough talking. I must leave now. I presume you have all well in hand now?"

"Absolutely," said Chef Pierre, sitting up straight. "You will not be disappointed. Rest assured, we will be there with cakes on. Haha!"

No one laughed.

Madame Bouchard stood up. "How you run your business is none of my concern. Just make sure any clients I send your way remain happy."

Chef Pierre pushed back his chair and got up.

"That's my priority, Madame Bouchard," He nodded with vigor. "And yes, you will have the spiced Black Forest cakes. They're Asha's best."

I raised an eyebrow. *He's already agreeing to the menu?* I wondered what else he'd promised to this woman.

Madame Bouchard gave a curt nod to Katy and me. "I know you will do your best, girls."

With an unsmiling smile, she stepped toward the entrance. Anne jumped up to open the doors for her.

It was only after Anne had gently closed the doors behind the Lady and herself, that I realized I'd been holding my breath.

I turned back to see Chef Pierre pulling out a whiskey decanter from his side cabinet. He put three glasses on the table.

"Every time I talk to that woman, I need a drink."

He filled the tumblers with the golden liquid and pushed a glass in my direction and another toward Katy.

"Ladies, this is a business decision," he said, picking up his glass. "You need to put your egos aside. If we do our job well at this event, we'll have the entire diplomatic community raving. Asking for us. This is not just a sweet sixteen birthday party. This is an opportunity for us to impress the wealthiest people on this side of the Atlantic."

He took a swig of his drink.

Katy and I held on to our glasses.

"Madame Bouchard loves your work," he continued, "Like me, she craves things that are uncommon, exclusive, exo..." He stopped and gave me an apologetic smile.

"Exotic?" I finished his sentence for him. Chef Pierre was always trying to be polite.

I knew my cakes were different. I added a few blended spices to the batter like my mother used to, spices from Asia and seasonings from East Africa. That was my secret sauce. Only Katy knew what my magic potions comprised.

"Madame Bouchard was the one who introduced me to the diplomatic world in America," the Chef was saying to his whiskey tumbler. "She's well connected, you see. Knows everything about everyone, and that makes her more powerful than the diplomats themselves. That's the only reason I summoned you. I know you won't disappoint us."

Everyone was summoning us these days, I thought.

We didn't have many choices. The CIA had us on a watch list, and I was sure Interpol and the Mossad had us in their databases.

Like David, the rest of us were just waiting for someone in a stuffy government office to decide to take us away in handcuffs. We were lucky to be sitting with Chef Pierre at all.

"You didn't ask the most important question," said Chef Pierre, bringing me to the present moment. "I did a price adjustment. Do you want to know how much you'll make from this job?"

"How much?" Katy asked before I could.

"Here's your advance." He pushed a cheque toward us and raised his glass in a toast.

"To the Red Heeled Rebels."

Chapter Twenty-Eight

Everyone was at the bakery that morning, except for David.

Tetyana was at the dojo, finishing the morning kickboxing class. Katy and Luc were preparing a routine order in the kitchen. Bibi was washing her Subaru in the alleyway, preparing for afternoon deliveries.

And David had taken the Red Beast for repairs at the armored car company.

I was thankful the car was finally getting fixed, even if it meant we had to hail down taxis or rideshares for now. Driving it around town with a bullet hole in the back was embarrassing. This being New York though, no one said anything. As far as I knew.

It was nearly lunchtime now.

I'd left Chef Pierre's office that morning half relieved to get the contract again, one with an even bigger dollar figure than previously offered. Maybe it was Chef Pierre's way of thanking me for not kicking up a fuss or making an "international incident."

I didn't know, and I didn't care anymore. As long as we were getting paid. And paid well.

A lifetime of hero-worshiping had ended that morning. I was struggling to not fall into a depression. Knowing I had to write a fake letter of apology to that family, for something I'd never even imagine doing, felt like a double punch to the gut.

I looked at the words I'd written so far on the pad in front of me.

"Dear Mr. Ambassador and Family," was as far as I'd gotten.

The more I thought about it, Sarah being in danger felt more real. Everything I'd seen and heard so far pointed to nefarious activity. And those last texts from her seemed genuinely frightening.

Kali was waking inside me. I knew what it was like to be in danger. I knew what it was like to feel hopeless and lost. I wasn't going to look away now. My blood boiled at the thought of Ahmed getting away with whatever he had planned for his own sister.

We still didn't know what crime she'd committed to warrant a death threat. Other than gorging on trays of cupcakes or screaming at her servants, I couldn't fathom what she might have done so wrong. Bibi was sure Sarah had hurt her family's "honor" somehow, and according to their culture, they wouldn't hesitate to punish her. Even if it meant committing murder.

In the pure light of day, and to anyone else, this might sound like crazy talk. But we were all convinced something was very wrong.

"Hey, they want our address, telephone number, a formal name and a picture of an official ID. What do I tell them?"

I turned my attention to the present. Win was sitting across from me at the table in the reception area of our bakery. She was looking at me over the top of her laptop, a question on her face.

We'd designed the reception room for customers to wait while their orders got ready, but we never had visitors. Everyone ordered online and got it delivered directly these days. Besides, we didn't live in the most inviting neighborhood.

Comfy couches and coffee tables were scattered across the reception area. In the middle was a large wooden bench that doubled as our team's dining table where we had meals together.

All morning, Win had been trying to contact Safe Horizon without giving too much away. She'd created several anonymous profiles with different email addresses and sent SOS messages to the organization. But each time, she'd got a reply asking for a telephone call to confirm the details.

It was understandable. They probably received false calls and even scams. We were staring at the email on Win's laptop, trying to think of the next best solution, when Tetyana stomped into the room.

"We're infested," she said, her face scrunched in disgust.

She held out her open palm. I peered at the strange black thing in her hand.

"What is it?" I asked.

"Wanna take a guess?"

"Is it turned off?" Win asked.

Tetyana nodded, pointing at a tiny switch. "Coms disabled."

"Where did you find it?" I asked.

"Outside, on the back door," said Tetyana.

"Lemme see," said Win, taking it and scrutinizing it.

"Do you think it's the CIA?" I asked.

Tetyana shook her head. "That's one thing I'm sure about. This is cheap stuff anyone can buy on the Internet. It's not them."

"Or it is them," said Win, "but they want us to think it's not them."

"Who would they want us to think it is?" I asked.

Tetyana shrugged. "All I know is if they wanted to listen in, they'd use something not this easy to find. Much higher grade than this."

How twisted could this get? I glanced around the room, wondering what else had crept inside our home, listening in on us, watching us.

"Either I missed it yesterday, which I don't think I did, or someone installed it right after they noticed the last ones had been pulled out." Tetyana's mouth was set in a grim line. "I'll check the security camera footage to see if we can get a visual."

I stared at the ugly thing, the size of a mini USB stick. In Tetyana's other hand was an electronic device with a short antenna. The bug detector.

"I'll be doing a sweep every hour from now on," she announced. "And I'm putting more cameras on the perimeter."

"As if you have extra time," I said, knowing she'd added more classes and was working around the clock to ratchet up our income to help Chanda.

"Gotta do what we gotta do."

The front door to the bakery banged open and Bibi walked in, water pail in hand.

"Who locked the back door?" she demanded.

"Oh, sorry, hun," said Tetyana. "I forgot you were outside."

Bibi shot her an irritated glance and marched into the kitchen, her wet Doc Martens making her sound like a small but angry army approaching enemy land.

The night before, Tetyana had thrown her old phone out and given her a substitute burner phone. Bibi had used it to text Sarah but hadn't heard back.

She was now sure Sarah wasn't replying because she didn't trust this unknown new number, which meant we would never help her, that Sarah would then disappear for good, and it was all Tetyana's fault.

Bibi was the queen of passive-aggressive tactics. We braced ourselves for the door slam.

A few seconds later, Luc opened the door and came out, rolling his eyes.

"Katy's mad at me 'coz I didn't clean up my mess in the sink fast enough. Now Bibi's mad at me 'coz I asked her how she was doing. What's wrong with everybody today?" He threw a kitchen towel on the table, grabbed a chair and plopped down. "Man, running a bakery is god-darn hard work."

"Much better than selling illegal stuff and sleeping on the streets," I said. "You're doing awesome work, Luc. You've got to be proud of what you're accomplishing here."

He nodded and looked away. Luc wasn't one to gush at compliments, but I knew that meant a lot to him.

"So, I hear we're back on for the diplo party on Saturday now?" he said. "Why the change?"

"One, we're getting paid good money. Two, it will keep Chef Pierre happy, which is important if we want to stay. And three, we get to check on Sarah."

"Three birds with one stone," said Luc. "I like it. Good thinking."

Win wrinkled her nose. "If Sarah's locked up somewhere, how are they going to have a birthday party without a birthday girl?"

"Guess we'll find out on Saturday," Tetyana said, straightening up. "Right now we have more important things to do."

Luc sat up, bug-eyed, suddenly noticing what she had in her hand.

"Is that what I think it is?"

"Not to worry," said Tetyana, "it's on its way to the recycling depot."

"Why don't you just stick it in the city garbage bin on the street?" I asked. "Why do you want to recycle that thing?"

"Don't plan to recycle anything. I'll smash this into pieces and it will all go in the dumpster behind the depot. It will look less suspicious over there. Too many eyes here. That CIA guard's out here all day, and who knows who else is watching. We seem to be quite popular these days."

"Can I keep it?" asked Win.

"What for?"

"So I can check it out. Maybe trace it back."

"Aren't they, whoever they are, going to know when you trace them?" I asked.

"Never done it before, but I can figure it out."

Tetyana and I exchanged glances. This was risky.

"On one condition," Tetyana said, handing the bug to Win. "I want you to show me exactly what you're going to do and how."

"Don't worry," said Win, cradling it. "I'll be careful. Besides, I think I know who they are."

"Me too," Luc said, reaching over and grabbing the device from her.

"Hey!" Win cried out.

Before anyone could react, Luc brought the bug close to his mouth.

"Mr. CIA? You're wasting your time. Why don't you catch real criminals for a change?"

"What are you doing?" I asked in a hoarse whisper.

Tetyana swiped at him. Luc jumped behind a couch.

"Mr. James, if that's your real name, your suit makes you look like a hundred-year-old fart."

"Stop it!" I mouthed, waving my arms frantically.

"Go buy some real clothes, you—"

Tetyana grabbed him and wrangled him to the ground. During the tussle, the bug fell on the floor. Win swept it up.

I watched all this unfold with my heart in my mouth. I didn't need any more excitement in my life at the moment.

Tetyana gave Luc a violent shake by the shoulders.

"What the frigging heck do you think you're doing?"

"It was off! It was totally turned off!" Luc flashed a wicked grin at her.

She let him go with a dark look that said she'd rather have killed him.

"He's right. It wasn't on," said Win, placing the bug carefully on the table.

"If they're gonna listen in on us, we should tell them what we really think," said Luc, turning on his heels and returning to the kitchen.

"Well, that was really mature," I said, falling back on my chair.

For once, Win didn't rush to defend her boyfriend. She threw a frustrated look in his direction.

Tetyana leaned in, picked up the device and rotated it between her fingers, thoughtfully. "You know," she said, after a few seconds, "maybe Luc had a brilliant idea without even realizing it."

This didn't sound good.

"What do you mean?" Win asked.

Tetyana's green eyes were shining. "They want to play games with us?"

"Tetyana," I said, in a warning voice.

She smiled at the bug in her hand.

"I'm gonna put this baby right back where I found it."

Chapter Twenty-Nine

Tetyana spent all afternoon pouring over the security camera footage.

But whoever put the bugs on our perimeter had been meticulous.

It was difficult to say if it was a man or a woman. They came in the early hours of the morning when we were in bed, well after the city worker/CIA guard had left for the night. The person on camera was slim built and wore a plain black hoodie, a black baseball cap, black pants, and white sneakers. The hoodie hid their face, and the entire operation took only two seconds. Then, they disappeared.

The grainy figure could have been anyone in the city. It could have been the CIA guard returning to this job when we wouldn't spot him. It was hard to say.

Tetyana got a hold of an even stronger, professional-grade bug detector from Olek and ordered a high-end camera system from his sources.

I'd asked her to invite Olek to the bakery for tea that day, but he wasn't speaking to the rest of us right now. He was petrified and in hiding, which was perfectly understandable.

Every hour on the hour, Tetyana or David swept the entire building, from the dojo's change rooms to the War Room, the bakery to our bedrooms and even the bathrooms upstairs. So far, they'd found nothing inside or out.

After David had returned with the car fixed, we'd gathered in the War Room with Chanda and Peace joining us virtually, and we'd brainstormed late into the night.

The more we talked, the more Tetyana's harebrained idea seemed plausible. From all the suggestions we'd bandied around, it was the only workable solution that could point us to who was wiretapping us. When we voted, the decision had been unanimous.

And now, everybody had a job to do.

The next evening, we huddled in a nervous circle inside the bakery kitchen.

"Everyone good to start?" Tetyana asked, looking around the room.

"All set," said David quietly.

"Ready or not, here we go," said Katy.

"I'm good." Bibi nodded.

Win jumped into position between Luc and me. "Ready Freddie."

"Let's start this show!" said Luc, pumping his hands in the air.

It was close to dusk, a time when everyone had gone home from work and was having supper in front of their televisions or screens or with family. It was the time of day when the alleyway behind the bakery was the quietest.

"Okay, starting countdown," Tetyana said. "Now."

I felt my shoulders tighten like I was readying for battle.

"In three."

My back tensed up.

"Two."

I can't believe we're doing this.

"One!"

She stepped to the back door and opened it noisily.

"Good to get some fresh air," she said out loud. "Finally."

I peeked out the door. Other than a homeless man dozing in his sleeping bag a block away, there was no one else around.

Luc, Katy, David, and I trooped out behind Tetyana and huddled next to the door.

"Dang kitchen's boiling," said David.

"I'm dying for a cigarette, man," said Luc.

"Want my lighter?" asked Tetyana.

"Jeez, what a long day," said Katy, with a groan. "I'm exhausted."

"Me too," I said, "but we gotta prepare for our next job pronto. No time to waste."

"So how much did you negotiate for the info?" asked Luc.

"A million," I replied. "That's our bottom line."

Inside the kitchen, Win opened a tap and Bibi pushed around a set of steel baking pans, making kitchen noises.

"Come on," said Luc. "That's not enough for a year in Ibiza. We'll have to find some nice digs and a few sweet rides. That's gonna cost us."

"Can we negotiate up?" asked Tetyana.

"I will try," I said. "They're not easy to deal with, but I may bend them at the last minute."

"Go for two million, I say," said David. "Or we give them nothing."

"I agree," said Tetyana. "We're offering gold here."

"Don't worry," I said, "A million is our bottom threshold. I'll start high and negotiate down if and as needed."

"Wouldn't we get a leg up if they came here?" Katy asked. "Home advantage and all that? We have a quick chat, they leave the cash and take the info. And we're done."

"Too risky," said Tetyana. "We don't want anyone seeing them near here. The fewer connections, the better. Besides, they'll already be at the party, snooping around, given all those foreign diplomats."

"So what's the arrangement for Saturday?" David asked.

"I put everything in a mini USB stick," said Tetyana. "All the names and the accounts are in a spreadsheet. Barbados, Jamaica, it's all there. I double and triple-checked. The stick's real easy to hide it. No one will know."

"Good work," I said. "I'll make two cakes and modify the second one. We can stick the USB in it."

"How do we make sure they don't pick the wrong cake?" asked Katy.

"The first one's a four-tier grand birthday cake we'll be rolling into the event hall. The second one's a single layer plain Jane we'll leave in the kitchen."

"No decorations, just white fondant?"

"Yup. I'll cut it in two, bury the stick before covering it up with icing. We'll leave it in a box and tell the kitchen staff it's the overflow cake."

"We've got to make sure no eats it or that'll be hell," said David. "That's a tiny USB. They'll never even notice it if they swallow it."

"If someone does," said Luc with a real giggle, "they're gonna have to take them away and wait overnight till the tiny ass stick comes out."

"With everyone worried about their weight and sugar and all that, no one asks for seconds these days," I said. "I usually bring the overflow cake home. We'll be good."

"We can't have anyone touching it, though," said Tetyana. "We'll be busy serving in the hall. So we'll need someone dedicated to this."

"Bibi can monitor it in the kitchen," I said. "Right, Bibi?" I hollered.

"Yup, I can do that," called Bibi from near the sink.

Good. Tetyana or David would be seen as major threats. A lone young delivery girl would be perceived as a pushover.

"How will we know it's them, though?" asked Katy.

"The code word is Christy Gordon," I said, "They'll be asking for her."

"Christy Gordon? Where did you get that from?"

"Deputy Director of International Ops. CIA."

A snicker went around the group. I was surprised at how realistically everyone was acting.

"So we have to be at the ambassador's house by five o'clock Saturday, right?" asked Katy.

"Yes," I said, speaking slowly, pretending to check something, "They'll let us in the back door as usual. And the guys will come by at eight."

"What about the money?" asked Luc.

"They'll bring it in a duffle bag and leave it under the kitchen sink," I said.

"It's going to be a long night," said Tetyana with a fake yawn.

"Hey, did you know the prince of Monaco will come to that party?" Luc said.

"Gosh, I hope I see him!" said Katy an excited gasp.

"Tons of celebs are coming," said Luc, "Hey, do you think can I take pictures?"

"Not if you want us to get kicked out," said David.

"All right, back to work, people," I said. "We've got stuff to do."

I opened the door, and the others shuffled after me, grumbling in low voices.

"Can someone shut the door?" Tetyana called out, before closing the door with a loud thud, herself.

Silence.

Nobody spoke for five seconds.

"That was cool," said Luc with a grin.

"Was it okay?" asked Katy, looking at me anxiously. "Felt patchy to me."

I gave her a thumbs-up. "Everyone needs acting lessons, but we did fine."

"The main message got through," said Tetyana, "that's the most important thing."

"Are you sure we're not going to get into trouble?" Bibi asked, worried.

"If it's a government body listening, they can accuse us of extortion," David said. "But there won't be any evidence because we haven't actually contacted them. They'd also have to have a warrant for that wiretap, but I doubt they do."

"And if it's Sophie's gang?" Katy asked.

"They'll know we're a hard bargain. We have the information and we can and will hand it over to the authorities. Which means they'll be there to check the cake out ASAP."

"I just hope they don't send anyone to check *us* out," said Luc, making a slicing gesture with his finger across his neck.

"I suggest we close shop for the day tomorrow and get some training," said Tetyana.

"Me too?" asked Win.

"Yes, you too," said Tetyana. "We'll be packing heat, so I need you all at the range for a few hours."

"Won't they have metal detectors?" asked Luc.

Katy shook her head, "Didn't see one. Haven't seen one in any in the houses we've been to so far."

"They have them at the embassies," said David. "They don't install detectors in the residences unless the family's under a specific threat. It depends on the country. You can bet the Israeli ambassador's house is locked down tight. We're good with the Saudis."

"If they have VIPs coming in," said Tetyana, "they'll be upping security. We'll have to be prepared for that."

"Remember, we're flying under Chef Pierre's banner and we'll be going through the back door like the other help," I said. "That'll give us good cover. They might check our bags, but I doubt they'll make us strip."

Tetyana nodded thoughtfully.

"It's a risk we have to take. As long as none of us makes any stupid moves, we'll be good."

Chapter Thirty

"It's a pleasure to see you again."

We'd been waiting in the dining room in the Saudi ambassador's penthouse for an hour.

I got up and stepped toward the ambassador, feeling my knees knock.

"It's nice to see you as well, Mr. Ambassador. Thank you for having us back."

He was his usual dapper and friendly self, his smile broad and his handshake warm. There wasn't a hint of anger.

Under instructions from Chef Pierre, Anne had forwarded my letter to this household the night before. It had been a peace offering, and it seemed to have worked.

I'd held my nose and written five tactful sentences, trying not to throw up on the paper. Bibi had sat across from me, encouraging me. She was the reason I'd been able to finish it. This would be our only chance to find out what had happened to Sarah.

I knew the apology letter had nothing to do with me, but more to do with them. When I signed it and handed it to Bibi to deliver it to Chef Pierre's office, I'd waived my rights to accuse anyone in this household of anything.

"I'm glad we got it all sorted out and are back on track for this very important gathering tomorrow," said the ambassador with a genial smile.

I glanced behind him. His second wife was hovering in the back, as women in this family tended to. She glowered at me like an angry bat, the frown lines around her mouth visible even from where I was. She didn't make any move to say hello. I wondered if this woman had ever smiled in her life.

My mouth was dry, but I had to do this. I lowered my voice. "Mr. Ambassador, how is Sarah doing?"

He jerked his head back slightly.

"Oh?"

He stared at me for a moment, but collected his thoughts quickly. "I, er, think she's doing fine now. I, er, haven't been home for a few days. Just returned last night..."

He turned back to his wife. "Your daughter is doing okay now, right?" he asked.

Your daughter?

The woman gave a curt nod and spoke back in Arabic. He replied in his language. I wished I understood what they were saying. We'd left Bibi and David behind when we needed them the most.

The ambassador turned back to me with a polite smile. "All is good, she says. Let's not refer to this incident again and upset her any further." He stopped to clear his throat. "Now, Chef Pierre assures me you will make some magnificent desserts to impress my esteemed guests, am I correct?"

"We certainly will, Mr. Ambassador."

A dark shadow entered the room, and I felt a chill go through me. It was the man I'd had nightmares about for the past few nights.

Ahmed looked like a slimy snake, an over-fattened slimy one. His eyes said anything but welcome. They were ugly, probing laser beams, filled with hostility. On his nose was a Band-Aid, probably to hide the cut I'd given him a few days ago.

He glared at me.

"We won't disappoint you," I said, turning my attention back to his father and forcing a smile.

With a nod, the ambassador moved to Tetyana.

While I was in my signature business suit and red heels to look the part of a businesswoman as usual, Tetyana wore her black leather pants, leather jacket and red boots. She looked like a modern-day Amazonian warrior. Minus her weapons.

Tetyana towered over the ambassador, but that didn't seem to faze the man. He greeted her the same way he did me, thanking her for coming.

Tetyana offered her hand and gave him a polite nod.

Luc stepped up next, flashing his charming smile that could overpower almost anybody.

"Bonjour, Monsieur l'Ambassadeur," he said, with a slight bow of his head, *"C'est un plaisir de vous rencontrer." It is my pleasure to meet you.*

Luc always knew how to rub important people the right way. Reverting to his native French always helped, especially with diplomats and celebrities who didn't even speak a word of the language.

I wished the son and the wife would disappear soon so I could speak frankly with the ambassador. I wouldn't get another chance to talk about his daughter. He had to know what happened to her, that she'd been asking us for help.

To my dismay, as soon as he'd greeted Luc, he turned around and walked out of the room with his son, excusing himself. The wife shuffled off behind them, her mouth still curved down.

I was thankful the dreaded preliminaries were over, but I kicked myself for missing my chance. I'd have to think of another way to get my message across now.

The one person left behind was the security goon with the yellow smoker's teeth. He slouched against the wall near the entrance, scrolling through his phone, ignoring us, as if nothing had happened between us before.

We'd just sat back down when the servant girl came in.

My heart leaped.

Reza!

It was the same girl who'd brought our tea in the dining hall before. And the same one, I gathered, who'd slipped the phone to Sarah when she'd brought her food.

She walked in, eyes downcast, a Moroccan tea tray in her hands.

I spotted the white card on the tray the minute she set it on the coffee table. I pounced on it.

"Girls, wait in room. I will join in half hour to discuss. - head of staff, Saudi Arabia Embassy Household," read the card.

I flipped it around. No pencil scratches. No secret messages.

"Let me see it," said Luc, pulling the card from my hands.

"Thanks so much for the tea," I said, taking the teacup from the girl and giving her a bright smile. "Excuse me." I paused. "May I ask what your name is?"

"Reza," she whispered with a shy smile.

"It's so nice to see you again, Reza. My name is Asha."

I offered my hand.

She glanced nervously at the security guard at the doorway. He was absorbed in his phone now.

Reza turned back and put her limp hand in mine.

I turned to Tetyana and Luc and introduced them to her. Another awkward moment as she hesitantly took Tetyana and Luc's extended hands.

"We'll be working in the kitchen with you on Saturday," I said.

She nodded. "The head of staff told me."

"Can you tell us a little about the kitchen?" asked Tetyana.

Reza nodded again.

"Why don't you take a seat?" I said, patting the empty chair next to me.

She gave me a shocked look and shot another nervous glance at the security man. He was texting something furiously, oblivious to us now. Or so it seemed.

"I stand," she whispered.

"Don't be silly," I said. "Sit down with us. We have a few questions for you about tomorrow."

She didn't move.

"Don't be afraid," said Luc, flashing her his most friendly smile. "We just want your help."

Reza gingerly took a seat at the edge of the chair and gave us a timid smile.

She started answering our questions in monosyllables, stumbling over words, and glancing over her shoulder every few seconds. It took ten minutes to get the layout of the kitchen and preparations for the party.

While the security guard had his nose buried in his phone and had turned away from us now, we didn't know if he was listening in. But as long as we stuck to kitchen logistics, we should be okay, I thought.

Reza started speaking more freely when he stepped out to take a call. She relaxed, became animated, and talked in longer sentences, happily gesturing with her hands.

She'd been working at the house for four years, she told us. Someone had found her in an Indonesian village and had "given" her to this family in exchange for a sum of money to her family. In return for twenty-hour back-breaking workdays, she got lodging and board. She was happy to see America and learn English, she told us. Her smile grew broader and her face softer as she practiced with us.

Though she shared her story lightly, my heart grew heavy. *A modern-day slave*, I thought. Just like I'd been at Mrs. Rao's house years ago.

The difference between me and her was I'd already finished primary school and had traveled with my parents before I'd got roped into servitude. I'd known how to read and write, which meant I'd known when to push back and get out. Reza had never been to school in her life.

But she seemed oblivious to her situation and grateful to be here. It was joyful to see her blossom from the fearful, demure girl to a smart and high-spirited one.

I glanced at the security man chatting loudly on his phone near the doorway. There was still no sign of the head of staff.

I wondered how risky it would be to ask about Sarah. I had many burning questions. *Where is she? How is she doing? Who locked her up? Does her father know what's going on? Was it her that added the SOS note to the back of the first card?*

"Hey, Reza," I said, leaning in and lowering my voice. "Do you know where Sarah is right—"

The head of staff barged into the room, startling us.

Her face turned purple at the sight of Reza sitting among us.

"Reza!" she bellowed, spit flying. *"Alkhuruj alan, alkalba!"*

With a startled shriek, the girl jumped from the sofa. She ran out of the room, her face ashen in fright.

Chapter Thirty-One

"I have the menu," said the head of staff in a cool voice.

There was no *hello* or *nice to see you*. No handshakes or small talk.

Maybe she was mad at us for entertaining a servant girl in their drawing room. Maybe she knew we'd seen Sarah in trouble and was nervous about it. Maybe she knew nothing about Sarah and was just having a foul day. It was hard to say.

She sat on the chair Reza had vacated.

"You will have Chef Pierre logo on every cake? Yes?" she snapped in my direction.

That wasn't a request.

I straightened my back and looked her in the eye. "I'm his official partner. I add his insignia on everything I make."

"Three hundred guests coming. Very important from around the world. We want logo. Big logo."

Of course, you do, you shallow—

"There is big walk-in fridge in the back kitchen. Cakes stay there until party starts, understand?"

"Sure, that makes sense."

"You stay in kitchen until I call. When I call, you come and serve in the hall. You know protocol?" She gave me a stern look.

"I'd be delighted to serve the cakes at the party," I replied unsmilingly. "I've catered many diplomatic engagements."

"Good. And the big cake. You have design?"

I pulled out the tablet from my bag and scrolled through the photographs Luc had prepared for this meeting. With a curt shake of her head, she dismissed them all, finding fault with each of them. After going through thirty photos, I began to despair. I was just about to give up when an idea popped to mind. I realized her rejections were the opportunity I'd been looking for.

"You know, it would be nice to talk to the birthday girl," I said, taking my tablet back from her disapproving hands. "This is her sixteenth birthday, after all. That's a very special day. Let's ask *her* what she likes."

The woman's eyes narrowed.

"May I speak with Sarah, please?"

Her eyes flickered.

"Birthday girls always choose their cake designs," I said. "It's tradition."

"I tell you what she likes," snarled the woman. She grabbed the tablet back from my hands and flipped through the photos till she found a multi-tiered cake with a climbing rose decoration. "This one," she said, stabbing the screen with her finger. "You make this."

I took my tablet back. "Absolutely. I'd be happy to make this cake for Sarah."

With a huff, she gathered her pen, paper, and phone and got up.

"You must know where to go on Saturday. Come with me."

I glanced at Luc and Tetyana. They caught my eye and nodded.

We followed the woman into the main corridor and toward the penthouse elevator.

I could hear the raspy breathing of the security guard as he lumbered after us. He made me nervous, but I knew Tetyana would subdue him in an instant if the need arose.

Luc and I were carrying our handguns too. My weapon was in my purse-holster and it was comforting to feel its weight. I hoped I didn't have to use it.

The head of staff showed us the path we had to take on Saturday, from the kitchen to the hall and back. We were to stick to the back corridors reserved for the help, contractors and lesser family members. That way, we'd be out of the way of the important guests.

We were on the top floor of the penthouse now, in front of the massive doors to the event hall. The security guard pulled out a set of keys from his pocket and opened the doors for us.

We trooped in.

It was a grand hall with high ceilings and floor-to-ceiling windows.

The head of staff pulled open the curtains to let the sunlight stream in. Then, she signaled me to follow her around as she chattered about where the buffet table would be set, how the tables and chairs would be positioned and where we'd have to wheel in the birthday cake.

I followed her, only half-listening, my mind whirring on more important matters. The security guard had annoyingly attached himself to my heels, and I couldn't wait to get rid of him.

A phone call gave me the break I needed. The head of staff moved aside to take it, dismissing me with a brusque wave.

"That's a super nice view you have here," Luc said out loud.

I turned to see him gazing out the windows at the end of the room.

I walked over to him, followed by the guard. The city of New York lay below us in all its glory. A view fit for royals.

The guard stood next to us, staring out the window too.

"Do you have views like this in Saudi Arabia?" Luc asked the man in his most suave voice. "I've seen photos of Riyadh. It's magnificent. Saudi Arabia is such an enchanting country."

I noticed Tetyana move quickly behind us.

The head of staff was facing the wall, intent on her call.

Good.

"Excuse me," I said, turning to the guard, "I need to use the women's washroom."

He gave me an annoyed look and turned back to Luc.

"Excuse me, the women's toilets?" I tried again. "I really need to go. It's an emergency."

"Outside, outside," he said, giving me an impatient wave and stepping away from me. I was sure dealing with such an inquiry was beneath him to even contemplate. Especially one coming from a woman.

"Do you know Petra?" I heard the man say to Luc. "It is very old site, very sacred."

"Of course, I know. What a beautiful place...," gushed Luc.

Good. Keep him talking.

I ran out of the hall, leaped into the elevator and went down one floor. As soon as the doors opened to the women's quarters, I jumped out, my heart thumping loudly.

I had no idea what I'd say if anyone asked what I was doing here. The only plausible excuse that came to mind was I was looking for the women's toilets and thought they were in the women's quarters.

A weak cover, but I could play dumb.

I knew one person in this household who'd never believe me, the person I didn't want to bump into, and that was Ahmed.

I scurried through the corridors, my heart in my mouth, trying to recall the route from the last time. It took me two minutes to find Sarah's bedroom.

Her door was closed, but the key was on the outside.

Making sure no one was around, I unlocked the door and turned the doorknob gently.

I peeked in.

The curtains were drawn but I could make out the inside.

I stared, my mouth open.

Someone had cleaned everything up.

All of her belongings had been moved out. There were no stuffed animals or pink cushions. No luxury coverlets or blankets. Even the posters of the pop stars had been pulled down.

Except for the naked bed and the empty dresser with drawers pulled out, the room had been completely emptied.

Part FOUR

Chapter Thirty-Two

"Hey everyone!"

We looked up.

It was David, popping his head through the bakery kitchen door. He was in his white martial arts uniform, with no T-shirt underneath. His hair was tousled, and he looked sweaty, like he'd just finished a class.

I stared.

Katy nudged me.

"Stop ogling," she whispered.

I looked away quickly, feeling my face go warm again.

"Got three more classes to teach," David said. He lowered his voice. "Tetyana, I won't have time to pack the hardware and check the gear for tomorrow. Could you...?"

She nodded. "I'll get on it as soon as the dishwasher's loaded."

Katy, David and the girls had been working in the kitchen all morning while the rest of us had been at the ambassador's house making final arrangements for the Saturday party.

Now we were back, the kitchen was crowded. We had much to do and everyone was helping out that afternoon.

Tetyana had jumped in to lend a hand after finishing a kickboxing class and doing a sweep of the building. Win and Bibi were taking turns to decorate the cakes under Luc's watchful eyes.

Steel trays with hundreds of cupcakes sat on the counter, looking pretty in pink. They were ready for a princess's birthday party, except we weren't sure if the princess would show up. These bite-sized cakes were for the guests. I still had to make the principal item for the cake-cutting ceremony tomorrow.

Back at the ambassador's house, I'd returned to the event hall after closing the door to Sarah's empty room. I'd made my way quietly through the corridors I wasn't supposed to be in but met no one.

I'd stopped every few feet to deposit the small devices Tetyana had given me. I'd stuck one under a coffee table, another on a vase, and another on a painting frame. I'd also stuck one on the side of the elevator door.

When I got back to the hall, Luc was chatting in French with the head of staff, his charm wattage at its fullest. He'd disarmed this woman who I thought wasn't capable of having a normal conversation.

At the other end of the room, Tetyana was keeping the security guard busy, pointing at something in the distance. I'd slipped into the room quietly, but no one had said anything. I didn't get another chance to find out where Sarah was or to speak with the ambassador alone before the security guard ushered us out of the apartment.

"So, are we ready for tomorrow's big day, then?" David asked.

"For the party, you mean?" I said.

"I was thinking more about our deadline," he replied, his voice somber.

"Midnight tomorrow," said Luc, looking up from the swirls of icing he'd fashioned on a cupcake. "That's when we turn into pumpkins, right?"

Katy had been measuring the ingredients in a corner, her face pink with exhaustion. She rubbed her eyes. "Oh, god, I'd forgotten all about it."

"How could you forget the CIA man?" asked Win.

"Just lost count of days," she said. "We've been running around so much. It's like a bad dream. Are we there already?"

"We will be," Tetyana said, stooping to take a clean dish out. "In twenty-four hours."

"And we still don't know who he really is," said David.

"Nope," said Win. "We checked everything."

With strict instructions to not hack into any system, we'd tasked Win to confirm William James's affiliation with the CIA. She and

Bibi had spent hours pouring over government sites, public directories, even Twitter feeds, but had failed to come up with an answer.

Like any good CIA operative, William LB James simply didn't exist.

"If we don't call him back, are they gonna put us in jail?" Bibi asked.

I turned off the electric mixture and looked at her.

I'd been hashing out our options, still undecided, but we were running out of time.

I put the mixer down and walked over to the far counter. I pulled the business card from my purse and stared at it, willing it to give me the right answer.

We'd already had a virtual summit on this with Peace and Chanda.

Peace couldn't find anything in the legal books that showed precedence. This wasn't the first time the CIA had conscripted civilians to do missions for them, but as expected, there was no official record. We had no idea what the risks would be of turning down an offer from the most powerful intelligence agency on the planet.

It had taken me a while to fully grasp what William James had proposed.

If we signed up with him—if he truly represented the CIA—we'd become paid slaves for life. Our salaries might bag us a car, a house and all the things a stable government job in the West would bring, but they wouldn't pay the growing bills of our orphanages in Africa.

Tetyana had been talking of expanding to Eastern Europe where "white slavery" was in full swing, bigger than ever before in the history of humankind. We could do so much.

Working with Chef Pierre meant our earning potential was limitless. The only question was how quickly I could find rich clients, meet their needs and grow my team. If I remained in good standing with the Chef, I could grow the Red Heeled Rebels brand, maybe even spin off and become a high-end franchise one day.

Working with a celebrity chef wasn't easy. We were at the mercy of him and his clients, their whims and desires. I also knew my popular spiced cakes could stop being the flavor of the month at any time. Madame Bouchard could tire of us one day and convince Chef Pierre to end the partnership.

Then where would we go?

At least the offer from the CIA, if it was a genuine offer, would give us stability, a permanent country, and education for the girls. We'd even get to live normal lives.

Everyone had stopped working and was looking at me intently.

"We have no obligation to call him," said Tetyana, noticing my conundrum. She didn't trust authority, any authority, even those supposedly on our side.

David leaned in through the doorway, a concerned expression on his face. "You know we'll lose our independence as soon as we sign on the dotted line, right?"

If anyone knew what it was like to work in that sector, it was David. Before I could answer, Tetyana spoke up again.

"We can kiss our freedom goodbye and become drones. Is that what you all want?"

"I'm not a drone," said Win, shaking her head.

"Me neither," said Bibi.

"Sounds like hell," said Luc.

Katy gave me an unhappy look. "I love our life just the way it is, even if we don't know what tomorrow's gonna be like. But I'm with you, whatever you do."

"I'd rather rot in jail than join them again," said David. "But I'll go with what you decide. We're in this together."

During missions, Tetyana and David turned into our tactical leaders, aggressive ones at that. Luc and Katy managed the bakery's daily operations and finances. But they all left the life-changing arrangements to me.

I knew they were looking to me for this big decision, just like they'd looked to me when I came to America to work for Chef Pierre. Even if they didn't agree and may scream about it for a bit, I knew they'd follow me to the end of the earth.

It had taken me a while to figure out why.

Then, I'd realized it was because I was the one who had brought them together. And I was the one who kept them together.

I gave them a reason to keep hope alive, something they'd all been robbed of in childhood.

Except for Peace and Chanda who'd come from single-parent families, the rest of us had been shunned, scorned or sold by our own. We didn't belong to a family, a community, or even a country. They'd all abandoned us a long time ago.

Though Peace had had a semblance of a normal childhood, he'd dedicated his life to fighting injustice, a cause that would make him one-tenth of what he'd get, had he gone into corporate law like his father wanted him to. Peace had a big brain and an even bigger heart.

Chanda had chosen her path when she was just a kid taken from Tanzania to Kenya in the back of a truck to work for the mines. She'd never given up on her goal to make a difference in others' lives.

Young Win had only one aim in life, and that was to become the best hacker in the world, all in the name of helping the most vulnerable in society.

While Luc liked to joke around, he worked hard at the bakery. I knew he yearned for a life with people who cared for him, and that was why he never went back to hanging out in the streets, dealing drugs for gangsters.

If all David and Tetyana had wanted was money, they'd have found lucrative work as hired mercenaries. They stayed with me because they were seeking redemption for their painful pasts.

And Katy, my loyal Best Friend Forever, had stuck with me through everything from the beginning and had never looked back. She was a sister, more than a friend.

The Red Heeled Rebels united all of us under one banner.

The bakery and the dojo were our fronts. Behind it all, we had a serious unspoken mission, and that was to do the right thing at the right time, no matter what. If that meant we had to fight injustice till we drew blood, till those who harmed innocents would feel the pain, so be it. This was why we stuck together. The Red Heeled Rebels gave us a purpose and a path to rebuilding our shattered lives.

I looked around me and my chest swelled up.

This was my family.

And they were waiting for an answer.

I slipped the card back into my purse.

I still had twenty-four hours to get back to William James.

Chapter Thirty-Three

The shrill sound of the alarm jerked me awake.

I looked around the darkened room with bleary eyes, my heart racing.

Is the house on fire?

From above me, a panther-like shadow pounced from the upper bunk. I nearly screamed.

Tetyana!

She was already at the door with her sidearm drawn.

I jumped out, still in my pajamas. She whipped around and hissed. "Get your Glock."

I dove under my bed and got my handgun out.

"Bibi, Win," said Tetyana, "stay right here. Don't move."

The two girls sat up in their beds, watching us in a daze. The clock on the nightstand said it was three forty-six am. The security alarm was ringing like mad. I was sure it was waking up the entire neighborhood.

Katy jumped out of her bunk and joined us, her gun in hand.

It was David's turn to be watchman that night. His job had been to stay inside the War Room, scanning live camera footage of our perimeter for unusual activity. He was supposed to alert Tetyana at any sign of trouble, but it seemed the alarm had been a surprise to her too.

A loud crash from downstairs made us jump.

David!

I was about to rush out when Tetyana pulled me back roughly by the shoulder. She put her finger to her lips and motioned Katy and me to stay behind her.

Holding her pistol in front, she clicked open the door.

The alarm clanged even louder. From the corner of my eyes, I saw Bibi put her fingers in her ears.

Tetyana motioned us out. We stepped out to the landing after her.

Luc was crouched behind the stairway railing, his face white, peering in between the wooden poles, his attention on the first floor.

I peeked over his shoulder.

At the foot of the stairs was David.

He was pointing his weapon at the connecting door between the dojo and the bakery, the one that led to the bakery's reception room and to the kitchen in the back.

He spotted us and motioned us to join him.

Tetyana turned to Luc. "Stay with the girls," she whispered. "Lock the door."

With a quick nod, Luc slipped into the girls' room. The door closed gently, and I heard the click of the bolt.

Tetyana took the first step down. We tiptoed behind her, keeping our eyes and ears peeled.

On the wall near David was the alarm console. The red danger light was blinking in tune with the nonstop electronic screeching.

"They had a decoy," David said when we joined him.

"Where?" asked Tetyana.

"Someone threw rocks at the dojo window. Thought it was some kids. When I went to check, another party broke into the bakery. Fifteen seconds ago. They're in there."

We turned to the connecting door.

Through the open doorway, I could see our reception room and the door to the kitchen. The kitchen door was closed, just as I'd left it the night before. I always locked up the kitchen. That was where I kept my cash register and my finished and unfinished cakes.

I could hear someone rummaging inside.

They're raiding my kitchen!

The evening before, I'd spent hours painstakingly preparing the final ingredients for the next day so we could meet our regular orders and Sarah's birthday party menu items. Everyone had been working long hours with little sleep, and we had to make time for the mandatory training Tetyana and David had planned for us. The last thing I needed was another hurdle thrown our way.

My blood pressure rose. *They'd better not ruin my cakes or I'll throttle them with my bare hands.*

Tetyana signaled to David. He nodded.

Shoulder to shoulder, guns aimed forward, they stepped inside the bakery reception room. Katy and I followed a few steps behind.

It sounded like a herd of marauding buffalo was rampaging through my kitchen, smashing things, making a mess.

My hackles went up. *I'll shoot them in the head myself, I swear.*

"Stay back," Tetyana whispered, motioning Katy and me into the shadows. "Cover us."

Katy and I kneeled near the connecting doorway, training our weapons toward the kitchen.

David and Tetyana positioned themselves on either side of the kitchen door.

Another loud clatter came from inside.

What are they waiting for? I gritted my teeth and fought the urge to run in guns blazing.

Tetyana and David crashed through the door, screaming at the top of their lungs.

"Freeze!" Tetyana yelled. "I said, freeze!"

"Get down!" David shouted. "Down!"

The herd of buffalo sounded panic-stricken now.

Katy and I scrambled after them. A cool draft of air hit us as soon as we entered the kitchen.

"Oi!" David hollered. "Stop!"

It was hard to see what was going on.

Someone slipped and fell. Someone cursed. The back door banged open. A ninja-like fellow in black dashed out the back door.

David and Tetyana gave chase, shouting. The door banged open and shut again.

Katy and I rushed after them.

"Hey!" I exclaimed as I slipped and landed with a painful thud on the floor. "Ow!"

"Aiiee!" cried Katy as she came flying down next to me.

It was just Katy and me in the kitchen now. I took in the mess around us.

The cabinet drawers had been pulled open. Cutlery, baking trays, and dishcloths had been flung all over the place. The cash register was open and someone had rummaged through it. That was what we'd skidded on. Slippery greenbacks were strewn over the floor, covered with baking soda.

I looked at the countertop. All my cakes were intact. Except one.

It was the cake I'd made the night before, the undecorated one, covered with only plain white fondant icing. It now looked like it had been smashed with a sledgehammer. They'd been looking for something. And I knew what it was.

I heard shouting in the alleyway outside.

I leaped up and ran out just in time to see two men in black balaclava masks jump on a motorcycle.

David was lying on his stomach near the Subaru, his gun angled from under the car.

"Down!" yelled Tetyana from behind the Red Beast, when she spotted me come out.

I dove next to David.

Where's Katy?

I looked around but couldn't spot her. I'd thought she'd been right behind me.

A gunshot rang out. I covered my head.

It was Tetyana. She'd shot at the men.

The men wobbled on their bike, trying to regain balance.

Did she hit them?

That was when I noticed their bike jackets looked bulky and stiff, like they had body armor underneath. A chill went through me. These were professionals.

The man in the back lifted a hand and pointed it our way. I spotted his black gun.

"Watch out!" Tetyana yelled.

I ducked and covered my head again.

The bullet hit the Subaru's side window, breaking it into a million pieces, showering David and me with broken glass.

Another shot rang out. The Subaru was getting pummeled.

The motorcycle roared off through the narrow alleyway.

David and I sprang to our feet to see Tetyana jump on her black Ninja.

She revved the bike.

"Wait!" I cried out. "Tetyana!"

She shot out of the alley on one wheel and blasted off without a glance back.

Chapter Thirty-Four

We had to help Tetyana, but the Subaru was useless.

Its front tires were flat and its windows had been blown right off. The Red Beast was back from the repair shop and had amazing horsepower and was armored, but that would be like using an elephant to run after a cheetah. We'd never catch up to the bikes.

David was removing the chains on his Yamaha when we heard Katy call out from inside.

"Guys! Get in here!"

David left his bike and we dashed inside.

Katy was in the bakery's reception room, her hair as wild as flames around her. "The dojo!" she said, pointing to the connecting door. "I heard a loud crash just now!"

I noticed Katy had shut the house alarm off. The screeching had stopped and it was deadly quiet inside the building.

We listened in for a few seconds.

Nothing.

"Asha, cover me," said David. He turned to Katy. "Barricade the back door."

"What about everyone?" I said, glancing up the stairway. Both bedroom doors were still closed.

"They're good," Katy said. "Checked on them just now."

A siren sounded in the distance.

Did someone call the police?

I stepped up to the window quickly.

There wasn't a soul on the streets, but a few lights had come on in the apartment block in front of us. Our fracas had probably woken half the neighborhood. I was surprised a SWAT team hadn't already barged in.

A line of neighborhood cars was parked alongside the road as usual. Nothing looked amiss except for the dark brown van with tinted windows at the end of the block. I tried to remember if I'd seen it before.

"Let's go," said David.

Leaving Katy in the bakery, David and I stepped toward the dojo.

Apart from David's office and our War Room hidden in the back, there were two changing rooms with toilets and showers. Most of the space in the dojo was taken up by the open gym. The floor was lined with thick wall-to-wall grappling mats. A smattering of gym equipment, including punching bags and Bob, the Rubber Man, sat along the perimeter of the room.

There were cameras everywhere here except for the change rooms. It would be next to impossible for anyone to hide in there.

David opened the door to the dojo quietly. I stood on the other side, gun trained forward, my throat dry, ready for an intruder to pounce on us.

He pulled the door open and we moved in, shouting, "Freeze!"

Nothing.

David flicked the lights on.

The dojo was empty.

We glanced around. Nothing looked unusual.

David walked over to the office and rattled the doorknob. It was secured with a biometric lock and a keypad. No one could get in there other than one of us, using our thumbprints and the secret code.

We turned our attention to the change rooms. That was the only place someone could remain hidden. We treaded quietly over the mats and jumped inside each room, shouting, threatening to shoot as we did.

But there was no one.

What did Katy hear?

We panned the room.

"Jeepers," said David suddenly, pointing at the window.

There was a long crack in the window furthest from us. In the shadows, it had been hard to spot.

How did that happen?

The dojo windows were made of a strong double-paned reflective glass. It would be difficult to damage these windows unless they'd been using something very strong.

I was just about to inspect it when David pulled me by the arm. "Stay back," he whispered and flattened himself against the wall.

An inky shadow caught my eye.

Someone's at the window!

We waited, not breathing.

They can't see inside, can they?

In the silence, I heard the police siren grow louder. It was hard to say if they were coming here or some place else. This was New York, where the emergency siren was the official anthem that played day and night.

David slid to the floor.

"Cover me," he said, as he began to crawl toward the window on his stomach.

I felt a slight breeze of frosty air. It was coming through the cracked opening.

Be careful, I said silently to David, keeping my eyes peeled on the window, on alert for the shadow to reappear.

When he got to the end of the room, David raised his head to take a peek.

Someone fired.

"David!" I cried out.

The bullet shattered the window over his head. It whistled through the room and hit something behind us.

David dropped to the mat, shards of broken glass falling on his body.

He grimaced and tried to re-position himself.

He's hit!

I army-crawled across the mats toward him, my heart thumping like mad.

David was clutching his shoulder, wincing in pain.

"Let me see," I asked.

Someone shouted from outside.

In a flash, I turned and fired through the hole.

A man yelped in pain or fear, I couldn't tell.

They're going to fire back.

I grabbed David's head and pulled him down.

Instead of more gunfire, we heard the squeal of tires on the asphalt. The smell of burning rubber came through the window.

The police sirens were getting close now.

"You all right?" I asked David.

"Just a scratch," he said. I couldn't see the wound but a bright red patch was forming on his shoulder.

"Oh, my god. That's not good."

"I'm okay," he said and flipped his thumb, pointing behind him. "But he's a goner."

I whirled around.

It was Bob, the Rubber Man. He was still standing on his steel pedestal at the corner of the gym, but his entire rubber face had been blown off.

I gave David a shocked look. *That could have been us.*

He nodded.

I felt sick to my stomach.

The police cars were now a block away. That was what made the goons run.

I picked up my pistol, got up and shook the glass shards from my shirt. Then I helped David stand.

I wondered how the others were doing upstairs and in the kitchen.

And where's Tetyana? Is she okay?

The sirens were right outside our door now.

My mind was racing a million miles a minute.

What do we tell them?

"I've got to warn the others," I said.

"Put the weapons away. Don't want to look too militant or have to answer too many questions," David replied in a weak voice.

He looked pale.

"You okay?" I said.

"Go," he said. "I'll manage them. They'll be more sympathetic to me in this condition."

Car doors slammed.

"Go!" he said.

Without looking back, I ran out of the dojo and scampered up the stairs, taking two steps at a turn.

"Katy!" I yelled. "Katy! Get up here!"

I got to our bedroom door and thumped on it.

"Luc! Bibi! Hey, Win!"

Someone was banging on the front door of the bakery.

"Police!" a man's voice shouted.

"Police! Open up!"

Chapter Thirty-Five

We heard heavy footsteps on the stairs.

Boots. Police boots.

Any moment now.

We braced ourselves.

The bedroom door got kicked open and two burly city cops rushed in, their guns drawn.

"Christ!" exclaimed one of them when he saw us huddled on the floor in our pajamas, our backs against the bunk beds.

They lowered their weapons. And stared.

We stared back.

"Everybody okay here?"

We nodded.

"Are they gone?" asked Katy with a scared look.

"Is David okay?" I asked in a shaky voice.

"We're gonna secure all the rooms. Y'all stay put, okay?" said the second cop, holstering his sidearm.

He turned to his shoulder mic. "Ten-ninety-seven. Five inside second-floor bedroom. Civilians. Kids. No visible danger. Code four. Over."

Code four? What does that mean?

"Ten-four. Continue to secure rooms," said a woman's voice. "Medical emergency here. Paramedic on site for one injured party. Over."

"Oh, no," said Win and Katy at the same time.

"David!" I scrambled up.

"Whoa there," said the second cop, putting out his hand. "This here is a crime scene."

"But we heard gunshots," I said. "Is he okay?"

"Hold it right there," the first officer said. "You'll have to wait till we get more details."

He made another radio call to his colleague. We waited, comprehending only half of what they were saying.

"Who's the oldest here?" he asked when he was done.

Katy and I put our hands up.

"Okay, you two can go down with this officer. Our sarge wants to talk to you."

He turned to Luc, Win, and Bibi, who were still squatting on the floor, eyes wide open, hair askew.

"You stay put right here till we give the green light. Just hang on, okay? You're safe now."

They nodded.

The second officer motioned Katy and me to follow him downstairs.

I was half-relieved help had come so fast. But the other half of me was worried sick about what would happen next. I wondered about Tetyana. *Where is she? Is she alive?*

Katy and I found David lying on a white stretcher on the floor of the dojo. A paramedic had her first-aid kit open and was digging in it for something with rubber gloves. She had cut out David's shirt and I could see his left shoulder was bleeding.

"David!" I ran up to the stretcher.

Katy joined me. "Hey buddy," she said. "You okay?"

He gave us a weak smile.

"Didn't go in," said the paramedic, unrolling an antiseptic gauze.

"Is he going to be fine?" I asked.

She nodded. "It'll heal. There'll be a scar, though. Something to show off to his pals, but otherwise, it's superficial."

David lifted his head to talk. "I'm feeling great," he said with a wonky smile.

"Move over," said the paramedic, pushing me aside. "Lie down," she commanded to David. He collapsed back on the stretcher.

She pulled him onto his side so she could get a better look at the wound. He grimaced but complied. She started to wipe the blood with a cotton pad.

I locked eyes with David. He gave me a slight nod and a thumbs-up.

At least he was being looked after. But Tetyana was still not back. *What if she comes in now? Can we keep our story straight?*

"You all live here?"

I looked up.

It was another NYPD officer. She was smaller than the other cops but had more badges on her shirt. Her face also said she wasn't someone you messed with.

I got up and dusted my pajamas.

"Yes," I said. Hearing my voice squeak, I cleared my throat. "Yes, we do."

"Who runs this place?"

"I run the bakery. And she works with me," I said, pointing at Katy. I looked down at David. "And he runs the gym."

"And you were here all night?"

"We sleep upstairs."

She nodded but was frowning. "Follow me back here, please."

Katy and I exchanged glances. This must be the sergeant.

"This way." She motioned us to follow her to the kitchen.

A lone male officer was inside. He had a phone in one hand and was panning the room, recording the scene.

The door was closed, but the room was cold. I glanced at the window. The bars had been ripped out and a large hole had been cut through the window. *That's how they got in.*

My heart fell seeing the mess again.

The clock on the wall said it was four fifteen in the morning. I'd set my alarm clock to four to prepare for Sarah's party. I hadn't bargained for any of this to interrupt my work.

"Did you have the house alarm on?" asked the sergeant.

I nodded. "We put it on every night."

"And it went off tonight?"

"Yes. We heard noises like someone had broken into the bakery. David went to check on things. Then we heard gunshots."

The sergeant surveyed the money on the floor.

"How much do you keep in your register overnight?"

"Around five or six thousand."

She gave me a shocked look. "Six grand?"

I nodded, keeping my eyes steady. We kept a lot more than that in the safe in our War Room, but I couldn't tell her that.

"Why in god's name don't you take that to the bank after closing?"

"I need it for my ingredients every day."

"Six grand to make cupcakes?"

"I cater to Chef Pierre's clients."

"Chef who?" She frowned.

"Chef Pierre, eh?" said the male officer, raising an eyebrow. "My wife loves his cooking show."

I nodded. "He works for diplomats and celebrities. I'm his business partner, so things are pricey."

"Ah," said the sergeant, her face clearing.

"Seen him on *Oprah*," said her colleague, with an admiring nod. "Pretty big shot. Frenchman, right?"

"Belgian."

The sergeant pulled her phone out.

"Okay, ladies, let's start at the top. Can you two give me your names, birth dates, occupations, and addresses to start the statement?"

As Katy and I finished giving our details, the two officers who'd been upstairs trooped into the kitchen.

"All clear, Sarge," one of them said.

I gave a quick glance at Katy.

What about the War Room?

"Altercations limited to the alleyway at the back of the bakery and the gym next door. Everything else locked tight. We have one casualty. Had a licensed handgun. Said he was defending himself when the men broke in. Said they came for the cash register."

"Took names and statements from the kids upstairs," said the second cop. "They never left the room. Locked themselves up as soon as they heard the alarm go off. Smart move," he added with a nod in our direction.

"How many?"

"Three upstairs. A little nerve-wracked, so I passed them a counselor's card."

"Good work." The sergeant nodded. "What else did you find?"

"Two bullet holes in the windows in the gym. That's where he got shot at."

"They shot up one of the cars in the back too," said the other cop. "There was quite the gunfire."

The sergeant turned to us. "How many were there?"

"We were upstairs, so we didn't see anything," I said, trying to swallow my shame for lying to a police officer. "But we heard people shouting."

Katy nodded. "And gunshots."

"How many?"

"I, er, don't know," Katy said, genuinely trying to think. "It was hard to say. Maybe four? I thought they killed David."

"We got reports of gunshots from your neighbors," said the sergeant. "And you didn't think of calling nine-one-one?"

Katy and I looked at each other.

"I, er, I guess we weren't thinking," I said, hoping I looked as frazzled as I felt. "It happened so fast, and I was worried David was getting hurt—"

Just then, their radios came to life.

"Ten-thirty-five," they crackled, "Repeat ten-thirty-five." The voice sounded urgent.

The officers stood to attention, heads cocked to the side, listening.

"116th Station. I repeat, 116th Station. Calling all patrols."

The sergeant looked at her team.

"Go! I'll take care of this. Report back at the office."

The men turned around and dashed out.

I broke into a cold sweat.

Did they find Tetyana? Is she in trouble?

The sergeant spoke briefly into her mic, telling the people on the other side she was sending reinforcement. The chatter on the radio increased, and the officer turned the volume low.

"Hey."

We turned toward the door. David was straggling in, shirtless. His right shoulder was bandaged. Behind him was the paramedic, her stethoscope around her neck.

"Minor blood loss," she said to the sergeant. "I'd prefer he come to the hospital so a doc can have a look, but—"

"No, I'm good," said David, "it's nothing."

We knew he was lying. His face was pale, his shoulders were limp, and he looked a mess.

"Your call, mister," said the paramedic, "That morphine won't last long."

"I'm fine."

She slapped the counter to say she was finished here. She turned to the sergeant and rolled her eyes before marching out.

The sergeant glowered at David. "I'm not sending anyone to take you to Emergency later. That's why she's here now."

"I'm good," David said, waving his good arm. "Really, I'm fine."

The officer turned to Katy and me.

"What I want to know is," she said, her eyes narrowing. "What exactly you all do here."

I swallowed.

This is how we're going to end up in prison.

Chapter Thirty-Six

"How long have you been at this location?"

"Six months."

"Where were you all before coming here?"

"Dar es Salaam, Tanzania."

Her eyebrows shot up.

"How did you end up in New York?"

"Chef Pierre recruited us to help his business because he saw my work at a party and liked it."

"You all have immigration papers in order?"

"Yes." I nodded. Maybe a bit too vigorously.

"I'd like to see them."

"I'll get them for you," Katy said, stepping out.

David pulled out a seat at the counter and put his head down on the table.

"What I don't understand is," the officer said, looking at the bills on the floor, "why you keep all this money in your cash register."

"I need to buy high-end ingredients and I hate lining up at the bank every afternoon to deposit money. Takes too much time."

"These yours?" she said, pointing at the glass case on the counter. Behind it lay four intricately decorated cakes with climbing flower designs made from icing. These would make up the birthday cake I'd assemble into tiers later that day for Sarah.

I nodded.

"How much does one go for?"

"Seven thousand," I said. "It comes in four-tiers."

Her eyebrows shot up again. "Are you kidding me? For some fancy flour mixed with sugar?"

"It's custom built and handmade with the best ingredients."

"Whad'ya put in it for that price? Crack and cocaine?"

"Black Pearl," I said. The last thing I needed was for her to think we were dealing drugs. "It's got half a liter of Black Pearl in it."

"You put pearls in this thing?" She bent over to inspect the cakes more closely, sniffing the glass suspiciously. "What happens if you swallow one? Won't it kill you or something?"

"Sorry, not real pearls. I meant Remy Martin Black Pearl. It's a cognac from France. Like champagne, but more expensive."

"Never heard of it. Guess you don't get that at the corner liquor store?"

"You have to order it from France. One bottle is around, er, fifty thousand dollars. That's why—"

She let out a low whistle. "Fifty K?"

"Some are around a hundred thousand a bottle. Depends on how long they've aged."

"This Chef Pierre and his clients must be loaded if they're commissioning thousand-dollar cakes."

She rocked back and forth on her heels, regarding me strangely, like I was a curiosity more than a threat.

"You got one of those bottles here?"

"Black Pearl?" I asked.

"What does it look like?"

I looked at her in surprise. *The sergeant wants to see a Black Pearl cognac bottle?*

I walked over to our liquor cabinet and opened it.

"Oh!"

I stared at the empty space in the front row of the shelf.

Where's my bottle of Black Pearl?

I whirled around, my heart beating a tick faster.

"Maybe Luc put it someplace else," I muttered to myself and pulled open the next cabinet door. I went from one cabinet to the next, opening and checking. Then, I ransacked through the open drawers.

The sergeant watched me without a word.

I closed the last drawer and looked at her in dismay.

"They took it! Those men stole my Black Pearl!"

She sighed.

"You start a new highfalutin business for someone who's on TV, and you leave a whole whackload of cash and this fancy-dancy alcohol lying around in *this* neighborhood? They were probably scoping you for weeks, trying to find the best time to break in. What were you thinking?"

"I, er..."

This was where I'd have to stop telling the complete truth. I looked at David for help, but he still had his head down.

Six thousand dollars wasn't a whole whackload of cash. Six hundred thousand in greenbacks was what we had locked away in the War Room. It was our emergency fund. I needed all the luck in the world for the local police to not start rooting around in our place. I crossed my fingers.

"Don't you have a safe in here?" the officer asked.

"A safe?"

"Yeah, a waterproof, fireproof, theft-proof steel box. You can get a small one at the hardware store for fifty bucks. That's what you need for your cash."

I swallowed. We had something even better than that in the boardroom. Our weapons storage was all that and bulletproofed too. "I, er, I guess I wasn't thinking...."

"Damn right, you weren't. Could have got yourself and your friends killed. Then, I'd have to send a team over to scrape you off the floor. It's what we do every other night around here."

I hated lying to her. She was on our side. She was probably the only person in uniform who'd ever tried to help us in our lifetime. But I was on full alert. I knew what happened when we trusted the wrong people.

I took a deep breath to settle myself.

If I screwed up now, this wouldn't just end with me in jail. Bibi, Win, Luc, and Katy would also be in danger.

Unlike David and Tetyana, who'd worked for paramilitary forces, none of them had ever picked up a gun or hacked an account with criminal intent. It had always been in self-defense. To stop an abduction. A rape. A killing.

If we got carted off to jail, that would be the end of the orphanages. Chanda didn't have access to any official funding channels. She was in hiding herself, living a double life, which meant we were the only source of her funds.

If we stopped our work, the kids we'd rescued would be back in the mines, under the thumb of their merciless masters, forced into backbreaking work in dark underground pits, getting whipped daily and finally hacked to death with a machete once they were too weak. Only to be replaced by another batch of stolen children. This was the evil we were fighting.

"I'm sorry," I said, looking down at the floor. "We really didn't mean to make trouble for you. I'm really sorry."

The officer watched me, her eyes narrowed. "You weren't making street payments, were you?"

"Pardon me?"

"No gangs came knocking asking for protection money, did they?"

"Protection money?" I asked, my eyes wide. I hadn't even thought of it. "No." I paused. "Is that a thing here?"

"No, it's not!" she snapped. "It certainly is not a *thing* here. If anyone did, that's reasonable grounds for arrest and prosecution. I'll happily see them off to jail myself."

"Oh," I said. "Sorry. I had no idea, but we never paid anyone anything. We were trying out this place because it's hard to find affordable rent. We were planning to move to a nicer spot once we started making a profit. Chef Pierre doesn't like us being here either, and he's refused to visit us here."

Katy walked in with our papers just then, her eyes red from all the stress.

"I told the others to stay in bed," she said. "They're a bit freaked out right now."

The officer nodded and took the identification papers from her.

With a grunt of acknowledgment, she started going through the documents one by one. She unfolded the visa papers carefully and held them to the light. She was a local city cop, not an immigration officer, but if she looked closely enough, she'd see problems on a few of the booklets.

Katy and I waited, leaning against the counter next to David who'd now fallen asleep, courtesy of the painkillers.

After a few minutes, the sergeant put the passports back on the counter and looked at us.

A slight snore came from David.

The sergeant sighed.

"Here's what I'm going to do," she said. "I will authorize a junior constable to monitor your place. Just for the day. It's rare these guys come back to rob a place they tried once, but it'll be a deterrent to anyone else." She gave us a strict look. "I can't send anyone for more than a day, you hear?"

I nodded, trying to look grateful.

The CIA was watching us. Someone else was listening in on us. Now the NYPD wants in on the action too? What happens when the watchers find out about the other watchers?

"I normally don't do this, but you kids are new here and still figuring things out, so I will see what I can do."

Thank you so much, Sergeant," I said.

"Thank...thank you, Officer," Katy stuttered.

"All right, you all have some cleaning up to do here. I'm going to let you go."

She'd just turned to leave when we heard the motorcycle roar up and stop with a screech at the back door.

Tetyana?

The officer whirled around and pulled out her sidearm.

"Expecting more company?"

Before we could answer, the door banged open and in stomped a tall, muscular woman, muddied from head to toe.

"Tetyana!" Katy cried out.

"What happened to you?" I asked.

Tetyana removed her grimy helmet. Dirt covered her arms and legs like she'd fallen into a wet sinkhole.

My eyes bulged. In her free hand was the bottle of my Remy Martin Black Pearl.

She stepped up to the kitchen counter and plopped the bottle on it, sending mud specks flying.

"Found it," she said to me.

I stepped up to the counter and picked up the bottle. It was mine, all right.

"And you are?" said the sergeant with a frown.

Tetyana placed her muddy helmet on the counter. Any other time, I'd have admonished her, but I had more important things to focus on. We had to get our story straight, plus, I had no idea how she was about to react to the officer.

"I work at the dojo," replied Tetyana in a clipped voice. "Heard the alarm and came to check."

"Tetyana," I said, before the officer could speak, "We told them about the break-in. But we didn't see the people who tried to steal our money. Did you catch them?"

With an understanding nod, Tetyana turned to the sergeant.

"One of them tried to run away with this on his bike. He didn't get far."

"Got a good look at the perp?" the officer asked, pulling out her phone again.

"Afraid not," said Tetyana, shaking her head. "They were wearing helmets. Too bad 'coz I wanted to see who it was too. But they won't be coming back."

The officer looked up. "Oh, yeah?"

Tetyana nodded.

"Chased them down a side street, got right close to the back wheel and made them slide across the asphalt. Pulled one guy up, punched him in the face a few times, gave a good kick to his balls, and pulled the bottle from his jacket. The bastards took off on their bike like cowards before I could do anything else." Tetyana's mouth curled in scorn. "Petty thieves."

The sergeant stared hard at Tetyana for a few seconds. Her phone rang, distracting her. She glanced at the screen and turned the ringer off.

She turned back to Tetyana. "I have to go now, but you need to come to the station today to give a formal statement. Maybe something about the bike can help us locate them."

The officer stared at each of us, one by one, even at David who was now dead to the world, snoring on the counter behind us.

"Don't know what it's like where y'all come from," she said finally, "but this ain't Kansas no more, you hear? Next time, don't go chasing intruders. Don't go punching robbers. Definitely don't go shooting anyone. Just dial nine-one-one. Makes this easier for everyone. Got it?"

We nodded silently.

"Welcome to New York, kids."

She blew an exasperated raspberry as she marched out.

Part FIVE

Chapter Thirty-Seven

"Mic check. Mic one. Can you hear me?"

"Loud and clear."

"Mic two. Can you hear me?"

"I hear you well."

It was almost party time. But none of us were in a party mood.

We were packed tight inside the Red Beast. We'd just arrived near the Saudi house and found a quiet, shady spot under a tree, ten blocks from the building, to prepare ourselves before we walked into the ambassador's home.

Everyone thought David should have stayed home, but we'd lost that argument. The painkillers were making him drowsy, but with a CIA hire monitoring us from the front and an NYPD intern watching us from the back, he'd felt claustrophobic.

He'd got in the car and refused to budge, saying he was feeling just fine. I wouldn't have wanted to stay home alone in that situation either.

Plus, we each had a job to do.

Win had transformed the furthest back seat of the Beast into an amateur espionage center, albeit a cramped one.

She was now in front of her electronic consoles, like a proud mother hen, watching over her brood of gadgets and audio and video equipment.

She was a fast study. I didn't think even Stanford knew what she was capable of. Bibi was sitting right next to her, absorbing everything.

I could teach anyone to bake and decorate. I could also hire a strong security team from anywhere. But Win's skills were rare. I was glad she was with us, and that she was happily teaching an eager Bibi too.

The two of them had worked on this setup all day. It had kept them busy, a diversion from the break-in and its aftermath.

They'd hooked up three laptops. One was recording our mics and another two captured the video footage from the hidden cameras I'd strategically placed around the ambassador's house during our last visit.

We had a view of the kitchens, the elevator, the main corridors and even the women's quarters, courtesy of my secret foray to Sarah's room. We also had an excellent vantage point of the inside of the hall from the small camera Tetyana had stuck on the frame of a painting.

Cleaning up the bakery that morning had been exhausting, but now, as we geared up, I was feeling a mix of excitement and apprehension. I was itching to start our mission.

"Sixty minutes to ETA," Bibi called out from the back.

"Roger that," said Tetyana.

In the space between Katy's seat and mine, I had carefully placed our cupcake boxes and tied them with baker's twine so they'd remain stable during the trip. Tucked in the middle of these boxes were my crème de la crème creations, the four decorated birthday cakes that had impressed the police sergeant. They were sitting in separate cardboard boxes, ready to be assembled once we got inside and into our prep corner, where Reza was waiting to help us set up.

Under my seat was a plain brown cardboard box. Inside was the overflow cake, the one we'd taunted our listeners with. Since the intruders had smashed the original, I had to bake another one hastily a few hours ago.

The break-in had rattled us.

But that wasn't going to stop our mission to find Sarah and maybe, just maybe, get a second chance at catching the people listening in on us. While nobody wanted to admit it, we were spooked, but we were all determined to finish what we'd started.

That morning, while David had slept off the painkillers upstairs, Tetyana had pulled Luc in and got to work. She'd first gone to the police station to give a statement, then rushed around to get our security system back in place and repair the bars and the broken windows.

It was a good thing we had a stash of emergency cash.

While our doors, windows and security systems were being reinforced, Katy and I had prepared the remaining menu items for the party. By the time the Red Beast was hooked up with the spy center and our home was secure again, the cakes had been decorated, boxed, and readied for delivery.

I was thankful we had two sentries outside while we were away. The CIA and NYPD were doing us a favor, at least that day.

"Asha?"

I jerked awake from my thoughts.

"Mic check time," said Bibi, tapping my shoulder.

After checking mine, she went on to Katy in the passenger seat. Next to her was Luc, the designated driver of the Beast that day.

For this event, Katy and I had ditched our business dresses and pumps. All Tetyana had to say was we had to be prepared to run And run fast. Just in case. That was enough to convince us.

She'd got each of us faux leather pants, waist-length jackets and red boots from a biker clothing outlet next to the hardware store where she and Luc had purchased the reinforced window bars.

Even Bibi had given up her Scottish kilt and T-shirt for the fresh look. I liked my new uniform. It made me feel like an unstoppable badass, though, I wondered what the head of staff would think when she saw us. Well, it was too late to change.

"All mics working," I heard Win say. "Cameras one to six are all on and the feed is clear."

"Good job, Win." Tetyana's voice came into our earpieces.

"Just remember if you get more than one thousand meters away from the van, I can't hear you."

"As long as it works on the eighty-fifth floor," I said.

"Don't you know GSM works in buildings a hundred stories high?" Win's indignant voice echoed twice, once through my earpiece and also from the back of the car.

"Sorry, honey, I'm learning these things every day," I said. "This is why we have you."

"My setups never fail. Also, everything's clean. If we lose a mic or a camera, no one can trace them back to us."

"Excellent work, sweetie," said Katy from upfront.

I sat back and closed my eyes to mentally prepare for the next few hours to come. We had no idea what to expect, but we had to be ready for anything.

My phone rang, startling me.

It was the ringtone I'd selected for Anne, Chef Pierre's personal assistant. I accepted the call and put the phone on speaker mode.

"Bonjour, Anne," I said, forcing a smile.

They say people can hear a smile across the airwaves and my role that day was to be the perky, happy celebrity chef ready to serve the diplomats of New York.

"Bonjour, mademoiselle," came the high-pitched, French-accented voice through the speaker. "*Tout est prêt?* Everything is ready?"

"Absolutely," I said. "We're on our way to the ambassador's house right now."

"*Bon, bon, bon.* Very good. Chef Pierre can't wait to see your cake."

"Chef Pierre?"

I looked at Katy. She gave me a questioning look back.

"Oui, mademoiselle. He didn't tell you? Madame Bouchard and the Chef have both been invited to the party."

I felt my stomach tighten. But I forced a wider smile.

"How wonderful. I'll be looking forward to seeing them both then."

"Chef said he will drop by the kitchen before the party starts so he can try a few of your cake pieces. You have an overflow cake, correct?"

I swallowed. "Yes."

"Good." Anne gave a high-pitched, whiny laugh. "If you ask me, he's trying to have his dessert before dinner. Like he needs more cake."

"Haha!" I forced a laugh. "He does have a sweet tooth."

I hung up saying a cheery goodbye, but feeling heavy, like another barrier had been thrown in front of us.

"Is the Chef's presence going to compromise our plan?" Tetyana asked.

Chef Pierre was never reliable during events. He always got distracted by a friend or pulled away by a journalist and had never visited the kitchen exactly as promised. Sometimes, he never even showed up.

I sat back to think of the worst-case scenario.

"If he comes early, we can manage this. We cut him a slice of the overflow cake, feed him, take some selfies and let him go," I said. "It'll only be a problem if he visits us while we're negotiating with the people we hope will come."

"Bibi will be in the kitchen alone while we'll be serving upstairs," said Katy. "Reza promised to help if we need her, but she won't be able to distract the Chef if it comes to that."

"I will come up," said Tetyana. "I was going to stay in the corridor to intercept the men in case they come early, but it might be best if I come inside."

"Guys." Win's voice made us turn to the back.

She had her nose stuck to one of the laptop screens. Bibi was hovering over her with a worried look on her face.

"What's going on?" asked Tetyana.

David, who'd been sitting quietly in the back seat, still recovering from his ordeal, leaned in to look.

"They're doing a sweep of the hall," he said. "I'd say it's a routine check, given the people coming today."

"The other locations?" asked Tetyana.

"Negative," said David. "They're good."

Win and Bibi crowded around the laptop, their eyes glued to the screen.

"Eek!" cried Win suddenly.

"Oh, no!" Bibi said, slapping her forehead.

"What's going on, guys?" asked Tetyana, her voice anxious.

David turned to us.

"We just lost camera one."

Chapter Thirty-Eight

The penthouse was buzzing.

Dignitaries, politicians, celebrities, and VIPs of the highest echelons of New York were here.

On a signal by the head of staff, two butlers opened the massive doors to the hall.

It was time.

Katy and I rolled in the gleaming chrome trolley which carried the four-tiered luxury birthday cake. The cake sat proudly on a gold-plated dessert tray, and on the three shelves beneath it were three hundred pink-iced cupcakes for the guests.

The room burst into applause. A wolf whistle rang out from somewhere in the back. We knew the clapping wasn't for us. Katy and I were playing a strange role, part celebrity pastry chefs and part hired staff, but we were just props. Props bringing in the crowning dessert, the fantastic finale to a sumptuous nine-course meal.

I taped a frozen smile to my face, trying hard to look the part. Earlier that afternoon, the head of staff had sniffed in disapproval at our new uniforms but had stopped giving us the evil eye once we strapped Chef Pierre's signature white, shin-length aprons around our waists. His logo was displayed prominently, and that was all that mattered.

As we pushed the cake cart in, I scanned the room discreetly, wishing we didn't have to go through such an elaborate show to find a missing girl.

I had to admit though, the birthday cake looked magnificent.

Pink fondant covered the cake, and Chef Pierre's royal emblem was stamped on each layer in white icing. Draping gracefully across the four tiers was a vine of pink roses, handmade by Luc. On top of the cake sat a sterling silver ornament with the number "16," and at the base of the cake tray were the words "Happy Birthday Sarah" in dark pink icing.

Chef Pierre had given me strict instructions from the beginning.

I had to follow all embassy requests no matter how outrageous, as long as they wouldn't land us in jail. He'd alarmed me with outlandish tales of diplomatic parties. "Some households are simply egregious," he'd said with a shudder of horror, followed by a story of how he'd once been forced to make a green and yellow polka-dotted cake in the shape and size of a baby elephant.

Surprisingly, the Saudi household gave no further instructions other than insisting on Chef Pierre's logo everywhere. I now knew why. This cake was a ruse. This entire party was a ruse.

We got confirmation the minute we heard the ambassador's welcoming speech to the guests. It was a long, rambling talk about international relations, trade, diplomatic ties, and allies and had nothing to do with a young girl's birthday.

It was only at the end when, as an aside, he mentioned Sarah wouldn't show up for the lavish dinner because of a bad headache, but that she would come out for the cake-cutting ceremony.

I wondered if Sarah was even in the house.

The last texts Bibi got from her had been difficult to decipher, garbled like Sarah had lost her ability to create complete sentences. Answers to Bibi's questions got progressively more confusing until neither Bibi nor David could figure out a word.

Bibi was sure Sarah was drugged and locked up somewhere in this house. Tetyana wondered if she'd been taken somewhere else. Since Sarah had gone silent a day ago, we had no way of knowing. Our best bet was to see if she'd come to her own birthday party.

Everything had gone according to plan so far.

Our car was in the back parking lot with the other service vehicles. David, having recovered somewhat, was in the driver's seat, ready to pull out at a moment's notice. Win was in her "control room" inside the Beast doing routine audio checks and monitoring the video feed.

Luc was leaning against a wall inside the event hall, next to the other servers, trying hard to blend in. He'd sweet-talked his way inside after befriending the head waiter and promising him expensive French cigarettes.

The head waiter thought Luc was just another starry-eyed subcontractor who'd wanted to get closer to the celebrities in the room. He didn't realize Luc was a walking, talking, live substitute for the camera we'd just lost.

The security team had only taken out one camera, but it was our most important video feed. As soon as that line went blank, Win hooked Luc up with a hidden camera. He promised us he'd wrangle his way into the hall before the cake-cutting ceremony.

He scanned the room now, ignoring us, turning slightly to the left or the right as instructed by Win from the Beast.

Tetyana was in the kitchen with Bibi, pretending to be my help. Reza, the servant girl, had cleared out a corner for us to set our supplies and for last-minute decorating touches. The head of staff had instructed her to be our guide, and most importantly, keep us out of the way of the territorial kitchen staff.

Reza had fussed around, happy to be useful. With us, she transformed into someone else. She walked confidently, chin up, shoulders straight, daring to laugh at Luc's jokes. She'd even talked back to the parking valet when he'd initially refused us a spot.

Parking inside the garage that day was for VIP guests and their chauffeured cars only. The entire building had been cordoned off, and the place was teeming with men in black suits and dark shades.

Reza had eventually found a spot in the back for us. We'd parked next to a white laundry van and waited while she found a pan rack on wheels to unload our cakes and take them up via the service elevator.

As "The Help," we'd become invisible. Just like Reza. With Reza leading us around and in our matching aprons, the security guards hardly gave us a second glance.

The applause in the hall died down and everyone started chattering among themselves again. The room settled into a slow party murmur as they waited for the ceremony to begin so they could taste one of Chef Pierre's own endorsed creations.

"Routine check," Win's voice piped in through our earpieces. "Can everyone give me your coordinates, please?"

"Tetyana. Kitchen. With Bibi."

"Bibi here. Reza's here too."

"Hall," said Luc's voice in between a pretend cough.

"Thanks," said Win, "David and me are in the car." She paused. "Asha, can you tap twice if you're in the hall and all is good? Four times, if not good."

I pretended to scratch my ear and tapped twice.

"Got it. Katy?"

Next to me, Katy smoothed her hair, and I heard two taps through my earpiece.

"All accounted for," said Win.

The head of staff had instructed us to roll the cake tray to the end of the room where the cake-cutting ceremony would take place. Katy and I kept pushing the cart, deliberately taking our time, our eyes darting around to glimpse any unusual activity.

If I'd really stopped to think about it, this was my moment. This had been a dream ever since I was a child. I'd had visions of introducing my cakes to admiring VIP partygoers, just like Chef Pierre had done before. Just like I was doing now.

And there he was. Chef Pierre, himself, at a guest table with The Diplomatic Dragon Lady.

He beamed proudly as we walked in, smiling and clapping louder than anyone else in the room. Thankfully, he'd gotten so busy catching up with his friends he'd forgotten to come to the kitchen and interfere with our plans.

I just hoped he wouldn't come afterward and hold us back. Our plan was to leave as soon as we were done with our mission.

With a friendly nod to the Chef, Katy and I kept rolling.

A few of the foreign dignitaries, men from cultures where staring at women was common practice, leered at us, creeping us out. I didn't need that, as I was already feeling self-conscious as it was.

The night before, Katy and I had tried on the bra holsters Tetyana had got for us for the first time. We were both carrying a concealed revolver attached to each of our bras.

Mine dug into my solar plexus, pinching me every time I turned or moved. While everyone assured me they couldn't spot a weapon under my shirt, my paranoia was running amuck.

Chapter Thirty-Nine

"We have a problem," said Katy.

I looked up at the podium. It hadn't been there when the head of staff had given us a tour of the event hall. She'd either pranked us or hadn't thought the logistics through.

The stage was elevated three feet above the floor. It was a beautiful setup. On the podium was a large rectangular table draped with an elegant white tablecloth with gold and pink trimmings. Someone had sprinkled pink rose petals on the table.

But to get to it, we had to climb five steps up. With our already assembled four-tiered cake. That weighed twenty pounds.

I looked around to see if anyone could help us.

One of the security guards halfway across the hall noticed our conundrum and smirked. He nudged his partner and two men laughed. No one else was paying attention to us except for Luc. We could have asked him, but that would turn the spotlight on us. The more we remained in the dark, the better.

Katy and I exchanged a glance. *The show must go on.*

We picked up the cake tray from both sides. Good thing we were wearing sensible boots. We worked our way up the steps and onto the platform two inches at a time. One wrong move and we'd never bake in this town again.

By the time we got to the top, we were sweating profusely. We placed the cake gently on the table.

I stopped to catch my breath. From here, I had an excellent vantage point of everyone in the room. While Katy and I worked, setting the plates and cutting knives and positioning trays of cupcakes around the main cake, I glanced casually around the hall.

The party guests were chatting away. Chef Pierre was having a belly laugh with a famous actress sitting to his left. The Diplomatic

Dragon Lady was in deep discussion with a regal-looking man who wore a red shoulder sash and an impressive mustache.

The ambassador's family was seated at the head table in front of the podium, under the main chandelier. They were mostly men, the ambassador's sons, brothers and male cousins, I suspected. While the ambassador was walking around the room saying hello to the other tables, his family didn't mingle.

At the head of the main table sat the man I loathed the most, and Ahmed looked like he'd already drunk quite a lot of the wine.

The servers were running around, offering tea and coffee and setting dessert plates and gold-plated cutlery at each table. The head of staff was at the back of the room, immersed in her clipboard and phone. The two security guards who'd laughed at us were flanking the main doors now.

But Sarah was still missing.

Who will cut the cake?

After setting everything up, Katy and I stepped down and quietly rolled our cart to the side of the hall. Once the speeches were done and the cake was cut, our next job was to carve perfect slices of the cake and plate it with the cupcakes. The waiters' job was to take the dessert plates from us and serve the guests, one by one.

Katy and I stood next to a small side door near the podium, hands clasped behind us, trying to make ourselves as inconspicuous as possible.

Luc was on the other side of the room, waiting patiently, studiously ignoring us as we were him.

Every few minutes, Win shared a routine status update through our earpieces. Tetyana and Bibi were the only ones who could reply openly, so we listened to their banter, scanning the room and waiting for the show to start.

I wondered about the people who'd bugged our home. We were now sure it wasn't the CIA. They were professionals, but not as organized or highly trained as intelligence operatives.

I wondered if they'd come tonight after the debacle at our bakery the night before. If we could get a glimpse of them, even a small clue as to who they were, our mission would be accomplished. If we were lucky, we might get to talk to them. Though after the break-in, I doubted they'd want to come close. It was going to be an interesting evening.

Suddenly, I felt goose bumps on my arms. Something made me turn my head toward the head table.

It was Ahmed.

He'd spotted me and was sending me a piercing look. It was an ugly, hostile gesture. After making sure I noticed, he turned away.

Was that a threat?

That was when the side door near us opened with a click. Startled, Katy and I shuffled out of the way.

"Oh, my god," came Win's voice. "It's *Sarah.*"

"Can you see her?" asked Bibi. "Is she okay?"

"On camera one," said Win. "She's standing right next to Asha and Katy."

Chapter Forty

Katy and I stared at the apparition that had appeared next to us. It was the ambassador's second wife who was accompanying Sarah.

Neither of them was smiling.

A hush fell in the room. Everyone turned to look. A few people clapped politely.

The wife's eyes scanned the room, then the cake. She stepped toward the platform, pulling Sarah by the arm, nodding unsmilingly at the applause. This woman was in her element, haughty and arrogant. In contrast, Sarah looked sickly. Her face was pale and her eyes were glassy. She wobbled along, following her mother's directions.

Katy leaned toward me and whispered in my ear. "Is it me or does she look drugged?"

I didn't get to answer.

"They're here."

Win's voice came muted, as if she was afraid to talk too loudly.

"Stand by," said David, speaking for the first time. "Getting a visual now." He sounded more alert than when we'd left him. The nap had probably helped.

"Where are they?" asked Tetyana.

"Parked near us," replied David. "Two cars down."

"Ooooh!"

The entire hall had let out a gasp.

I looked up.

Sarah had fumbled over the first step and had almost fallen. Her mother pulled her by the arm, shook her and whispered a sharp word in Arabic. We were close enough to see she was gripping the girl's arm so tightly Sarah's skin had gone a shade of pink.

Like a zombie, Sarah took another lethargic step up, her face a mixture of confusion and fear. She staggered a second time and clutched at the railing to steady herself.

The audience let out another gasp.

Ahmed threw his phone on the table, pushed his chair out and stood up with a scowl. He stomped over to the podium and grabbed his sister from the other side. Together, the mother and the brother pulled Sarah roughly to the top, almost manhandling her.

The audience took their seats, hesitating, unsure of what would come next.

Sarah stood in front of the cake, swaying. The birthday cake gleamed under the lights of the chandelier.

At least my cake's looking good, I thought.

Just when I thought all was okay, Sarah wobbled again. Katy and I instinctively took a step forward, but she straightened herself by grabbing on to the tablecloth. Her mother pulled her hand away.

I breathed a sigh of relief. For a moment, I was sure she was going to go down and take the cake with her. I felt bad for the girl. She looked awful.

"They're getting in. Showed some ID to the security guard in the back. He let them in without questions. Must have come prepared." David's voice came in my ear, urgent, anxious.

"How many?" asked Tetyana.

"Two men in blue worker overalls," replied Win. "They're dressed like electricals."

"You mean electricians?"

"The sign on the van says Johnson Electricals."

"David, how do you know it's them?" asked Tetyana.

"Gut feel but it never lets me down," he replied. "Came in white van with tinted windows. Stayed inside for ten minutes before coming out. Maybe they took a call. Maybe they scoped out the area. I don't like the way they walked."

I tried to keep my eyes on Sarah while listening to the conversation in my ear.

"Why?" asked Tetyana.

"Like they're packing."

"Could be the goons I chased this morning," said Tetyana. "I'm going to the corridor in the back. I'll leave this with you, Bibi."

"Don't you need it for cover?" came Bibi's voice.

"That thing is made to serve cakes, not fight hooligans."

She'd probably removed her apron. *Be careful, Tetyana,* I said silently.

A movement near the back of the hall caught my eye. Luc was slipping out of the room through the main doors.

Good. She needs all the help she can get.

The ambassador came bounding up the podium steps and picked up the microphone. He beamed at the crowd. They clapped. The show was about to start.

Seemingly oblivious to her surroundings, Sarah reached over and touched the base of the cake, pulling a pink rose off. It bounced off the table and fell to the ground.

Ahmed leaned over and slapped Sarah's hand. She pulled back, wincing.

What a way to treat a birthday girl.

"At this most auspicious occasion of my youngest daughter's birthday...," the ambassador started his speech with a grand smile at the audience. His wife and son stood a few steps behind him, looking like severe bulldogs, keeping a hand each on Sarah. The girl was barely holding up.

"Got a visual," came Tetyana's voice. "Two men in blue overalls. Don't look like CIA material."

"That's what I thought," said David.

"If it's not CIA, who are they?" asked Win.

"I'd bet on hired private goons," said David. "Not well trained."

I'd been clenching and unclenching my hands as I tried to split my attention between what was happening in the hall and the conversation in my ear.

There was no way for Katy or me to leave this room with no one noticing. We were near the podium, right behind the birthday party and only a few feet away from the head table. All eyes were trained our way. I was sure the head of staff would hunt us down and kill us if we veered from her instructions.

I badly wanted to be out there with Tetyana and David, but I couldn't abandon Sarah now. My mind raced, trying to think of our best next step.

I heard mumbling from David. He was talking to someone.

"No, I'm telling you," he said in an agitated voice. "The ambassador will be very unhappy. He'll get even more angry at you. Do you want that?"

What's going on?

I felt a trickle of sweat go down my back. My stomach churned with worry. I could feel Katy twitching nervously next to me.

Bad timing. This is terrible timing.

"Coming over for backup," said David. "Am in service elevator."

"How did you get through?" asked Tetyana, her voice sharp.

"Told them we forgot a special tray of cakes. The apron helped."

"I'll meet them near the service elevator banks in the back corridor," said Tetyana. "Don't want to alert the ambassador's security team. No need to get them involved."

Then the earpieces went silent. I strained to listen. I could hear a background hum, like the sound of an elevator. That was probably David. *But what about Tetyana?*

"Hello?" said Tetyana suddenly.

"Good afternoon."

It was a man's voice with a slight accent. *Is that European? Eastern European?* It was hard to say.

"May I help you?" Tetyana asked.

"We're looking for someone."

"Who would that be?"

"Er, a staff member." I could hear the hesitation in his voice.

I glanced at the side door, our closest exit. It was only five feet from us. I looked out at the crowd. All eyes were on the ambassador now.

Next to me, Katy had her head bowed, her hand over her ear, listening to what was going on outside, trying to block the ambassador's sonorous voice.

"What's their name?" Tetyana asked. "I'll be happy to get them for you. There's a big event happening inside right now."

"Oh? It was...he said refrigerator needs urgent work."

They clearly didn't want to talk too much. My spider senses tingled.

"That's strange. The fridges are all running smoothly. Did they give you a name so I can help find them for you?"

"Maybe we can go in and look ourselves."

"Which company do you work for? So I can let them know you're coming in."

We heard the rustle of papers.

"Johnson Electricals?" Tetyana asked. "Which one of you is Johnson?"

"Johnson is the boss. We, er, we work for him."

"So, who called you here?"

More hesitation.

"Christy Gordon," said the man finally. "We're looking for Christy Gordon."

It's them!

I felt an electric shock go through me.

Crash!

Katy and I jumped, startled.

The sound had come from inside the event hall. I looked at the scene in front of us, my mouth open.

Sarah had collapsed.

The crowd was staring at the podium in horror.

The ambassador had gone silent. His face was white, like he was about to faint himself.

Sarah lay motionless. The top half of her body was sprawled across the table, her arms limp to the sides, her face buried in my cake. Pieces of sugar roses, fondant icing, and buttercream confection were splattered across the room.

With an irritated grimace, Ahmed flicked a piece of cake from his jacket.

Part SIX

Chapter Forty-One

The mother's shrill screech echoed through the hall.

Ahmed grabbed Sarah by her shoulders and yanked her upright.

The poor girl stared blankly at the audience, icing covering her face and chest.

The room erupted in confusion.

Several got up to take a closer view, talking all at once. Some turned away, embarrassed by the spectacle. Others stared with their mouths open. A few snickered into their golden-trimmed napkins.

"Oh, my god," Katy whispered next to me. "Oh, my god."

I watched horrified, my hand over my mouth.

"My apologies, ladies and gentlemen," I heard the ambassador say. "Everybody, please take a seat. There is no need to panic. It's just a small medical issue. We will have a doctor check on her. I should have not encouraged her to come today. She really should be in bed. My sincere apologies. Please take your seats..."

The head of staff, waiters and security guards stared, rooted to their spots, afraid to do anything that might upset their employer even more. The male family members around the head table merely looked on in disgust, like they wished to be anywhere else but here.

The mother continued to wail with her hands over her head, distracting the ambassador and confusing everyone even more.

Behind his parents' backs, Ahmed pulled Sarah to the podium floor.

She collapsed to her knees, gasping for air, blinking uncomprehendingly. As Katy and I watched in horror, he slapped her face. She let out a small yelp.

What a jerk!

He'd been careful to hit her when she was down, hidden behind the table. No one saw what had happened, except us.

My eyes swept the room and returned to the platform, my mind whirring, trying to think of how to help the girl. That was when I saw Ahmed's fist strike out.

No!

Sarah lurched as his fist slammed to her side. She swayed and clutched at the air, seeking something to hold on to.

I jumped forward and grabbed the girl.

"Stop it!" I hissed.

Ignoring me, Ahmed let go of the girl, straightened up and joined his father, smoothing his jacket.

Between Katy and me, we got Sarah off the podium before her sick brother changed his mind and hit her again.

"I do apologize profusely for my daughter's condition." The ambassador was desperately trying to keep the audience calm.

Sarah sat crumpled on the floor behind the podium, holding on to Katy and me.

"She had the flu for a few days and wasn't feeling well, as you can see. We told her she can't come today, but she insisted because she didn't want to miss her party. Girls, you know. But I'd like to now invite my son to say a few words about his recent trip to Turkey..."

I looked up. Ahmed grabbed the mic and put a smarmy smile on his face.

The ambassador had regained his composure. His wife had stopped wailing and his son was now giving a funny talk. The audience was listening awkwardly, but the room had settled down at least.

Katy grabbed a napkin from the dessert cart and wiped Sarah's face. Dull brown eyes stared back at us.

"Sarah?"

No answer.

"Let's get her out of here," I whispered, pulling her up.

"I got her," whispered Katy, taking Sarah by the other arm.

Katy and I pulled her up gently and got her to stand. She didn't resist, but started trembling. She needed medical help.

I glanced at the side door.

The two security guards were standing by this door now. How they'd got here in a flash, I had no idea. They didn't look friendly. But we had no choice.

"So, later on that night, the honorable Japanese ambassador asked me if I liked sashimi and I said, but your excellency, I come from a desert..." Ahmed rattled on. Saving face, I realized, was far more important than the health of his sister.

Doesn't anyone care about the girl? Can't the ambassador see what's going on? Why doesn't he turn around?

Katy and I walked Sarah toward the side door. When we moved out of the shadow of the podium and into view, I felt the eyes of every guest on our backs, but I didn't look behind me. We kept moving, step by step, toward the exit.

The guards quickly stepped behind us as if to obscure the view from the audience. One of them opened the door and we ushered Sarah through. I heard the door shut behind us, thankfully. It was a relief to get out of that stifling place.

"She needs a doctor," I said.

"Let's take her to her room first," Katy said.

We walked at a snail's pace through the corridor and got into the elevator.

Though she was just a teen, Sarah was bigger and felt heavier than Katy and me combined. Every few minutes, her body twitched like she was about to convulse. Her breathing was heavy, and every step was laborious for her. Something was wrong with the girl.

As the elevator took us down to the women's quarters, I wondered how Tetyana was dealing with the two men outside.

Our earpieces had gone unnervingly silent since Sarah's collapse.

During our planning meetings, we'd all agreed that Win could turn off earpieces selectively if she detected anyone listening nearby or if too many things were happening at once that could compromise our chief mission. Right now, Katy and I were liabilities.

I'm sure Tetyana and David have everything under control, I thought. If things had turned sour, Win would have turned our earpieces back on and called for help.

I kept my eyes open and my ears trained. The gun digging into my solar plexus felt reassuring.

The elevator door opened and we walked out into the women's quarters. It was a relief to see Sarah's garish pink bedroom again.

We walked the girl to her bed and turned her around so she could sit. All there was left was the naked mattress, but it would have to do.

Sarah's face was pale. Her eyes were empty and her body twitched. When Katy kneeled to take the girl's shoes off, she let out a low moan, like she was hurting.

I held her by the shoulders. "Sarah, we're here to help, okay? We'll call a doctor for you. You'll be fine."

"I feel bad," she mumbled. "They made me sick."

"What made you sick?" I asked.

"The pills and...the injection," she said, in between raspy breaths.

"An injection? For your flu?"

Sarah shook her head. "Don't have flu."

Her eyes fluttered erratically and her mouth opened ever so slightly.

"He wants to kill me," she whispered.

She closed her eyes and her chin fell to her neck.

"Sarah?"

She sat motionless.

I shook her gently. "Sarah?"

"She's fainted," whispered Katy. "I'll clean her face. Maybe that will wake her up," she said, stepping into the en suite bathroom.

I laid Sarah gently on the mattress, trying to decide if I'd heard her right.

That was when I heard the click behind me.

I whirled around.

Someone had closed the bedroom door.

I stepped over to it and pulled on the handle. It didn't budge. I stared at it for a second before trying again.

Nothing.

I jerked the handle. It rattled in my hand, but the door remained shut.

"Hey!" I shouted and banged on the door.

Katy ran out of the bathroom, a wet towel in her hands. "What's going on?"

I turned to her. "They locked us in."

Chapter Forty-Two

"Girls are back on," came Win's voice in my ear.

"What the heck happened, guys?" Luc's voice crackled next.

I breathed a sigh of relief. Win had turned on our earpieces again.

"Luc? Win?" I said. "Everything okay?"

"What about you?" asked Luc, his voice anxious.

"Still alive," said Katy. "It's so nice to hear you guys."

"Don't worry," said Win. "You weren't totally cut off. We could hear you, but only me and Luc."

The sound of running footsteps came through my earpiece.

"Tetyana? You all right?" I asked.

"Those frigging idiots got away," she replied, panting hard. "Crashed through the fire exit door. Bloody amateurs."

"Don't get too close," said David's voice. "They can ambush you from below at any time."

"Don't think they have the balls. Scuttled like rabbits when they saw my Glock."

"They're not getting away yet," said David. "I'm on the ground floor. I'll catch them when they come down."

"Should have taken the goddamned elevator," said Tetyana, sounding annoyed. "I'm stuck here now with only one way down."

Is she in the stairwell?

"Did you check the doors?" asked David.

"Locked. All of them. Security feature," said Tetyana, panting heavily. "Probably get unlocked automatically when the fire alarms go off."

"Hey," Luc's voice came on. "Maybe if I pull the—"

"No!" Tetyana and David yelled at the same time.

"Don't touch the alarms," said Tetyana. "No need to attract the city's entire emergency squadron here."

Everyone went silent after that, and all we could hear were Tetyana's footsteps echoing through the concrete stairwell.

"Guys," said Win, hesitating, "don't panic, but Katy and Asha are locked up in Sarah's room."

Tetyana swore.

"Jeepers," said David. "How did that happen?"

"Sarah's seriously sick," I explained. "Long story short, she passed out at the party. The family didn't care, so Katy and I brought her to her room so she could lie down. She said someone was trying to kill her and then she fainted."

Sarah let out a moan. Katy walked over to the bed.

"While we were watching her, someone locked the door," I continued. "I didn't see anyone. Didn't even hear anyone come behind us. Not sure if it was those two security guards in the hall or someone else."

"No harm?" asked David.

"Not a scratch," I replied. "They let us leave, then locked us in."

"Hang on," Luc said, "I'm coming over."

"Where are you?" I asked.

"In the kitchen."

"The key could still be on the outside unless they took it," I said, remembering how we got in. "Come only if it's safe."

"Sure thing."

"Win, do you have a visual yet?" David's voice came on. "Can I get an ETA for when the men will get to the first floor?"

"No," Win said mournfully. "We don't have cameras everywhere, only inside the apartment."

"I know exactly where they are," said Tetyana, "four to five floors below me. Making a damn ruckus. And I'm more than three quarters down."

"Thanks," said David. "I'll be ready for them here."

"Who the heck builds frigging skyscrapers to live in?" said Tetyana, cursing under her breath.

"Remember, there's only one way out for them too," said David.

We waited for Tetyana to reply, but all we heard was her laborious breathing and her boots stomping on the stairs.

"Asha, Katy, I'm on your floor." Luc's voice came in a whisper into my ear.

I jerked around. "Already?"

"Just got off the elevator."

"Didn't bump into anyone?"

"Nope. Elevator was empty. Everyone's in the kitchen or at the party hall. No one saw me coming."

"Luc!" It was Win. "Find a hiding spot! Fast."

"What?"

"Someone's coming along the corridor," she said in a panicked voice now. "Two men."

Katy and I listened in. We heard a rustle, then Luc went silent. We couldn't even hear him breathing.

I crossed my fingers. I was sure now it was the two security guards who'd locked us in. It must be them walking toward the elevator now.

Behind us, Sarah whimpered and opened her eyes. I walked over to the bed. Katy offered Sarah a glass of water, but she struggled to sit up.

Flu, my foot, I thought as I helped her lean against the headboard.

This girl didn't have a cold or even a fever. Someone had pumped her with something bad. I glanced around the room for any signs of medication or syringes, but whoever had cleaned the room had done a good job.

The ambassador's reaction in the hall had disappointed me. Harshness from Ahmed and the mother was expected, but Sarah's father had turned his back on her when she needed him the most. I wondered if he knew what was going on and if he just didn't care.

With every sip of water, Sarah got some of her color back.

"They're hanging out in the elevator lobby," whispered Win in our ears. "Stay where you are, Luc. Don't move until I say."

We waited silently, wondering where Luc had hidden, praying they wouldn't find him. It seemed like the men would never leave.

"What are they doing?" I whispered.

"Checking their phones," replied Win. "They're on the settee next to the elevator and they don't seem like they're in any rush."

I thought I heard a funny noise, a stifled groan from Luc, maybe.

"Oh!" said Win.

We perked up.

"Someone just came out of the elevator. It's one of those covered-up women."

We waited.

"She's coming your way, Katy, Asha." She paused. "Funny...."

"What?"

"She's checking all the doors. Strange."

"Be careful," said David in a low voice, "could be a man under that robe. Stay sharp."

Katy and I exchanged looks.

"Time for Plan B," I said.

Katy reached into her bra and pulled out her pistol. I did the same.

"Watch out! She, he, whatever, is outside your door!" whispered Win.

A scratch at the door made us jump. I watched with widening eyes as someone tried the handle. But the door didn't open.

Katy took one side of the door and I took the other. We weren't going down without a fight.

The person was jiggling the handle now.

Thankfully, Sarah was dozing and not making any sound.

It took another minute before we heard something at the door again. This time, it was the click of a key being inserted into the keyhole.

I put my finger on the trigger.

The door opened toward Katy.

It was a woman in a black robe.

I leaped next to Katy, ready to fire.

"Get down!" I snarled.

She put her hands up.

A muffled voice came through the veil. "Don't shoot! It's me!"

"Bibi?"

Chapter Forty-Three

Bibi pushed the veil off her head and hurriedly closed the door.

"Where did you find that getup?" I asked.

"Reza gave it to me. She's taking care of our stuff in the kitchen."

"Luc, the men just got into the elevator but stay where you are," said Win. "It's too risky for too many of us to be running around there."

"We'll join you soon, Luc," I said.

A loud groan came through our earpieces.

"Where are you?" asked Win. "I can't see you."

"Behind the big plant," Luc said. "I'm cramped like hell. Hurry, people."

I turned toward the bed. Sarah was sleeping now. We'd never get away quickly with her in tow. She was a big risk.

"She can barely walk," said Katy, reading my mind.

I stepped up to the bed and kneeled next to the sleeping girl.

"Hey, Sarah," I said, shaking her gently by the shoulder. "Sarah? Wake up."

She opened her eyes, gave me a glassy look and said something in Arabic.

I waved at Bibi. "What's she saying?"

Bibi stepped up and leaned over her.

"Where am I?" Sarah said in English this time, sounding like she had marbles in her mouth.

Bibi answered her in Arabic. Katy and I watched as the two girls spoke in their language.

"Hurry, guys," I heard Luc say in my ear. "If those dudes come again, I'm in trouble."

"Hang on, just one minute, Luc," I said. I tapped Bibi on the shoulder. "We have to move soon."

"She wants to come with us," said Bibi, turning to me. "Her brother's threatened to slit her throat tonight."

"*Slit her...?*" I couldn't get myself to finish that sentence.

"Reza told me she wants to leave too. He does bad things to her too. She hates this house. I told you it's a bad place."

Sarah struggled to sit and fell back exhausted. She looked at us, tears running down her cheeks, her face a picture of despair. She clutched my arm, her nails digging into me.

"I'm scared. I want to come with you."

I nodded.

"We got you," said Katy taking her by the other arm. With Bibi encouraging her in her language, Sarah got off the mattress and onto her feet.

"Good job," I said, nudging her forward, toward the door. "Take one step. One more, now."

"Wait," said Bibi, stripping off her burqa. "Here." She thrust it into Sarah's arms. "They'll never know it's you. Put it on."

We waited till Bibi helped the girl put on the robe.

"Win, are we clear?" Katy asked once Sarah was fully ensconced inside the garment.

"All clear outside," said Win.

We stepped out, with Sarah hanging on to Katy and me. Bibi closed the door behind us, locked it and pocketed the key. "Give us more time if they come to check."

"Smart thinking," I said.

Sarah walked with us, shakily, but at least she was moving.

Bibi led the way, tiptoeing along the corridor, scouting the area. Katy and I followed her, holding Sarah, watching for any signals to stop and hide, or draw our guns. It took us longer than I expected, but we got to the elevator banks without bumping into anyone.

"About time," said a voice in my earpiece.

I glanced around.

"Where are you, Luc?" Katy whispered.

"Right next to you."

I whipped around to see Luc's face peeking from an oversized house plant next to the elevator doors.

The whir of the elevator startled us.

"*Merde,*" said Luc. "Someone's coming down."

"The party's over, guys," Win called out. "They just opened the hall doors. People are leaving. Guards moving all over the place now."

"Oh, no," Katy said.

"Can you hide somewhere?" said Win. "Till things calm down?"

Bibi scrambled over to the room nearest the elevator.

"It's unlocked. I checked it before."

Dragging Sarah behind us, Katy and I trooped in after her. Luc came after us and closed the door just as we heard a ping from the elevator outside.

Katy gasped.

I put a finger to my lips.

We stood in a circle, wide-eyed, trying not to panic.

I heard the elevator doors clatter open and voices come from the lobby. They faded as the people walked into the corridor and away from the room.

But we were playing with time.

"How do we get out of here?" whispered Luc.

"The elevator's a trap," I said, trying to think of our options.

Think girl, think.

Katy gave me a worried look. "What about the stairs?"

"Fire exit's at the other end of the corridor," said Win in our ears. "You'll have to go all the way back, and that's not good. Those people are still in the corridor."

I surveyed the room.

It was half the size of Sarah's. Reza had told us the servants slept in the dorm rooms next to the kitchen, so this had to be the chamber of a lesser wife, a younger daughter or someone lower in the family hierarchy. The room was as messy as Sarah's had been. The closet was wide open and dresses lay crumpled on the carpet. Piled in one corner, as if ready for laundry day, lay a heap of women's clothes.

There was no place for us to hide here. There was also no other exit than the door that opened to the lobby. If anyone came in here, we'd have some serious explaining to do.

"They got off the ground floor," David's voice came in our ears. "Heading to the main elevators."

"They'd better be going down, not up," said Tetyana, sounding exhausted.

"Their van's still here," said Win. "They're probably coming here."

"Almost there," said Tetyana. "One more floor to go."

"I'm on their tail," said David. We heard footsteps.

"Win," said Tetyana. "Don't move. Keep low, okay?"

"But the windows are tint—"

"I said stay low," said Tetyana. "They can react in ways we're not prepared for."

"Okay."

"David?" said Tetyana. "Hold fire unless absolutely necessary. Remember, we need them alive and talking."

"Roger that."

A gagging noise made me turn around.

Sarah was bent over, heaving. I looked around and grabbed a plastic bag with a half-eaten shawarma still inside. I tossed the food in the garbage and held the bag under Sarah's nose. She took it, tipped her face into the bag and retched. The smell made me want to throw up.

Katy had a stronger stomach than me. She kept Sarah's veil away from her face and rubbed her back as she vomited. Bibi found a box of tissues lying on the floor and held it in front of Sarah.

We watched the girl, feeling helpless.

After a minute, Sarah looked up from her bag, and wiped her mouth with a tissue. Her chest heaved, but her eyes were no longer glassy.

"How are you feeling?" I asked.

She pulled another tissue from the box and wiped her face. "Lot better," she mumbled.

"You threw up whatever they gave you," said Katy, contemplating the girl. "Must have been some kind of pill to keep you sedated."

"She needs water," I said, looking for the bathroom door, but Luc had beat me to it. He came out of the small en suite washroom with a filled glass.

I nodded. "We really need to get her to a clinic—"

"Hey, guys?"

We turned to Bibi, who was hovering near the closet.

"There's enough here for all of us."

She was holding up a black robe she'd found from the laundry pile on the floor. "They'll never know it's us."

We stared at her.

Luc went over to pick another robe from the pile. "Jeez, it stinks. Probably been sitting here for weeks." he said, holding it away from his nose, "but I guess it'll have to do."

"Brilliant," said Katy. "Absolutely brilliant."

"Let's do it," I said, feeling like we'd finally found a way out of this crazy place.

To get out of here this house safely, we had to become invisible. And these garments were designed just for that.

Chapter Forty-Four

The elevator doors opened with a loud *ding*.

Two men in expensive tailored suits and a tall woman in a white Chanel suit stared back at us.

Madame Bouchard!

I gulped. It took me a few seconds to realize she couldn't see me.

The smell of their overpriced cologne and perfume wafted our way. I didn't know which was worse, the overpowering scent of their exorbitance or the grimy, smelly interior of my robe.

"Why don't you all take the next one," said The Diplomatic Dragon Lady with a sniff, as she reached for the buttons.

A woman's voice called out from somewhere behind us.

"Get in!" Win's urgent voice came in our ears. "Two women are coming your way. They'll see you!"

Just as the elevator doors began to close, I pushed Sarah inside, almost knocking the Dragon Lady down.

Everyone piled in, helter-skelter, after us. They'd heard Win's warning, too. The two men and the Lady scuttled to a corner and regarded us like we were a pack of rabid raccoons.

I jabbed at the close button.

We'd been lucky someone from the household hadn't been in the elevator, or they'd have wondered where a troop of fully covered women was heading. Maybe they'd have even challenged us.

It took an eternity to get to the first floor. The Diplomatic Dragon Lady was the first to vault out of the elevator, holding her nose. A man dressed in a concierge uniform held the doors open for us, head bowed. He was a staff member, not a security officer. He gave us a curious glance as we piled out, but didn't say a word.

We got lost among the sea of guests and slipped out of the main penthouse entrance. Everyone was speaking in indistinct murmurs.

From their hushed demeanor and gossipy voices, I guessed the party hadn't ended as well as they'd expected.

A few security guards were in the foyer, but they were standing quietly to the side, too starstruck by the celebrities, or too busy preening and looking important to notice us.

The family would be preoccupied, saying goodbye to their guests and trying to make up for the disaster. The only person or people who worried me were whoever locked us in Sarah's room. They'd check up on us soon.

We didn't have a lot of time.

Guests were lining up to take the main elevator down to the building entrance where their valets would be waiting with their cars. It would be hard for us, conspicuous in our black robes, to blend in as the crowd thinned. We had to find another way down.

Katy tugged at my arm. "Look," she whispered.

Bibi, or who I thought was Bibi, was casually strolling away from the crowd, toward the back of the foyer. Luc, I guessed from the male swagger under the robe, was following her at a distance. They were heading to where the service elevator was.

"You guys coming?" Luc hissed into the earpiece.

Pulling Sarah in between us, Katy and I broke away from the party and followed them to the back, walking as nonchalantly as we could.

Just as we caught up to them, the service elevator light turned on.

"Someone's coming up!" said Luc.

"This way," I heard Bibi say.

She crashed through the exit door.

Fire exit!

We all rushed after her, bumping into each other, almost tumbling down the stairs.

Behind us, the service elevator door opened with a clatter. I was the last one in, and I turned to peek through the slit in the door.

Three security guards stepped out.

They hadn't noticed us, but they didn't move too far. They stopped a few feet away from the elevator, their backs to us, watching the crowd from afar.

I closed the door softly.

"What do we do now?" whispered Katy.

"Wait for them to leave," replied Bibi.

"Could take forever," I said. "Plus, when everyone leaves, they'll spot us within seconds in the foyer."

"Make it quick, everyone." It was Tetyana's voice coming through the earpieces. "Get in the car and wait for us. We'll be leaving soon."

Luc pulled off his robe, threw it in a corner and sneezed violently.

"That was sick," he said before leaping down the stairs. He stopped after a few steps and looked up. "You all coming or what?"

We didn't wait.

We ripped off our robes, threw them in the pile and scrambled after him. I took the rear, pulling Sarah behind me.

She was slow and her breath was coming loud and raspy. I had no idea what running down eighty-five floors would do to her, but we didn't have many choices.

"Coming down service stairwell," Katy said through her earpiece.

"Run, people, run," said Tetyana. "We'll be moving soon."

"Win!" David's urgent voice came through the airways. "Win!"

Oh, no. What's happening now?

"What the heck are you doing?"

"Sorry," said Win, sounding a tad guilty.

"Get back in the car!"

"Okay, okay."

"Oi," Tetyana's angry voice came next. "You wanna get shot?"

"I wanted to help." Win sounded embarrassed. We heard the car door close with a soft thud. "And I—"

"You can help by staying exactly where I told you to stay put!" snapped Tetyana.

"Sorry," came a small voice.

I'd been so focused on the conversation I hadn't noticed Sarah had stopped in the stairwell behind me.

"Hey, Sarah," I said, turning around, "Keep moving."

She leaned over the banister, her chest heaving. "I feel sick," she said in between breaths.

"I know, honey, but we have to keep going. You can do this." I reached out. "Here. Take my hand."

She stared at me, her face pale from the exertion.

"Asha?" Katy shouted from below. "You okay?"

"Sarah needs a break."

"I'm coming up," called out Bibi. "I can talk to her."

"No!" I said. "Keep going. We'll catch up. Go."

Sarah gave me a scared look. "I can't do this."

I reached out to take her hand, but she pulled away and plopped down on the step. "I can't do this anymore!" she cried, letting her head fall into her hands.

With a sigh, I stepped up and sat next to her. "Sarah, do you want to stay in your home?"

She gave me a frightened look. "No!"

"Then we have to hurry. We have to get out of here before they find us."

She didn't move.

"Listen, it's up to you. You have to decide if you're coming with us or if you want to stay with your family."

She turned away from me and stared at the handrail, her face a mixture of emotions.

The image of her brother hitting her behind the podium flashed into my mind. I didn't think that was a one-time incident.

Katy had told me a long time ago that when someone shows how they treat you once, believe it. Never make excuses or wait for a second time. That's how you get killed, she'd said.

She was right.

"Sarah," I said. "Is there anyone in your family we can trust?"

"Papa!" Sarah gave a wild look up the stairs and stood up halfway.

I grabbed her arm. "Wait! What are you doing?"

Neither of her parents had even turned around to see if she was okay, their priority being how they looked in front of their celebrity audience. I cringed at the memory.

"Do you really think your father will help you?"

"You're right," she said, sitting back down crestfallen. "Papa's off to Vienna tonight. A car was waiting for him after the party. Probably gone by now."

"And your mother?" I already knew what that woman was like, but I wondered if there was some hope for Sarah there.

She shook her head. "She hates me. She hates my aunties too, the other wives, I mean. All she cares about is shopping on Madison Avenue."

"And your brother? Why does he treat you like that?"

Her eyes narrowed at the mention of Ahmed. She looked down, silent for a few seconds.

Below us, I could hear everyone scampering down, encouraging each other on.

"He's gonna kill me, you know that?" she said, turning to me, her cheeks red. She wiped her face with her palm. I noticed she was trembling. "Ahmed said I broke honor to our family. He told me I'm an embarrassment. He told me he was gonna kill me tonight. On my birthday."

I stared at her silently. What do you say to a girl who tells you her own sibling thinks she doesn't deserve to live?

"I don't wanna go back," she said, sniffling. "I hate him! Ahmed makes my life hell!"

"Then we need to get outta here now," I said, taking her hand. "If all you can do is crawl, Sarah, I'm going to crawl with you. I will be here next to you, but we've got to keep moving. Can you do that?"

She didn't reply. That glassy look came over her eyes again.

I tried again. "If your brother or his men come down here and find you, what will they do?"

"They'll take me back to the warehouse."

"What warehouse?"

"Our jail. They'll slit my throat and after that, they'll kill the other girls too."

"What other girls?"

"The Iranian girls."

Something banged upstairs, making me jump. I looked up, my heart racing. We were seven floors down from the penthouse, which meant they could catch up to us within minutes. But it was hard to see anything from where we were.

Did they find us? Is someone coming down?

I tried to listen, but all I could hear was the din everybody was making below. If anyone opened that fire door, they'd know instantly where we were. We were sitting ducks.

I remembered how those men hadn't hesitated to shoot the back of our car in an open garage. There was no guarantee they'd spare us here.

This was a death trap.

"We've got to move," I whispered.

"I feel really sick," Sarah said.

"Take one step down with me. Please?"

She gave me a stubborn pout and shook her head. "I'm tired."

"Sweetie, they'll kill us all if we—"

She flashed me an angry look. "I told you I'm tired! Can't someone carry me?"

It was the old Sarah raising her head, the self-absorbed, obnoxious girl. I stared at her. We'd put everything at risk to help her, and here she was now, putting her life and ours on the line. I wanted to shake her.

I took a deep breath.

"Sarah," I said, gritting my teeth. "Get your ass in gear and get down the stairs right now."

She looked at me, startled.

"Do you want to get out of here?" I said, putting my face within five inches of hers, drill-sergeant style.

She nodded.

"Then move it!" I bellowed in her face. "Now!"

She got up and bolted down the stairs.

"Frigging hell!" Tetyana swore into my earpiece. "I was gonna come up and shove her down the stairs myself if she didn't start moving."

Chapter Forty-Five

"David," came Tetyana's voice again, this time low and cautious. "You have company."

"I see them," said David. "I'm behind Fire Door One."

My earpiece suddenly exploded. Male voices shouting in Arabic. The sound of car engines being fired up and driven away, one after the other.

Valets?

"Do you have a visual of our targets?" asked Tetyana.

"Negative. Last I saw them was behind the gold Lexus."

"Which one?"

"I see only one."

"Three gold Lexus in my line of sight. All with diplo plates."

"Jeepers. We lost them."

"We have to wait till the crowd clears," said Tetyana with a sigh. "Stay put."

Our earpieces went silent after that. The only sound was of our feet hitting the concrete steps. It was dry and dusty in the stairwell and with every floor we passed, I felt like the walls were closing in.

Next to me, Sarah was panting loudly, but she was moving, clutching tightly to my hand. Everyone else was three or four floors below us. I kept a tight hold on Sarah, nudging her every few minutes.

I felt bad for her. She was fighting the drugs they'd pumped into her, dealing with the exertion of scrambling down a claustrophobic stairwell, and grappling with the decision to leave her family. And she was only sixteen. Today.

We were now on floor number twenty. So far, so good. There had been no casualties, no heart attacks, no one dropping dead. Sarah was still breathing.

Even with our daily training, none of us had been prepared for a marathon run down a skyscraper. Thank goodness we were running down, not up. Even then, we had to take a few breaks every four to five floors. Sarah desperately needed the pause, and it helped the others too.

That was when I realized why the men hadn't come after us.

They hadn't expected us, least of all Sarah, to run down eighty-five floors. They probably thought we were still in the room. If they'd discovered us gone, they'd search the house. There were plenty of places to hide in that six-thousand-square-foot, three-story apartment.

"They're here!" Win cried out, startling us.

"Who?" asked Tetyana.

"The electricals!"

"Where?"

"Near their van."

"The bastards are getting away," grumbled Tetyana. "David, can you get to them?"

"On my way."

"You don't have to rush," said Win, a slight smug tone in her voice.

"Why?" Tetyana's voice was suspicious.

"They're not going to go anywhere."

"Why?" David repeated.

Win was silent for a second. "I, er, I slashed their tire."

"You did what?" Tetyana asked.

A chorus of exclamations came through the earpieces.

"It only took a minute. Their van was so close and the guys were in the stairway, so I took a knife to their tire."

"All four of them?" asked Luc, admiration in his voice. "How long did that take you?"

"Used David's super-duper Japanese knife," she replied, sounding proud of her handiwork. "I only did one tire, because David saw me and told me to get back in the car."

"Oh, boy," I heard David say. I could almost see him shaking his head. "Oh, boy."

"But there was nobody outside," said Win, "the guards were on their smoke break far away. It was super safe."

Tetyana was lost for words for once. We heard her take a deep breath.

"If someone saw you, you could have... Damn, girl! That was risky. Just don't try anything else, okay? David and I are gonna get those men soon."

"You're welcome!" called out Win. I could see her grinning to herself, alone in back of the car.

"Good job, Win," Luc whispered. I could hear the smile in his voice. "Proud of ya."

"Almost there," said Katy, panting, exhausted. "Floor five."

"When you get down, get to the car, people," said Tetyana. "Make it quick."

"I'm done!" said Bibi, first to finish the trek, "I'm on the ground floor. I'm at Fire Door Two."

"Hang on till everyone comes down," said Tetyana.

Sarah and I were two floors behind the others. "Right behind you," I called out.

"Oh, no!" said Win.

"Crap!" said David suddenly.

"Frigging heck." That was Tetyana.

"What's going on?" I asked.

"Someone called the cops," said David. "I almost ran into them."

"I didn't even hear them come," said Win. "They stopped at the back entrance. They've got their flashing lights on now."

"Are they here for us?" Bibi asked in a scared whisper.

"Everyone, get yourself to the bottom and stay near the closest exit," said Tetyana. "Wait for instructions."

It took Sarah and me two minutes to catch up to the rest of the team at the stairwell on the ground floor.

We joined the huddle in the cold stairwell foyer, hoping no one would walk in on us. Luc and I pressed our ears against the fire door, trying to hear what was going on outside with the cops, but the door was as soundproofed as it was fireproofed.

We waited, everyone trying to catch their breaths and slow their heart rates after the marathon run down. We needed the break.

Two minutes later our earpieces crackled to life again.

"Okay everyone, too many variables right now." It was Tetyana. "Our job's to get out of here ASAP," she said. "Win, without getting up or out, what can you see?"

"The cops are with a security guard and the two electricals. The men are showing a paper to the cops. They're near the back door."

"Has anyone noticed one of the van's tires has been slashed yet?" I asked.

"No one looked at the van," said Win. "They're just talking and talking and talking."

"How far is Fire Door One to where the men are, Win?" asked Tetyana.

"Right next to it," said Win.

'What about Fire Door Two? Where everyone is at."

"On the other side of the building."

"How far is the Beast from Fire Door Two?"

"I dunno...hmm..."

"How many cars lengths away, Win?"

"Maybe ten?" said Win, unsure. "Ten Minis or four like the Beast..."

"Thanks. Now tell me, are there any cars parked between the door and you?"

"Just one."

"It's not the cop car, correct?"

"Nope."

"Or the men's van?"

"It's an empty laundry van. The cop car is near the back door right next to the sign that says, *do not block door*. The electrical van is three rows in front of me."

I shook my head. "They'll spot us coming out right away. There's seven of us. And there's not much cover."

"Can't we go through the main door and tell them we're the dessert caterers?" asked David. "We all have our aprons on, don't we?"

"I ditched mine in the kitchen," said Tetyana.

"We left ours upstairs," said Katy. "It was getting too hot with the burqas."

"And smelly," added Luc.

"Sarah can't walk out in the open," I pointed out. "They'll flag us right away."

"Why don't we just army-crawl to the Beast from here? One by one?" said Luc. "They won't see us then."

"They'll see the door open and close if they're looking this way, even if they don't see us," said Katy.

"We do it in one or two-minute intervals to reduce that risk," Luc said. "Does anyone have a better idea?"

No one spoke.

"Sounds like a workable plan to me," said Tetyana.

"But how do we get out of the parking lot without them noticing?" asked Katy. "The Red Beast isn't easy to ignore."

"We'll cross that bridge when we get to it," said Tetyana. "Let's first get in the car."

"We can hide Sarah in the back and say we were just leaving after our job," I said.

"They're preoccupied right now," said David. "Let's hope their attention remains with the men."

"Worse comes to worst," said Tetyana, "we're bulletproofed and we have access to our weapons."

I exchanged a glance with Katy. I hoped it wouldn't come to that.

It took David and Tetyana thirty seconds to join us, as they stealthily maneuvered their way through the corridors.

David was our guinea pig.

Tetyana opened the door quietly, and he slipped out on his stomach. And that was the last we saw of him.

It was a relief to hear his voice when he said, "I'm in." We hadn't even heard the car door open and shut.

After an excruciating one-minute interval, Katy and Bibi went next. After another wait, Luc went to the car, army-crawling all the way.

Then, after what felt like forever, it was my turn to go with Sarah. We'd given her instructions and now I had to trust her.

Holding on to Sarah's hand, I crouched on the floor.

Tetyana put her finger to her lips.

I looked at Sarah. "Ready?"

She nodded.

Tetyana opened the door a few inches. I slithered out, pulling Sarah with me. We couldn't keep the door open any longer than necessary.

Sarah and I moved across the asphalt as fast as we could, getting closer to the Beast. I was thankful for my leather jacket. Sarah was getting road rash in her party dress I was sure, but she kept going, a determined look on her face.

The side door of the Beast opened silently as we got to it. Luc's face popped out and his hand came out to pull Sarah inside. I crawled in after her.

We stayed heads down, without speaking for another minute, waiting for Tetyana to join us.

Outside, one officer talked to his shoulder radio while the second cop walked over to the men's van. I wondered what the two men were being questioned for. *Trespassing? Impersonation? Home invasion?*

They looked their part, quietly leaning against the wall. The security guard stood next to them, fingers looped in his belt. It couldn't have been too serious because no one was hurrying or panicking or running. Everyone seemed to be cooperating.

While we watched anxiously, the officer did a cursory search of the van, but didn't notice the slash on the tire. The impact of what Win did would only show once the vehicle started rolling.

The Beast's door opened and Tetyana crawled in.

We breathed in relief. Everyone was here now.

David was in the driver's seat, his eyes peeled in front of him, watching the men. Tetyana slipped into the empty passenger seat in front.

"This is a good thing," she said, buckling up. "With the police here, we're safe."

"How is that good?" asked Katy.

"The family will be discreet," I said. "They won't come running out to find where Sarah is or where we're going."

"Let's go, David," said Tetyana. "No sudden moves."

David started the engine. We slowly backed out of our stall and inched toward the exit.

I watched the cops from the corner of my eyes, but other than a brief glance our way, they didn't stop us.

We got to the main road.

Traffic was heavy on both sides, much of it coming from the party that had ended early. Supersized luxury SUVs, white stretch limousines, Bentleys, Bugattis and two of those gold-plated Lexus drove by as we waited to turn.

David pulled onto the road when a space became available.

"We'll never find out who those men are now," Katy said, looking wistfully behind her.

Chapter Forty-Six

A sad howl came from the back of the car.

It was Sarah.

She was sitting next to Bibi. Her face was puffy. Her eyes were red. And her cheeks were wet with tears and snot. She'd been sobbing since we left her home, and Bibi had been trying to calm her to no avail.

I had no idea what we'd do with her.

She needed medical attention and psychological counseling, at least. *But what will she do after that?* We didn't have room at the bakery. We were bunking together as it was.

Katy turned to the girl. "Honey, no one will hurt you anymore. Don't you worry now, sweetie."

"Hey, Sarah," Luc said. "You're free now. How cool is that?"

Sarah took a tissue from Bibi and blew her nose.

"Hey, hon, do you mind if I ask a question?" I said, turning around in my seat when she'd calmed down a bit. "Was it you who texted me to come to your room the other day?"

Sarah nodded.

"What about the note? The one with pencil marks on the back of that card?" I asked. "Who sent it?"

"Reza."

I suddenly felt bad for the servant girl, stuck behind in that madhouse. I wondered how she was doing. I wondered what it would be like to be a slave to that family for life. A shudder ran through me.

"Do you know why she wanted to help you?"

"Because she knows what happens to girls like me."

Everyone fell silent.

There were so many missing pieces to this puzzle, but while I was dying to know more, we couldn't interrogate her. She'd had a harrowing day, maybe a week, even a month. But Tetyana didn't seem to have any qualms. She turned around in her seat to face Sarah. "What I want to know is this. Who's threatening you? And why?"

Sarah answered with a sob.

"It's her brother," replied Bibi on her behalf. "Ahmed's threatening her. Just like what happened to me."

"I have to listen to everything Ahmed says," said Sarah in between her sobs. "He tells me what I can wear, who I can talk to, when I can go out of the house, who I can marry. If he tells you something, obey or you're dead."

While Sarah's story may have sounded fantastical, I knew how common this was around the world. Though no one wanted to admit it.

"Does he think he owns you?" asked Tetyana with a scowl.

"He does. Because I'm his sister," howled Sarah.

"It's our culture," explained Bibi.

"Culture. Religion. That's just window dressing for power," David said in a sober voice from up front. "Power of husband over wife. First wife over fourth wife. Brother over sister. Rich over the poor."

We listened quietly. If anyone knew about these things, it had to be David.

"Girls matter little in these places," he continued. "They're chattel, only good for making babies, sex and housework."

"And if you're a girl and you don't listen to your family," said Bibi, "you dishonor everybody. It's super bad if you say no to a marriage. They can kill you and say it's honor killing."

"Five hundred years ago, maybe, but today?" said Katy. "What kind of honor do they think they get from killing a girl? That's just twisted."

"Did they want you to marry some old man from Saudi Arabia, Sarah?" I asked, softening my voice.

She took a deep, shaky breath before answering. "I just wanted to see Tom."

"Who's Tom?" asked Katy.

"My boyfriend."

"Where did you meet him?"

"School." She paused. "My family didn't want me to see him, but I texted him anyway. And he texted me every day. Tom said he wanted to kiss me and Ahmed saw the message. He's angry because I didn't listen to him."

"He's mad enough to kill you because of a text?" Katy asked, shaking her head. "And everyone's fine with that? Even your parents?"

"Papa doesn't talk about family stuff because he's always busy. Ahmed's in charge at home and he pretends to be Papa when he's away." Sarah sat up, suddenly agitated. "I need to call Papa. Does anyone have a phone? Can I use your phone, Bibi?"

"Sarah, I don't think that's a good idea," said David. I heard the warning in his voice.

"He doesn't know what Ahmed's doing. I have to tell him."

"I'm from Yemen," David said, "I know how it works. Your father will never punish a son. Sons are protected. They do whatever they want and get away with murder. Literally. You need to think carefully before calling your father."

"But, but..." Sarah tried to speak again, but her voice cracked. Bibi put an arm around her.

"It's not my place to give you advice," said David, "but if I were you, I wouldn't go to your father without evidence of what Ahmed's doing or he'll disown you."

Sarah looked crushed. "Disown me?"

David didn't reply.

She buried her head in Bibi's shoulder and sobbed.

The rest of us fell silent again.

I wondered if I'd put too much faith in the ambassador. I'd been sure if we shared everything with him, he'd understand. I'd thought if someone outside of his family explained, he'd help Sarah.

I looked out the window.

New York's night lights blinked at us. It was like they were calling us to come down and have a party. We were living in the most exciting city in the world. It was a beautiful Saturday evening. We should have been out having fun. But here we were, lying to the authorities, trying to catch the men watching us, and kidnapping a diplomat's daughter from her own family.

Life couldn't get any weirder than this.

The day, at least, was over. We were finally on our way home. All I wanted was to take a warm shower and crawl into bed.

Everybody in the car seemed lost in their own thoughts. Every now and then, I heard a sob from Sarah in between soft murmurs from Bibi.

I glanced behind me.

Win and Luc were sitting the furthest back in the Beast, lost in their own worlds, noses stuck to the screens as they browsed something. In the seats in front of them were Bibi and Sarah, their heads bowed low, almost touching, talking in low voices.

My heart went out to them.

They should be at school, learning things, having fun, meeting boys, dreaming of their future. Not like this. No one in this vehicle had been immune to the horrors of life, but it was heartbreaking to see it unravel in real time like this.

I sat back and wondered for the hundredth time if this was a good time to call the authorities for help. And for the hundredth time, I vetoed my own question.

"Hey, everyone," Bibi said, rousing us from our thoughts. "You need to hear this."

Everyone stirred and sat up, but no one answered.

"There are three more girls. Iranian girls."

My hasty conversation with Sarah in the stairwell came back to me. I turned around.

"Who are these girls?"

"They're gonna punish them because of me," said Sarah. "Because I ran away."

"Where are they right now?"

"In the warehouse."

"What's this warehouse?" asked Tetyana with a frown.

"That's our jail. Ahmed brought me to the house today for the birthday party, but after that, he was going to take me back there."

Katy and I exchanged confused looks.

"Start from the beginning, honey," said Katy. "So these girls, are they your friends?"

"Yes, they go to my school."

"Why are they in a warehouse?"

"Some men from Iran want American visas so their families told them they have to marry them. My friends didn't want to though. Because after they marry, the men won't let them come to school no more," Sarah explained. "But Ahmed said if anyone tries to run away from the jail, he will kill the others. He said it was going to be an honor killing. He said it was to teach everyone to obey their family."

"Oh, my god," said Katy.

"Frigging hell," said Tetyana. "Where's this warehouse?"

"Don't know."

"Can you describe it?" asked Luc.

"It's noisy. Lots of people shouting. There was a lot of big honking."

"Cars honking?"

"No, really loud like a ship."

"You mean a foghorn?" asked Luc.

"Maybe. Like from a cruise ship, you know?"

Sarah was big for her age that I had to keep reminding myself she was only sixteen. She'd probably never walked on the streets by herself, let alone driven a car. She'd probably been chauffeured with the womenfolk in her household and knew very little of her immediate surroundings or the city.

"The shipyards, maybe?" said David. "On the other side of Brooklyn Bridge."

Win started typing furiously on her keyboard.

"Hey, can you tell us more about the place?" asked Luc.

Sarah shook her head. "I don't remember anything. Ahmed covered my eyes."

"He *blindfolded* you?" Katy asked.

"In the car. He took it off when we got into the warehouse."

"How long did they keep you in there?" I asked.

"I don't know. It was like forever. But I wasn't alone."

"Can you tell us about the other girls?" Katy asked. "What were they doing there?"

"Their families didn't want them to run away. They were going to take them to Dubai and force them to marry those men soon so they were really, really scared. They cried a lot." Sarah swallowed a sob. Her voice rose in pitch. "One girl said she was gay. She told them she was never going to marry a man. So they took her away and..."

She started fidgeting with the tissue box in her hands. I noticed she wasn't looking at us anymore.

"They said they were going to teach her not to be gay. So she can be ready for her husband." She was speaking mechanically now. "She screamed a lot. But they held her down and hurt her. All of them. Even Ahmed."

Sarah started to cry again.

An arctic chill had settled inside the cabin of our vehicle.

No one spoke for a very long time.

Now, I was sure.

Sarah wasn't making any of this up. *No one could make that up.* I felt heavy, like all the world's problems had settled on my shoulders again.

"Hastein," I heard Win say from the back, but I barely registered it.

"Hey, everyone," Luc called out louder. "We found the warehouse."

Part SEVEN

Chapter Forty-Seven

It took us half an hour to get to the commercial district.

Win found the fastest route to our new destination and programmed David's phone GPS.

We were now driving across the iconic Brooklyn Bridge, taking in the city lights spread around us for miles on end. It would have been a stunning scene if we weren't on our way to an ominous warehouse with jailed girls, not knowing what to expect.

I no longer felt tired but had a vague premonition of danger. The others must have as well, because a watchful silence had fallen inside the Red Beast.

Up front, Tetyana was quietly double-checking everyone's handguns and the extra magazines. David was skirting around the night traffic so we wouldn't lose precious time.

Katy was messaging Peace in Boston to let him know where we were heading. "Just in case," she said.

Sarah had stopped crying as soon as we rerouted. She sat clutching Bibi's arm, eyes wide open, looking half-frightened and half-hopeful.

In the back, Win was tapping away on one laptop while Luc was glued to the second one.

"Peace thinks we should call the police," Katy said, after a few minutes of texting back and forth with him.

"Not going to happen," said Tetyana, not even looking up.

"The FBI?"

"Double not going to happen."

I thought of the business card I had on me. "William James," I murmured to myself, but Katy heard me.

"Think the CIA can help?" she asked.

"Not their jurisdiction," said David.

"Isn't our deadline tonight?" asked Bibi.

"Yup," said Luc from the back. "Call or we turn into pumpkins."

"We still don't know if he's real," Tetyana said, looking up sharply.

I exhaled loudly and leaned back in my seat. My brain was telling me to say yes as it would solve many of our problems. But my gut was telling me that decision would be wrong. Plus, no one else was in favor of a *yes*.

But what would happen if we said no? Would we get blacklisted? Deported? Imprisoned?

I felt a sharp jab of pressure between my shoulder blades. The stress was building inside of me. I stretched my back and took a few deep breaths to calm my nerves.

"I'll call him at exactly midnight," I said. "We still have a few hours to go."

With a shrug, Tetyana went back to her guns.

"But tonight, let's find these girls and get them the heck out of this hellhole," I said.

"Roger that," chimed Tetyana and David at the same time.

We were cruising around the perimeter of the shipyard now.

Bright spotlights on top of massive cranes illuminated the entire area. We could hear the deep whir of ships docking, the whine of commercial cranes as they swung back and forth, and the clanging of iron chains against the steel containers.

We could even see workers on steel bridges high above the ground, looking as small as insects in the distance. This was a twenty-four-hour world-class industrial complex.

How are we going to find anyone in here?

"Sarah?" Tetyana turned around. "I need you to focus, okay?"

Sarah nodded.

"I need you to think back and tell us everything you saw, so we can get to the right place."

"What do you want me to tell you?"

"Start at the top," said Tetyana. "How did you leave the house and end up in the car or truck or whatever they took you into the warehouse?"

"Papa's limousine. I don't remember getting inside, but I woke up in the back."

"In the trunk?"

"Back seat."

Tetyana gave her an encouraging nod. "Did you see any landmarks on your ride to the warehouse?"

Sarah turned to Bibi. I heard the word "landmark" thrown around. Bibi translated.

"No," replied Sarah, "because the windows are dark. I didn't see anything, and I was feeling really sick."

"Who was with you?"

"Ahmed. Someone, not our regular driver, was driving and another security man was in the front."

We were inside the complex now, driving along a small asphalt road in between nondescript brick buildings. Oversized equipment sat abandoned in parking lots. This was where bulldozers, excavators, cranes, backhoes and small trucks went to sleep for the night. It was quiet in this part of the complex. Overhead, the arena-sized spotlights gave the sky an eerie, unnatural glow.

David was driving at the speed limit, taking care not to attract any attention.

"Did they talk about where they were going? Did you hear them say anything?" Tetyana asked.

Sarah picked at her dress. "No," she said in a quiet voice. "I didn't hear their talk because he was hitting me."

"Oh, Sarah," Katy whispered.

"Ahmed likes to hit us when he's angry. He even hit our mother when he thinks she's not following a house rule."

"My goodness," I said.

"He slapped me on my head and my face. When I told him to stop and he started screaming at me."

Bibi reached over to squeeze Sarah's arm.

"What was he yelling about?" I asked gently.

"He told me I lost my honor. I told him I never even kissed Tom, but he didn't listen. He told me I was losing my culture and I was a bad girl because I didn't obey my family. He also told me if I told anyone anything I saw in the warehouse, he was going to kill me."

"Do you remember how long it took you to get to the warehouse?" asked Tetyana, softening her tone.

"Don't know. I just wanted him to stop hitting me."

"When did he blindfold you?"

"When we stopped."

"Did you hear anything?"

"Big machines and construction things, like right now."

"What happened after the car stopped?"

"Ahmed pushed me out. He was holding my shoulder really tightly. It hurt. He kept pushing me. I just remember the sound of the stones."

"Stones?" asked Katy. "Gravel, you mean?"

"Hey, everyone." It was David.

We looked up.

He pointed at the mid-sized gray building we were slowly driving by.

"We've arrived."

A steel fence and a line of trees hid the building from the road, but we couldn't miss the oversized gray sign in front.

Hastein Industries Limited.

Chapter Forty-Eight

It wasn't a fortress, but someone wanted to keep intruders out.

The fenced-in warehouse had a half a dozen security lights, but the place looked dark and forbidding. Through the iron gate, we could see a massive roll-up garage door, the only entry, it seemed, to the building.

Parked in front of this entrance was a sandy-colored Humvee, one of those obnoxious vehicles driven by city folk who'd never gone off-roading in their life. But it wasn't alone. Two black pickup trucks flanked it.

"Ahmed!"

We turned to Sarah. She looked like she would throw up.

"That Humvee," she said, pointing with a shaky finger, "It's my brother's."

"Oh, my god," said Bibi and Katy at the same time.

"Secure the vehicle," Tetyana said.

David turned off the headlights. He maneuvered the car around the block slowly with only the streetlights to guide him. We peered out of the window to find a safe spot to park.

Halfway down the block, David pulled the Beast into a lot next to a building with a sign that said, *Industrial Fishing Supplies Incorporated*. A fleet of small trucks with a blue fish logo was parked along one end of the parking lot, giving us perfect cover from anyone looking in from the street. We were now a five-minute walk to the main entrance of Hastein's warehouse.

David shut the engine off.

Everyone at the Industrial Fishing Supplies Incorporated had gone home for the day. The building was dark with only a few external lights on. There were no security personnel in sight.

"Listen up, everybody," Tetyana said, turning sideways in her seat to face us. "This is a reconnaissance. Some of you are coming with me. Some of you will stay here. We will all have jobs to do. All right?"

Everyone nodded, even Sarah.

This was Tetyana's territory. She was our lead now.

"For the first leg, David, Asha, and Katy, you're with me."

We nodded.

"Luc, Win, Bibi, and Sarah, you guys hold fort here."

They nodded.

"We don't know for sure if we have the right place—"

Sarah's face fell. "But that's Ahmed's car. I know it—"

"I believe you," said Tetyana, cutting her off. "There are too many uncertainties here. A recon means we'll check things out before we decide on a strategy to get inside. That's all I'm saying."

Sarah stared at her in confusion.

I wished we could have dropped her off somewhere safe. Bringing her into a full-blown mission was a mistake and a risk to her, but we had no choice. We were here now. The sooner we got those girls out, the better.

Tetyana got up stooping, so her head wouldn't hit the ceiling. She clicked open an overhead compartment and pulled down a long, sleek black box. Small white balls fell through the opening, raining on Katy and me. We covered our heads and ducked.

"What's all this?" asked Katy.

"Who plays golf?" Luc asked.

"Ping-pong balls," said David, reaching over and collecting them. He tucked them into the glove compartment while Tetyana opened the side door and got out. We all spilled out of the vehicle, following her outside.

She placed the black box on the asphalt ground.

No one bothered to ask what a handful of ping-pong balls were doing in the overhead bin. We were now too busy watching Tetyana unlatch the black box.

"Wow!" I said.

Even in the dark, I saw the gleaming chrome and steel nestled inside their foam protection.

"Whoa!" Luc said as he scrambled out to get a look.

Tetyana assembled the pieces quickly while the rest of us gathered around her, watching intently.

In seconds she had a fully assembled AK-47 which she handed to David to double-check and load. Then she went to work on the second weapon.

"It's like we're gonna take down terrorists," Luc said, his eyes shining. "Wish I could come with you."

"They're terrorists for sure," Tetyana replied in a grim voice, as she clipped something on top of the rifle. "Not political ones, maybe, but that's what they are and we're gonna treat them exactly like that."

"What they did to that Iranian girl is pure terror," said David in a low voice, not looking up from his task. "Those men will get what they deserve tonight."

David had good reason to feel the way he did. His only sister had been killed in Nairobi after Saudi traffickers bought her from a corrupt refugee camp organizer. They gang-raped her in front of him while he watched, screaming. She'd only been nine. He'd been seven.

Tetyana also had the right to feel how she did. After losing her brother in a Russian torture camp, she was always ready to fight anyone on the wrong side of human decency.

From a large duffel bag Tetyana had pulled out from the trunk, she dug a few items out and started distributing them among us.

"What's this for?" Katy asked, holding up the black leather gloves she'd just been handed.

"You want your prints on a crime scene?" Tetyana replied, throwing a pair at David, and another at me. "If everything goes as planned, the FBI will come sniffing around and one of our primary goals is not to leave a trace."

She dug out black ski masks from her bag and held them out. "Small for the girls and big ones for the boys."

"Wow, you came prepared," said Katy, trying hers on.

"Here, this one's for you, Asha."

I looked up at what Tetyana had brought out of her bag next.

"Kevlar vest and night-vision goggles?" I asked.

I also wanted nothing more than to eradicate evil from this earth, but I half wondered if we were approaching this mission as if it were more dangerous than it actually was. We were going to rescue three girls from a warehouse held by a bunch of diplomatic goons and an ambassador's overweight son. We weren't planning to fight the Russian army.

"Courtesy of Olek."

"How much did these things cost?"

"Good ransom money, but we'll need them tonight."

"How come I didn't know?" Katy asked.

"I put it under dojo reno costs."

I had felt the dojo was siphoning a lot of funds over the past few months, and I'd been planning to ask David about it. I thought Katy had it under control, but now I knew where it had gone to. I couldn't fault Tetyana's decision though. Not tonight, anyway.

"Can I have a goggle too?" Win asked.

"Here," Tetyana tossed one her way, "I only have two extra. These were pricey."

I tried mine on. "I can't see. What do you—"

"You need to adjust them manually," said Win. "Give it to me."

I handed mine to her. After fiddling with it, she passed it back to me. I slid it over my head and peeked out the front windshield. My world suddenly turned an eerie green.

"Wow," I said, as my eyes swept the area. I could see through shadows now.

I pulled it off to compare it with the "real world," and everything dimmed around me again, the only illumination coming from the weak lighting on the building next to us.

Next, Tetyana handed us a handgun each. They were bigger and more powerful than the mini-revolvers we had earlier.

I slid mine into its holster, glad Katy and I had ditched our dresses and heels for more sensible wear. I looked at the others. We look like a police SWAT team, I thought.

"Keep these nearby, Luc," said Tetyana, passing a sidearm and David's Japanese knife to him. "Stick the knife in your boots," she commanded. "You'll be safe here, but just in case. I always prefer to have a Plan C."

I wondered what Plan B was. And, for that matter, what Plan A was.

"What about me?" Bibi asked. "I want to help too."

"Some of those men may not speak English," said Tetyana. "Remain on standby. Listen to the CONVOs carefully and help me out when we need you, okay?"

"I can do that," she said, nodding vigorously.

"Win," Tetyana said.

"Yup?"

"Monitor the coms."

"That's my job." Win nodded. "I'll turn coms off on our end so we can hear you but you can't hear us in the car. That okay with you?"

"But we want to hear each other out there."

"You can still do that. I'll keep all your channels open. You just won't get distracted by what happens here."

"Fine. You know how this works. I'll leave that up to you."

"Sarah, I have a job for you too," Tetyana said, her voice gentle but firm. "Stay in the car and remain as calm as you can, without making a single noise. Keep your attention on the earpiece and be prepared to answer my questions. Can you do that for me?"

"Okay," Sarah squeaked. She'd been watching us gear up with a look of alarm on her face.

Win passed an extra earpiece to her and Bibi helped her to put it on.

"Luc, you're the oldest, so you're in charge when we leave."

"Yes, ma'am," said Luc, giving her a salute.

Tetyana's eyes narrowed through her ski mask as she squinted at Bibi, Luc and Win in the back. "Under no circumstances should any of you leave this vehicle. Got it?"

They stared at her.

"You heard me?"

"Understood," said Luc.

The girls nodded.

Tetyana turned her attention to David, Katy and me, her ragtag reconnaissance crew.

"Ready to take down some bad guys?"

"Yes," the three of us nodded earnestly.

Chapter Forty-Nine

We approached the warehouse from the side, the gravel crunching softly under our boots.

My Kevlar vest felt snug and heavy, but it was comforting to have it on. The eye goggles took some time to get used to, but I could see so much better while wearing them.

Tetyana and David carried their rifles slung across their backs. They'd seemed like overkill a few minutes ago, but as we got closer to the warehouse, I was glad we had them.

Tetyana had made us do a few trial runs with our gear around the Fishing Supplies building before we headed to the Hastein warehouse. She promised to include this in our regular training from now on so we could be better prepared next time.

David and Tetyana moved stealthily along the length of the fence, looking for entry points. Katy and I moved behind them, mimicking their movements, sticking to the shadows. Our black outfits and gear helped to keep us hidden.

I felt like I was part of a professional SWAT team, except a SWAT team would have been better trained, better equipped, and have several dozen armored vehicles and an entire city police force as backup. All we had was an SUV full of teenagers and two partially trained civilians—Katy and me—going straight into battle. Thank goodness for David and Tetyana.

So far, so good. We hadn't bumped into anyone.

An electric wire ran along the top of the fence which stopped at the main gates. The double gate to the warehouse opened to a driveway where the vehicles were parked. It was secured with an electronic keypad, one I was sure Win could break into within minutes, but Tetyana motioned us to keep walking.

We found a much smaller single gate on the west side of the building, locked by a hefty padlock. David picked it in less than a minute, the skills he'd learned in his former profession coming in handy.

We closed the gate behind us and slipped in quietly.

I wondered how many people were inside the building, where the girls were and if they were still alive. All this sneaking around in the dark was nerve-wracking, but I knew if we went in guns blazing, we would harm the very girls we were trying to rescue.

We got within a hundred feet of the west side of the warehouse when Tetyana stopped and put her arm out. We halted behind her, awaiting instructions.

We were near the tree line. From here, we could see the front of the building and could still remain hidden. The Humvee and the two pickup trucks were still there, parked as we first saw them.

Tetyana cocked her head to listen.

I glanced around. There wasn't a soul in the area.

We were now further away from the busiest part of the shipyard. I could hear the bangs and screeches of machinery, but the sound was dim. The warehouse and its vicinity were desolate. The men had picked a perfect spot to hide their evil deeds.

"Pair up," she whispered. "David, Asha, you two to the back."

"Ten-four," said David.

I nodded.

"Look for entry points. Meet back here in five. If you see anyone, withdraw immediately. This is a recon. Keep coms to a minimum."

"Roger that," said David.

"Got it," I said.

David and I turned left while Tetyana and Katy turned right.

David tucked his sidearm into his holster and brought his rifle in front of him. I felt my heartbeat tick faster as I followed close behind him. We stepped into the shadows of the building in the back and walked steadily and quietly, keeping an eye out for windows, doors, security guards or even dogs.

But no one was around.

The warehouse had been built of thick concrete slabs. There were no windows, no doors, and no entrances, except for the large roll-up loading dock in front.

I scanned the area for security cameras, but there were none, at least that I could see. Strange. I'd expected more surveillance around this place.

Industrial-sized plastic bins lined the wall in the back, making it difficult for us to maneuver around them quickly. David checked each one as we made our way down the line.

Our earpieces had gone silent. It seemed like everyone in the Red Beast was waiting anxiously, listening quietly. No sound was coming from Tetyana and Katy on the other side either.

My brain questioned if there was anything here after all. But my gut felt uneasy.

On one hand, it made little sense for an ambassador's son and his security detail to be hanging out at a darkened warehouse in the industrial district in the middle of the night. On the other hand, if you wanted to do evil things, this place, built like an above-ground bunker, was the perfect spot to lock people up and do untold things to them. No one would ever know.

"Guys!" Win's panicked voice came through our earpieces. "Watch your backs!"

I whirled around, pointing my pistol. But there was no one. David motioned me toward the wall. We flattened ourselves against the concrete and waited, our guns at the ready, furiously scanning all sides.

"They know we're here!" Win said.

"Found a tracking device under our car," Luc's voice came next.

My heart raced.

Who tracked us? The CIA? The people watching us? Or was it Ahmed and his goons?

"Hey." It was Bibi's voice now. She sounded like she'd been running. "I threw it under a big eighteen-wheeler parked on the next block. To give us time."

"Good job, but get back in the car asap," Tetyana hissed. "Time to find another parking spot."

"We're moving," said Luc.

The Beast purred to life.

The sound of the garage door being rolled open silenced everyone. The hair on the back of my neck stood straight up.

I glanced at David. He was listening intently.

Luc, Win, and Bibi had fallen silent too.

Someone hollered. A truck engine started. The vehicle moved and we heard the crunch of the tire on the gravel. The car stopped. The clang of the gates came to us as they opened and closed.

David and I remained where we were, plastered to the back wall, not moving. I wondered where Tetyana and Katy were. We waited, without breathing, until the sound of the truck dissipated down the street.

That's one or two fewer men to fight, I thought.

Luc spoke up. "Found a spot close to the shipyards. All the other parking lots had gates."

"Don't turn lights inside car," whispered David. "Keep a low profile."

"We're doing that," came Luc's voice.

"Hey, there's someone over there." Katy's voice came over the airwaves. "Over there. Is that—"

"Get back," came Tetyana's hoarse whisper.

"But I think I saw...."

A woman's shriek deafened us.

My heart lurched. Oh, my god, was that Katy?

"Katy!" I whispered urgently into my earpiece. "You okay?"

She didn't answer.

"Get the hell back!" Tetyana's angry holler made me jump.

A burst of gunfire broke out.

David jumped out and raced along the wall.

I ran after him, my handgun at the ready, wishing I had a rifle too now.

"Come out or I will kill her," said a gruff voice.

I recognized that voice. It was the yellow-toothed guard who'd threatened Katy and me in the elevator the other day.

A chill went through me. *Does he have Katy?* I felt sick to my stomach.

"Drop your weapon or I'll have your head!" Tetyana's voice came into my ear and echoed across the grounds.

David got to the end of the wall and stopped. I halted right behind him. He tiptoed to the edge and peeked out. Whatever he saw made his body go rigid.

"Let her go now!" Tetyana shouted.

"I cut her throat," snarled the man.

"Let me go!" That was Katy. "Get your hands off me, you pig!"

"Stop moving, you fat cow, or I cut you."

"I said, lemme go!"

"Shut up or I'll shoot you, bitch!"

Then I heard the single shot.

"Katy!" I screamed without thinking.

Silence.

"Get out!" shouted the man in our direction now. "Or I kill the girl."

David pushed me back roughly and stepped out of the shadows, his shoulders stooped.

"Drop it."

David pointed the rifle down and dropped it.

Oh, my god, oh, my god, what did I do?

My heart hammered. My mind raced.

What do I do now?

I tiptoed back fast until I felt the recycle bins on my back.

I dropped to the ground and slipped behind the nearest one. There were some advantages to being five-foot, ninety pounds skinny. I squeezed myself into the space between the bin and the wall and stayed quiet, my weapon clutched tightly in my hand, not daring to breathe.

Through my earpiece, I could hear people shouting, tussling, and Tetyana and David cursing.

What happened to Katy? Is she…? Did he…?

I couldn't get myself to even think of the words.

I was just about to peek out when I heard footsteps coming my way.

Chapter Fifty

A group of people strode past the bin, hollering in Arabic.

My mind swirled. *How many men are there? What happened to Tetyana and David? Where's Katy?*

There was no sound from my friends. Either they'd decided not to talk, or they'd been gagged. I badly wanted to peek out and see where they were being taken, if they were okay, if they were even alive.

The footsteps moved toward the front of the building. Then I heard the loading dock roll up.

It made me sick to my stomach to think of what I'd just done. *Did that man shoot Katy or cut her like he threatened?* If I'd kept my big mouth shut, David and I could have saved them.

This is all my fault.

The garage door rolled shut. Through my earpiece, I heard echoing footsteps, like the group had entered a large open hallway.

I prayed no one would find the earpieces. They were small and embedded well enough that you had to look really close to see them. I hated to think of what might happen if the men discovered them.

They continued to talk boisterously as they moved inside the warehouse. A door opened and shut. More walking. More echoing footsteps. Suddenly the men started to shout at each other. It was like an argument was breaking out.

I was sure Bibi and David knew exactly what they were saying, but David was not in a position to speak and Bibi was probably too petrified to talk right now. I listened carefully, thankful I hadn't heard any more gunshots.

The sound of something being scraped back screeched in my ear. Then, a loud metallic clang.

What's that?

More shouting. More arguing and more yelling.

The metal clang echoed in my ear again.

And everything turned silent.

Eerily silent.

I could no longer hear anything from inside the warehouse. *Did Win turn off all coms?*

I waited, not breathing.

Nothing.

Silence had fallen on the grounds too.

I didn't know if any of the men had remained outside. I waited in my crunched position for another two minutes, ignoring the pain shooting up my shins, listening for signs of life.

Everyone in the Beast had gone quiet too.

I wondered about the recent gunfire outside. Would someone have heard it? Would they have called the police by now? Or were we too secluded for anyone to hear what happened here?

The shipyard workers were too far away and everyone seemed to have gone home for the day in this part of the complex. Besides, the sounds of the heavy machinery would have drowned out any noise.

It was only me and my handgun now.

What do I now? Think, girl, think.

My legs were cramped, my back was stiff, and my brain felt mushy. This was exactly when I needed Kali to come alive inside of me, but she refused to make her presence whenever I felt fear.

I took a deep breath to steady myself.

Those men aren't going to get away with this. We're gonna get them out.

I uncurled myself and peered out from behind the bin. There was no one within sight.

A second truck engine started near the front, starling me. I listened intently, wondering if they were taking my friends away from the building.

I checked the magazine in the pistol. All good.

Time to stop hiding and do something.

I crouched low to the ground and slipped out, half expecting someone to pounce on me, but there was nobody outside.

"Asha!" said a voice in my ear, making me jump. My heart raced.

"You okay?"

I tapped my earpiece.

It was Luc.

"I was behind the bins," I whispered. "They took them inside."

"We saw that," said Win.

"How?"

"You and Katy have cameras on your goggles," said Win. "I put them there when you asked me to adjust them for you."

This wasn't the first time Win had embedded audio or video equipment on us without telling us. I pushed back the immediate thoughts that popped into mind and instead gave Win a silent prayer. I just wished she'd tell us these things beforehand.

"Did you see Katy?"

"Still standing," said Luc. "Those were warning shots. The men gagged the three of them and marched them inside."

"Can you see them now?"

"Cameras cut out a minute ago together with the coms," said Win. "Wherever they are, there's no transmission for audio or video."

My heart sank.

What does that mean? Are they locked up somewhere? Are they still alive?

"What else did you see?"

"There's a big garage behind that roll-up door," said Luc. "From there, they took them through a long corridor and then into a huge warehouse, full of stuff. The main part of the warehouse, we think. Everyone gathered in the middle of this big hall. We couldn't see what was going on but heard a metal door open. I think they got pushed inside. That's when the audio and video stopped."

"What were the men arguing about?"

Bibi answered. "They were arguing whether to shoot them or not."

My blood ran cold.

Suddenly Sarah's voice came, high pitched, agitated.

"Oh, no!" cried Bibi.

"What's going on?" I whispered.

Frightened, hushed voices came in my ear. They were speaking urgently, about what, I couldn't make out.

"Guys?" I said, tapping my earpiece. "All okay?"

"A black truck just drove by," said Win. "Sarah thinks she saw a security guard inside, someone who works in her house."

"Merde!" said Luc. "It stopped at the end of the road. Don't know if they saw us."

"Oh, my god, it's turning back," said Win.

"Get down, Sarah!" said Luc, his voice angry. "Don't move!"

A subdued bleat from Sarah told me she was complying. At least, I hoped.

"Cutting coms," said Win. "In case they pick us up."

I nodded, even though they couldn't see me.

Silence.

I waited in the dark, crouching next to the bins, racking my brain, trying to think of my options.

I could run back to the car and give Win, Luc, and Bibi backup. I could also shoot my way into the warehouse to rescue the others. Both seemed foolhardy.

I could get caught, and then what? At least from the outside, I had more agency. I had to think this through.

Think, girl, think.

Everyone in the car was still quiet.

I vacillated on ideas until I felt pins and needles on my legs and arms. I was just about to turn around and move toward the loading door when I spotted the shadow emerge from the grounds behind me.

It was heading my way, coming fast.

I whipped out my gun and trained it in the movement's direction.

"Freeze!" I hollered. "One inch closer and I shoot!"

Chapter Fifty-One

"No, don't! It's me!"

It was Bibi. I knew it, even with that ski mask on. She must have dug it out of Tetyana's duffel bag.

I uncocked my gun and lowered it, my heart still pounding. This was the second time that day I almost shot Bibi.

"What are you doing here? I could have killed you!"

She ran toward me. I noticed the handgun in her hand.

"What happened?" I asked. "Is everyone okay?"

"Win's got trouble turning coms back on again. She's fiddling with it right now. Luc found another box in the back and this," she said, showing me her weapon. I came to tell you we're all okay."

"What about the truck?"

"It turned around and went away."

"Did you see the license plate?"

"Nope. We stayed down for a long time. But we heard it drive past us and get back on the main road. I think they were checking us out. It was super creepy."

"We've got to figure out how to get the others out of here," I said. "That's our priority."

I checked my earpiece. It still wasn't working.

I looked at Bibi.

"Are you ready for some recon work?"

She gave me a determined nod. "What do you want me to do?"

I gestured her to follow me and advanced to the loading dock, the only visible entrance to this concrete vault.

When we got to the edge of the wall, I peered out, holding my pistol ready. The Humvee was still parked in its original position, but the two black trucks were gone. I expected to see a sentry, but no one was in sight.

"We're back!"

For the third time that night, I jumped.

It was Win's voice in my ear. "Guys, we're back!"

"All okay?" I whispered.

"Tetyana and David stored enough arsenal for an army in here," said Luc. "Do you know there's a secret compartment near the spare tire well? How come they never told us about it?"

"I didn't know, but that's good. Keep checking for more weapons," I whispered. "We might need it all. Stand by."

I turned to Bibi. "Follow me."

We crouched low and shuffled on our haunches toward the loading dock, our eyes and ears on full alert.

"Win," I whispered when I got to the door. "There's a keypad on the garage door."

"What's on it?"

"Regular numbers and letters. Like a normal keypad."

"What's the brand?"

"Heinrich. Model four thousand."

Through my earpiece, I could hear her tap away on her keyboard.

While Win was checking, Bibi and I inspected the door. It was a garage door big enough to roll a small truck through.

"There's no handle or anything mechanical. The keypad opens this electronically," I said.

"No space to jack it up either," said Bibi, running her fingers along the bottom of the door. "Super tight everywhere."

A regular roll-up garage door would have been a challenge, but this one was reinforced.

"There's got to be another way in," I said.

"We could wait for them to come out and tackle them then," said Luc in my ear. "It'll be risky if they have prisoners with them though."

"That could also take forever," said Bibi. "Maybe they won't come out till tomorrow. Who knows what they'll do to everyone..."

"If we can't find a way in, we fracking blast our way in," said Luc. "We have the ammo and more weapons now."

"What kind?" I asked.

"Two more Glocks, a T3x with a scope, two semi-automatics and a suppressor which I think is for the sniper."

I shook my head. "We'll need something more powerful to blast our way through this. Too bad the grenade launcher is at the dojo."

"We can make a run at the door with the Beast," said Luc. "Like you guys did before."

"When did that happen?" asked Win.

"Didn't Asha run through the barrier in the parking lot the last time?" asked Luc.

"That was a plastic pole," I said. "We're talking a full-on, reinforced steel loading dock here. We'll kill ourselves on impact."

"Can you think of a better idea?"

"Guys! Take cover!" It was Win. "That truck is coming back."

Bibi and I turned around to run and hide behind the sidewall, but it was too late.

We'd been listening so intently to the conversation in our earpieces, we'd missed the sound of the vehicle coming our way. I cursed myself.

The truck was pulling in through the main gates now. There was no way we could get away without them seeing two figures disappear to the back.

I looked around in desperation. "Here!" I cried, pulling Bibi by the arm and scrambling under the Humvee.

The truck's tires crunched on the gravel as it pulled up next to the Humvee. The engine turned off.

We waited, flat on our stomachs, hearts hammering, our heads just touching the steel floor pan of the Humvee. Our earpieces had gone quiet. Win had turned everything off again.

We could hear Middle Eastern music blaring from the cab, accompanied by rowdy male laughter. Whoever it was, they were having a party. And it was taking forever for them to get out.

I twisted to the side and pointed my gun at the front door of the truck, waiting for them to step out. If it was just one man or two, I could take them in the ankles and force them to take us inside.

We waited for the right moment, frozen in our places.

Finally, the front cab door opened and a sleek pair of men's dress shoes stepped out. I cocked my gun. Another pair jumped out from the back. Then, another. And another.

How many are there?

Whoever they were, they had come well dressed. I wondered if this was more of Sarah's family.

From underneath the Humvee, I counted the feet. There were at least five men.

My stomach tightened. Five of them against the two of us. And neither of us were experienced shooters.

Should I risk it?

"*Yalla, Yalla!*" one of the men hollered.

Another shouted back and laughed.

It sounded like they were getting ready for a celebration. They weren't taking any precautions to keep the noise down, and that worried me. It told me they were sure no one would hear them here.

In between their boisterous laughter, I heard guns and weapons being checked. These men weren't here just to have a party. They were here to have a killing party.

If they find us here, they'll shoot us execution-style.

Suddenly someone clicked open the driver's door of the Humvee.

My heart jumped into my mouth. Bibi clutched at my arm. We froze.

If they drive this car out, we're dead.

I closed my eyes.

Maybe this is how we're going to die.

But the man didn't get in the car.

He jumped on the running board, leaned in and rooted around inside before pulling back after finding whatever he'd been looking for. The Humvee rocked back and forth as he jumped off and slammed the door shut.

Chatting loudly, the men stepped away from the vehicles.

Through the chatter, I heard someone punch the keypad. Within seconds, the loading dock door rolled up, and the men disappeared inside.

Bibi and I stayed under the Humvee for fifteen seconds after the men left. I counted silently in my head, surveying the area, looking for feet left behind or anything suspicious in any direction.

"Clear," I whispered as I crawled out all stiff and dusty, and helped Bibi out from underneath the vehicle.

"You guys okay?" came Win's shaky voice in my ear.

"Those men are horrible," whispered Bibi.

"They didn't see us," I whispered into my earpiece.

The thought of getting discovered and being summarily executed had temporarily paralyzed my brain. My legs felt like they'd give way any moment, but seeing Bibi's pale face made me stand a little straighter. I had to stay strong, plus, we had to get everyone out. Soon.

I motioned her to follow me to the side of the building where we had better cover.

"Those men, those men..." Sarah was babbling in our ears. "They're my brother's friends. They said they came for a rape party...." She broke off, choking.

"That's what I heard too," Bibi said, her face contorted in horror.

"Geez," said Luc.

I felt nauseous.

"Help them!" Sarah cried, her voice piercing my ear. "Please help my friends."

Bibi shook her head in frustration. "We have to do something. Anything. They're horrible!"

I nodded, trying to think.

"Hey, Asha?" Luc said in my ear. "I found something in the glove compartment I think you need to see."

Chapter Fifty-Two

It took us ten minutes to get ready.

While Bibi and I made our way back to the Beast, Luc and Win had ransacked the car, digging up everything Tetyana and David had tucked away. The long-barreled rifles, the handguns, the tanto knives, the nunchucks, and the crowbar would help. But it was Luc who'd hit on the idea of using the ping-pong balls. An exceptional solution any way you looked at it.

Everyone had scrambled to action, including Sarah, who was ready to do anything to rescue her friends.

She was in the Beast now with strict instructions to stay in the driver's seat with the engine running but the lights off, ready to drive over to the warehouse when we called.

Sarah was our getaway driver.

She'd assured us she'd driven before. Three times in total. Tom, her boyfriend, had taken her out in his car and shown her how, she'd said. That was good enough for me. We had no choice.

Luc, Win, Bibi and I were back on the warehouse grounds now, having slipped in through the side gate on the west end.

From behind an elm tree near the fence, I watched as Bibi bent to light the ping-pong balls we'd carefully lined up against the loading dock door.

My world was doused in that eerie green light of night-vision goggles again. Win and Luc flanked me on either side, their weapons trained on the garage door, the two extra goggles snug around their foreheads, awaiting my instructions.

I wished Katy was here with us. Her archery skills would have been perfect for this job. As I waited for the world to blow up around us, I wondered how much better it would have been to take these men down silently with arrows, one by one. *That would really freak them out.*

Bibi had a handgun and the crowbar on her. Luc and Win were carrying their handguns, which they both had used before. I had my handgun tucked away in my bra holster and David's sniper rifle with the suppressor on in my hands, a weapon I'd trained on a few times with David.

Except for that crowbar, we'd all used these weapons at the range, but none of us were anywhere near prepared to fire live ammunition in a hostile environment.

The T3x in my hands felt heavier than I expected. I wasn't carrying just a deadly weapon, I was shouldering the weight of my decision as well.

But if there was one thing we'd learned from our pasts, it was to improvise and adapt in any situation. Otherwise, none of us would have survived this far.

And we were all raring to go.

While Luc, Win and I stayed behind the trees, flat on our stomachs on the ground, Bibi lit the last ping-pong ball, gave us a wave and dove behind the side of the building. She was well hidden now.

The pin-pong balls started smoking right away. Luc had been right. They made the perfect backyard smoke bombs. A silly prank he played as a kid was coming in handy now.

I waited, my palms sweaty, my heart racing, in anticipation of the smoke to cloud the entrance.

"Now!" I hollered to Luc and Win.

Their gun fire came fast and furious. My ears began to ring like mad, but I kept my eyes focused on the scope.

After a few rounds to the door, I yelled, "Stop!"

We needed to save our ammunition for the next step.

It didn't take long for the garage door to roll up.

A shadow careened out through the smoke, shouting in confusion. A second shadow lurched out on the other end, shooting blindly. Behind the trees, we crouched even lower.

My instructions to the team had been simple. Our goal was to inflict maximum damage on the maximum number of men as quickly as possible.

The dark forces of Kali were fully alive inside of me now. My pep talk inside the Beast had been short but brutal. Half of our family was imprisoned inside, their lives on the line. There were girls being prepped for a rape party. We had to see these men as the monsters they were. This was not the time to be squeamish or submissive. We would bring them down, one by one.

"There will be blood," I'd said, "And we will stop the evil."

I watched the men through the scope, my finger on the trigger.

After giving them a few seconds, I honed in on the nearest man and pulled the trigger. A surprised yell came from him as he fell to the ground, clutching his stomach. With a terrified look, the second man turned to run.

I aimed at the next man and pulled the trigger. Another bullet. Another man down. My training had come in handy.

"Good hit," I heard Luc breath next to me.

We knew there were more to come.

We waited silently, biding our time.

Not hearing any more gunfire, another shadow crept out of the side of the door, crouching low, holding automatic weapons in his hands. Then another man slithered out. And another. It was like watching insects crawl out from a dark hole.

They whirled around, hollering to each other, the smoke disorienting them. I gave them a few seconds.

One man moved toward where Bibi was hiding. I trained my scope on him. From where I was, I could see her shadow. She had her weapons ready, but that would not be enough.

"Luc, keep an eye on right. I'll take man on left first."

Luc aimed at the man huddled over one of his dead comrades on the ground. He made an easy target, but I didn't want him to shoot yet. I had a noise suppressor while he didn't.

My first target was the man walking toward Bibi. I squeezed the trigger. He fell with a surprised cry. Another man dove to the ground and tried to crawl under the Humvee for cover, but I got him before he could.

The last man standing spotted us or heard us. He pointed his gun our way and a burst of bullets hit the trees.

"Heads down," I said, as I frantically resettled my rifle to take aim and fire in his direction. One shot and the man stopped dead. His gun fell with a loud clatter next to his body.

We waited, our senses on high alert, watching, listening, waiting, but an eerie silence had fallen on the grounds now. It was like even the wind had stopped. Bibi was still crouching in her corner, her handgun trained, just in case.

The garage door was wide open now.

"Time to go in," I whispered, pulling my weapon back.

We got up and silently surveyed the damage we'd done.

"I'd be surprised if we haven't disabled half the team," said Luc.

The thought we'd just taken human lives hadn't fully registered with me yet. Like the last time, I knew I'd pay for my sins. I always did. But I didn't have time to think. Or reflect. Or philosophize. That would come later. Right now, I had to focus. My adrenaline was pumping hard, and I was ready for our next task.

I waved at Bibi to let her know we were coming over.

"This way," I whispered, as I stepped to the right, further into the trees.

The tree line curved with the fence and gave us good cover. The trick was to get in the garage door before they closed it and without getting shot at. We scampered behind the trees, keeping low, making as little sound as possible.

Every now and then I looked up to see if anyone was at the dock door.

But there was no one.

Either they were in hiding and waiting for us inside, or too busy in the back to hear what had happened to their team. We had to be prepared for either scenario.

As soon as we were out of sight of the garage door, we scrambled toward the sidewall where Bibi was waiting for us. I lifted my eye goggles as we got to the building and placed them on my head to see better, now there was more light. The others did the same.

It was hard to see what they were thinking as their masks covered their faces well.

"All okay?" I asked.

Three masked heads nodded.

I slung my rifle on my back and pulled out my handgun. Then, I flattened myself against the concrete, and motioned everyone to follow me. I inched toward the main door, sticking to the wall, hoping the element of surprise would be on our side once again.

A few feet from us, lying in pools of blood, were the bodies of the men I'd just taken down. One of them had a tattoo of a scimitar on his forearm. I turned my eyes away quickly. I needed to focus on my task. The last thing I needed was to get unnerved from seeing the carnage I'd left behind.

When I got to the opening, I waited ten seconds, not breathing, listening for signs of anyone waiting to ambush us.

Nothing.

On my signal, Luc and I rushed inside the doorway, training our weapons.

It was brightly lit but empty.

We'd stepped into a garage big enough to fit five small trucks. Lined along the walls were mid-sized shipping cartons. There was a door on the other end which was slightly ajar.

Where is everyone?

"All clear here," whispered Luc.

I nodded and stepped up to the door that seemed to lead to the principal part of the building.

Bibi and Win were following us, their weapons drawn.

When Luc and I got to the doorway, we trained our guns in front, praying nobody was waiting for us on the other side, ready to trap us.

Luc kicked the door open and stepped in. I followed him in.

Nothing, again.

We were at the beginning of a long, narrow corridor lit by white fluorescent light. At the other end was a massive double door made of steel. There were four smaller doors set on both sides of the corridor. All were closed.

It was empty, stark, and cold here.

I remembered Win and Luc talk about seeing this corridor through Katy's body camera. From what they said, this led to the main warehouse where Tetyana, David, and Katy had been taken. That was where all communications had ceased.

I prayed they weren't getting tortured while we were racking our brains trying to find out how to get in.

A sound made me turn.

As I watched, the handle of one door depressed ever so slowly.

I stood petrified for a second.

"Geez," Luc whispered.

"Get back," I whispered. "Ready to fire."

We took two steps back, stood shoulder to shoulder, and focused our guns on the door.

Chapter Fifty-Three

The door creaked open an inch.

Someone peeked out. Then, the door shut as quickly as it had opened.

"Who's there?" I called out.

I heard a yelp.

It was a girl.

I lowered my weapon. "We're here to rescue you," I said, "we're here to take you home."

The person behind the door tried to say something. She sounded muffled, like she was having a hard time talking.

I was just about to step up to the door and try the doorknob when I heard a stinging slap. The sound echoed through the corridor, chilling my blood.

I ran up and banged on the door. "Oi!" I shouted. "Open up! Come out!"

"Or we shoot down the door!" hollered Luc.

The door opened.

A frightened girl, barely a teen, with her hands bound stumbled out.

We jumped back, staring at this phantom of a girl. Her face was thin and pale and covered with bruises, old and new. She was bleeding on her arms and thighs.

She gave us a terrified look.

A grim shadow loomed behind her. It was the yellow-toothed security guard from the ambassador's house.

His eyes widened when he saw us. He didn't know it was us behind the masks. All he saw were two figures dressed in black, balaclavas on their faces, night-vision goggles perched on their heads and handguns in their hands. Pointing his way.

But he recovered fast. He pulled the girl in, one hand wrapped tightly around her shoulders and the other pushed a gun to her head.

"Let her go!" I said.

Without a word, the man dragged the girl backward, toward the end of the corridor where the massive door was.

Luc and I sprang forward. We followed them, our guns trained on the man.

"Let the girl go, you asshole," I said, glaring at him.

"You rat bastard rapist, leave her alone," said Luc.

"I will shoot her dead if you come close," he snarled, and jabbed the gun further into the girl's neck. She winced in pain but didn't say a word.

We slowed our movements but kept watch, waiting for the right moment.

Five feet from the end of the corridor, the man stopped. He glanced behind him to see how far the main door was. In that split second of distraction, Luc and I pounced.

Luc pulled the girl away.

The man turned around with a shocked expression on his face.

I lunged at him, slamming him against the wall with my rifle. His weapon fell to the floor, clanging against the bare concrete.

With an ugly roar, he brought his fist up high. I ducked to the left, giving a swift kick to his shins as I did.

That did nothing, but I evaded the punch.

I saw another fist come down. I ducked to the right and slammed my knee against his balls. He doubled over. Remembering Tetyana's classic move, I raised my rifle and whipped it across his bowed head.

Once. Twice. Three times.

He screamed in pain.

Kali was out in full swing now. Knowing how he must have treated these girls, every hit felt strangely satisfying.

He fell to the floor, clutching his bloodied head. I gave another kick to his side and he doubled over.

Luc moved in fast, handgun out. He pressed it to the back of the man's neck.

"You're a dead duck," he said and cocked the gun.

"Wait," I said, "we need him to find the others."

I pulled the goon up by his collar. He covered his face with his hands, afraid I'd hit him again.

"Get in there, you scum," I ordered, pointing to the room he'd come out of. "Now!"

Still covering his head, he wobbled toward the open doorway, encouraged by the thrust of my gun barrel on his back.

"I'll check the other rooms," said Luc.

I nodded.

"Hey, girls!" I called out.

Win and Bibi came out of the shadows and into the corridor.

I pushed the man inside the room and turned to Bibi. "You're with me," I said, not wanting to use her name in front of this thug.

She followed me inside.

The room was bare. It had one uncomfortable-looking chair, a plain steel table and a naked, dirty mattress for furniture. It smelled so foul in the room, I nearly gagged.

"Oh, my god. What do they here?" Bibi asked.

I glanced around. "I can only imagine," I said, feeling sick.

"They're evil," said Bibi, looking nauseous.

I turned to the man who was staring at us with his mouth open. Hearing two female voices, and seeing us having the upper hand, probably confused him. Or angered him.

"Down!" I barked.

To my surprise, he shouted back in Arabic, spittle flying from his lips, his face contorted into hate.

Halfway through his diatribe, Bibi gave an angry snort.

"I said get down and put your hands up!" I shouted, pointing my rifle at his chest. "Your life depends on one question, you hear me?"

Bibi translated, her voice carrying more venom than I'd heard before.

She really didn't need to translate. He understood every word I was saying. He was merely refusing to comply.

He kept screaming at us. Though I didn't understand any of it, I was sure most of it were obscenities or threats. Then, without warning, he turned to Bibi and spat on her face.

Bibi didn't hesitate. She shot his knee.

The man fell, screaming.

I stared at Bibi. She'd taken an angry stance in front of him, feet apart, crowbar in one hand and a smoking gun in the other. As far as I knew, this was the first time she'd shot anyone.

"What do you want to ask him?" she said, without looking up, her fiery eyes focused on the man squirming in pain at her feet.

I recovered from my shock.

"Ask him where they took everyone. Where are they now? Also, where are the girls, the Iranian girls?"

Bibi translated.

The man didn't respond. He curled up, crying.

"Answer me!" she screamed. "Or the next shot will be to your head!"

That made him look up. His eyes were filled with fearful, hateful tears. He whimpered, regretting his actions already.

Bibi pointed her pistol at his face and took a step closer.

The man put his hands up and raised his eyes to the heavens as if calling for divine help.

That didn't fool Bibi. Her words came out harsh and fast. I had no idea what she was saying, but the man's reactions told me enough. He started talking. Bibi listened intently.

Finally, some answers.

I waited to the side, letting Bibi take the lead. I was ready to react in case he tried to get away or attacked her, though in his condition he'd fail miserably on both fronts. Still, a desperate man should never be trusted. I watched him closely.

"They're inside the warehouse," Bibi translated, her eyes steadfastly on him. "Underground. In a basement chamber."

"A basement? In here?"

"A secret room. They built it to hide the girls they brought from East Asia and Eastern Europe. Sounds like several Middle Eastern diplomats are clients here."

"My god."

"There's a metal door on the floor," Bibi translated, her eyes still on the man. "Somewhere in the middle of the warehouse. Our friends are with the girls."

"Are they...?" I asked, not sure I wanted to hear the answer. "Did they...?"

"Still alive. Supposedly, that's all he knows."

The man was pleading with her now, hands clasped in front, sweat and tears streaming down his face.

Bullies like him were cowards when cornered. I'd seen it all the time.

"That's all you know, eh?" Bibi asked in a dangerous voice.

The man babbled in Arabic. I caught a few words here and there, words I'd learned from David and Bibi over the years. "God's will." "Good man." "Pray."

Bibi's eyes filled with contempt. "You pray to God after you rape little girls? To cleanse yourself?" Her voice dripped with poison. "You think your praying makes it right?" she shouted.

I'd never seen this side of her. Her voice was strong and steady, echoing off the bare walls. She was standing straighter than usual, looking like a mighty Arabian warrior queen. I watched, not able to take my eyes off this extraordinary transformation.

The man replied something.

"A gift? A gift to you from God?" Bibi asked in shock. "No god would allow this horror. These are children. These are women. What you did was rape. You tortured them for your sick pleasure, you twisted animal! You belong in hell!"

As I watched, jaws open, she brought the crowbar down and slammed it across his neck. The man screamed.

"That's for what you did to that girl," shouted Bibi.

She slammed him on the nose next. Blood spurted from his face.

"That's for all the other girls you hurt." Next, she aimed at his head. "And that's for being the scum of the earth you are."

The man cowered, sobbing, bleeding, trying in vain to shield himself from her vicious blows.

Never in a thousand years would I have imagined myself encouraging violence. There was a part of me that knew anger and savagery were never the answer. I knew too well how revenge brought only sleepless nights. I should have stopped young Bibi, but I didn't.

The Indian goddess of war, Kali, whom my grandmother had worshiped and said would always protect us, was strong inside of me. Wherever I saw injustice, whenever the strong wreaked havoc on the weak, Kali came up, waking me, spurring me to fight back. And right now, I was silently cheering Bibi on.

She gave one last blow and the man fell to the ground, a bloodied mess.

"All clear," said Luc, coming in.

He glanced at the man writhing on the floor and looked away with a grimace.

"All rooms are empty and the door to the warehouse is locked," he said.

"Where are the girls?" I asked.

"Outside. That girl we found is traumatized." Luc gave me a grim look. "Can't even talk."

"Do we need a key or a code for the big door at the end?" I asked.

"A code," said Luc.

I didn't have to ask. Bibi was on the man in a flash.

She put the crowbar on the man's neck, pulling him back on his knees and pinning him against the wall, choking him. She barked at him. He flailed, trying to push the crowbar away, but Bibi was in full control.

She said something and released the bar. He grabbed his neck and spluttered for a few seconds before speaking in a hoarse voice, trembling.

"Five, Seven, Nine, Three, Two, Six," Bibi translated.

With a nod, Luc hurried out to try the code while I looked around for something to gag the man with. He was already physically incapacitated, but I didn't want to risk him calling attention from his friends.

"We don't have much time. Let's tie this sicko and get everyone out. Do you see any rope?"

Bibi walked over to the table and pulled open the drawer.

"Oh!"

I stepped toward her and peeked over her shoulder.

A black blindfold. A ball gag. Two packets of condoms. A rusty knife. And yellow utility rope.

I felt sick to my stomach.

"Rape kit," I said, pulling the gag out with the butt of my gun.

Part EIGHT

Chapter Fifty-Four

A high-pitched shriek startled us.

We'd just blindfolded, gagged, and tied the ambassador's security goon to give him a slight taste of his own work. He was bleeding heavily from the wound in his throat and nose where Bibi had cut him. He wasn't going to last long.

But before we left him in the room, Bibi told him we had spared his life so he could reflect on his sins. I doubted he heard.

We'd just locked the door and were about to join the others when we heard the scream.

"Is that Win?" I said, my heart hammering again.

Luc dashed out of the main warehouse door and ran past us toward the entrance, giving us a panicked look. We scurried after him.

Win and the girl we'd saved were sitting on a crate near the entrance. Win had a shocked expression on her face. The girl looked frightened, but neither was in imminent danger.

"You okay?" I called out as we ran up to them.

"Yeah," Win said, "but someone—."

The screech filled our ears again. I tapped my earpiece.

Who is this? What's going on?

"Lemme gooo!"

I recognized that cry. It was the same scream I'd heard at the ambassador's penthouse while I looked over the catering contract in the dining room. It felt like eons ago, but I could never forget that voice.

"It's Sarah," I said, my heart sinking.

"She was alone in the car," said Bibi, her hand flying to her mouth..

"Someone found the Beast," said Luc.

"Sarah?" I said, tapping my earpiece, "Can you talk? What's going on? Talk to us, Sarah."

She didn't answer.

We heard scuffling, then something heavy being moved. Suddenly Sarah wailed. "Leave me alone. I just wanna go home!"

A car door slammed shut. Whoever she was with wasn't talking.

"Stop it! Why aren't you listening to me?"

She sounded more angry than frightened.

Thunder exploded in my earpiece like someone had hit me inside my head. I jumped back involuntarily. Everybody did.

Did someone just slap her?

Sarah screamed and a torrent of fierce Arabic came through the airwaves. She wasn't taking her attackers serenely.

Luc and I exchanged a quick look. He nodded. I knew what we had to do.

I turned to Win and Bibi. "Go, hide in the rooms. Wait for us."

They reached to help the girl up. She shrank back, wide-eyed, mumbling something.

"I don't think she wants to go back to those rooms," said Bibi.

I could understand that, but we couldn't afford to lose any more of our team right now.

"Hurry," I said. "Please. This is for your safety." I wasn't sure if she understood, but she got up. Dragging her, Win and Bibi ran into the corridor. It was a relief to hear a door shut behind them.

Sarah's voice screeched in our ears again. "I don't wanna go with you! I told you already!"

Another car door slammed. An engine started.

Are they stealing the Red Beast?

We listened, heads cocked to the side.

"That's not ours," said Luc.

"You're right," I said.

I'd driven the Beast a hundred times and knew its special growl. When David bought the vehicle, he'd taken it to a local garage for an upgrade. With an engine more enhanced than any car its size or make on the road, it sounded different. What I heard right now was the subdued hum of a regular car.

"They're taking her away," I said, not moving.

But Sarah wasn't going quietly. She shrieked and struggled like an angry banshee. I was surprised they hadn't gagged her already.

I racked my brain. *Who is taking her? Where are they taking her? What do we do now?*

"Do we go after her in the Beast?" Luc asked, his brow furrowed.

I could see he was torn like I was.

We couldn't abandon Katy, Tetyana and David. I had no idea if more men were lurking in the back, or if they were planning an attack on them as we stood here, deliberating. Time was running out.

"What did you see inside?" I asked Luc.

"Not much. Just a huge warehouse with containers, equipment, and stuff."

"No one around?"

"There's a door to a room on the other end. Looked like a big office of some kind. A light was on, but it was hard to say if anyone's in there. The main warehouse, though, was empty."

"What about that basement?"

"Looked for it but didn't get a lot of time 'coz I heard Sarah scream."

I nodded.

"So, what do we do?"

"We get everyone out of here first," I said, making a decision. "Then we find Sarah."

"Sounds like a plan," he replied.

I was about to turn and go back into the corridor when we heard a car drive up to the building.

We should have expected it. But the headlights shining through the front gates took us by surprise.

My heart skipped a beat.

"They're coming here!"

The gate opened, and the vehicle drove in, its wheels crunching on the gravel. I felt sick with panic. *They'll spot the dead men soon. And if they find us here, we're done for.*

The truck roared up the driveway and halted, brakes screeching to an abrupt stop. A man let out a shocked yell. Another man screamed. Car doors opened and slammed shut. Then we heard footsteps. Running. Scampering about.

"They're coming inside!" said Luc.

I looked around me in alarm. Before I could say anything, Luc grabbed my arm and pulled me behind the closest crate.

The footsteps slowed, more cautious as they approached the open door riddled with bullets. We stayed huddled behind the wooden crate, not sure what to expect.

Someone stepped inside the garage.

We stopped breathing.

I heard low voices, then the sound of someone walking around the room.

We could hear Sarah's voice through our earpieces and echoing across the grounds now. She was crying, pleading, and shouting. I wondered if anyone was with her in the car or if they'd abandoned her in there, locked up.

I peeked out from my corner.

Two men in black suits were panning the room, guns in their hands. I'd seen them before. They were from the ambassador's security detail. They walked in a circle around the room in a daze. They stepped into the corridor and tried all the doors, banging on them, calling out names.

I prayed silently for Win and Bibi. *Please have your door locked.*

The main door at the end of the corridor screeched open, and the men's voices dissipated as it closed behind them.

In my pocket was the key to the room where the security goon was tied up. I fingered it, thankful Bibi had gagged him well.

After ten excruciating minutes, the men returned to the entrance and hollered at someone outside. Someone shouted back.

I counted.

That makes three men. There could be more.

Luc and I waited.

Soon, we heard the sounds of something heavy being dragged inside.

I peered outside and got the shock of my life.

The dead body of a man stared at me from across the room. He was propped carelessly on the floor in a half-seated position against a crate. He had a gaping wound on the side of his head, his jacket was steeped in blood, and his eyes were wide open. Lifeless. Staring right back at me.

But it was the tattoo of the scimitar on his arm that caught my eyes. He was one of the men I'd just shot.

I withdrew with a shudder. That face would haunt me for the rest of my life.

The two security men got to work, dragging and resettling the dead bodies in a row across from us. Five dead men in all.

Luc and I stayed behind the crate, petrified, praying they wouldn't search back here.

A truck door opened and Sarah's screams echoed across the grounds louder.

"Noooo! I don't wanna go back there! How can you do this to me?"

Someone was forcing her inside.

Ahmed?

I peeked out one more time.

Sarah staggered in through the open doorway. She wasn't gagged or bound, but she looked incensed.

I suddenly realized why.

Behind her, with an angry scowl on his face, walked her father, the ambassador himself.

Chapter Fifty-Five

He pushed Sarah across the room, toward the corridor.

The two men followed the father and daughter inside.

We heard them step through the main door into the warehouse. We waited a whole minute, counting silently under our breaths. After a quick peek outside to make sure no one was around other than the dead men, I tapped my earpiece.

"Win, Bibi?"

"We're in the room," whispered Win. "You okay?"

"Good," I whispered back. "But the ambassador's here. He kidnapped Sarah."

"What?" said Win.

"I knew it," said Bibi.

"Here's what I want you to do," I said. "Get back to the car and secure yourselves. Luc and I will find the basement and get the others out."

"Scope out the car and the area before getting in, okay?" said Luc. "Make sure it's safe. Use your weapons if you have to."

"Don't worry about us," said Win.

"Wait one sec," I said. "We'll cover you."

I took a deep breath and raised my gun. I turned to Luc. "Ready?" I stepped out from behind the crate, purposefully avoiding the bodies, and tiptoed toward the corridor with Luc next to me.

We crouched at the doorway to the corridor, listening intently. It was quiet. Even Sarah had gone silent. I wondered if they'd separated her or if they'd pushed her into the underground room with the others.

We trained our weapons on the main door at the end of the corridor.

"You can come out now," I whispered.

The girls unlocked their door and slipped out, followed by the Iranian girl.

"Run!" Luc said.

Holding hands, the three girls ran, disappearing behind us.

We waited in our position till we couldn't hear their footsteps any longer.

With a quick nod to Luc, I tiptoed along the corridor to the warehouse door.

It looked like a massive fortress once I got up close. Luc joined me and punched in the code he'd memorized earlier. While I trained my pistol at the door, he pushed the handle and opened it an inch. It was a heavy door, made of reinforced steel. Bulletproofed too, I was sure.

No sounds came from inside. It was spookily quiet, like everyone disappeared into a black hole once they entered this room.

Luc and I slid in and closed the door behind us gently.

I'd expected bright lights, but it was dark with only the fire escape lights illuminating the room. The place had been shut down for the night.

Massive shipping containers lined the walls. Forklifts, pallet trucks, carts, pulleys, trolleys, and other equipment sat haphazardly next to them. One container lay open, exposing its cargo: metal sheets and pipes. Another container carried crates piled to the top. It was what you'd expect to see inside a working warehouse near a shipyard.

A door creaked open and a stream of yellow light fell on the floor. Someone was coming out of the room at the far end.

Luc and I scrambled behind the nearest container.

A heavyset man walked toward us, carrying a handgun. His brow was lined with frustration and he slouched like he was exhausted. I'd seen him earlier, dragging the dead bodies in.

He walked to the main door, five feet from where we were hiding, checked it and lumbered back to the room, grumbling to himself.

Did they hear us come in?

We waited a full minute in case he'd appear again.

When we were sure we were alone, we scooted across to the nearest forklift. Then to the next and the next, staying hidden in the shadows. We did this until we got to the midway point. From here, we panned the room to see if we could spot a trap door or an entrance to a basement.

"Do you see it?" Luc asked in a whisper.

"Not yet," I whispered, shaking my head. We'd have to examine every inch of the floor to find it, but that meant we'd be out in the open and the men in that room could come out any time.

"Hey," a voice said in my ear.

I clutched Luc's arm. He gave me a terrified look.

"Who's this?" I whispered. "Win?"

"Tetyana," said the voice.

"What?" Luc and I exclaimed at the same time.

"Shhh..."

She was silent for a few seconds. "We lost contact when they put us in here. If I stand in one corner, though, I can hear you if you're close enough. Patchy but good."

"Where are you?" I whispered.

"Under the warehouse," she said.

"We're inside the warehouse," said Luc.

"Thought so. That's why we can connect," said Tetyana. "Opening's halfway across the room, smack dab in the middle, next to the yellow container."

Luc and I tiptoed out, looking for the container. It wasn't hard to spot.

"Found it," I whispered. "Now for the door."

Our eyes were glued to the ground but our ears were perked up, listening to any hint of a sound so we could run back to safety.

"There!" Luc whispered, pointing.

My heart gave a leap.

It was a gray latch on the floor, flushed with the concrete. I kneeled in front of it, praying it wasn't locked. There was no keypad or keyhole, just the latch that blended with the concrete. If we hadn't been looking for it, we'd never have spotted it.

"Think we found you," I whispered.

"Great. It's locked for us. See if you can open it from the outside."

Luc flipped the latch open.

This was too easy.

I looked up anxiously, waiting for an alarm to blare or a security light to go off. But it stayed quiet. If this had triggered anything, we'd have to take our chances.

Summoning all our strength, we pulled on the latch.

The concrete slab moved underneath us.

It was heavy, and it would make a lot of noise if we moved too fast. Working quietly, we shifted it an inch at a time. Once we'd pulled the block a few inches, I peered into the darkness.

"Hey," came David's voice from below. "Nice to see you."

It was too dark to see his face, but I could make the forms of people in the shadows beneath us.

I felt a pang of joy. But this wasn't the time for emotions. Luc and I kept working on the block, moving it slowly and steadily, inch by inch.

Once we'd opened it fully, I leaned back and surveyed the warehouse, looking for a ladder or a stepping stool.

"They're good," said Luc, nudging me.

I turned around to see David's hands clutch at the opening.

He pulled himself up and jumped out silently, like a puma. Within seconds, he was bending into the hole and pulling Katy out, while Tetyana gave her a leg up from the bottom.

"There are five more girls," David whispered as he plucked out a strange girl I'd not seen before. One by one, he pulled the rest of the occupants out. Tetyana came last and didn't need anyone's help.

I wanted to hug them, but we didn't have time.

With David's help, Luc and I put the slab back in place quickly and silently.

"They took our guns," whispered Tetyana. "They had these girls by the throat so we had to, or there'd have been a massacre."

The girls huddled in a group, frozen with fear. They looked too terrorized to speak.

None of them looked like Sarah. They looked more like Win, from South East Asia or thereabouts, except for one, a lanky blonde teenage girl. That was when I remembered what the security goon had told Bibi in the room under duress. *"A secret room. They built it to hide the girls they brought over from East Asia and Eastern Europe for the diplomats."*

One girl looked barely nine. She stared at me with fearful brown eyes, trembling. Like a frightened baby deer, I thought. At that moment, all I wanted to do was to pull her in, comfort her and cry with her. Cry for them. Cry for all the girls subjected to the unspeakable things humans are capable of.

"We have to hurry," Tetyana whispered. "Sarah's friends are in the far room. They took them there."

I swallowed my tears and touched my earpiece. "Win, Bibi?"

"Right here," Win's voice came through, to my relief.

"You okay?" Luc asked, anxiety in his voice.

"Car's secured. We moved to a new location closer to the shipyards."

"We have more girls here," I said. "Five in total."

"We know," said Bibi. "We can hear you. It's the basement that cuts the connection."

I looked at Tetyana. "What's the plan?"

"I'll need two of you with me and David," she said. "Someone needs to get everyone else to the car."

Luc stepped up. "I'll take the girls. And I'll stay with them in the car just in case."

"Roger that," replied Win through our earpieces. "We'll drive over to the side gate to pick you up. Bibi knows where it is."

"Good," Tetyana nodded. "Make it quick. Stay alert."

"We need weapons, though," said David. "I'd like my AR-15 right about now."

"You can have this," I said, handing the T3x sniper rifle to him. "There's more in the car. We'll go get them."

While Tetyana and David inspected the warehouse and made a plan, Luc ushered the girls out into the corridor. Katy and I escorted the group till we reached the side gate where the Red Beast was waiting, engine humming but lights off.

Once we said goodbye and the Beast drove off, Katy and I slipped back into the warehouse, carrying our stash with us.

We now had two semi-automatic rifles, two more handguns with extra cartridges and the nunchunks. We walked back, listening keenly to our earpieces for any signs of Tetyana and David being in trouble. So far, all we got was their urgent whisperings.

Katy and I had just got inside the warehouse doors when a sound came from the room at the end. We spread out, scrambling behind the containers, flattening ourselves against the wall.

From where I was, I saw two men walk out of the room. It was the security men who'd come with the ambassador. They were carrying much bigger guns now.

I did a double take. Even in the darkness, I recognized Tetyana and David's rifles, the ones they'd confiscated.

The men walked confidently toward the middle of the warehouse, to exactly where we'd been only ten minutes before.

They stepped up to the gray latch.

I froze.

I didn't dare look at the others, but I was sure they felt the same. They'd find the basement empty and start searching. We could stay hidden only for so long. I felt terror rising inside of me. I clutched my pistol.

This is how I will die. In a hail of bullets in a gunfight in a nondescript warehouse in the middle of nowhere.

One man reached down and pulled the latch open while the other man kneeled next to him and watched, holding on to his gun. It took the first man some time to pull the concrete block away.

My stomach lurched.

But instead of looking inside, the two men pointed their rifles into the basement and pulled the triggers.

The thunderous sound of bullets pumping into the cavern below echoed off the steel containers.

Chapter Fifty-Six

They only stopped when they ran out of bullets.

They threw the empty guns to the side, picked up the concrete slab and slammed it into the hole without even pausing to check their handiwork. They jumped to their feet and returned to their room without a glance back.

I don't know how long I stood frozen, horrified at what had just happened. Was Kali watching over me and my friends?

A tap on my shoulder made me turn. It was Tetyana signaling me to come out. Her eyes were expressionless.

I couldn't move. It was like my boots were glued to the floor and all the blood had been drained from my system.

"Can I take this?" she whispered, pointing at the extra weapons in my hand. Without waiting for an answer, she reached over and gently pried the rifle and the handgun off my numb fingers.

She slung the rifle on her back. "Get your Glock out," she whispered, as she racked the slide on her handgun. "And keep it ready."

I noticed David had the sniper rifle across his back and was holding the AK-47 in front of him.

Next to me, Katy looked as pale as I felt. She was staring, like a zombie, at the discarded weapons on the floor.

If we'd been behind by just ten minutes... I shuddered to even think of it.

"Listen up," said Tetyana. "From now on, only use initials to call each other, got it?"

Katy and I gave her an inquiring look.

"What's the pla—" I started, but David and Tetyana were already marching toward the office at the far end of the warehouse.

Katy and I followed them in the shadows, wondering what our plan of attack was.

Tetyana and David were no longer in stealth mode. They were making a beeline toward the door in a military stride. Their faces were taut and their eyes looked deadly. Katy and I moved out of the shadows and picked up our pace.

The faster we walked, the more confident my posture became and the more I felt I was ready for battle. Anyone coming out now would think twice before confronting us.

We were heading toward the warehouse supervisor's office. On one side of the room was a small kitchenette and on the other, a washroom with a sign that said "Men Only." Parked across from the office was a fleet of shiny new forklifts.

As we approached the area, we heard voices of men arguing in Arabic. The heated debate raging inside meant no one had heard us stomp up to their hideaway.

Sarah was still silent. I wondered if she was inside this office or if she was even alive.

Tetyana motioned Katy and me to hide. I selected the nearest forklift behind which I could remain hidden but still see through the space between the steel bars. Katy slipped behind the forklift across from me. David took position behind Tetyana and aimed his rifle at the door.

Then, to my surprise, she stepped up to the door and knocked.

The voices inside went quiet.

I aimed my gun at the door and held my breath.

Tetyana knocked again.

"Pizza delivery!" she called out.

Silence.

"Pizza delivery for the ambassador!"

The door flung open and the ambassador's enraged face popped out.

"Who the hell—?"

Tetyana had her handgun on his forehead in a flash. She grabbed him by his jacket collar, pulled him out and slammed his head against the wall.

"One move and you're a dead man," she growled before he could utter another word.

Pandemonium broke out in the room.

Men hollered. David shouted to everyone to put their hands up and come out, or else he'd put a bullet right through them.

"Get out, you motherfuckers!" yelled Tetyana.

"Hands in the air! Out!" shouted David.

I wished I had a better view inside the room, but I dared not move. There was a reason they wanted us armed and ready, hidden behind this machinery.

The two men who'd happily gunned the basement room stumbled out, shaken. David pulled them out by the collar and pushed them down, forcing them to crouch on the floor, their backs against the wall, hands in the air.

I squinted at the scene. Someone was missing from this picture. The girls and Sarah, yes, but there was someone else. Before I could formulate my thoughts, I heard the ambassador laugh a crude laugh.

We turned to him.

"I have trained security men, and you two punks think you can threaten us?"

Tetyana didn't skip a beat.

"Agent K!" she called out. "Find us some rope, please."

It took a second for Katy to realize Tetyana was referring to her. She stepped out with her gun, her flaming hair looking like an angry lion's mane, her mask making her formidably frightening.

The men stared at her, bug-eyed.

"On it," Katy said, with a smart salute.

A flicker of fear went through the men's faces. Their eyes darted around the warehouse, worrying about who else might be concealed behind the containers and machinery. Right now, it was just me. I leaned into the shadows even more and clutched my pistol, waiting for my turn.

I now knew what Tetyana was banking on. The element of surprise. The more shocks to the system, the more unnerved these men became, and the easier to control. Her rebel warfare experience was reemerging.

Katy rooted around a nearby workbench and brought out a thick yellow rope.

"Tie the bastards," Tetyana said, not looking up.

She still had the ambassador pinned against the wall, her arm against his chest, holding him in check. In her other hand was her handgun, its barrel pushed into the soft part of the man's stomach. I'd hate to see the mess if she pulled the trigger now.

While David kept watch over the security men, Katy tied them. That was when it dawned on me. *Where's Ahmed?*

My eyes swept the warehouse. I knew he wasn't among the dead men out front.

A strange muffled sound came from inside the office.

I peeked through the forklift's bars. I could only see a slice of the inside. It was well lit and from where I was, I glimpsed an elegant Persian rug and a plush coffee table with a hookah pipe on it.

Again, that sound, a muffled thudding, like it was coming from far away.

"Sarah?" Tetyana called out. "Is that you?"

Do they have another basement under this warehouse? Are more girls hidden in here?

Silence.

"Done," said Katy.

"Watch them," said David, stepping into the office.

We waited.

A faint smile crossed the ambassador's face.

That was when we heard the click of a key.

We turned toward the sound. The toilet door was opening slowly.

I felt a chill go down my back.

The door scraped on the ground as it opened wider.

"Who is it?" shouted Tetyana.

David jumped out of the room.

Freeze!" he yelled, turning in the direction of the toilet.

The pale faces of two adolescent girls thrust into view. Their hands were tied behind their backs and they were gagged, just like the other girl we saw. These must be the two other Iranian girls Sarah talked about.

Ahmed stepped out behind them. He had a smug smile on his face and a handgun in his hand. The gun was pointed at the girls' heads.

My heart sank.

Katy and David were pointing their guns at him now, but there wasn't much they could do. There wasn't much I could do either. The girls would get hit either way.

"Real men don't threaten little girls," Tetyana said. "You should be ashamed of yourself."

"They broke family honor!" Ahmed spat out.

"And how did they do that?" Tetyana asked in a charming voice.

That irritated the ambassador. "We don't have to tell you anything!" he yelled, his spit landing on her mask.

She didn't flinch.

"You can either talk to me now," she said in the calmest voice I'd heard from her. "Or you can talk to the FBI later."

The men on the ground stiffened at the mention of the FBI.

"I have diplomatic immunity!" roared the ambassador in Tetyana's face. "I'm not afraid of your FBI!"

Tetyana smashed him against the wall. "I'm worse than the FBI," she said with gritted teeth.

He exploded in her face, screaming in Arabic.

"You hit my father again and I kill these girls!" screeched Ahmed.

Tetyana thrust the gun against the ambassador's throat.

That shut them both.

"You may have all the immunity in the world," she said, "but how would your reputation hold if what you and your men did to these girls ever got out? Have you thought of that?"

The ambassador glared at her.

"No more cocktails. No more fancy parties. No more invitations to special committees. Zilch. Nada. The world will stay away from you, like the dirty rotten skunk you are."

The ambassador remained silent.

"Forget immunity. What about your credibility? There goes your prestigious job. Do you think your country will want your face to be shown on their diplomatic roster?"

"I'm a powerful man," he replied, clenching his teeth. "And you're just punks. Who are you anyway?"

"Oh, I'm sure you'd love to know," she said, and paused, glancing at the girls quivering in front of Ahmed. "First tell me, what did these girls do that was so bad, they had to be punished like this?"

The ambassador growled. "If our women disobey us, we punish them till they learn. How dare you question what I do with my own property?"

Property?

He was frothing at the mouth, his face contorted into an angry sneer. You could see how much he loathed answering to a woman.

"You stupid Westerners will never understand. I own them and I will do as I wish to them."

A crash from the office made us jump, including the ambassador.

"I'm not your property!"

We turned to look.

It was Sarah. She staggered out of the office, her dress ripped, her face red with rage.

Chapter Fifty-Seven

Ahmed's eyes widened.

"How did you get out?" he asked in a surprised voice.

"You think I'm just a stupid little girl!" Sarah turned on him, her eyes spitting fire. "You put me in a rape room. And I'm your sister! You treat me like a prostitute!"

"You are a prostitute!" shouted Ahmed, eyes bulging. "You run after white boys!"

"He's my boyfriend!"

"Don't talk to your brother like that!" snapped the ambassador, forgetting the position he was in.

Sarah took a bold step toward her father, who was glaring at her like an angry lion ready to rip its cub's throat out.

Tetyana tightened her grip on him. David and Katy stood their ground, their weapons trained on Ahmed's head. I leaned in. No one could say how this would end up.

The last thing we needed was for Sarah to start a physical altercation and make us lose control over the situation. Not that we had much control anymore.

Sarah was a foot away from her father now. She stared at him, her shoulders square, looking ragged but defiant.

"I don't belong to you! I don't belong to nobody!" she screamed. "I'm not your *property*!"

Her words echoed through the warehouse.

It took a minute for the ambassador to recover from his shock.

"You, you...*woman*!" he spat out as if that alone was an insult. "How dare you talk back to me?"

"You treat Ahmed like he's a prince and you treat us like animals!" Sarah shouted right back.

Ahmed scowled at her. "I will whip you with my belt if you don't shut up, dumb girl!"

Sarah ignored him.

"You black-hearted, ungrateful little cow," said the ambassador. "It's your duty to obey your father."

"Why?" Sarah matched her tone to his. "Why do I have to obey you? Who says you can treat me like a dog? Why does our culture say girls are nothing?"

Her face was flushed pink. There was a fire in her belly and it was growing strong. She was no longer a sniveling girl. She was blossoming into a young woman, finally discovering her voice.

From behind the forklift, I watched her in admiration. I hadn't known she had this in her. *You go, girl,* I said, silently. *You stand up for your rights. Stand up for your life.*

"I will thrash you for this! You have no shame!" cried the ambassador.

"You're gonna hit me because I wrote a love letter?" Sarah's voice was breaking now. "Just because I wanted to have a date with Tom? At least he treated me good. He even wanted to meet you and ask for your permission."

"You have no honor, you stupid girl!" Ahmed said, curling his mouth in disgust. "Back home, they'd take you to the town square and behead you. That's what happens in a civilized culture. Not like these barbaric westerners."

"You got off easy," said the ambassador. "The Iranians ordered the men to teach these girls a proper lesson. At least I told them to not touch you."

My eyes went to the two bound and gagged girls. Silent tears were streaming down their terrified faces.

"I should have never taken your mother, that worthless village whore. You're no better." The ambassador's face had turned purple. He raised his voice. "From now on, you will never set foot in my home again. You will no longer have a family. I disown you, you worthless woman!"

Sarah's face crumbled. She collapsed to the floor, her spirit gone.

"Oi!" Tetyana had had it. "Enough!"

"Father, why do we waste time with these unbelievers?" Ahmed spoke from behind the girls. "Let me get rid of them. Maybe I can have the other girls before I send them to hell where they belong."

The more I watched Ahmed, the more I expected him to spring horns on his head and fangs in his mouth. Even the devil, I was sure, had more humanity than him. I felt nauseous. *It's you who belongs in hell,* I wanted to yell, but I held my tongue.

"You touch one hair of those girls or of anyone else and your father's a dead duck," said Tetyana in a deadpan voice.

"Let my father go, you pagan bitch!"

"Let the girls go first," said Tetyana. "They've suffered enough."

He sneered at Tetyana. "You think I take orders from a woman?"

Tetyana pushed her gun barrel deeper into the ambassador's throat. He choked and spluttered.

"Wait," the ambassador spoke up, his voice hoarse. "No shooting. No more shouting." He paused for a second. "Perhaps we can negotiate."

All eyes turned to him.

"What do you suggest, Mr. Ambassador?" Tetyana asked.

"Let me and my men go and I will shower you with gold," he replied in a low tone. "Small unmarked coins."

Tetyana remained silent as if contemplating his offer.

"A million in real gold," added the ambassador.

"You know what?" she said, not letting her grip slacken. "I think you're a very savvy diplomat. I'd be happy to negotiate." She paused, her eyes gleaming. "But is that all you can offer?"

"What else do you want?" the ambassador asked her suspiciously.

"Here's my proposal," said Tetyana. From her tone, I could imagine a wicked smile breaking across her face behind that mask. "You will book a private jet to take us to a condo in Dubai with a few house-slaves, paid for. And two Lambos in the garage."

"You're mad." said Ahmed.

"How is that mad? We were looking for a summer vacation house. We'd also like a cheetah. You keep exotic pets back home, doncha? I'm sure you can spare one for us."

"You ask a lot," said the ambassador, grumbling.

"Well, it's your life you're bargaining with here. I'm sure it's worth more than just a million coins." She jabbed him with the pistol, making him gasp in pain.

"And, one more thing," she said.

He gave her a wary look.

"That Reza girl you have in your house in New York?"

A flicker of fear went through his face. He still didn't know who we were. I was the only person who'd spoken more than a few sentences to him before today, and he hadn't heard my voice. Not yet.

"I want you to call your head of staff right now and tell her today's her last day."

He blinked.

"Reza needs to be in a taxi in ten minutes and she needs to have twenty thousand US dollars in cash on her," Tetyana said, giving him a look that said, *Don't argue*. "A household like yours will have ample cash lying around. Rustle it up. Put it in a bag and give to it the girl. Then let her go."

He stared at her uncomprehendingly.

"Why don't you get your phone out and instruct your staff? No hanky panky. One of my team here speaks Arabic even more fluently than you."

It took a few seconds before he realized she was serious. He cautiously pulled his phone from his pocket.

"Agent K? Dial the number, please."

Katy stepped up and took the phone. She dialed the head of staff at the ambassador's house using the contact list on her own phone. She put the ambassador's phone on speaker mode and held it to his mouth. The two spoke in Arabic, so I turned to David to see his reaction.

From the conversation, it seemed the head of staff didn't at first believe him but acquiesced quickly. A direct call from the ambassador himself would be a rare occurrence for her.

"It's done," said the ambassador.

David gave Tetyana a slight nod.

"You're a very smart man," said Tetyana. "If I find you're lying, or if Reza is not free, the world will hear of your little operation here."

"They will follow my instructions."

"Wonderful. Now, how about the other promises?"

"A million dollars in unmarked small denomination gold coins. And you can buy your own condo and goddamned cheetah."

He was getting bold.

"Three million," snapped Tetyana. "Condos in Dubai are expensive."

"Two. Delivered by car in an hour to anywhere you want."

"How about here?"

"What do you mean?"

"Get them to deliver it here, to this warehouse. We'll be waiting."

The ambassador's face was now lined with sweat.

"Call them," commanded Tetyana.

He pulled out his phone again and made a call.

Something about the way David shifted told me the ambassador wasn't being honest. But David didn't intervene. He exchanged a quick glance with Tetyana. She'd felt it too.

"Okay," said the ambassador when he was done with the call. "My men will come with your gold in half an hour."

Tetyana nodded. "Sounds like a deal to me."

"So, now you must let me go," said the ambassador.

"Only if you let the girls go," said Tetyana.

"Only if you let my father go," snapped Ahmed from his corner.

Tetyana let out a sigh.

"Let's do this together in a civilized manner, shall we? On the count of three." She glared at Ahmed. "We both release our respective hostages at the same friggin' time. Understood?"

He glared back, challenging her.

"Deal?" said Tetyana, louder.

The son glanced at his father.

"Do as she says," the ambassador said in a tired voice.

"Deal," grumbled the son.

Tetyana turned to the ambassador. "Tell your son I'll have his head if he doesn't honor this agreement."

"You have my word," said the ambassador. "I'll have his head too."

"All right then, let's start," said Tetyana.

"One!"

No one breathed.

"Two."

The air got sucked out of the room.

"Three!"

Tetyana removed her gun from the ambassador's throat and stepped back. Ahmed pushed the girls away. They fell on the floor with a cry. Katy pulled them away from him.

Ahmed turned his weapon at Sarah, who was sitting in a crumpled mess on the floor.

"Sarah!" I shouted. "Watch out!"

She whipped around to see her brother aiming at her and screamed.

I stepped out and shot Ahmed in the chest.

Chapter Fifty-Eight

Ahmed fell to the ground, floundering and screaming.

The ambassador stared at his son in shock.

Ahmed was damaged but not dead. Not yet, anyway. If the man died, it would be for a good reason. *A justified killing,* I thought, gritting my teeth.

I looked up to see Sarah staring at me, her mouth agape, her face a mix of relief and horror. I walked over and pulled her up. She burrowed her face in my shoulder and broke into sobs.

Katy started removing the ropes and gags from the two terrified girls.

Tetyana didn't waste time. She started with the ambassador first.

The crack of the gun whipping his head startled us. In a few minutes, with David's help, she had him bound and gagged and seated next to his men.

One man kicked her as she passed by. Tetyana raised her pistol. He shrank back, regretting his decision. The sound of her weapon smashing across his face echoed through the warehouse.

Katy dug out water bottles for the girls from the kitchenette. They drank like they'd been stuck in a desert for years. One started washing her face, spilling most of the water on her dress. She pulled at her skin vigorously as if she wanted to rip off all the horror and pain she'd endured over the past few days.

The ambassador sat with his head buried in his bound hands. His two security goons hung their heads, resigned to whatever was coming.

Tetyana secured Ahmed despite his bullet wound. Ignoring his screams, she bound his hands and feet. Then she pulled him over to the others, leaving a trail of blood on the floor, and deposited him roughly next to his father.

He spat at her. In return, Tetyana whacked him with her gun, pulled a ball gag they'd used on the girls and stuck it in his mouth.

"What about the other men?" I asked Tetyana. "The ones supposedly coming with the gold coins."

She gave a sideways glance at the men on the floor who were staring at me now. She gave me a discreet motion to remain silent. That was when I remembered. The ambassador and his crew knew my voice.

I swallowed, hoping they'd not remember.

Or did they?

Tetyana motioned Katy and me to join her and stepped up to the men on the ground. Katy and I stood on either side of her, not sure what she was up to. The men looked up at her, fearful. I wondered if the girls they'd hurt, raped and murdered had looked at them the same way they were regarding us now.

Tetyana poked the ambassador with the butt of her rifle.

"Oi, we're leaving you alive so you can tell your people, your criminal cabal around the world, this is what happens to those who kidnap, hurt or mess with girls. You hear me?"

He stared at her with evil in his eyes.

"You hear me!" she roared and brought her weapon down with a sickening thud. The ambassador balled up instinctively, but he didn't have a chance.

I didn't need instructions. Screaming like Kali gone mad, I slammed my gun on Ahmed. Next to me, Katy whacked the two security goons, raining blows on their heads, their backs, their legs.

I was about to finish Ahmed off when someone pulled on my arm.

"That's enough."

It was David.

I stopped, trying to catch my breath.

He pulled Tetyana by the shoulder next.

"We don't need to do this. Let's get out of here."

She took a step back and looked at the men whimpering in a fetal position at our feet.

"Yeah, time to get outta here," she said.

After a final and thorough check around the warehouse to make sure we hadn't missed anyone or anything, we walked silently toward the main entrance and out to the parking lot.

In the dark, it was hard to say there had been a bloodbath here. But daylight would show the bullet holes and the pools of blood.

Tetyana called the Beast and agreed on a meeting spot three blocks from the Industrial Fishing Supplies building. We jogged toward the side gate of the warehouse, flanking the Iranian girls and Sarah, holding on to them, encouraging them to keep up.

I was still operating on pure adrenaline. My brain was whirring, trying to think about how we'd get away with all this.

Tetyana stopped us just as we slipped out of the gate.

"One last job," she said, taking out her phone. "Gotta call the cops."

"No!" Katy and I said at the same time.

"Yes," she replied. "This is why I got us burner phones with a voice change app."

She dialed a number.

We waited silently.

"Hello!"

Her voice came warbled through her mask, anyway. The app was a bonus, I thought.

"Oh, man, heard shooting at the shipyard. On the south side, I think. Hard to say. Sumthing's going on there. Crazy shit. You better come check, man." After blabbering like an overexcited citizen, she gave a fake name and address and hung up.

She turned to Katy. "Your turn. Put on your best New York accent."

After Katy, it was my turn. We decided David's voice might sound too suspicious, so he got a pass.

Once done, Tetyana removed the SIM cards and threw our phones in the bushes. Two blocks away, she scattered the SIM cards in a ditch.

"You do realize those men aren't bringing any gold," said David. We were jogging along the tree line now, staying as far away from the road as possible. "He called for reinforcement. He couched his words, but I knew he was speaking in code."

"Thought so," replied Tetyana. "But if they bring gold, it'll be a bonus."

"How?" Katy asked.

"One more suspicious activity for the authorities to investigate. That'll keep the heat off us."

"What will happen when they see the dead men in the garage?" I asked, trying to shake off the first pangs of guilt coming over me.

"That's why I gave you gloves and masks," said Tetyana. "They won't find a trace of us, even if they had cameras."

"There were no cameras," David said, "I checked. They wouldn't want any evidence of their own criminal activities, anyway. So that was helpful."

"The best thing that happened," said Tetyana, "was when they fired our guns into the basement. Did you notice they weren't wearing gloves?"

I shuddered at the memory. It was still too fresh. Still too raw. All I knew was we'd been lucky. Very lucky.

"Their fingerprints will be all over those guns, and the bullets from those very guns will be inside the dead men," said Tetyana. "It's a perfect setup. Unplanned but perfect."

"But won't they get away?" asked Katy. "Diplomatic immunity and all that? I feel like they'll be back doing bad things somewhere else."

I worried about the same thing. These girls were safe now, but I hated to think these men would get another chance to wreak havoc on other children, elsewhere.

Maybe we should have finished them.

"Even with immunity, there'll be lots of questions. Especially if someone brings bags of unmarked gold coins to the incident. Not to speak of the dead men, the weapons, the bullet holes, the rape kits..."

Chapter Fifty-Nine

We got to the Beast in ten minutes. It was hidden behind a nondescript office building.

"All good?" asked Tetyana as we dashed up to the car.

I looked in. All the doors and windows were open, and Win and Luc were hovering outside. Our super-sized SUV was full.

"It's gonna be tight in there," said Luc, surveying the three extra girls with us.

While Bibi ushered Sarah and the two new girls inside the car, the rest of us huddled next to the building.

We had many questions but no answers.

What were we going to do with everyone? How were we going to get them to safety, a place where they could get the help they needed?

We couldn't call a taxi or a rideshare for the girls. Even if we took them home, I couldn't turn the bakery and dojo into a refugee camp. If a health inspector came around, that would be the end of my contract with Chef Pierre and the end of our stay in America.

Our own presence in New York wasn't guaranteed. And our home wasn't safe. Unknown men were watching us and had even broken in. A mystery we still needed to solve. And we already had our plates full funding the orphanages back in Africa.

The whine of a crane made me look up.

I looked back at the girls. They'd each got blankets and water bottles. Bibi had the first-aid kit open and was tending to one girl's wound. The children looked drained. I couldn't even imagine what was going through their minds right now.

They need a place to sleep, to eat, and a place where they'd get proper care by doctors, nurses, and psychologists. And these kids can't wait.

Suddenly I knew. "The docks," I said, pointing up.

"What about them?" asked Tetyana, her eyes following my finger.

"We take the kids to the docks, as close as possible. They'll be safer. More traffic. More people around. Plus, seeing migrants near the docks isn't farfetched." I paused. "And we don't have to be involved."

"Win, Bibi, and Luc still have phones," said Katy, nodding. "So we can call for help with that voice app thing."

"Not the cops," I said. "But we can try Safe Horizon and tell them we found lost migrants at the shipyards."

David nodded. "These kids need serious help from people who know what to do with trafficked children. City cops will be as lost as we are."

Katy put her hand up to shush us.

"Hear that?" she said.

A police siren wailed in the distance.

"We need to move fast," Tetyana said.

"I saw a bus shelter on our way in," said David. "It's probably the middle of the night shift so no one will be around. We can park a block away and escort them there."

"We don't have space for everyone in the car," I said. "One or two of us can drop the kids off and meet the rest somewhere safe."

"David, Asha, you two get the kids to the bus stop," said Tetyana, nodding. "Keep a low profile. I'll stay here with the rest of our gang." She surveyed the area. "We'll find a place to hide and we'll radio so you can pick us up when you're done."

"I found Safe Horizon's emergency number," said Win, looking up from her phone.

Luc pulled out his mobile. "I can call them too."

"Give fake names and addresses," said Tetyana. "When you're done, hand over your phones."

While they made the calls, David and I closed the car doors and jumped inside the Beast. David took the wheel and got the car on the road.

I turned around in my seat to see how everyone was doing.

Sarah was gently rubbing the back of one of the Iranian girls who was lying on her lap. The others were sitting quietly, most with eyes closed, leaning against each other for comfort, huddled under the emergency blankets, hugging their water bottles.

I didn't know if anyone spoke English, but it was worth the try.

"Hey there," I said, showing them my hands, palms out, to look as nonthreatening as I could—as a black-clad, masked foreigner, one they'd seen carry a rifle only half an hour ago could, I guessed.

I spoke softly so as not to startle them. "You're all going to be safe now."

The few who were awake gave me blank stares.

I tried again. "You're free now."

I wished I knew their languages. I also wished I could take off my mask to make them feel safer. But Tetyana's orders had been strict; we were never to take our masks off during missions.

Sarah was the only person who understood what I was saying, and even she was regarding me cautiously.

"You know those bad men in that warehouse?" I continued. "They won't hurt you anymore."

More confused looks. This was harder than I thought.

"Sarah, I need your help."

She nodded.

"This group needs a guide. Can you be their leader?"

She sat up, interested, but I could see she was still wondering where this was going.

"I can do that," she said. "I'd like to do that. What do you want me to do?"

"A group of people will come to help you soon. When they arrive, tell them everything that happened to you." I paused. "But would you tell them you didn't see our faces? That you don't know who we are? Can you do that?"

She gave me a confused look.

"You see these girls?" I said, pointing to the kids in the back. "We can rescue more children like that if nobody knows who we are. But if anyone finds out, we'll have to stop this work. That's the only reason we could help you this time."

Her face cleared. She nodded. "I can cover for you. I know what happened to them. I want to help them and I want to help you too."

I sighed in relief. Every decent person usually wanted to support us when they knew what we were doing. I knew we could depend on her.

"Thank you, Sarah. We truly appreciate that."

A few of the girls had sat up and were leaning over to listen in to our conversation now. My heart went out to them. I wondered about their families back home. I wondered if anyone here had been sold by their own parents like Win had been. Or cast away like Luc had been.

"Don't be scared," I said, turning to them. "The police will be here soon. They're good police here. New York police. We also called a group who can help you. They will pick you up tonight and they'll make sure you get a safe place to clean up, get clothes, get food, get sleep, and—"

Sarah's face fell. "I thought I could come and stay with *you*."

I looked away, feeling guilty. I took a deep breath before speaking. Sarah flashed me a disappointed look as if she anticipated my answer.

"I'm so sorry, Sarah. You need professionals, honey. Someone who can find you a safe home and a good school for you. That's important." I sighed. "This is as far as we can go. We're not the right people to help you from here on."

I noticed the tears in her eyes. I reached over, squeezed her arm and held her for a while.

"I have no family now," she said, crying.

"None of us do," I said. "But we turned out all right. You'll be fine, Sarah. You're strong. You're smart. You're a powerful young woman. What you did today was very brave. You're a hero, you know that? That's how we all see you. Never forget that."

She looked away and wiped her eyes, but I knew she was listening.

"Can you make one promise to me?"

She nodded through her tears.

"I want you to finish school. Do well. When you're done and have passed all your classes, I want you to come and knock on our door. You can help us then."

Part NINE

Chapter Sixty

"Is the strawberry shortcake done?"

"Done like dinner," said Katy in a singsong voice. "Here it comes."

It was steaming inside the kitchen. We'd been baking since dawn, rushing to prepare an order for a high tea party at the Hungarian embassy.

David and Tetyana had closed the dojo for the day, feigning the flu. That kept everyone away. And that was good, because they had important work to do.

I'd had little time to think about the past forty-eight hours. My brain had strategically moved those memories to the back so I could focus on my task at hand.

It was nice to be in my bakery doing what I loved. The more I pretended life was normal, the better I felt. And that was what we all needed. A sense of normalcy.

Luc was decorating the chocolate crumpets. Katy was placing rows of colorful macaroons in a white box. The scones and finger sandwiches were done and already packaged. The silver trays with Chef Pierre's emblem were stacked on the counter waiting for the party.

We usually asked for extra hands from the culinary school when we had a big order like this, but I was glad it was just us in the bakery. I couldn't handle strangers coming in and out of our home right now.

I'd given Bibi and Win the day off, telling them to play a computer game, go on a shopping trip or to the nearest spa. Anything, I said, rather than sitting around moping or reliving the last few days.

Win had wanted to play a game and Bibi had wanted to go to the spa. In the end, they'd compromised and decided to get their nails done at the corner salon, get a massage and then come home to play video games till dinner.

As I piled the cakes boxes in a corner, I half wondered if we should find a therapist in town, someone the girls could talk to. No one, let alone teens, should be exposed to the things we had in the past forty-eight hours. But where would we even find someone to talk to? Someone safe? Someone who'd not call the authorities? I had no idea.

At least we had each other.

Now that the day's work had slowed down, my mind wandered again.

I wondered what David and Tetyana were up to. They'd walked over to the Russian bar to meet Olek for breakfast and talk about buying more hardware. They would also rethink our security system and come up with a more rigorous training plan for all of us.

I picked up the menu Anne had sent me that morning.

I needed a clear mind to make sure everything was ready and for that, I needed space to think. I stepped out of the kitchen and walked into our reception room. I pulled out a chair and took a seat at the table, glad to get off my feet.

I went through the menu items one by one, ticking each line and making notes in the margins for where we'd had to rustle up gluten-free, allergy-free specials. But it was hard to focus.

My mind kept shifting back to the kids. I knew I'd never erase the memory of the expressions on their faces as David and I waved goodbye. They'd looked so vulnerable. Their faces said, *Why are you abandoning us like this?*

We'd told them we weren't going far. We'd told them we'd watch over them till help arrived.

David and I had hidden behind a discarded steel container just around the corner from the bus shelter, waiting for Safe Horizon. But that didn't make me feel any better. It had taken enormous willpower to not bawl my eyes out on the way back.

We'd also taken a gigantic risk hiding close by, but we'd had a good backup story. If we heard footsteps, David and I were going for a heavy make-out session behind the container and we'd pretend surprise and embarrassment if we got caught.

That had been the plan. We'd never had to put that plan into action.

Two police cars arrived within minutes, their sirens screeching and their lights flashing, frightening the children. Somewhere behind us, I heard more police sirens, like the entire NYPD was rushing over to the shipyards. I just hoped they wouldn't make it hard for us to get out.

What we hadn't bargained for was for Safe Horizon to call emergency services when our calls went in. A police car with a siren could get to the kids faster than they could with their regular vehicles.

So, the four officers stood guard over the kids, talking into their walkie-talkies, scanning the area, but not doing much else. They seemed slightly overwhelmed at finding half a dozen migrant children cast away, alone, in the middle of nowhere like this, at night no less.

When the Safe Horizon team came and got out of their van, the four officers stepped aside to let them do their job, looking relieved.

One of the crew kneeled down and spoke to the youngest child. We couldn't make out what she was saying, but after a few seconds, Sarah stepped forward to speak. She was taking the lead.

This was our cue.

The officers would go on full search mode soon. We had to get away. And quickly.

David and I backed away from the container and walked silently to the Beast, which we'd parked nearby, holding tightly to each other's hands.

Though my heart felt burdened, my head knew we'd done the right thing. Those kids needed to get reunited with their families, wherever in the world they were, or find asylum here. They needed safety and security, which we couldn't guarantee.

This was what Bibi and Win needed as well, and god knew, the rest of us.

An emergency siren wailed in the distance, forcing me to the present, back to the bakery reception room.

I looked down at the menu in my hands, trying to focus. I had almost everything ready for the order, except for the special hazelnut coffee our guests wanted. I still had to brew a pot.

The siren was getting closer and closer. *Maybe there's an accident on the highway.*

I really needed to get back to the kitchen and finish my chores, but my mind shifted back to Saturday night. I wondered about Reza. *Did she get away? Where is she now? Did Sarah break down and tell the authorities about us?*

I pushed that last thought out of my head and was just about to push my chair back and get up when I felt something cold and hard on the back of my neck.

"Move or I shoot you dead."

My blood ran cold.

I knew that voice.

How did the ambassador get in here?

Without turning my head, I raised my eyes and scanned the reception area. All I had to protect myself was a plate of sample cakes, today's menu and my pen.

I took a deep breath to steel myself.

Behind me, the ambassador was wheezing heavily. He smelled like he'd not washed for days. A stinging whiff of antiseptic came from him. They must have patched him up and let him go, his diplomatic immunity kicking in.

Strangely, time seemed to have slowed down. My senses had heightened tenfold. I was feeling calmer than I should have been.

"I knew it was you," he growled. "When I heard your voice."

"What you were doing to those children was inhumane," I replied.

"You bitches got involved in something that wasn't your business," he replied, slurring like he was drunk.

The gun shook momentarily, but it pressed against my neck quickly. Behind me, I felt the ambassador sway. I wondered how he was even standing after the whacking he got from Tetyana.

From inside the kitchen, I could hear Katy and Luc chatting, the sounds of a tap open and close, a spoon against china.

"When evil happens," I said, "it becomes my business."

I closed my eyes and waited for the inevitable shot.

"Because of that, you and your stupid friends will die today."

Something stirred in me. Something strong, something black, something fiery. Kali was waking up.

"You embarrassed my family," he was saying. "And you killed my son."

I raised my eyebrows. *Ahmed is dead?*

"My son is dead! My only son." His voice broke. "I'm left with some useless women now. And my family's honor is all gone."

I snapped my head up.

"Your honor?" I said, gritting my teeth. "Your honor left you a long time ago."

Kali was fully awake now. I wasn't going to die today without a fight.

He laughed crudely. He seemed to enjoy this, toying with his victims.

I was holding the pen in my hand so tightly I could feel my nails digging into my palm.

I knew what I had to do.

I snapped around and slammed the pen right into his eye.

Chapter Sixty-One

The ambassador screamed and staggered back.

With a Kali warrior roar, I lunged forward and stabbed him in the face again and again and smashed his jaw with my right hand.

He dropped the pistol and covered his face with both hands.

Luc and Katy rushed out of the kitchen.

The police sirens were right outside our door. People were shouting. Car doors slammed.

"Asha!" Katy cried out.

"What the heck's going on?" said Luc, his eyes wide in shock.

A dark shadow crashed through our front door.

"Freeze!" a voice bellowed. "Police!"

I froze, and my pen fell to the tile floor with a clatter.

Two officers in full tactical gear stood on the bakery's threshold, aiming massive guns our way.

"Hands up!"

I brought my hands up. Katy and Luc did the same.

The ambassador uncovered his face and glared at the cops.

"You!" the police hollered at him. "Get your hands in the air! Now!"

The ambassador's face turned purple. He looked ready to implode.

"I'm a diplomat!" he roared.

A spittle of saliva streamed down one side of his mouth. His unbrushed hair stood on his head like he'd been electrocuted. And his left eye was bleeding from my stabbing. All this only made the police more nervous.

"On the floor! Down! Now!"

"Do you know who I am?" the man squawked in reply, beating his chest. "I'm an ambassador, you morons! How dare you shout at me! You have no control over me, you son of a donkey ass mother's dog!"

They closed in on him, bellowing, "get on the floor! Now! Down! Down!"

But the man didn't seem to hear them. He beat his chest and yelled, a man gone berserk.

His expensive suit was torn and dirty, and he had blood streaks all over his jacket. I could still see the scratch marks on his face where Tetyana had pistol-whipped him. He looked like he'd spent the night on a hospital floor or in a jail cell.

If he'd been in full form, I'd never have escaped him just now. I wondered about the state of his mind.

Without warning, he grabbed my plate of cakes and threw it at the cops.

They ducked.

He picked up my chair and smashed it over an officer.

That did it.

They lunged forward and slammed him, face-first, to the floor. He fought back, screeching like an enraged child. Within seconds, our little bakery was swarming with an army of cops.

Katy, Luc and I stood to the side, backs to the wall, stunned, watching the officers stream in and surround the ambassador's jerking body, trying to hold him down.

After handcuffing him, they peeled him off the floor and hauled him out. He hadn't stopped hollering and struggling, so it took four men to carry him out. The others trooped out after them.

The last remaining officer walked around the room as if checking for something. He peeked into the kitchen, then turned to us. We were still standing with our arms in the air.

"No one hurt?"

We shook our heads, too shocked to speak.

"You can put your hands down."

We obeyed.

"We followed him here. Stole a car at the hospital and hit two pedestrians on the way. Pretty badly. We nabbed him just in time."

We stared at him mutely.

He squinted at us from under his helmet. "Know the guy? Any personal connection?"

"We, er, made his daughter's sixteenth birthday cake," I replied. There were some things we couldn't hide. "The party was on Saturday."

He raised his eyebrows.

"Sounds like he didn't care for our cake that much," Katy piped up, poker-faced. "The party didn't go too well either. His daughter passed out on the cake."

He gaped, trying to find a suitable response. He finally took a step back. "You'll get called to the station to make a statement later today. Okay?"

We nodded.

With that, he stomped out the door.

We were standing rooted to our spots when the front door creaked open again.

I inched closer to my friends, wondering what fresh hell was going to come through those doors now.

It was William James, the CIA man.

He stepped in, looking professorial as ever.

"May I come in?" he asked from the threshold.

I stared at the apparition.

Taking our silence as a yes, he stepped in, closed the door, and walked up to us.

We watched him, warily.

"You didn't call me this weekend," he said, shaking his head. "I thought we had an agreement."

It took me a while to find my voice.

"I just had a man hold a gun to my neck," I said. "And you want to know why I didn't call you?"

He didn't answer. He stood there, rocking on the balls of his feet, surveying us.

"I know where you were two nights ago," he said.

Katy, Luc and I exchanged quick glances.

There was no accusation or hostility in his expression. Just disappointment.

Before we could reply, the door opened, and in marched Tetyana and David, looking grim. They stopped short when they saw James.

"Come on in," he said, seeing them. "Just wanted to have a quick chat with you all. Come right in."

Something about that made me snap. "This is our home!" I said. "Don't tell us if we can come or go into our own home!"

That didn't seem to faze the CIA man.

"I was merely being courteous, Ms. Kade," said James, holding up his hands. "Speaking of which," he turned back to Tetyana and David, "no problems coming in, I trust? I put a word in for you."

David gave him an angry look.

"Oh, nothing to bother about," said Tetyana, her lips curled in scorn. "Just had to walk by a dozen cop cars, a screaming maniac and a team of riot police who wanted to see our ID. Every one of them."

I searched the man's face.

"Why are you here?"

He sighed and rubbed his face as if trying to find the right words. When he spoke, it was in a regretful voice.

"You do realize you have committed so many crimes on American soil this weekend that you could be put away for a long time?"

He waited for an answer, but no one spoke.

We all knew silence was a tactic to make us blurt out everything. David had told us about the interrogation techniques of the intelligence world. *We might be novices, but we're not that naïve.*

I was thankful Win and Bibi were at the spa. They'd not have kept quiet for too long. I didn't know what would happen next, but whatever it was, I was glad they weren't here to see it.

Luc spoke first. "So, you're here to haul us off to jail, is that it?"

The man shook his head. "The CIA does its business overseas. I have no jurisdiction here. Not in this city. Not in this country."

He paused and looked at us. I thought I saw a glint in his eyes. "Would you like to know how the children are doing?" he asked in a soft voice.

I glimpsed a warning in Tetyana's and David's faces.

"How are they doing?" Katy asked before anyone could stop her.

The man's demeanor changed. He seemed to relax a little.

"They'll survive. They need a lot of help and it will be a long journey to recovery, but they'll make it through," he said. "They're with ORU now."

"ORU?" Katy asked.

"Operation Railroad Underground. A rescue organization headed by one of our own retired officers. They'll take good care of them."

"The, er, kids tell you anything?" asked Luc.

I closed my eyes again. *Wrong question.*

The man shook his head.

"I saw photos of the scene. Foreign diplomats and all that, so a good friend at the FBI let me take a peek. I must admit, you did an expert job covering up your tracks."

Chapter Sixty-Two

"We don't know what you're talking about," said Tetyana in a guarded voice.

"Look," said the man, his brow furrowed, "it's a little too late to make up stories. This operation has your signature all over it. If you think you're fooling me, you're wrong."

No one spoke.

"Didn't I tell you not to get involved with these diplomats?"

"And leave those kids to be treated like animals?" Katy snapped. "Do you think any of us could have lived with ourselves if we did that?"

"You know what your problem is?" James replied. "You're idealists. Idealists are lovely, but they don't think. They only feel. And that's what gets you in trouble and makes you muck up jobs."

"We did a bang-up job!" cried Luc. "We got eight kids out of a hellhole. They'd still be there getting tortured or killed if we hadn't got them out!"

I closed my eyes again. This man was good at making us talk.

"You've got one thing working for you. Local cops think it's foreign gangs fighting foreign gangs. They're still trying to figure out who did what to whom. It was messy. Real messy." He paused and regarded us gravely. "But you already knew that."

He knew way too much.

"The Saudi government has intervened and demanded the bodies be flown to their country. The FBI doesn't want to lose evidence, so they will fight it. But no one wants the media involved or an international incident of any sort. So this investigation will drag under the covers for months. Maybe years."

I listened, half-fascinated to know what was happening behind the scenes, half-fearful of where this was going to take us.

"The fact that all this took place in a Hastein-owned warehouse makes it even more challenging."

It was my turn to forget not to speak. "Is there a connection here to the head of the State Department?"

"No one knows for sure yet, but I'll tell you this. This doesn't look good for anybody. Least of all for the Secretary of State. Someone will put a lid on this if they haven't already."

"Wow," said Luc.

"Right now, the ambassador's story isn't cutting it. His daughter is ready to give a testimony, and that is enough to expel them all. The spotlight will be on them."

"Where's Sarah now?" asked Katy.

"In a safe house with the other kids. In exchange for information, she should get asylum but no one will admit to this, of course. Her family is ready to get on a plane and get back to Saudi Arabia without her tomorrow. They don't care. They're just worried about their reputation." He paused. "They skipped our jail because of immunity. But if you ask me, they won't get a warm welcome when they land at home."

"Hope not," I said. "They don't deserve a welcome from anyone, anywhere."

James nodded. "I've been in this business for a long time. The Saudi government's going to distance themselves from the ambassador. They'll put him in jail and make a big public relations fuss. And we can rest assured the Saudi jails will be far more hellish than anything he'd face here in the US."

He turned grave eyes on us.

"Though between you and me, we all know the madness will continue under the radar. Women will be imprisoned for wanting freedom. Girls will be kidnapped for torture. And slaves will be sold and bought from Asia and Africa. That's regular business."

He looked genuinely sad. Weary, like all the world's problems had settled on his shoulders. I detected a hint of regret in his voice, like he was trying to atone for his past. I wondered what kind of work he'd done before. For a split-second, I felt for him. The CIA man almost looked human.

"Can we see them?" asked Katy. "The kids and Sarah, I mean."

He shook his head. "I wouldn't advise it. You've done enough. More than enough. You want no connections between this incident and any of you. My advice is to lie low."

"Why are you telling us all this?" asked David, who'd been watching, his arms crossed and a deep frown on his face. "What do you have to gain?"

The man looked crestfallen. "Well, I'd hoped you'd all chime in and say very nicely *thank you, Mr. James.*"

"Thank you?" Tetyana said with a scowl.

"Do you know how many favors I had to promise to get this information? The FBI are hoarders. Those buggers hate sharing. I'll let you know, I threw in a few red herrings to make sure your tracks remain covered."

"Why are you protecting us?" David asked.

"Because my original offer still stands. You are talented, but you need training. Badly. If you want to change lives, you have to learn the business. We can make change together."

I shook my head. "Not going to happen," I said, quoting one of Tetyana's favorite lines. Even though I saw a flicker of human in this man, I still didn't trust him.

"Look," Tetyana said. "Like you said, there's no point hiding our past. Between all of us, we've made enemies on four continents. How do we know you're not someone sent to get us?"

"Your imagination's running a bit wild, isn't it?" he replied. "Didn't I give you the name of my superior in Washington to call and confirm?"

He had, but calling any authority wasn't something any of us wanted to do. One wrong word and we could get expelled, deported, jailed, even. *Who knows?* As if we'd take that risk.

"People planted bugs in our building," Katy said. "They broke in here in the middle of the night, and you're wondering why we're a little suspicious?"

Luc nodded. "We have the right to be paranoid as heck."

"Ah, yes," said James, as if remembering something. "That was unfortunate. The officers let those two men go. They convinced them they were in the wrong building for some electrical work, and the cops and security believed them." He shook his head. "If I'd got to them in time, I could have at least questioned them or got someone with the right authority to do so. That was bad timing."

"So, they're out there somewhere?" asked Luc, nervously.

"One more reason for you to join us," quipped James.

We stared at him.

"You'll be one of us, and we take care of our people. Now, that's a formidable weapon to have on your side."

I had to agree. He had a good point.

"I'm going to give you some time to think about this." He paused. "Ladies and gents, next time you even *think* about doing something like this again, call me. I won't be able to save your buts again, post facto."

With that, he turned around and walked out, hands in his pockets and head down, like he'd just had a disappointing conversation with a bunch of failing students.

The five of us stood in a circle staring at each other.

I was sure everyone's brains were buzzing like mine, but no one spoke.

The bakery phone rang, startling us all.

Katy stumbled over to it and turned it on.

"Bonjour!" the jovial voice of Chef Pierre boomed into the room.

"Bonjour, Chef Pierre," Katy replied.

"How are you doing today, Mademoiselle Katy?"

"Good," said Katy, not at all sounding good, "Er, excellent, thank you. And you, Chef?"

"Magnifique! Is Mademoiselle Asha there?"

"I'm here, Chef," I said, leaning toward the phone. "It's nice to hear from you."

"Marvelous, marvelous, even after that incredible fiasco at the Saudi ambassador's house. Can you believe it? Haha! It was madness. Poor girl though," he said. "Too bad about your beautiful cake. Well, it wasn't your fault. I can tell you the diplomatic community is buzzing with dirty gossip right now. It'll keep them occupied for months."

He had no idea.

"Mademoiselle Asha. I have a scoop for you!"

He sounds smug, I thought. I really didn't want any more scoops. I'd had enough for a lifetime, but I couldn't tell him that. I forced a smile on my face.

"I can't wait to hear the news, Chef."

"We've been invited to cater to the biggest fundraising gala in the country! Everyone will be there. Texas tycoons. LA celebrities. Politicians and diplomats from Washington. Former presidents."

He paused, waiting for my reaction.

"Wow. That sounds amazing," I said, trying to perk up. What I really wanted to tell him was I was done with diplomats. Forever. But I couldn't do that. "How marvelous, Chef. Congratulations!"

"Madame Bouchard worked her charms, as usual," Chef Pierre was saying. "There was a lot of competition but they wanted me, *bien sur.* Voila, mademoiselle! And we have a beautiful contract. Didn't

I tell you we will make inroads into America together? I'll be as famous here as in Europe!"

I took a deep breath. "I cannot tell you how happy I am to be part of this journey with you."

"Mademoiselle Asha," he boomed. "Get your team ready. You're going to the City of Angels!"

• • • •

—THE END –

• • • •

Read the first chapter of the next Red Heeled Rebels book here.

The Girl Who Knew Their Names

Chapter One

Two pairs of white-gloved hands pulled open the massive double-doors for us.

With a nod to the butlers, Katy and I stepped inside the most elegant ballroom I'd seen in my life. We were on the penthouse floor of a five-star hotel on Sunset Boulevard. It was a venue fit for royals. This was where the pampered celluloid kings and queens of the City of Angels hung out.

It was a swanky gala dinner, graced by the glamorous glitterati of this town. This lavish celebration was being streamed live across the globe for the masses to watch as they sat on their couches, chomping on popcorn and sipping on sodas. The world was watching, glued to their screens, eager to glimpse their favorite silver screen stars, keen to gossip about their hair-dos, outlandish dresses or irrational love lives.

Little did they know they were about to witness a murder in real time.

The hand-selected guests in this room had received their invitations tucked in white gift boxes wrapped with gold ribbon. As if the exclusive invitation alone wasn't enough, inside those boxes had been jewelry pieces encrusted with precious stones, hand-carved platinum pens and miniature jade carvings that together would have cost more than a small car. This was not a proposal one declined lightly.

Hollywood never played small.

I tried not to gawk. Everyone here was stunning, dressed in simmering ball gowns and stylish tuxedos. The flash of gold, platinum, silver, diamonds, pearls and precious stones twinkled to us from all corners of the room.

Though Katy, with her fiery red hair, impossibly long legs, and slender Irish genes, could have passed for a starlet, we were clearly the odd ones out. I was especially out of place, a petite half-Asian girl in my little black dress and signature red heels. I had my hair up in a bun and wore my makeup light. This was our semi-uniform as the official catering partners to the celebrity Chef Pierre from Europe. He was the caterer every high-society VIP clamored to have at their functions around the world.

The gala was celebrating its twenty-fifth anniversary, and The Red Heeled Rebels catering company had been commissioned to make the honorary cake on behalf of Chef Pierre. Katy and I weren't at this party as guests. We were working.

We glided discreetly into the room, maneuvering our way around the celebrity tables, rolling our shiny chrome trolley on which sat the most extravagant five-tier cake I'd ever made. Stamped on the base of each royal blue tier was Chef Pierre's famed logo in silver-colored icing.

My heart thumped louder with every step I took. I couldn't believe I was here. My dream had come true. This was why I'd spent copious hours pouring over recipes and experimenting for years until the day I found the exotic secret formula that hooked Chef Pierre and his discerning clients.

My life had changed the day he'd discovered my talents. Never in a thousand years had I imagined a girl from the slums of India would end up serving to Hollywood's finest. I'm sure Katy felt the same way. She began her life as a runaway in the back alleys of Toronto, digging for scraps of food in garbage bins.

We had finally made it.

What I really wanted to do was somersault down the center aisle. Instead, I pasted a polite smile on my face, the kind that said I'm happy to be here but I know my place. I knew the famous A-listers smiling our way, were smiling at my cake. Not us. We were invisible to them.

"Hey, Asha?" Katy whispered with a giddy look. "Can you believe this? What are we even doing here?"

"I know. Crazy, isn't it?" I whispered back.

Keeping our professional smiles intact, we pushed the cake to the front of the room, where the Master and Mistress of Ceremony stood, waiting to announce the lucky person who'd get invited for the cake-cutting ceremony.

As Katy and I had practiced more than a dozen times before, we carefully transferred the cake from the cart onto the podium. I plucked a silver-plated cutting knife from the cart and placed it on a gold-trimmed serving plate.

Our first job was done.

We stepped back, dissolving into the background. We still had work to do. After the cake-cutting ceremony, our next job was to slice the cake and serve it to the tables, greeting guests in French and leaving them with a taste of the old continent—exotic yet dignified. Chef Pierre had trained us well.

"Mr. Eddie Manx, would you do kindly the honors?" boomed the Master of Ceremonies into the mic.

The room broke into applause.

Everyone knew who Manx was. Even me. He was the most prominent Hollywood director who'd just been acknowledged for a lifetime of film making that evening.

I watched the silver-haired man push his chair back and get up. He brushed his lapel and flashed a smug grin at the actress sitting next to him. She was wearing a gorgeous maroon lace gown and her hair pulled back into a high ponytail. I recognized that distinct unibrow. She was Maria Pablo, an eighteen-year-old who'd moved to LA from Mexico City only a year ago. Her fast rise to fame had surprised many and had set the tabloid tongues wagging.

I noticed she didn't smile back. She didn't even clap. Even from where I was standing, hidden in the wings, I could see an unhappy darkness on her face. She looked down and pretended to play with the purse on her lap.

Manx strode up to the front, chest out, arms swinging, a cocky expression on his face, like he owned the place. In fact, he did. He'd made the careers of most of the actors and actresses here. It was clear he'd expected to be called up for the honor.

A strange movement at his table made me turn.

It was Maria.

She was getting up slowly but deliberately, her heavy makeup gleaming under the lights of the crystal chandelier above her table. A black handgun glistened in her hand. Her face was taut. Her dark red lips were set in a grim line. She knew exactly what she was doing.

I watched her petrified, feeling like I was viewing a slow-motion movie scene. I wanted to scream to everyone to watch out, but my mouth refused to open.

Her tablemates gawked at her, too frozen to speak, to call out, to stop her. None of us, it seemed, believed what was happening right in front of us.

The shot rang out.

Manx crumpled to the ground, grasping his chest, two feet from my beautiful cake.

The Master and Mistress of Ceremonies stepped back, horrified.

The room erupted in screams.

• • • •

CONTINUE THE ADVENTURE...

Do you want to know what happens to the Red Heeled Rebels next?

You'll find out in the next book in the Red-Heeled Rebels series.

Asha thinks she's snagged the most coveted catering job in Los Angeles. But she doesn't realize she's about to face the most powerful predator in town on her first day...

The Girl Who Knew Their Names is a gritty tale of crime and deception that will take you on a crazy jaunt from the dingy back alleys of the City of Angels to the glitzy Hollywood galas where you will rub shoulders with stars and starlets, but where you can trust no one.

Click on the book cover or here to get The Girl Who Knew Their Names.[1]

www.books2read.com/TheGirlWhoKnewTheirNames[2]

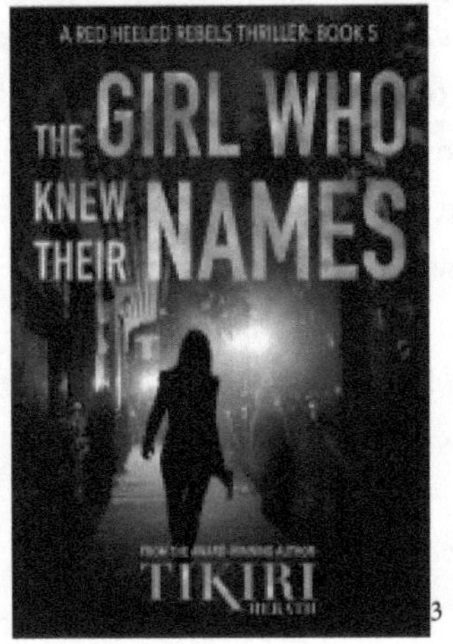

[3]

1. **http://www.books2read.com/TheGirlWhoKnewTheirNames**
2. **http://www.books2read.com/TheGirlWhoKnewTheirNames**
3. http://www.books2read.com/TheGirlWhoKnewTheirNames

Your Gift

Would you like to find out what happens to Sarah?
Download your exclusive copy of the epilogue short story here:
Epilogue story for The Girl Who Broke Free[4]
www.BookHip.com/PJPGJ[5]

4. http://dl.bookfunnel.com/uflzbon7z3
5. http://dl.bookfunnel.com/uflzbon7z3

The Red Heeled Rebels Series

In a world where justice no longer prevails, six iron-willed women rally together to seek vengeance on those who stole their humanity.

This is a story where the thrill of *Kill Bill* meets the wrath of *The Girl with the Dragon Tattoo.*

If you like gripping thrillers with flawed but gutsy heroines, vigilante action in exotic locales and twists that leave you at the edge of your seat, you'll love these books by multiple award-winning Canadian novelist, Tikiri Herath.

Pick up the Red Heeled Rebels books for a heart-pounding international adventure without having to get a passport or even buy an airline ticket!

• • • •

WHAT READERS ARE SAYING on Amazon and Goodreads:

- "Fast-paced and exciting!"
- "An exciting and thought-provoking book."
- "A wonderful story! I didn't want to leave the characters."
- "I couldn't put down this exciting road trip adventure with a powerful message."
- "Another award-worthy adventure novel that keeps you on the edge of your seat."
- "A heart-stopping adventure. I just couldn't put the book down till I finished reading it."

- "Kept me mesmerized and captivated with the rich descriptions which made me feel like I was actually inside the story."

- "This is a fantastic read that will have you traveling the globe. I absolutely loved this book. You won't be able to put it down!"

- "A real page turner and international thriller. Reminds me of why I've always loved to read. Because I can visit worlds and places I wouldn't ordinarily get to see."

To learn more about this addictive series, go to www.RedHeeledRebels.com[1]

• • • •

PREQUEL: THE GIRL WHO Crossed the Line

A reckless girl. A grave mistake. A fateful destiny.

All she wanted was to belong. Then, she committed an unforgivable crime...

• • • •

BOOK ONE: THE GIRL Who Ran Away

An estranged orphan. A treacherous plot. A perilous journey that could kill her.

She'd just survived a fiery car crash in the middle of nowhere. Both her parents are dead, but that's nothing compared to what she would face next...

• • • •

BOOK TWO: THE GIRL Who Made Them Pay

1. http://www.RedHeeledRebels.com

A kidnapped friend. A forbidden house. A precarious journey to escape their captors.

They are fleeing a fate worse than death. They think they're finally safe in London, when one of them is snatched into a waiting black cab. And now, she will do anything to find her friend...

• • • •

BOOK THREE: THE GIRL Who Fought to Kill

A lost cousin. A heinous crime. An impossible rescue that risks it all.

She was ready to cross oceans to hunt down her stolen cousin. But she didn't know the terrifying stakes waiting for her on the other side that will test her resolve and courage...

• • • •

BOOK FOUR: THE GIRL Who Broke Free

A sweet sixteenth birthday banquet. A missing diplomat's daughter. A menacing family secret.

She thought she'd finally made it when she was invited to cater for the swankiest party in upscale Manhattan. But she didn't realize the birthday girl's family has other plans and the banquet is a ruse for something more perilous than she could ever imagine...

• • • •

BOOK FIVE: THE GIRL Who Knew Their Names

A glittering Hollywood gala. An actress with a dark vendetta. A cold-blooded murder among the stars.

She thought she'd snagged the most coveted catering job in Los Angeles, and a chance to meet A-list celebrities. But she didn't realize she was about to confront the most powerful predator in town on her first day...

• • • •

BOOK SIX: THE GIRL Who Never Forgot

A girl from the swamps. A family gripped by darkness. A killer on the loose at the Mardi gras.

She was invited to cater a lavish ball where New Orleans' blue-blooded families celebrated Mardi gras in style, away from the cacophony of common street parades. But she didn't realize a murderer was lurking in the shadows, waiting to frame her for their deed...

• • • •

AWARDS & PRAISE FOR The Red Heeled Rebels books:

- Grand Prize Award Finalist - 2019 Eric Hoffer Award, USA
- First Horizon Award Finalist - 2019 Eric Hoffer Award, USA
- Honorable Mention General Fiction - 2019 Eric Hoffer Award, USA
- Winner First-In-Category - 2019 Chanticleer Somerset Award, USA
- Semi-Finalist - 2020 Chanticleer Somerset Award, USA
- Winner in 2019 Readers' Favorite Book Awards, USA
- Winner of 2019 Silver Medal - Excellence E-Lit Award, USA
- Winner in Suspense Category - 2018 New York Big Book Award, USA
- Finalist in Suspense Category - 2018 & 2019 Silver Falchion Awards, USA
- Honorable Mention - 2018-19 Reader Views Literary Classics Award, USA
- Publisher's Weekly Booklife Prize – 2018, USA

Asha Kade Murder Mystery Series

How far would you go for a million dollar payout?

A private investigator gets a million dollars from an eccentric client's estate every time she solves a cold case.

Asha accepts this bizarre challenge, but what she doesn't bargain for is to be drawn into the dark underworld of her past again.

The only thing that propels her forward now is a burning desire for justice.

• • • •

TRYING TO ESCAPE HER troubled past, Asha Kade starts a new life in New York as a celebrity baker for the city's socialites.

Business is booming. Her high-society clients love her creations. She is engaged to the love of her life and she is surrounded by her closest and most loyal friends.

Things are looking up.

Finally.

Until one day, an unusual bequest from a former wealthy client draws her back into the dark underworld of murders, kidnappings, and the haunting crimes of her youth.

For every cold case she will solve, her client's estate will award her a million dollars. But this reward comes with a twist. It must all go to a charity registered to help trafficked and orphaned children.

Asha has no choice.

She is compelled to fulfill the dying woman's last wish.

Especially as the benefactors of her work will be those who have endured horrors much like she had in her youth.

Fighting her own past demons, Asha gets drawn further and further into a new life of investigating cold cases no one else can crack. Cases someone would rather she not solve....

But there is no turning back for Asha now.

• • • •

IF YOU LIKE GRIPPING mysteries with twists and turns that leave you at the edge of your seat, and a strong female protagonist who isn't afraid to look villains in the eye and fight for justice, you'll love this murder mystery series by multiple award-winning Canadian novelist, Tikiri Herath.

Pick up the Asha Kade Murder Mystery books for a pulse-pounding, bone-chilling adventure from the comfort and warmth of your favorite reading chair at home.

Can you find the killer before Asha does?

• • • •

BOOK ONE: MERCILESS Legacy

BOOK TWO: Merciless Games

BOOK THREE: Merciless Murder

BOOK FOUR: Merciless Lies

BOOK FIVE: Merciless Secrets

BOOK SIX: Merciless Silence

• • • •

TO LEARN MORE ABOUT this exciting new series, go to www.TikiriHerath.com/mysteries[1].

1. http://www.TikiriHerath.com/mysteries

Dedication

This book is dedicated to Tuti Tursilawati, an Indonesian maid, who defended herself during a violent rape attack from her Saudi owner by killing him in 2018. For trying to save herself from a life of mental and physical terror, Saudi Arabia responded by summarily executing her by beheading, with no due process.

She is one of many migrant women who have lost their lives to this brutal, misogynistic and barbaric regime.

• • • •

TRUTH IS HARSHER THAN Fiction

These are a few women who have dared to escape the misogyny of Saudi Arabia and it's neighboring nations. They have shown courage in the most difficult of circumstances, some paying with their lives in their quest for freedom:

- Rahaf Mohammed - https://www.bbc.com/news/world-us-canada-46873796

- Rotana Farea and Tala Farea - https://nypost.com/2019/01/26/why-women-are-so-desperate-to-escape-saudi-arabia/

- The Reem and Rawan sisters - https://www.theguardian.com/world/2019/mar/25/now-i-own-my-life-saudi-sisters-who-fled-family-granted-asylum

- Dina Ali Lasloom - https://en.wikipedia.org/wiki/Dina_Ali_Lasloom

- Mashaal bint Fahd al Saud - https://en.wikipedia.org/wiki/Mishaal_bint_Fahd_bin_Mohammed_Al_Saud

- Samar Mohammad Badawi - https://www.hrw.org/news/2018/08/01/prominent-saudi-women-activists-arrested

- "Laura" (Anonymous) - https://www.wbur.org/onpoint/2019/01/17/rahaf-mohammed-saudi-arabia-women-escape

- The secret network of women who watched over Rahaf Mohammed's escape - The Fifth Estate - https://www.youtube.com/watch?v=VQW5_P6XNsk

- Women are trying to escape Saudi Arabia, but not all of them make it - ABC News - https://www.youtube.com/watch?v=4_NppxAt_cY

- Most women in the Arab world are disadvantaged socially - Business Insider - https://www.businessinsider.com/arab-women-of-privilege-have-it-worst-of-all-2019-2

• • • •

"The world will not be destroyed by those who do evil, but by those who watch them without doing anything." - Albert Einstein

AS I RESEARCHED, PLANNED, and wrote these novels, I spoke with women and men from around the world, some of whom I'd never met before. They included women who are tirelessly fighting for equality and dignity in South Asia and the Middle East despite the push back and hostility from their own families and communities.

They included former military officers and peacekeepers who had been deployed to conflict zones and saw the heart-wrenching plight of children, but had neither the resources nor the permission to assist them.

Regardless of where they came from, they all shared with me their stories. They read mine. Most importantly, we discussed the difficult topics in these books frankly and without prejudice. I gained many insights through these chats, but one lesson I took away was there are good people everywhere.

These are the good people who do not apologize for harmful traditions nor tolerate cultural dogma. These are the good people who yearn to change age-old customs that subjugate our daughters and alienate our sons. These are the good people who desire to create a better world for all humanity, for now and for the future.

I was surprised to see how much of our world views we share, regardless of differences in gender, vocation, political views, sexual orientation, or nationality.

We all have more in common than not. And this gives me hope, hope for a wiser, kinder, open, and more connected global community that uplifts us all.

Acknowledgments

To my amazing, talented, superstar editor, Stephanie Parent, thank you, as always, for coming on this literary journey with me and for helping make these books the best they can be.

••••

TO MY FANTASTIC INTERNATIONAL team of beta readers who helped me through this adventure, who cheered me on as I toiled, and who gave me their frank feedback, thank you. In alphabetical order:

- Blessmore Chikwakwa, Zimbabwe
- Carolyn Pennett-Staresinic, Canada
- Cyndi Wannamaker, USA
- Julie Young, USA
- Michele Kapugi, USA
- Otivbo Akhigbe, Nigeria

••••

A SPECIAL THANKS GO to Scott Jones (Canada), H. K. Slade (USA), and J.P. Medved (USA) who read my manuscript to give me expert advice on the language around training and usage of weapons, law enforcement practices and key relevant topics. I owe a debt of gratitude for your time, your extensive knowledge and for your generous advice.

••••

TO ALL THE KIND AND generous readers who take the time to review my novels and share their frank feedback, thank you so much. Your support is invaluable.

• • • •

I'M IMMENSELY GRATEFUL to all of you and will owe you all a glass of wine or several when you come to Vancouver next!

How would you like to write your own life story?

The Rebel Diva Self-Empowerment Series
www.RebelDivas.com[1]

• • • •

THE REBEL DIVA BOOKS are life-changing practical guides that take you on an adventure of a lifetime. Uncover your purpose, your passions, and your talents to create a step-by-step masterplan to achieve your life goals. You will read a story in these Rebel Diva books, and that story will be yours.

• • • •

WHAT READERS ARE SAYING:

- "One of the most motivational and thought-provoking books I have ever read."
- "This book is phenomenal! This book is written for real people; no platitudes or empty promises."
- "A very inspirational read. This is highly recommended, especially if you're seeking to do and make a difference."
- "The author is teacher and cheerleader. She gives solid guidelines to help you figure out your goals and action plans, and she truly comes across as someone who cares."
- "This isn't just another self-help book—instead, this incredibly useful book includes a clear method and helpful exercises to help you uncover your dreams, passions and purpose."
- "Very inspiring. Even though I am older, this book made

1. http://www.RebelDivas.com

me want to go after some of my dreams that I thought I was too old for. The book comes with a link that you can download a 100-page workbook. I plan on giving my daughter a copy too."

- "Proudly considering myself a Rebel Diva after taking this journey to self-discovery!"

• • • •

SIGN UP TO GET YOUR exclusive Rebel Diva gift!

The Fear Buster is a short Rebel Diva workbook that shares three essential tools to help you overcome any fears or doubt and make both small and big decisions quickly. Go to the Rebel Diva site to get your personal copy as a gift.

www.RebelDivas.com/FearBuster[2]

2. **http://www.RebelDivas.com/FearBuster**

About the Author

Tikiri Herath is a multiple-award-winning Canadian author. Born in Sri Lanka, a tropical island in the Indian Ocean, she spent her childhood in South East Africa, and has lived and worked in Southeast Asia, Continental Europe, and North America.

She started her adult life as a lone immigrant girl, but went on to receive a bachelor's degree from the University of Victoria, British Columbia and a master's degree from the Solvay Business School in Brussels.

For fifteen years, she worked in risk management in the intelligence and defense sectors, including in the Canadian Federal Government and at NATO.

Tikiri's an adrenaline junkie who has rock climbed, bungee jumped, rode on the back of a motorcycle across Quebec, flown in an acrobatic airplane upside down, and parachuted solo.

When she's not writing or plotting another thriller scene, you'll most probably find her baking in her kitchen with a glass of red wine in hand and jazz playing in the background.

To say hello and get free travel stories from around the world, go to www.TikiriHerath.com.[1]

1. http://www.TikiriHerath.com.